image® COMICS PRESENTS

GLITTERBOMB

VOLUME ONE: RED CARPET

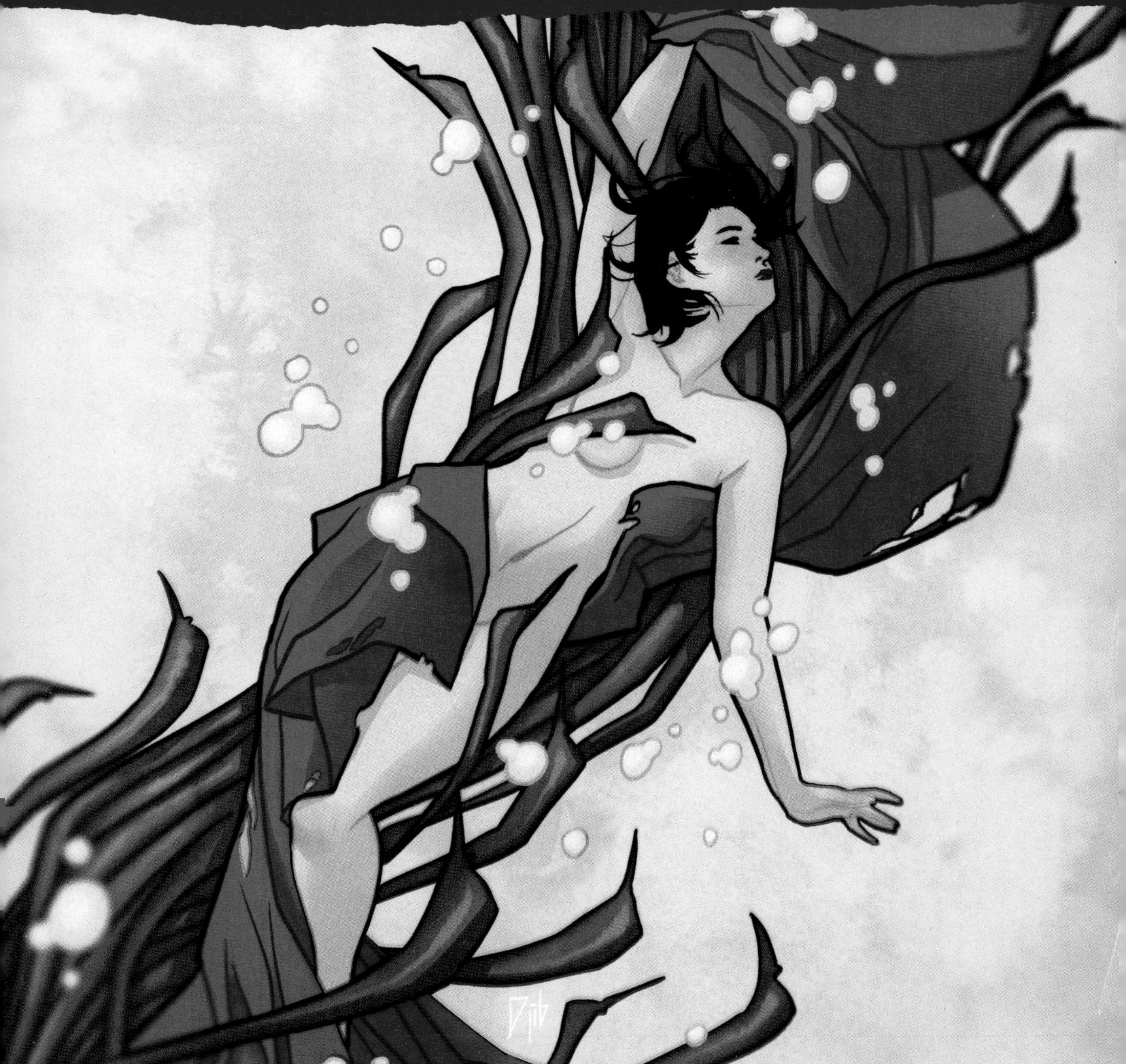

CREATED BY JIM ZUB AND DJIBRIL MORISSETTE-PHAN

IMAGE COMICS, INC.
Robert Kirkman—Chief Operating Officer
Erik Larsen—Chief Financial Officer
Todd McFarlane—President
Marc Silvestri—Chief Executive Officer
Jim Valentino—Vice-President

Eric Stephenson—Publisher
Corey Murphy—Director of Sales
Jeff Boison—Director of Publishing Planning & Book Trade Sales
Chris Ross—Director of Digital Sales
Kat Salazar—Director of PR & Marketing
Branwyn Bigglestone—Controller
Susan Korpela—Accounts Manager
Drew Gill—Art Director
Brett Warnock—Production Manager
Meredith Wallace—Print Manager
Briah Skelly—Publicist
Aly Hoffman— Conventions & Events Coordinator
Sasha Head—Sales & Marketing Production Designer
David Brothers—Branding Manager
Melissa Gifford—Content Manager
Erika Schnatz—Production Artist
Ryan Brewer—Production Artist
Shanna Matuszak—Production Artist
Tricia Ramos—Production Artist
Vincent Kukua—Production Artist
Jeff Stang—Direct Market Sales Representative
Emilio Bautista—Digital Sales Associate
Leanna Caunter—Accounting Assistant
Chloe Ramos-Peterson—Library Market Sales Representative
IMAGECOMICS.COM

GLITTERBOMB VOLUME 1: RED CARPET. ISBN: 978-1-5343-0051-4. First Printing. March 2017. Published by Image Comics, Inc. Office of publication: 2701 NW Vaughn St., Suite 7
Portland, OR, 97210. Copyright © 2017 Jim Zub. All rights reserved. Originally published in single magazine form as GLITTERBOMB #1-4. "GLITTERBOMB," its logos, and the likenesse
all characters herein are trademarks of Jim Zub, unless otherwise noted. "Image" and the Image Comics logos are registered trademarks of Image Comics, Inc. No part of this publica
may be reproduced or transmitted, in any form or by any means (except for short excerpts for journalistic or review purposes), without the express written permission of Jim Zub or Ime
Comics, Inc. All names, characters, events, and locales in this publication are entirely fictional. Any resemblance to actual persons (living or dead), events, or places, without satiric inten
coincidental. PRINTED IN THE USA. For information regarding the CPSIA on this printed material call: 203-595-3636 and provide reference #RICH — 726082.
For international rights, contact: foreignlicensing@imagecomics.com.

STORY
JIM ZUB

LINE ART
DJIBRIL MORISSETTE-PHAN

COLOR ART
K. MICHAEL RUSSELL

COLOR FLATS
LUDWIG OLIMBA

LETTER ART
MARSHALL DILLON

ALT COVERS
STEVEN CUMMINGS
CHRISTIAN WARD
MARGUERITE SAUVAGE
VIVIAN NG
TREVOR JAMEUS
RAY FAWKES

BACK MATTER
HOLLY RAYCHELLE HUGHES

PROOFING
OLIVIA NGAI
STACY KING
MELISSA GIFFORD

SPECIAL THANKS
BRIAH SKELLY
JIM DEMONAKOS

GRAPHIC/LOGO DESIGN
JIM ZUB

PART 1: CIRCULAR HOMICIDE

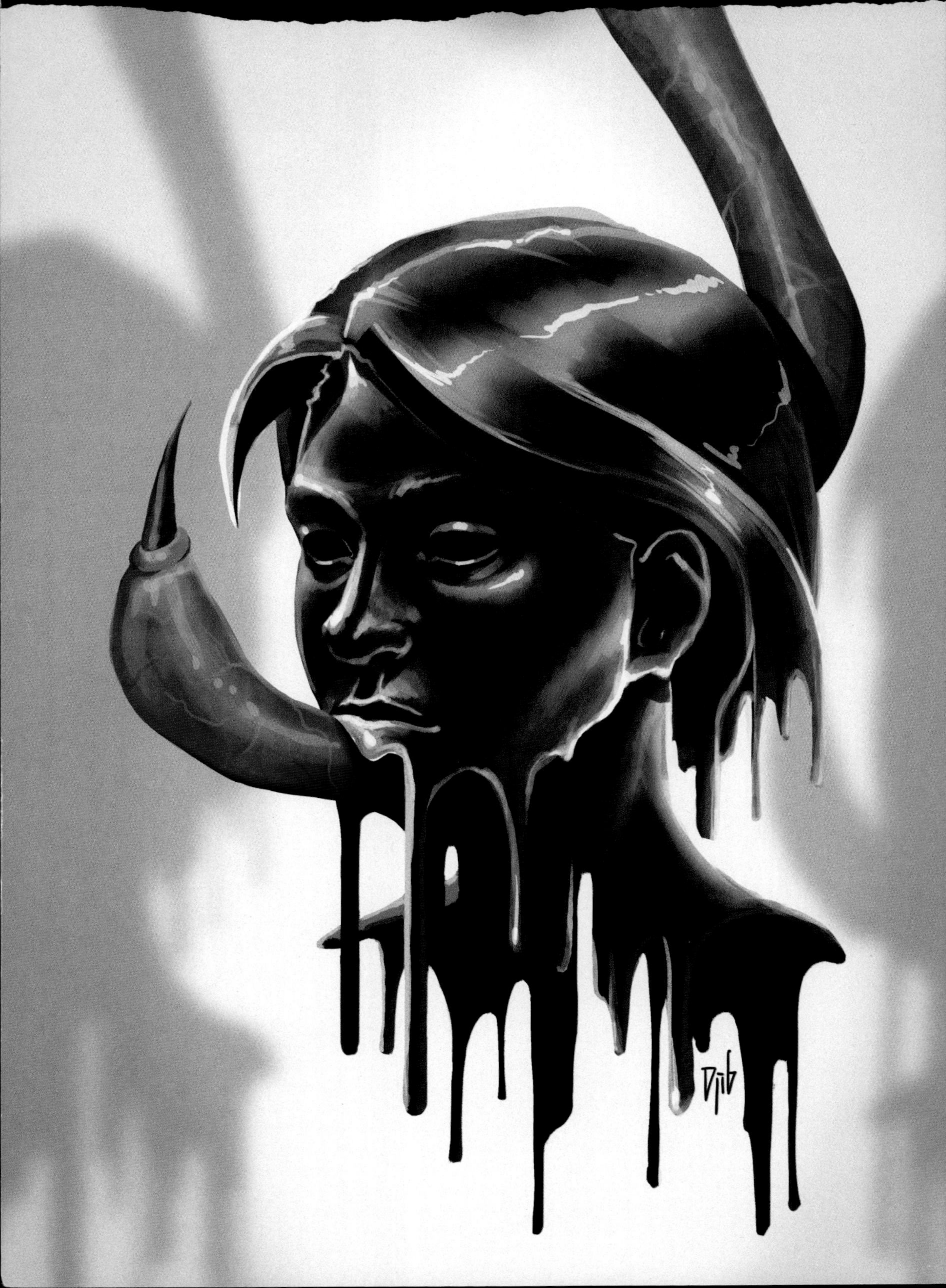
Djib

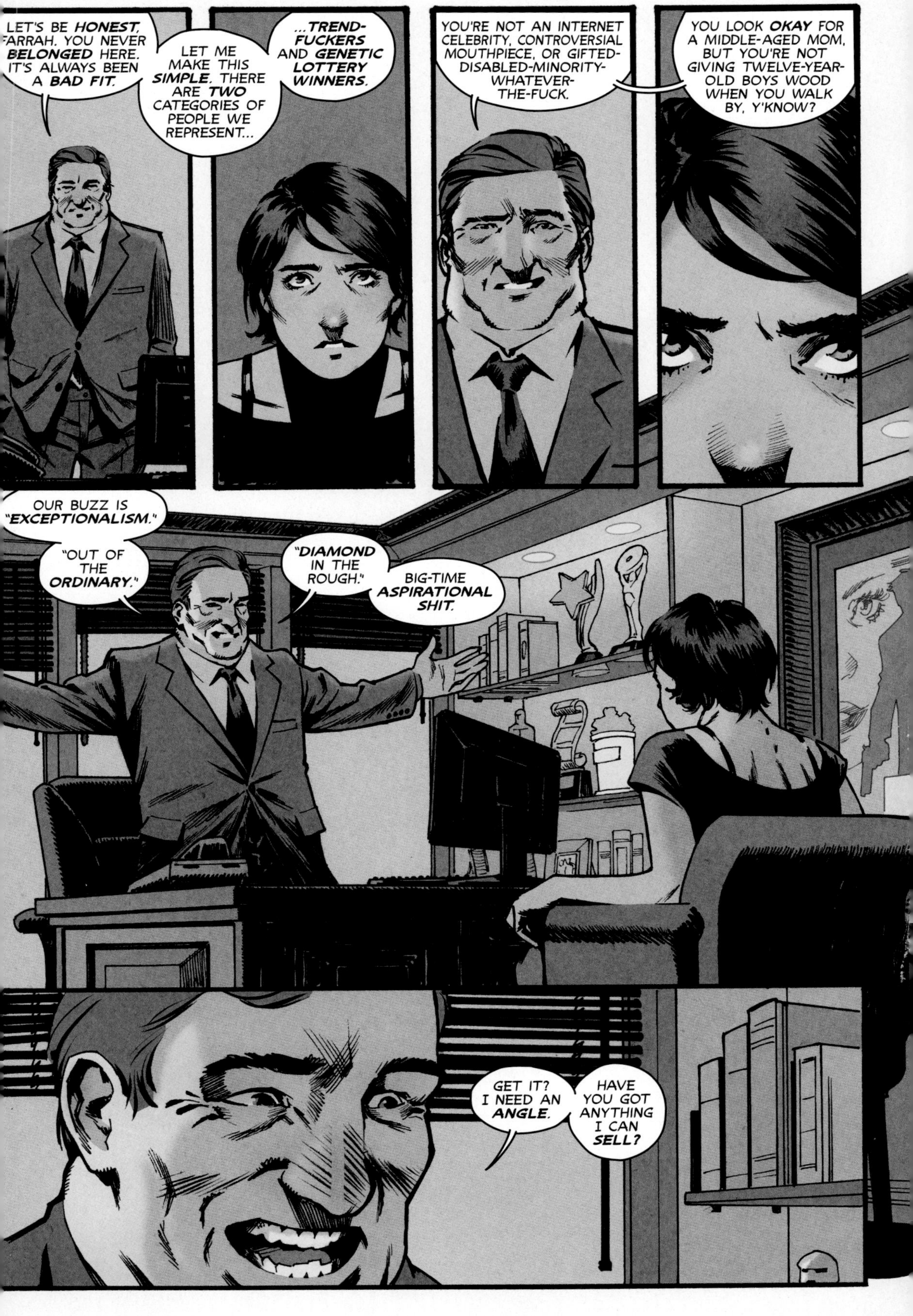
LET'S BE HONEST, FARRAH. YOU NEVER BELONGED HERE. IT'S ALWAYS BEEN A BAD FIT.
LET ME MAKE THIS SIMPLE. THERE ARE TWO CATEGORIES OF PEOPLE WE REPRESENT...
...TREND-FUCKERS AND GENETIC LOTTERY WINNERS.
YOU'RE NOT AN INTERNET CELEBRITY, CONTROVERSIAL MOUTHPIECE, OR GIFTED-DISABLED-MINORITY-WHATEVER-THE-FUCK.
YOU LOOK OKAY FOR A MIDDLE-AGED MOM, BUT YOU'RE NOT GIVING TWELVE-YEAR-OLD BOYS WOOD WHEN YOU WALK BY, Y'KNOW?
OUR BUZZ IS "EXCEPTIONALISM."
"OUT OF THE ORDINARY."
"DIAMOND IN THE ROUGH."
BIG-TIME ASPIRATIONAL SHIT.
GET IT? I NEED AN ANGLE.
HAVE YOU GOT ANYTHING I CAN SELL?

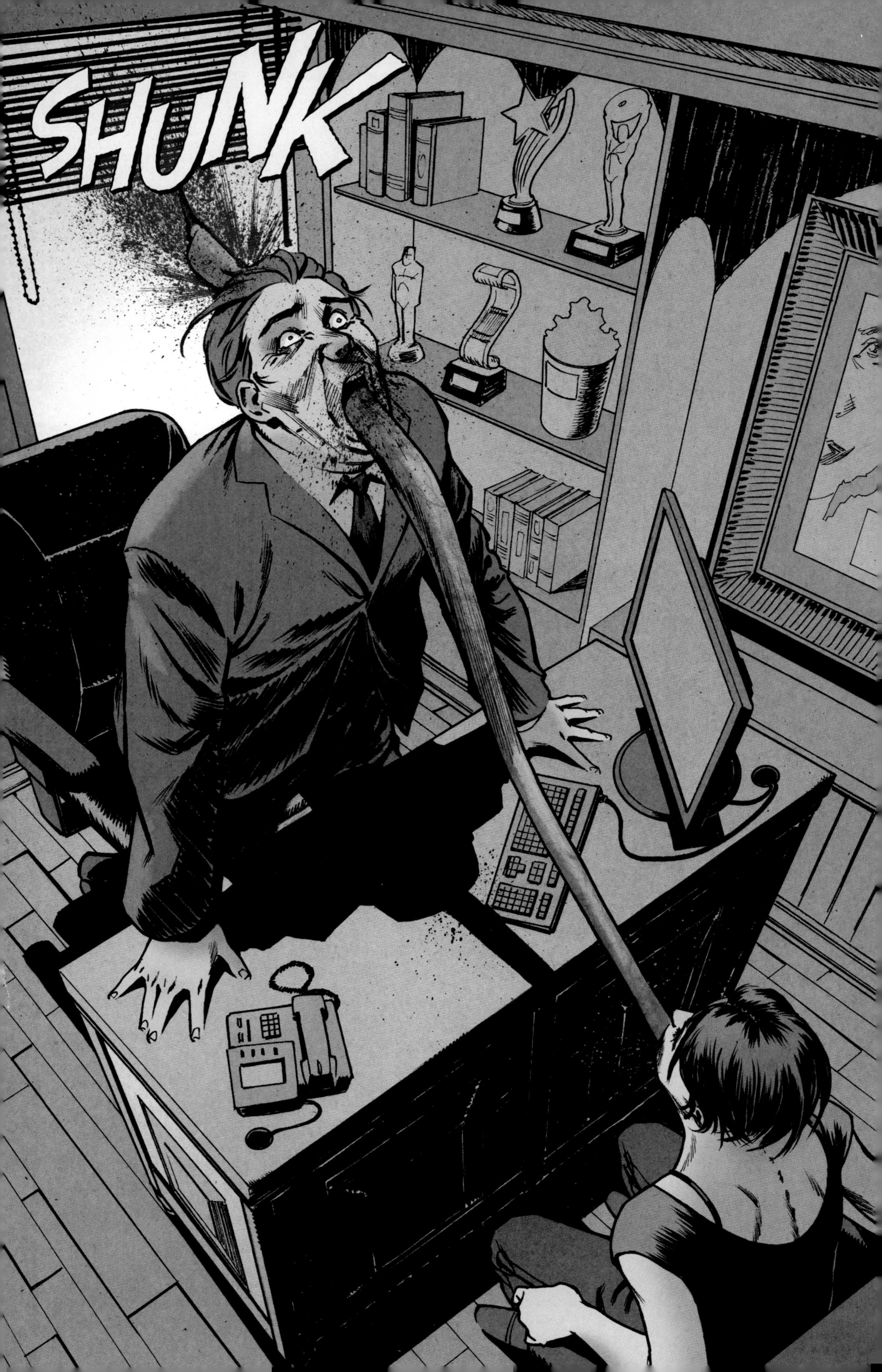
SHUNK

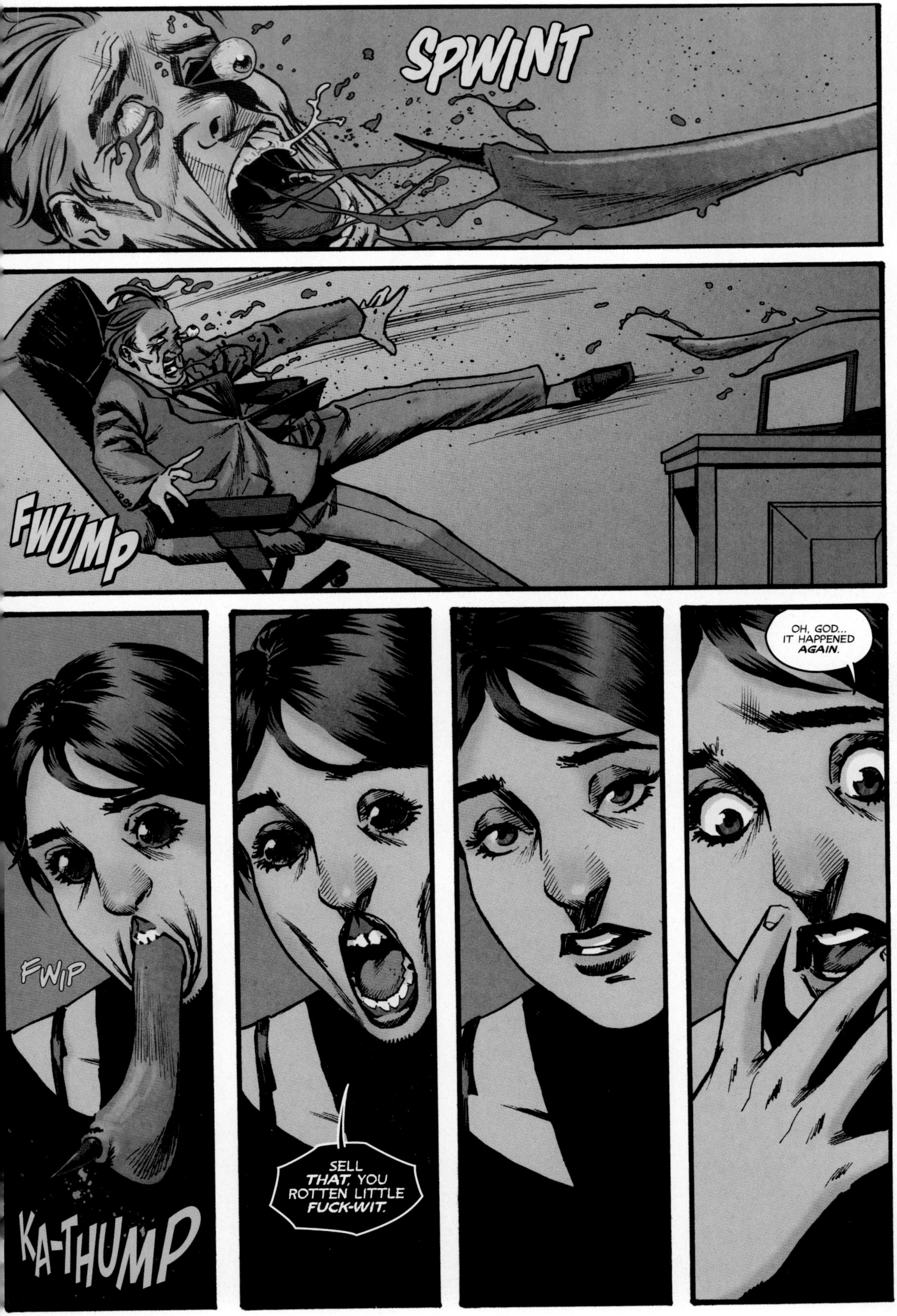
SPWINT
FWUMP
FWIP
KA-THUMP
SELL THAT, YOU ROTTEN LITTLE FUCK-WIT.
OH, GOD... IT HAPPENED AGAIN.

GLITTE

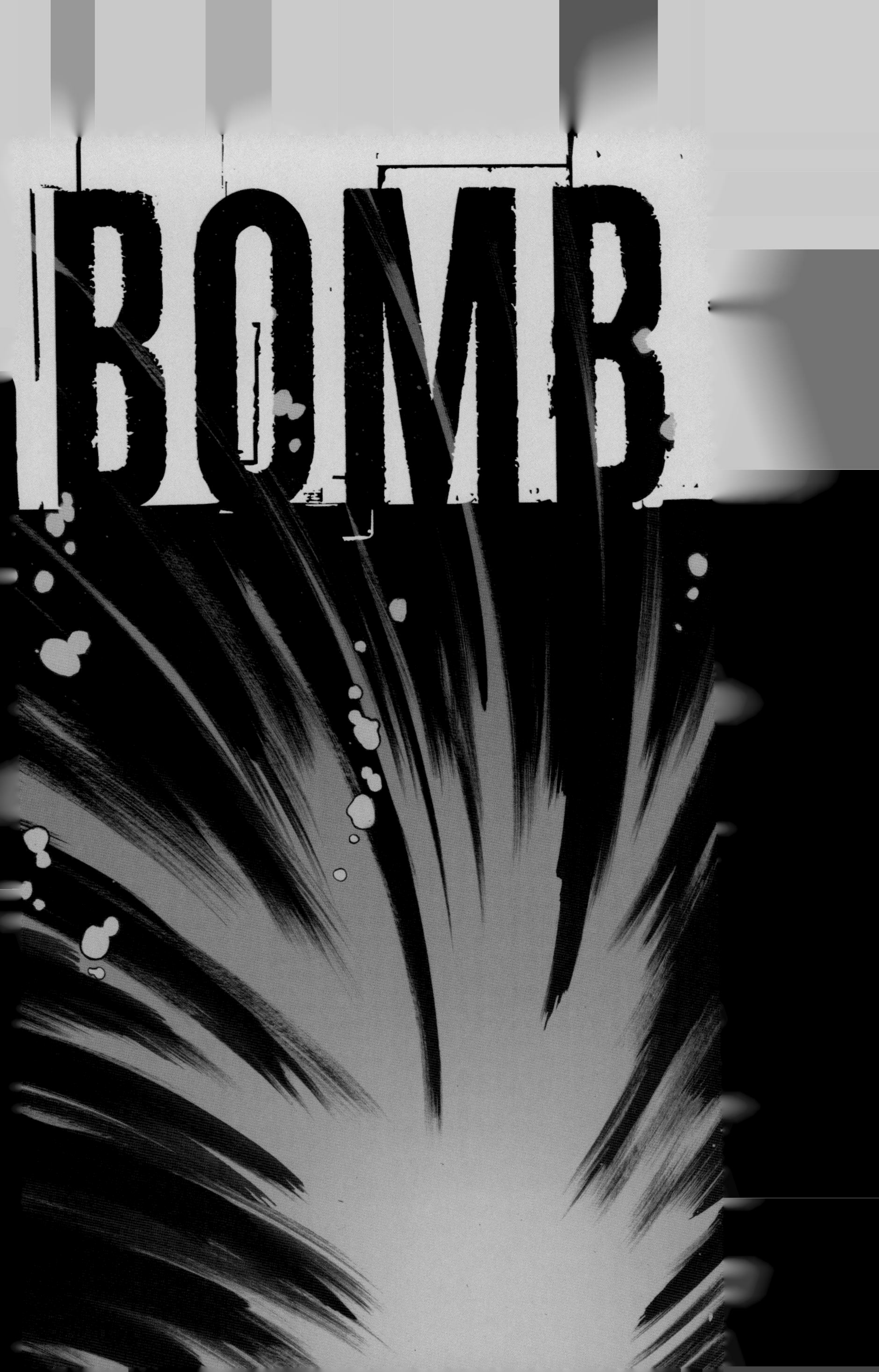
BOMB

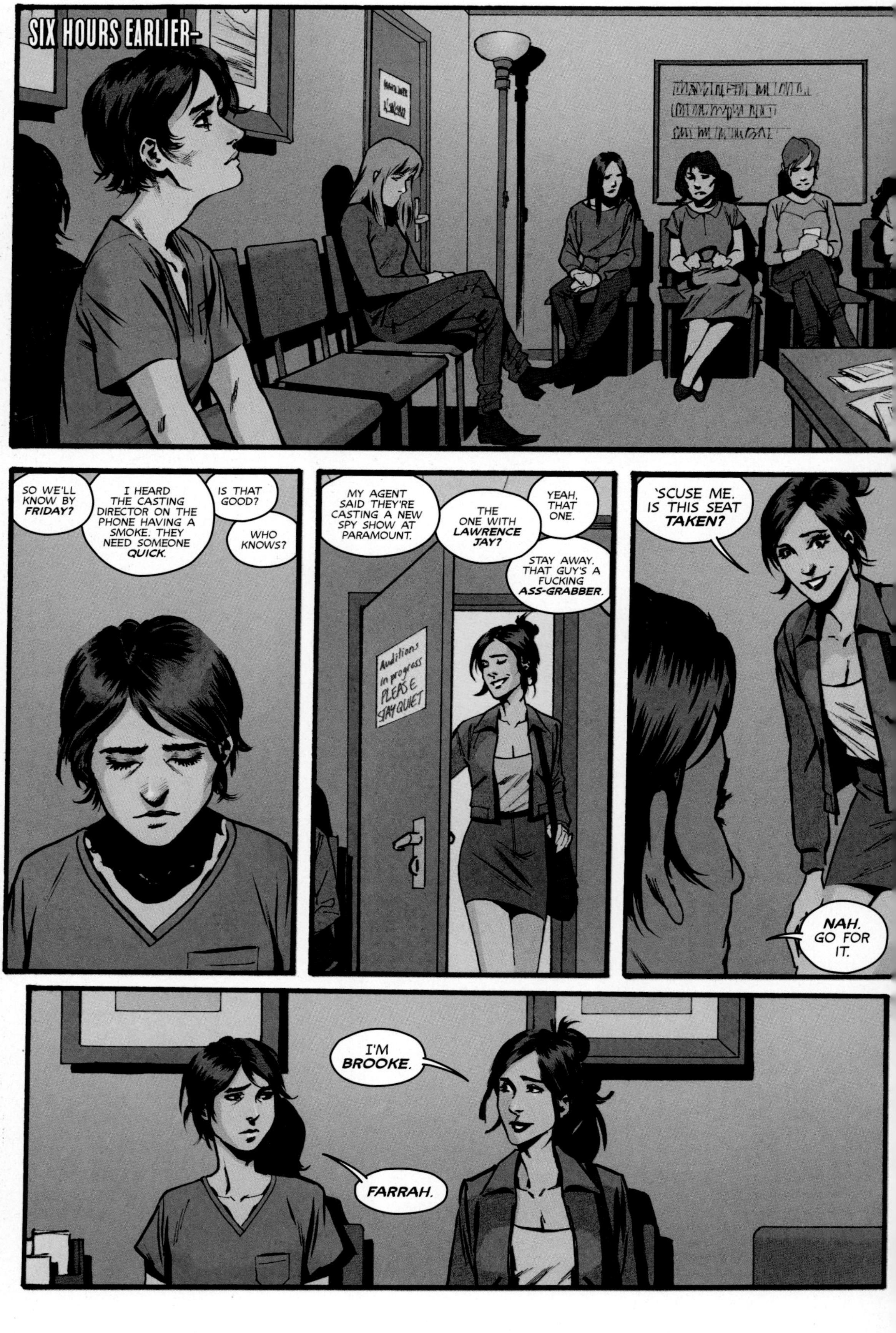
SIX HOURS EARLIER–
SO WE'LL KNOW BY FRIDAY?
I HEARD THE CASTING DIRECTOR ON THE PHONE HAVING A SMOKE. THEY NEED SOMEONE QUICK.
IS THAT GOOD?
WHO KNOWS?
MY AGENT SAID THEY'RE CASTING A NEW SPY SHOW AT PARAMOUNT.
THE ONE WITH LAWRENCE JAY?
YEAH, THAT ONE.
STAY AWAY. THAT GUY'S A FUCKING ASS-GRABBER.
Auditions in progress PLEASE STAY QUIET
'SCUSE ME. IS THIS SEAT TAKEN?
NAH. GO FOR IT.
I'M BROOKE.
FARRAH.

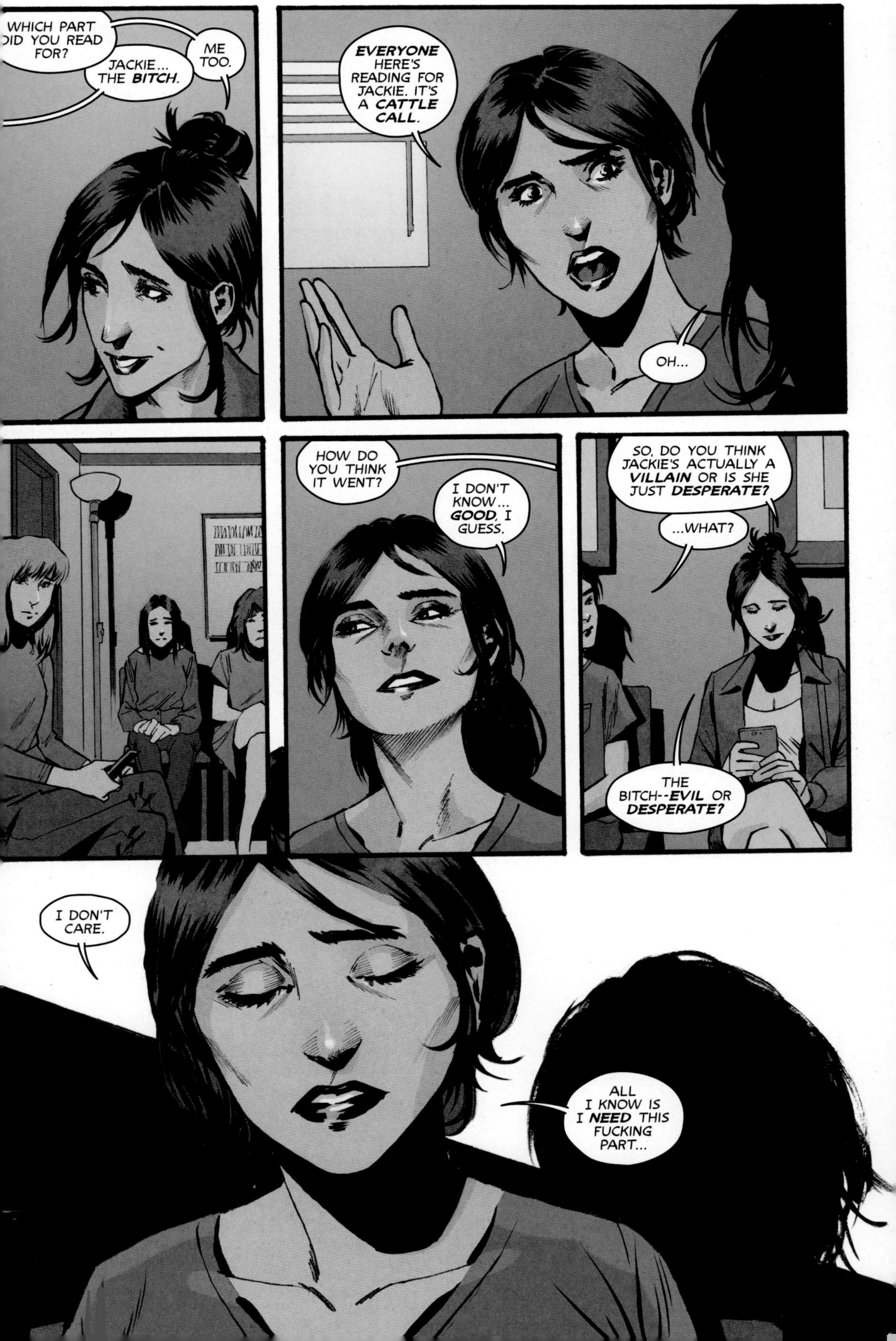
WHICH PART DID YOU READ FOR?
JACKIE... THE BITCH.
ME TOO.
EVERYONE HERE'S READING FOR JACKIE. IT'S A CATTLE CALL.
OH...
HOW DO YOU THINK IT WENT?
I DON'T KNOW... GOOD, I GUESS.
SO, DO YOU THINK JACKIE'S ACTUALLY A VILLAIN OR IS SHE JUST DESPERATE?
...WHAT?
THE BITCH--EVIL OR DESPERATE?
I DON'T CARE.
ALL I KNOW IS I NEED THIS FUCKING PART...

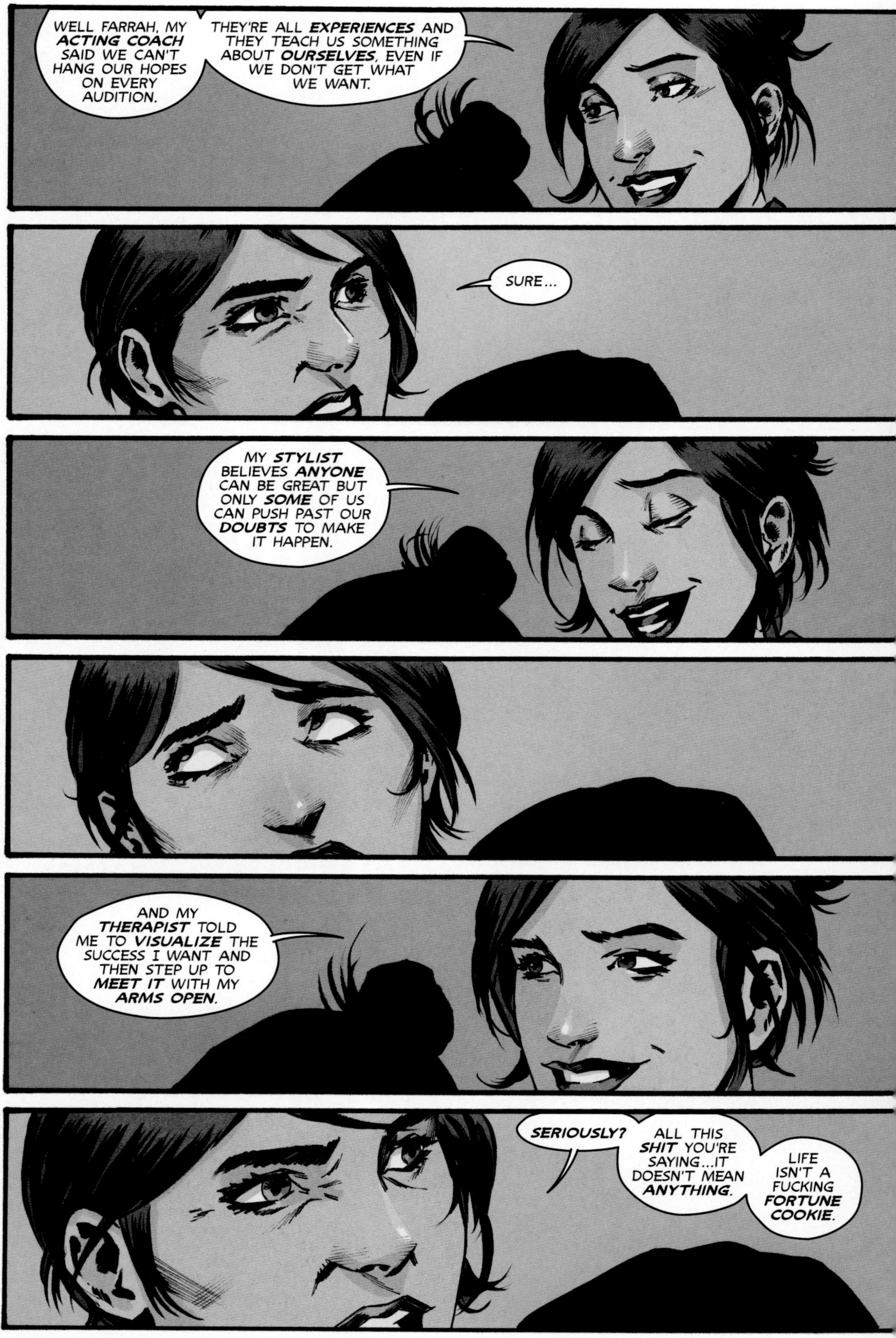
WELL FARRAH, MY ACTING COACH SAID WE CAN'T HANG OUR HOPES ON EVERY AUDITION.
THEY'RE ALL EXPERIENCES AND THEY TEACH US SOMETHING ABOUT OURSELVES, EVEN IF WE DON'T GET WHAT WE WANT.
SURE...
MY STYLIST BELIEVES ANYONE CAN BE GREAT BUT ONLY SOME OF US CAN PUSH PAST OUR DOUBTS TO MAKE IT HAPPEN.
AND MY THERAPIST TOLD ME TO VISUALIZE THE SUCCESS I WANT AND THEN STEP UP TO MEET IT WITH MY ARMS OPEN.
SERIOUSLY?
ALL THIS SHIT YOU'RE SAYING...IT DOESN'T MEAN ANYTHING.
LIFE ISN'T A FUCKING FORTUNE COOKIE.

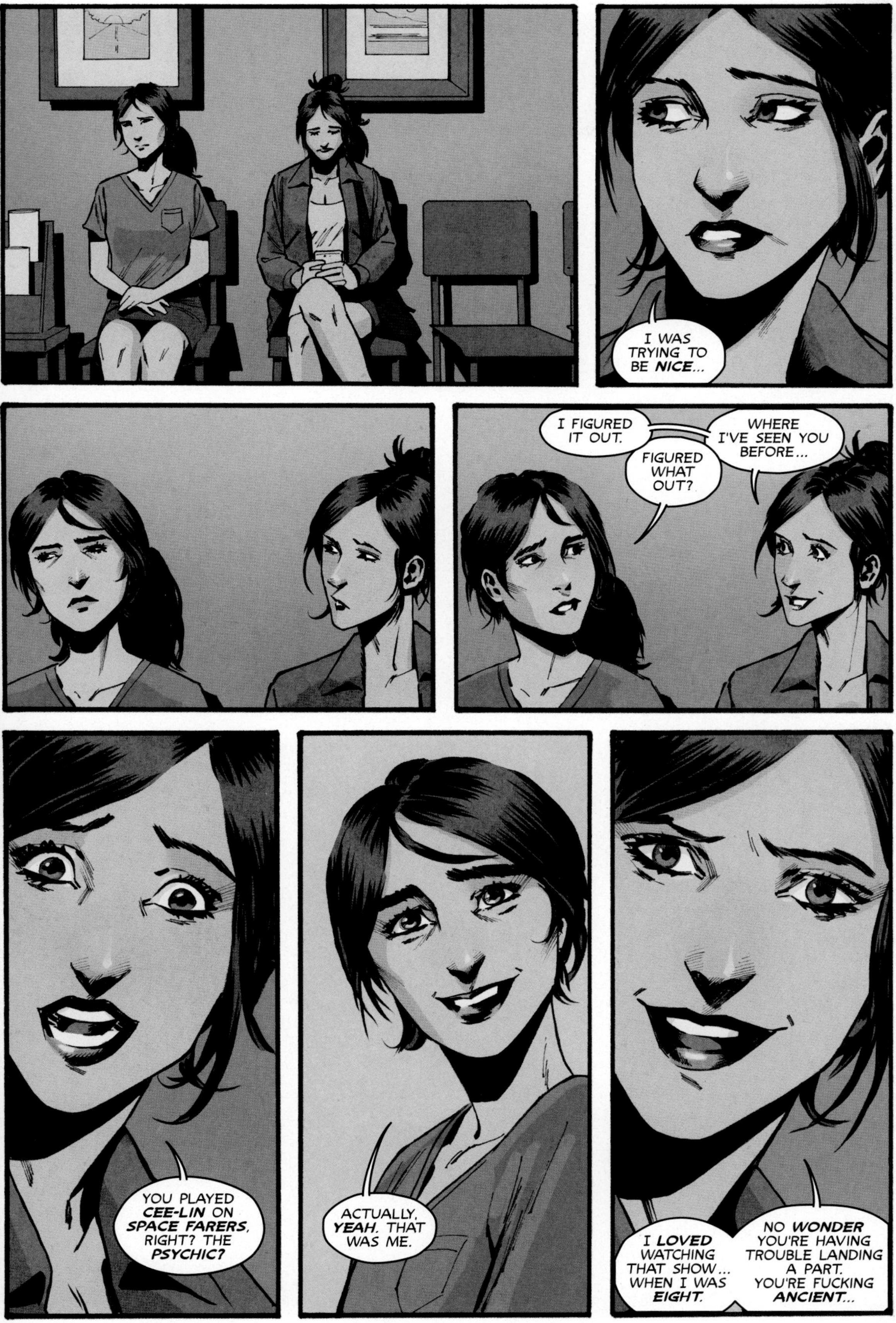
I WAS TRYING TO BE **NICE**...
I FIGURED IT OUT.
FIGURED WHAT OUT?
WHERE I'VE SEEN YOU BEFORE...
YOU PLAYED **CEE-LIN** ON **SPACE FARERS**, RIGHT? THE **PSYCHIC?**
ACTUALLY, **YEAH**. THAT WAS ME.
I **LOVED** WATCHING THAT SHOW... WHEN I WAS **EIGHT**.
NO **WONDER** YOU'RE HAVING TROUBLE LANDING A PART. YOU'RE FUCKING **ANCIENT**...

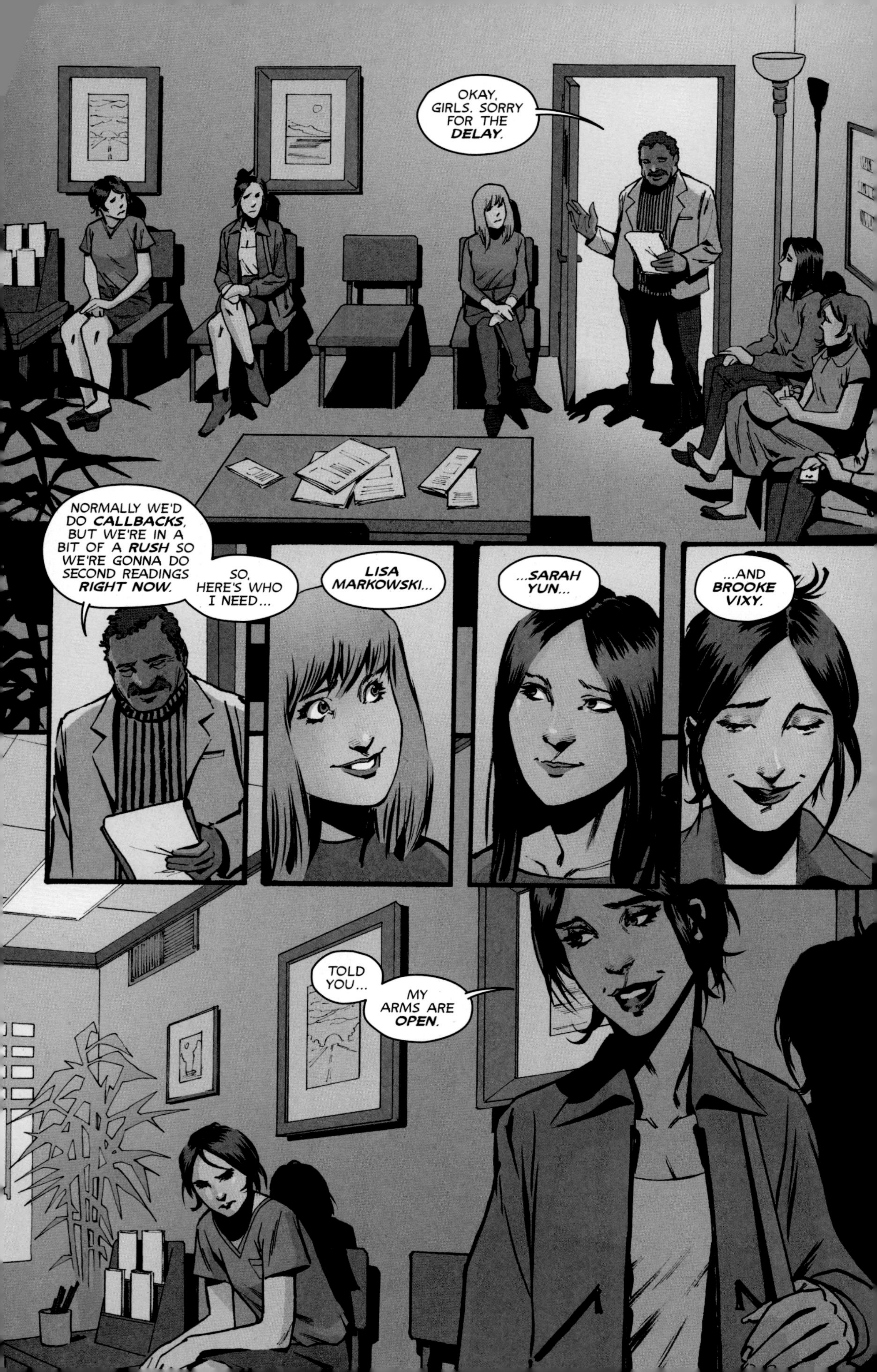
OKAY, GIRLS. SORRY FOR THE DELAY.
NORMALLY WE'D DO CALLBACKS, BUT WE'RE IN A BIT OF A RUSH SO WE'RE GONNA DO SECOND READINGS RIGHT NOW.
SO, HERE'S WHO I NEED...
LISA MARKOWSKI...
...SARAH YUN...
...AND BROOKE VIXY.
TOLD YOU...
MY ARMS ARE OPEN.

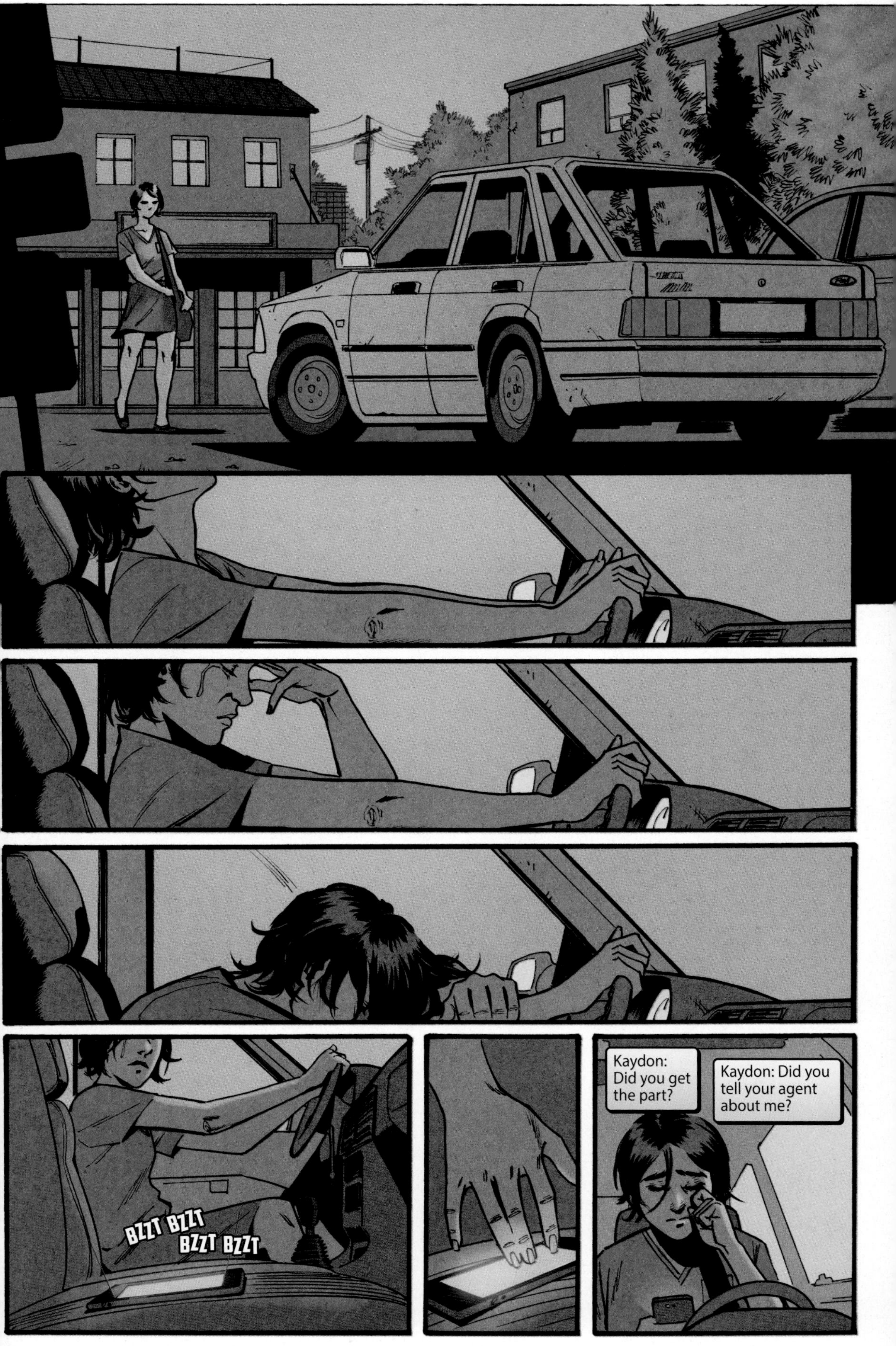
BZZT BZZT
BZZT BZZT
Kaydon: Did you get the part?
Kaydon: Did you tell your agent about me?

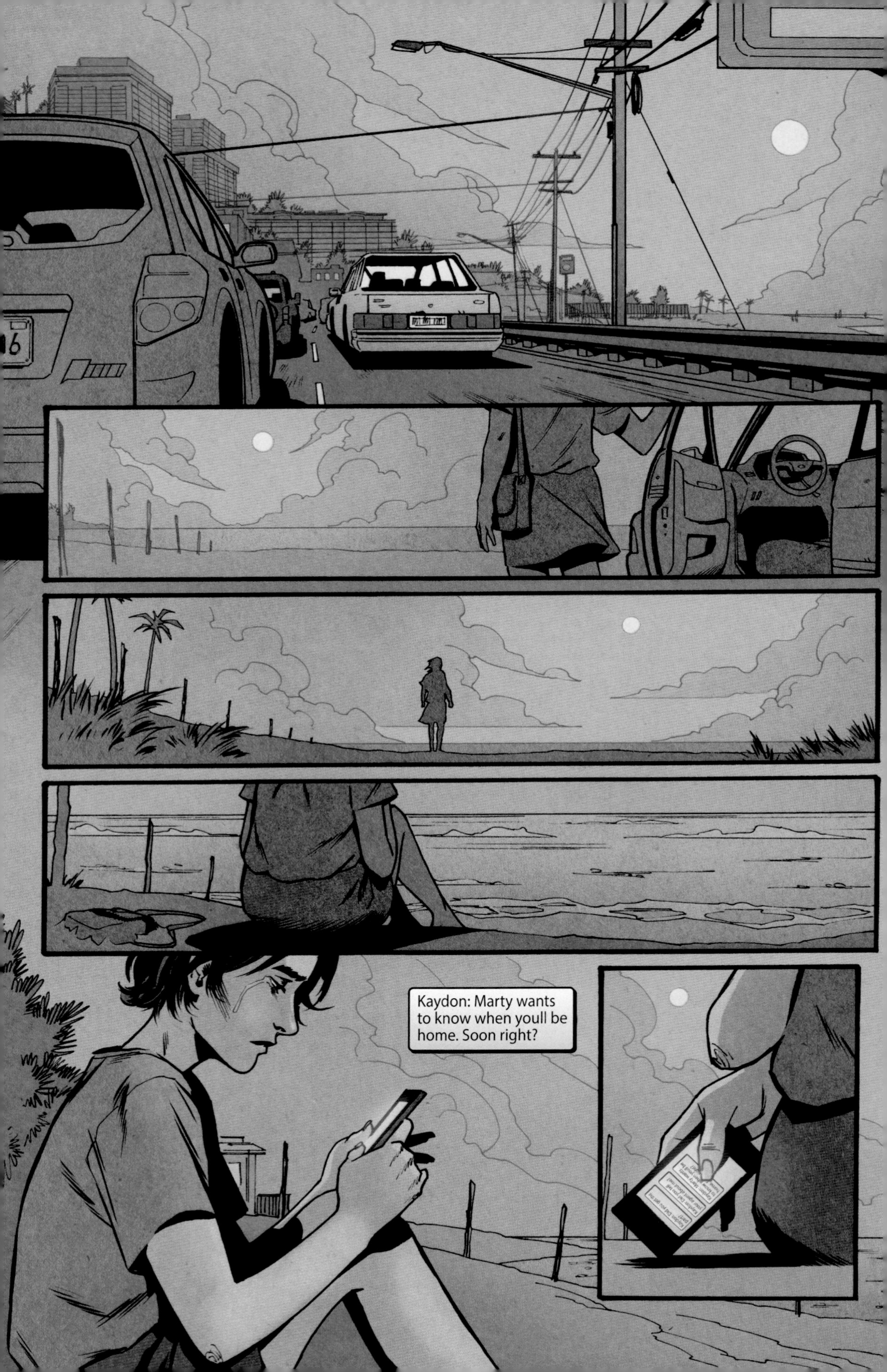
Kaydon: Marty wants to know when youll be home. Soon right?

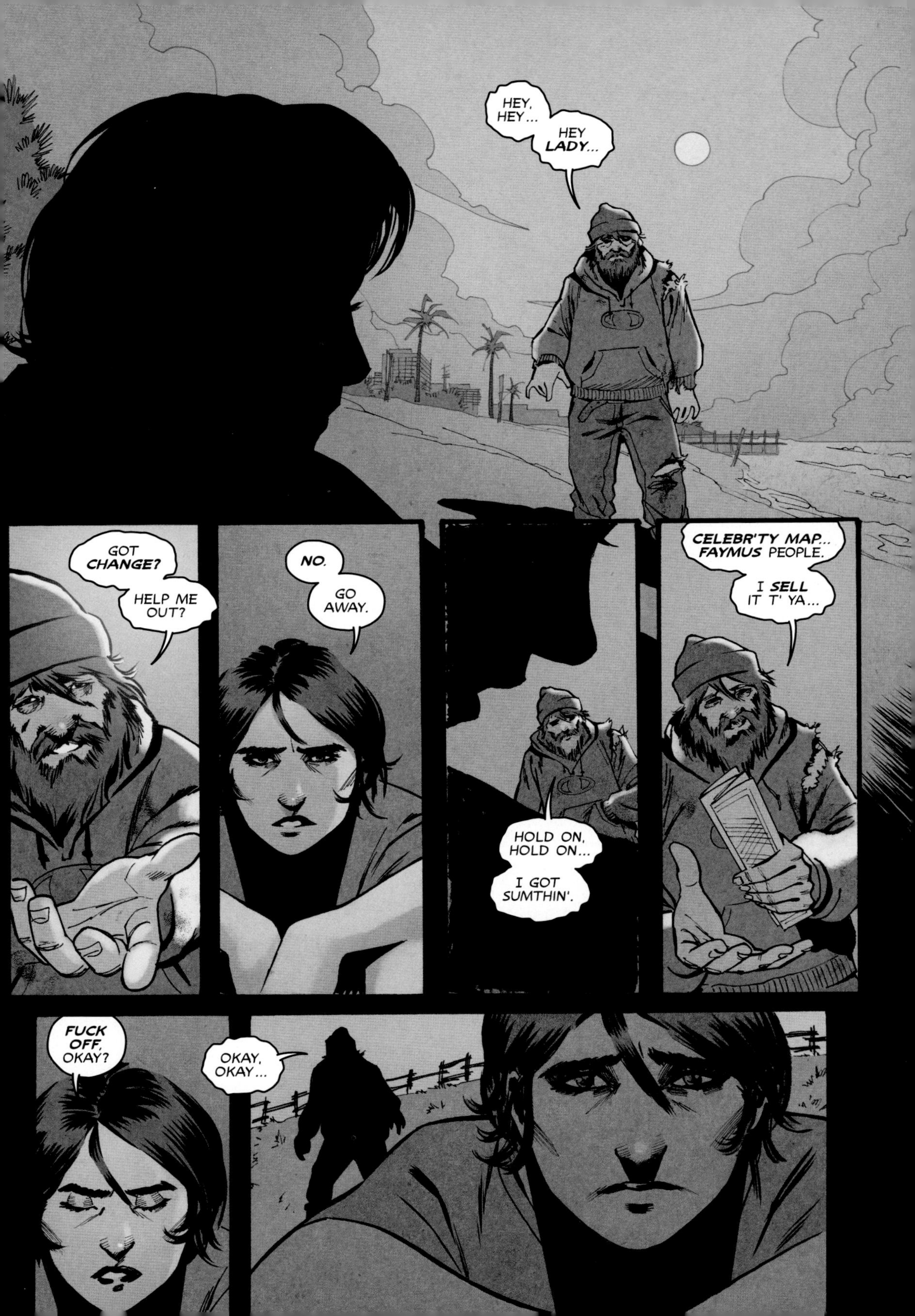
HEY, HEY...
HEY LADY...
GOT CHANGE?
HELP ME OUT?
NO.
GO AWAY.
HOLD ON, HOLD ON...
I GOT SUMTHIN'.
CELEBR'TY MAP... FAYMUS PEOPLE.
I SELL IT T' YA...
FUCK OFF, OKAY?
OKAY, OKAY...

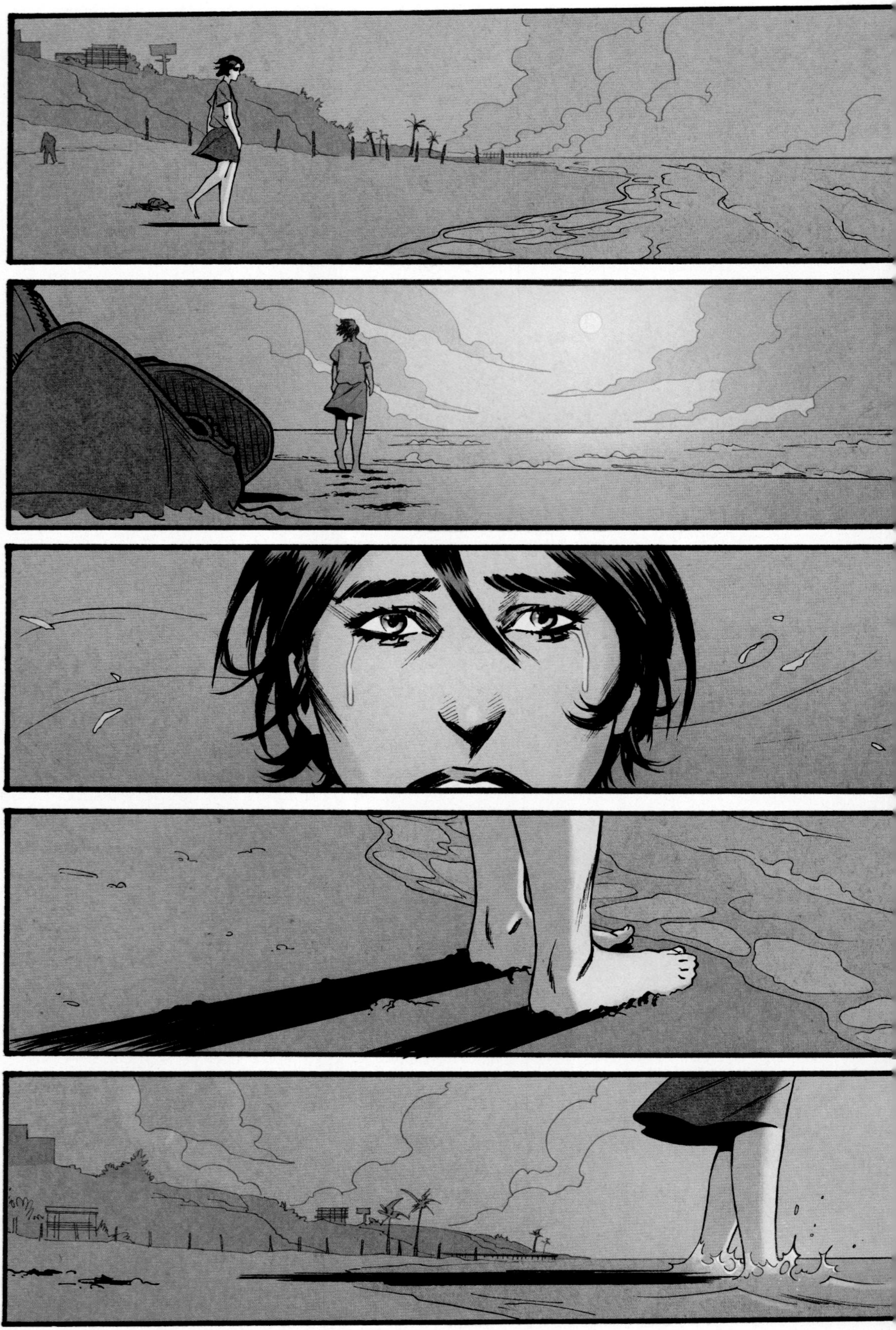

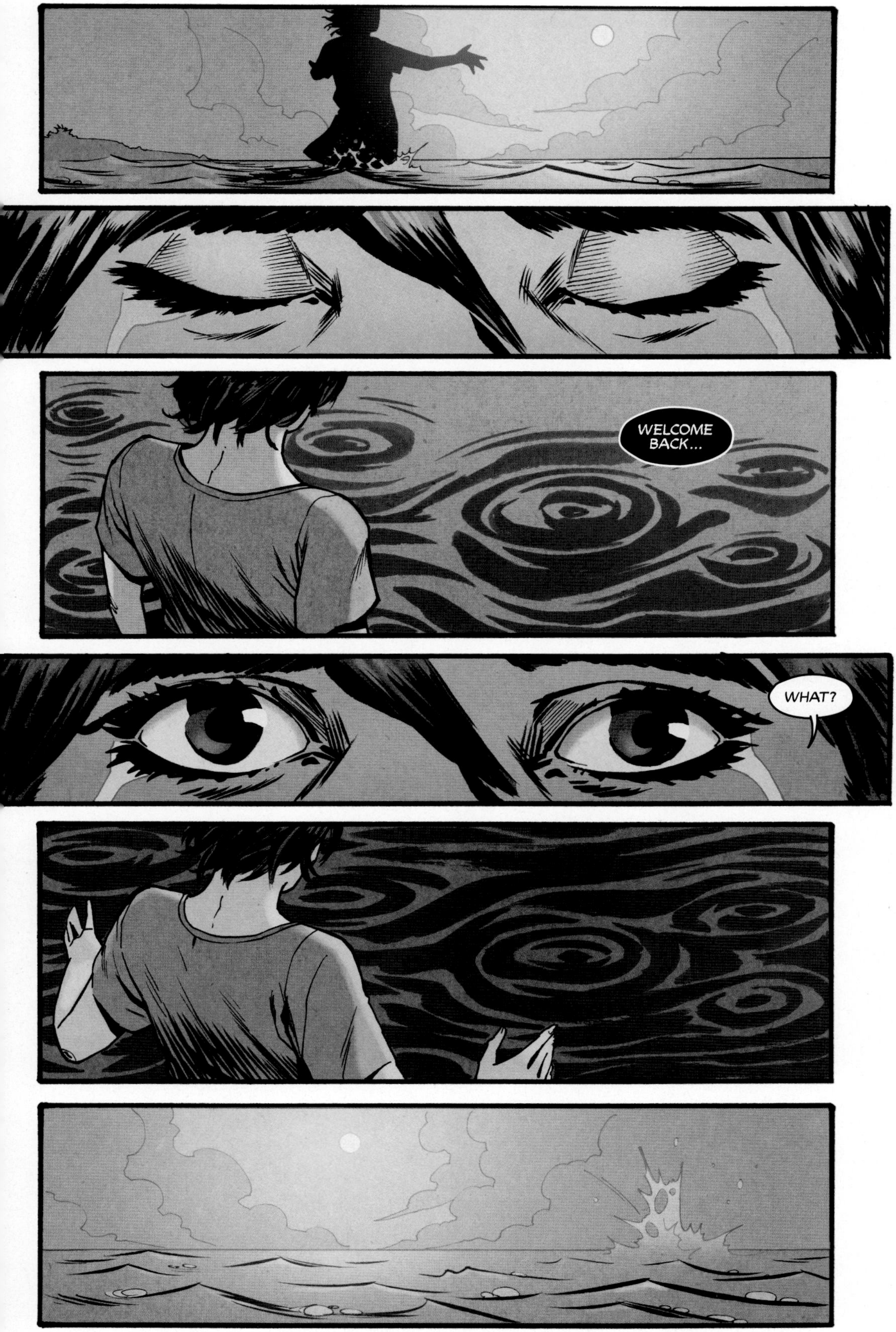
WELCOME BACK...
WHAT?

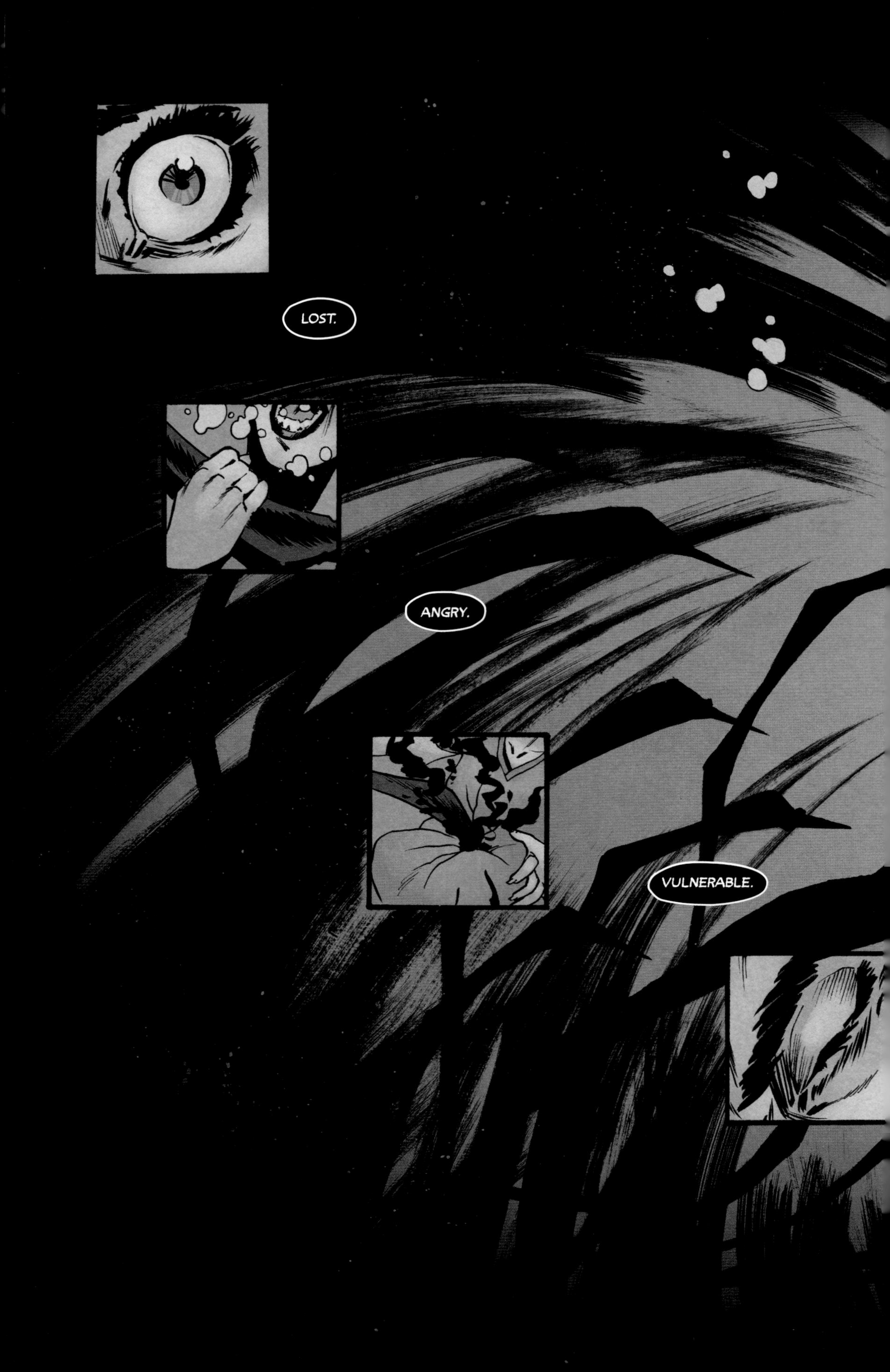
LOST.
ANGRY.
VULNERABLE.

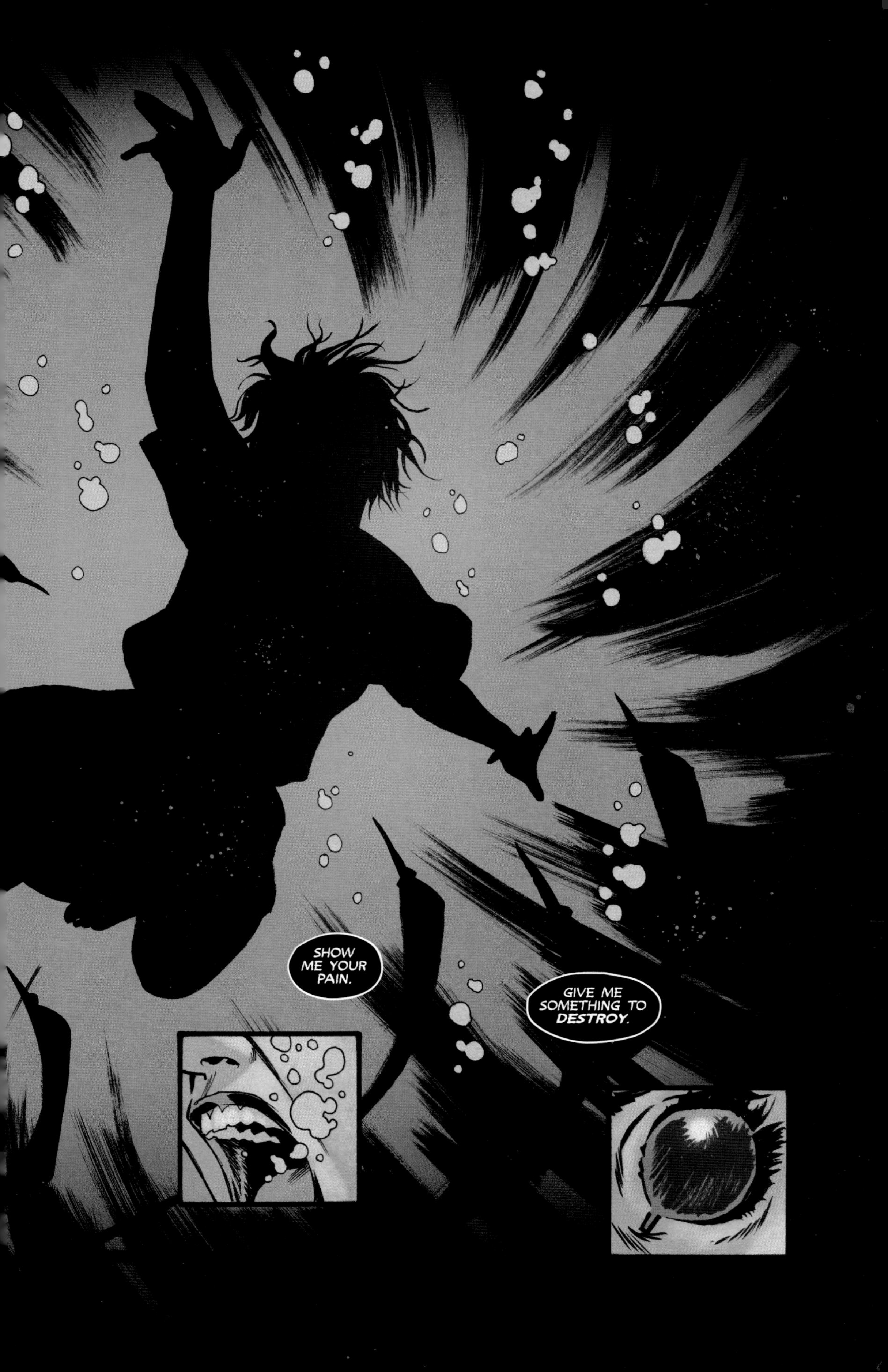
SHOW ME YOUR PAIN.
GIVE ME SOMETHING TO DESTROY.

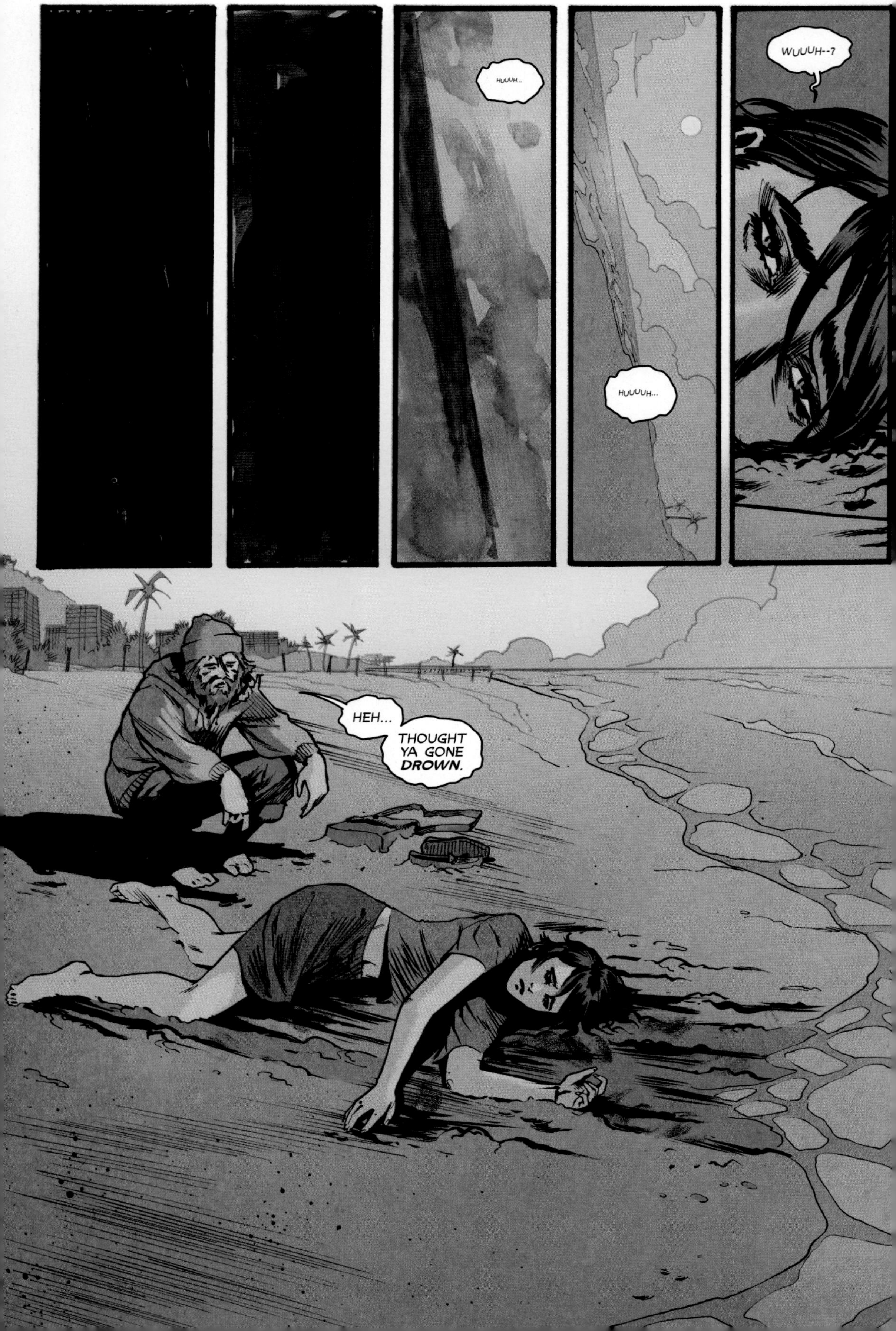
HUUUH...
HUUUUH...
WUUUH--?
HEH...
THOUGHT YA GONE DROWN.

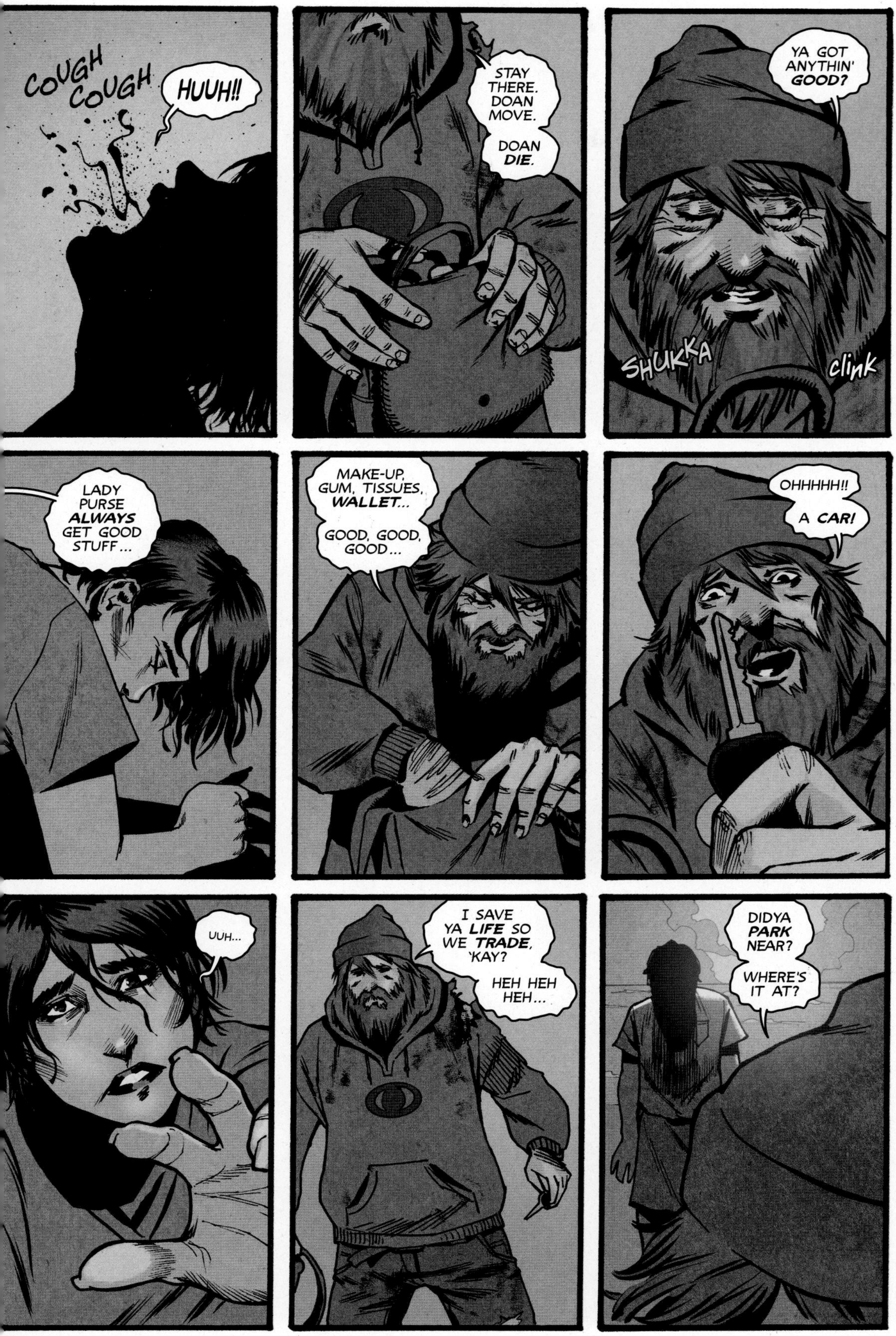
COUGH COUGH
HUUH!!
STAY THERE. DOAN MOVE.
DOAN DIE.
YA GOT ANYTHIN' GOOD?
SHUKKA
clink
LADY PURSE ALWAYS GET GOOD STUFF...
MAKE-UP, GUM, TISSUES, WALLET...
GOOD, GOOD, GOOD...
OHHHHH!!
A CAR!
UUH...
I SAVE YA LIFE SO WE TRADE, 'KAY?
HEH HEH HEH...
DIDYA PARK NEAR?
WHERE'S IT AT?

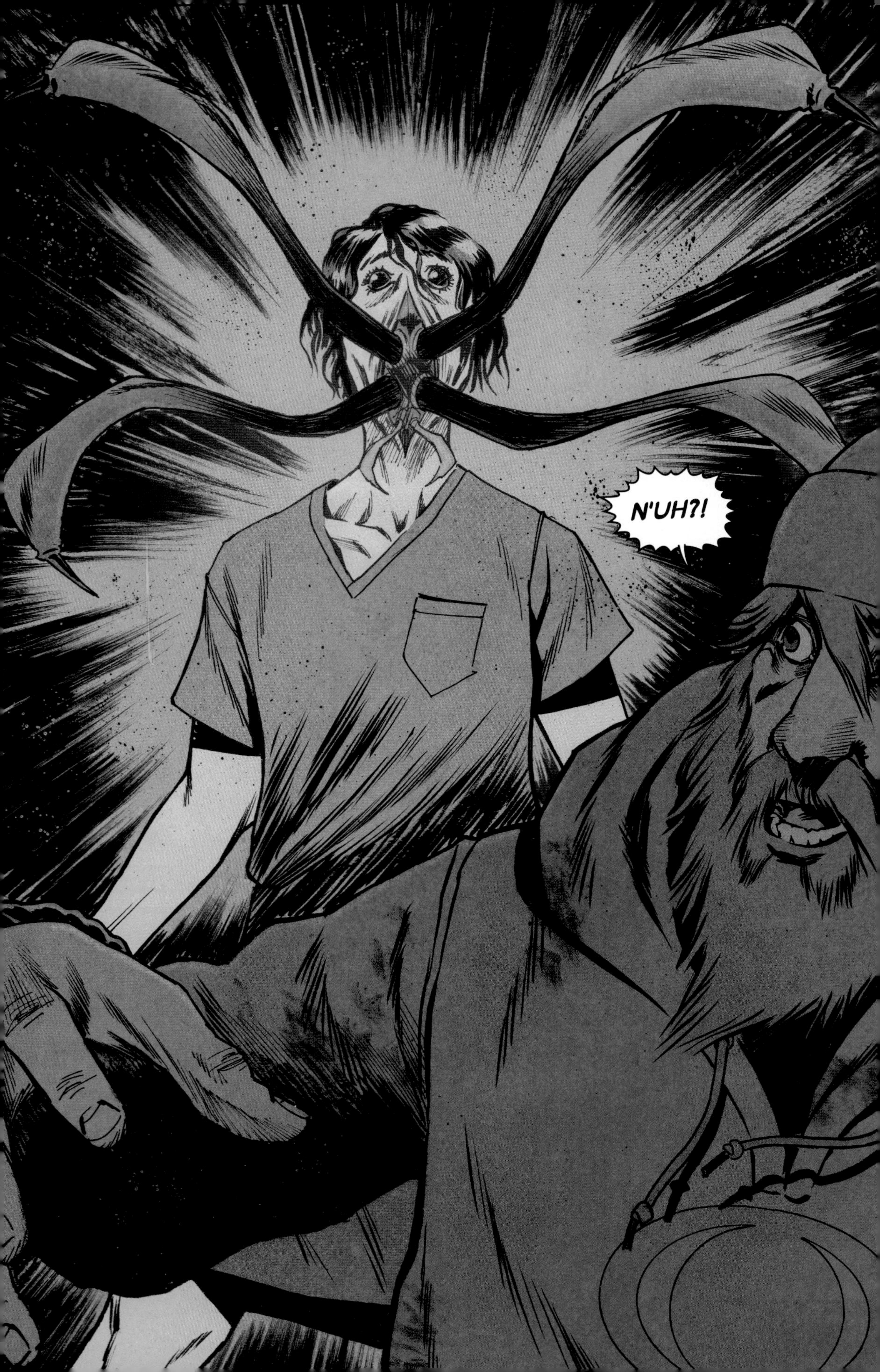
N'UH?!

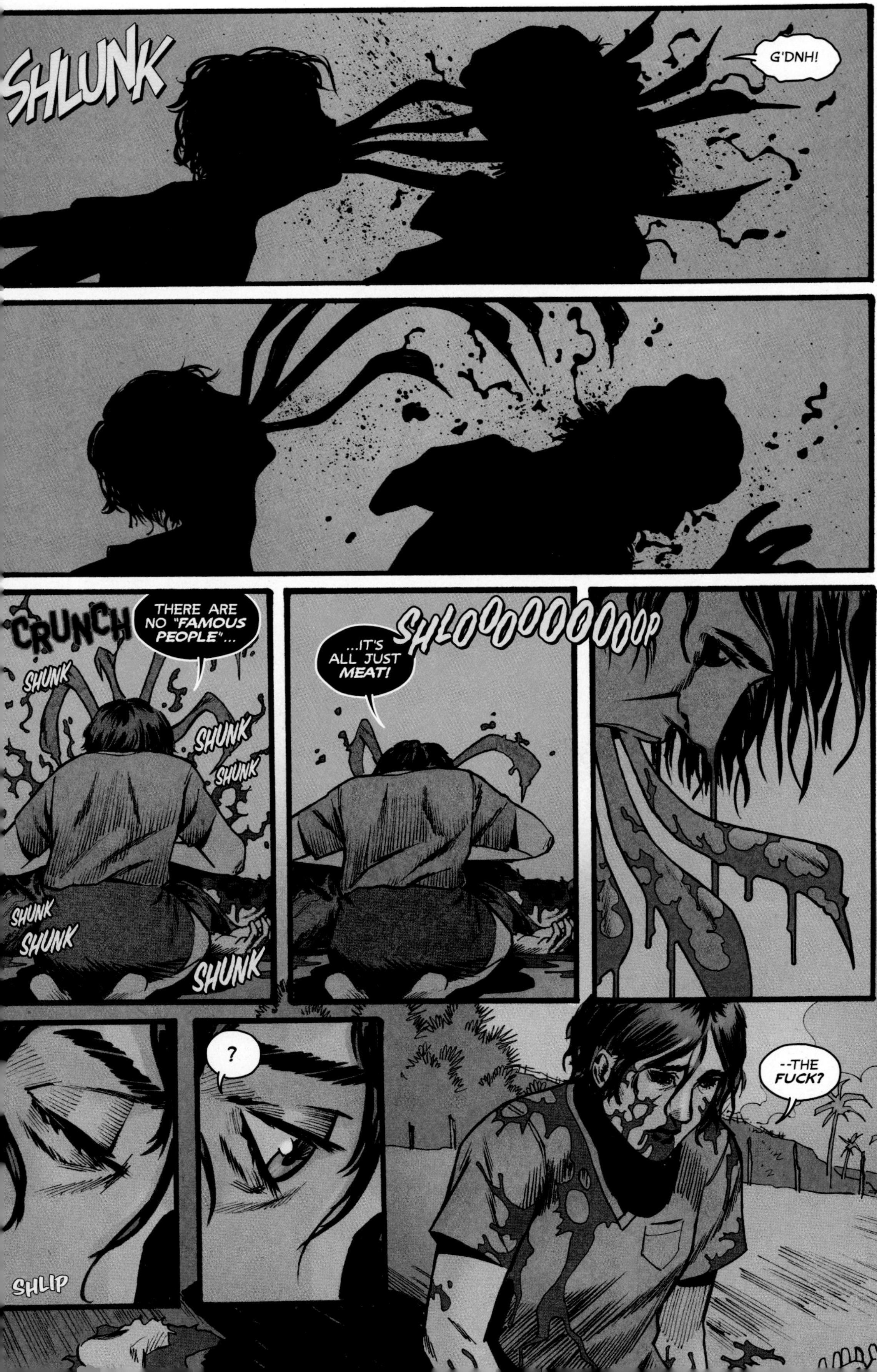
SHLUNK
G'DNH!
CRUNCH
THERE ARE NO "FAMOUS PEOPLE"...
SHUNK
SHUNK
SHUNK
SHUNK
SHUNK
SHUNK
SHLOOOOOOOOOOOP
...IT'S ALL JUST MEAT!
SHLIP
?
--THE FUCK?

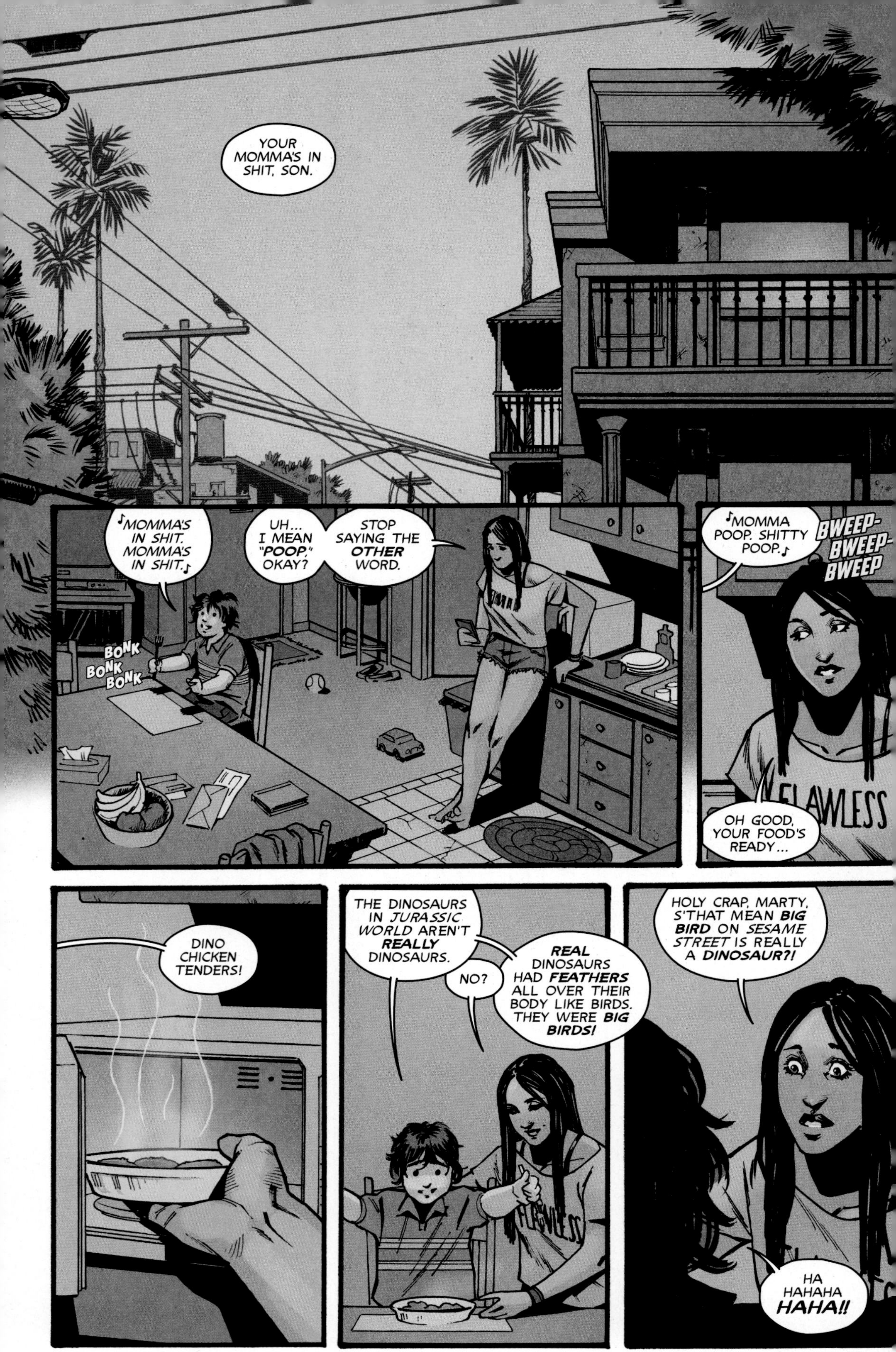
YOUR MOMMA'S IN SHIT, SON.
♪MOMMA'S IN SHIT. MOMMA'S IN SHIT.♪
BONK BONK BONK
UH... I MEAN "POOP," OKAY?
STOP SAYING THE OTHER WORD.
♪MOMMA POOP. SHITTY POOP.♪
BWEEP-BWEEP-BWEEP
FLAWLESS
OH GOOD, YOUR FOOD'S READY...
DINO CHICKEN TENDERS!
THE DINOSAURS IN JURASSIC WORLD AREN'T REALLY DINOSAURS.
NO?
REAL DINOSAURS HAD FEATHERS ALL OVER THEIR BODY LIKE BIRDS. THEY WERE BIG BIRDS!
HOLY CRAP, MARTY, S'THAT MEAN BIG BIRD ON SESAME STREET IS REALLY A DINOSAUR?!
HA HAHAHA HAHA!!

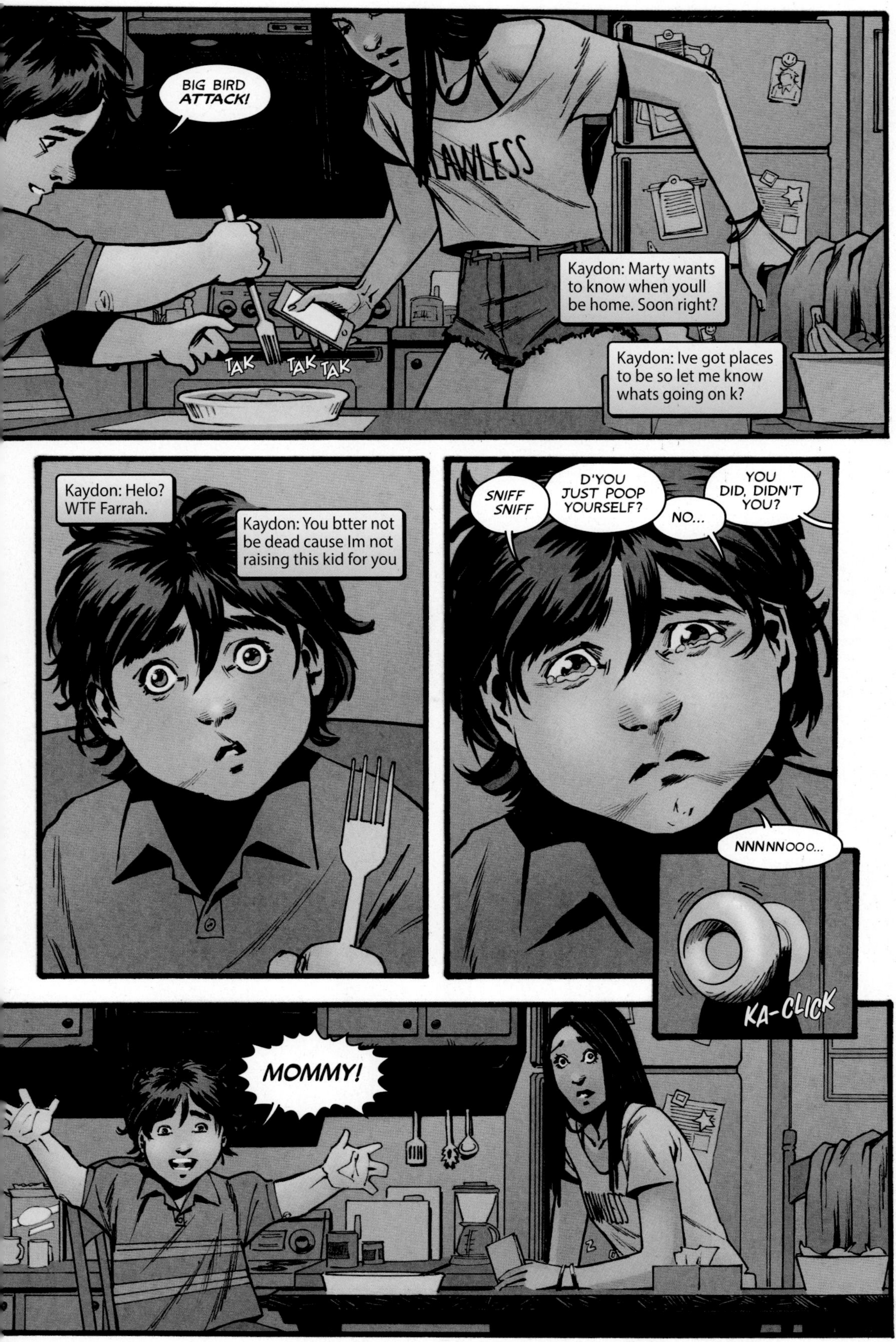
BIG BIRD ATTACK!
FLAWLESS
Kaydon: Marty wants to know when youll be home. Soon right?
TAK TAK TAK
Kaydon: Ive got places to be so let me know whats going on k?
Kaydon: Helo? WTF Farrah.
Kaydon: You btter not be dead cause Im not raising this kid for you
SNIFF SNIFF
D'YOU JUST POOP YOURSELF?
NO...
YOU DID, DIDN'T YOU?
NNNNNOOO...
KA-CLICK
MOMMY!

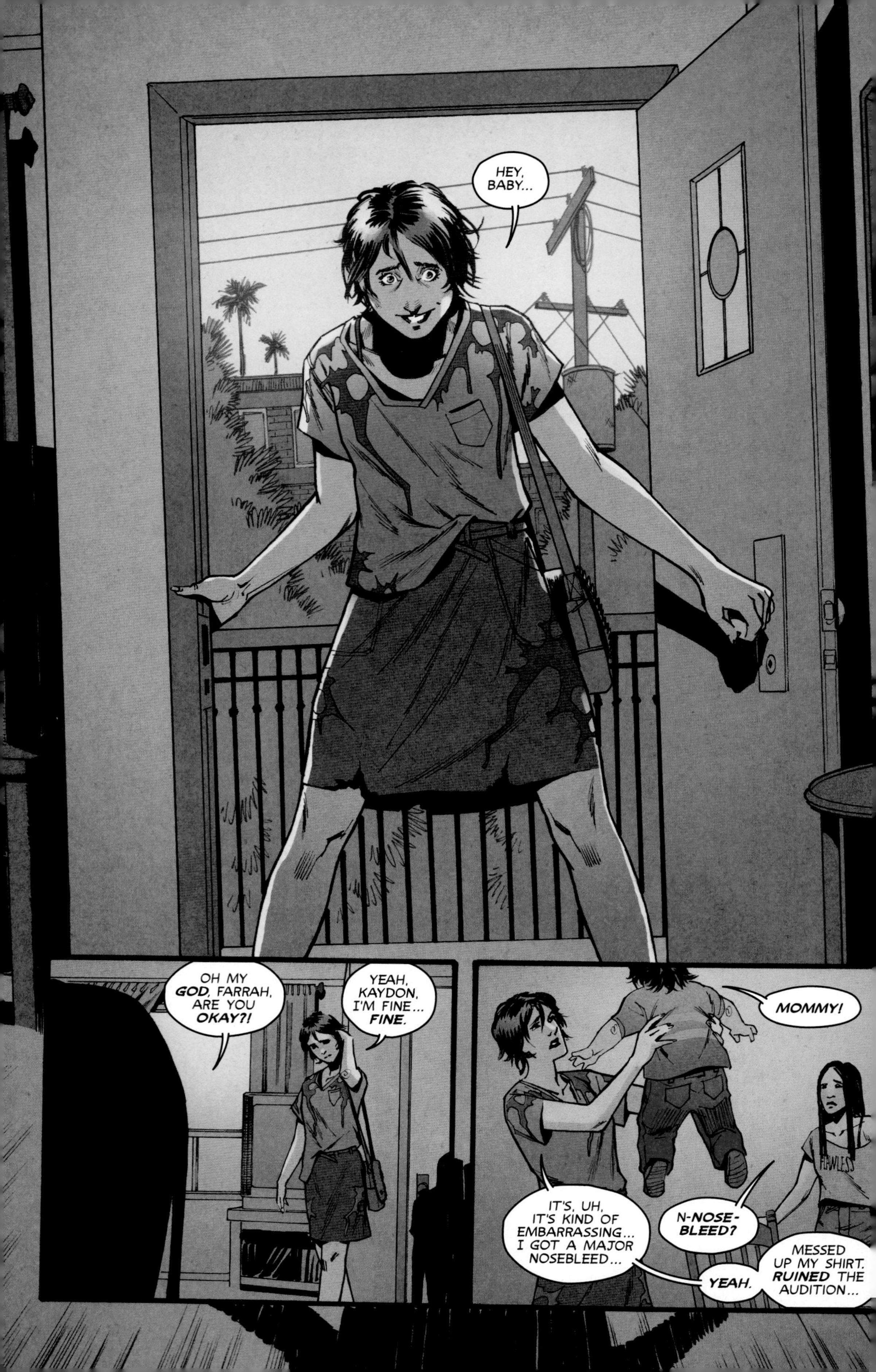
HEY, BABY...
OH MY GOD, FARRAH, ARE YOU OKAY?!
YEAH, KAYDON, I'M FINE... FINE.
MOMMY!
IT'S, UH, IT'S KIND OF EMBARRASSING... I GOT A MAJOR NOSEBLEED...
N-NOSE-BLEED?
YEAH.
MESSED UP MY SHIRT. RUINED THE AUDITION...

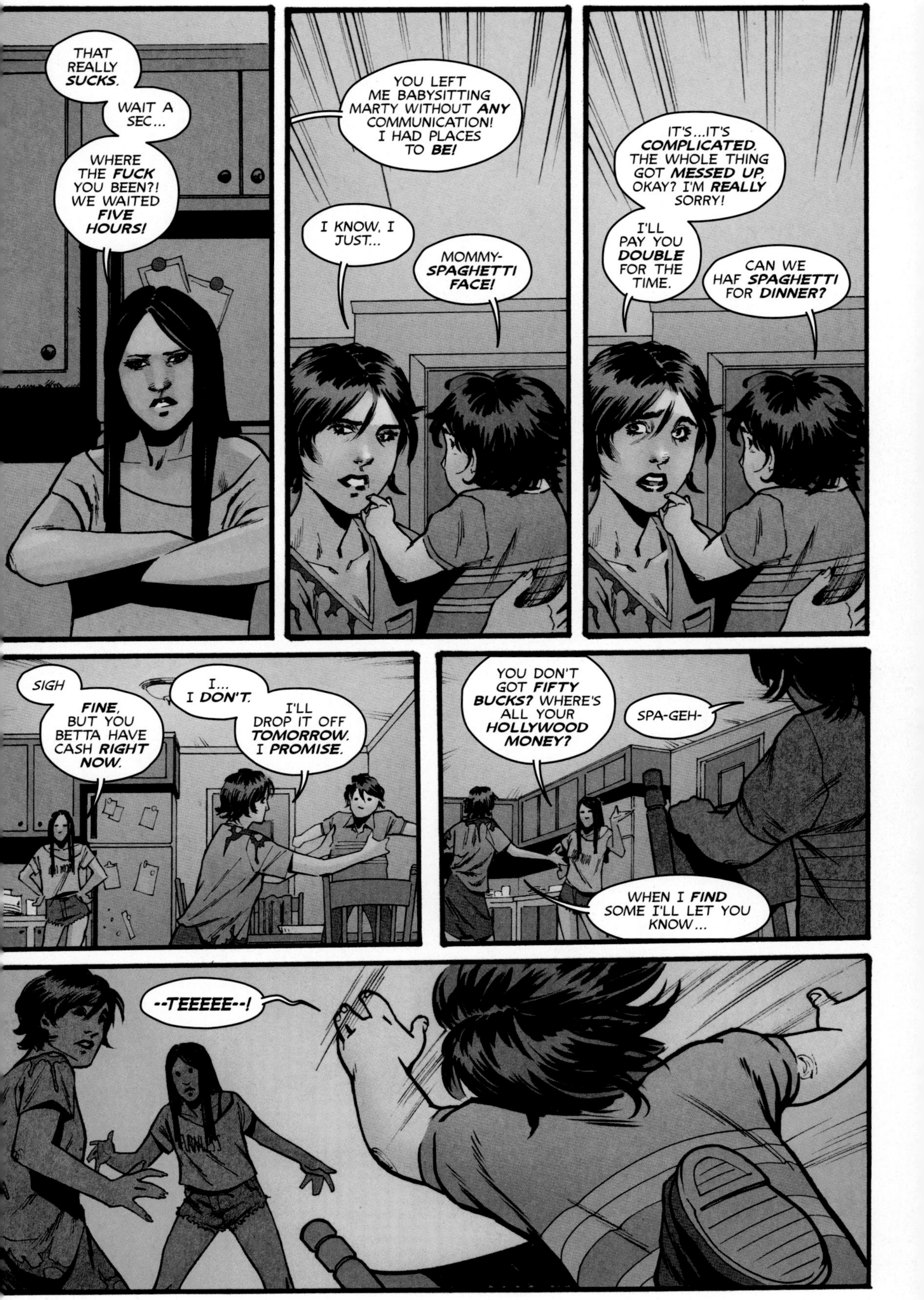
THAT REALLY SUCKS.
WAIT A SEC...
WHERE THE FUCK YOU BEEN?! WE WAITED FIVE HOURS!
YOU LEFT ME BABYSITTING MARTY WITHOUT ANY COMMUNICATION! I HAD PLACES TO BE!
I KNOW, I JUST...
MOMMY-SPAGHETTI FACE!
IT'S...IT'S COMPLICATED. THE WHOLE THING GOT MESSED UP, OKAY? I'M REALLY SORRY!
I'LL PAY YOU DOUBLE FOR THE TIME.
CAN WE HAF SPAGHETTI FOR DINNER?
SIGH
FINE, BUT YOU BETTA HAVE CASH RIGHT NOW.
I... I DON'T.
I'LL DROP IT OFF TOMORROW. I PROMISE.
YOU DON'T GOT FIFTY BUCKS? WHERE'S ALL YOUR HOLLYWOOD MONEY?
SPA-GEH-
WHEN I FIND SOME I'LL LET YOU KNOW...
--TEEEEE--!

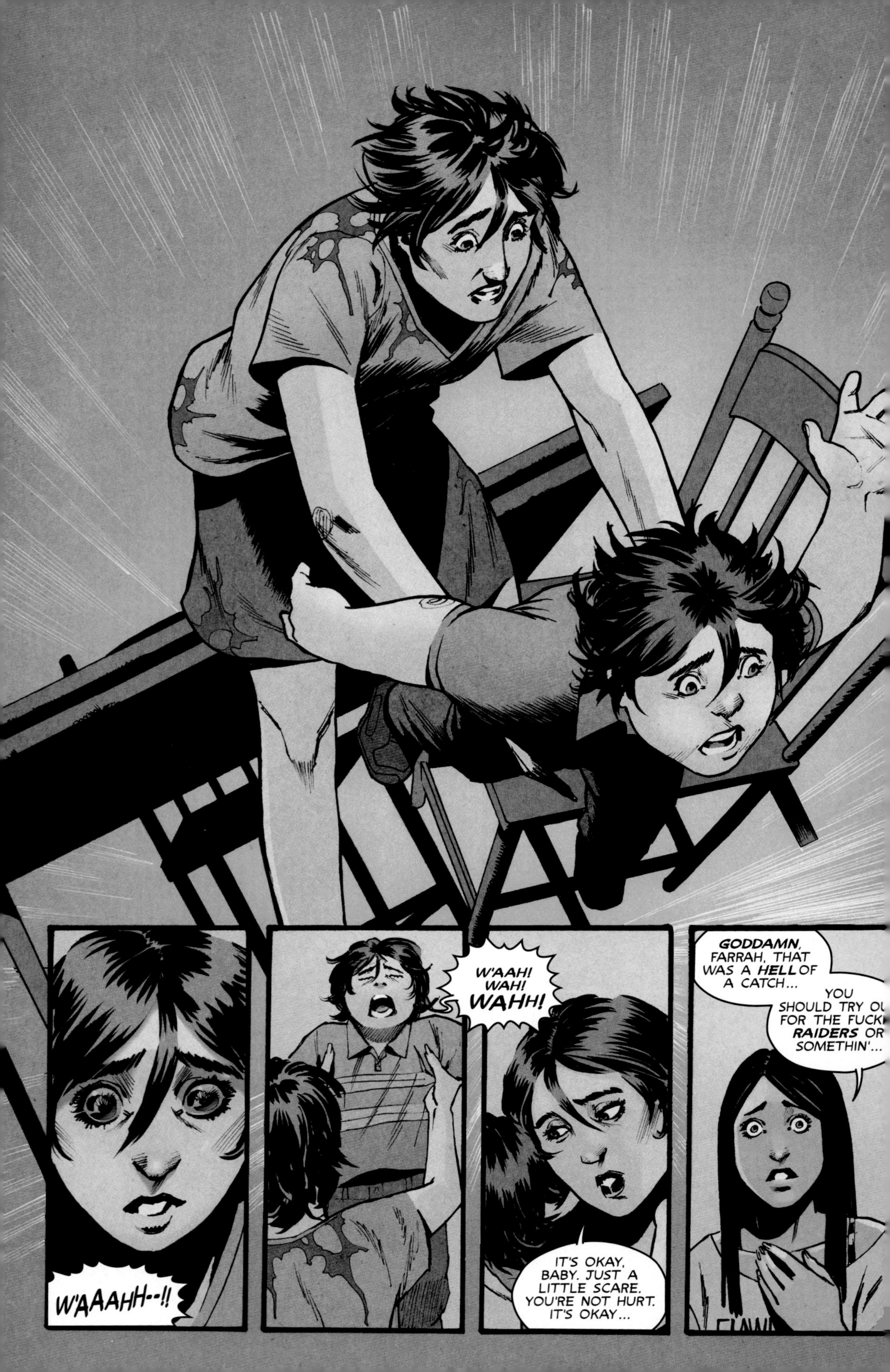
W'AAAHH--!!
W'AAH! WAH! WAHH!
GODDAMN, FARRAH, THAT WAS A HELL OF A CATCH...
YOU SHOULD TRY OU FOR THE FUCK RAIDERS OR SOMETHIN'...
IT'S OKAY, BABY. JUST A LITTLE SCARE. YOU'RE NOT HURT. IT'S OKAY...

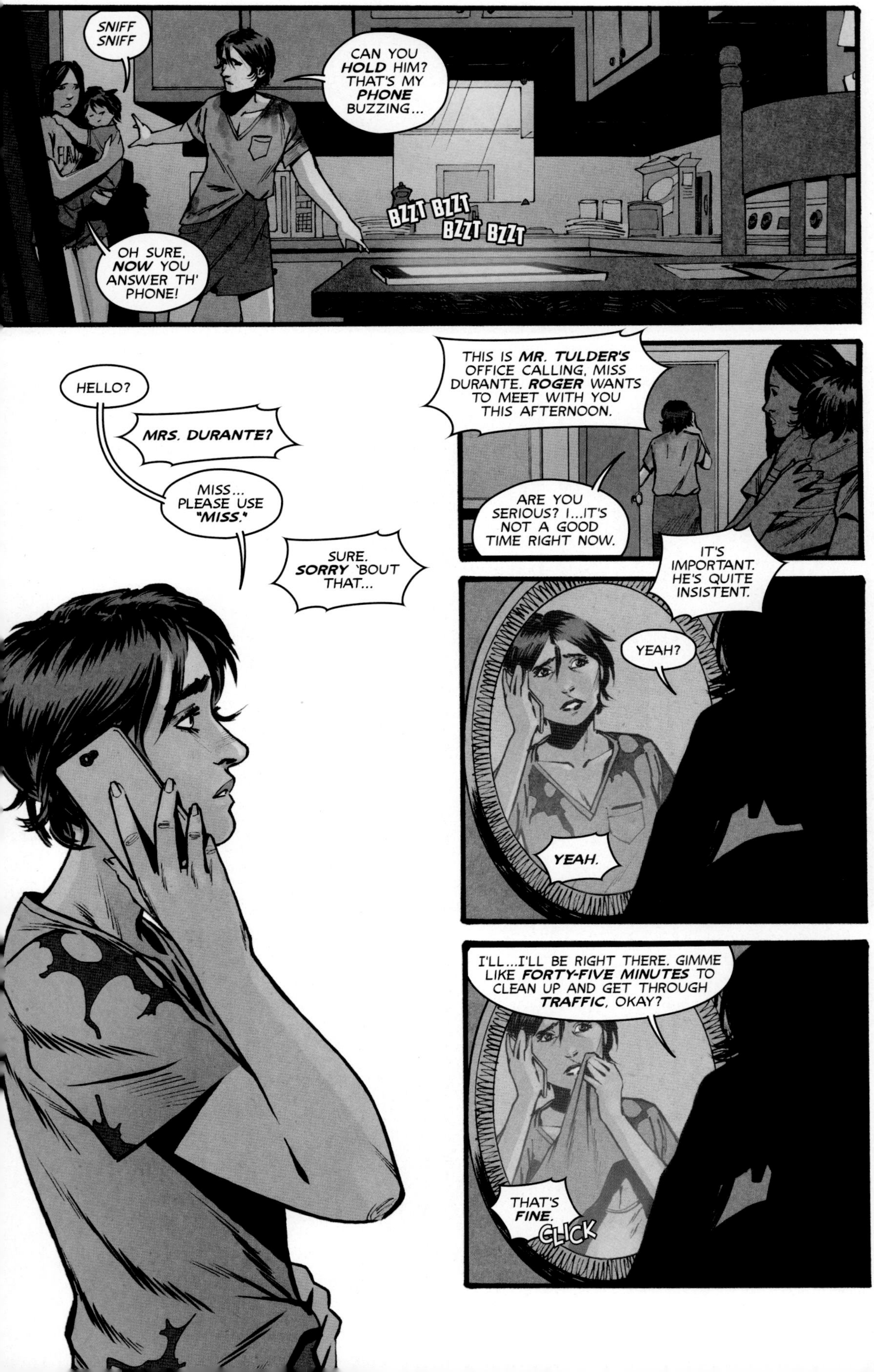
SNIFF SNIFF
CAN YOU HOLD HIM? THAT'S MY PHONE BUZZING...
BZZT BZZT BZZT BZZT
OH SURE, NOW YOU ANSWER TH' PHONE!
HELLO?
MRS. DURANTE?
MISS... PLEASE USE "MISS."
SURE. SORRY 'BOUT THAT...
THIS IS MR. TULDER'S OFFICE CALLING, MISS DURANTE. ROGER WANTS TO MEET WITH YOU THIS AFTERNOON.
ARE YOU SERIOUS? I...IT'S NOT A GOOD TIME RIGHT NOW.
IT'S IMPORTANT. HE'S QUITE INSISTENT.
YEAH?
YEAH.
I'LL...I'LL BE RIGHT THERE. GIMME LIKE FORTY-FIVE MINUTES TO CLEAN UP AND GET THROUGH TRAFFIC, OKAY?
THAT'S FINE.
CLICK

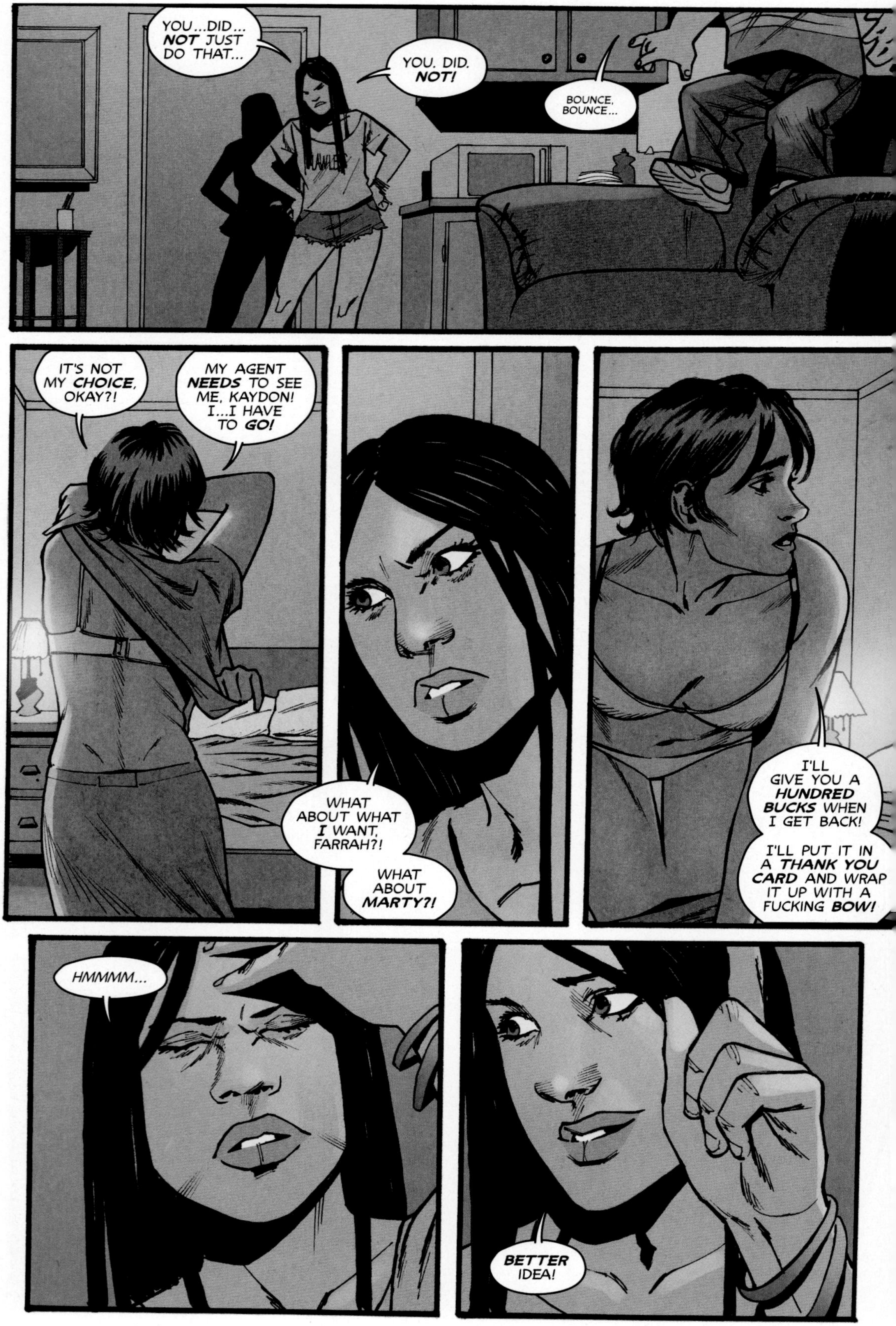
YOU...DID... NOT JUST DO THAT...
YOU. DID. NOT!
BOUNCE, BOUNCE...
IT'S NOT MY CHOICE, OKAY?!
MY AGENT NEEDS TO SEE ME, KAYDON! I...I HAVE TO GO!
WHAT ABOUT WHAT I WANT, FARRAH?!
WHAT ABOUT MARTY?!
I'LL GIVE YOU A HUNDRED BUCKS WHEN I GET BACK!
I'LL PUT IT IN A THANK YOU CARD AND WRAP IT UP WITH A FUCKING BOW!
HMMMM...
BETTER IDEA!

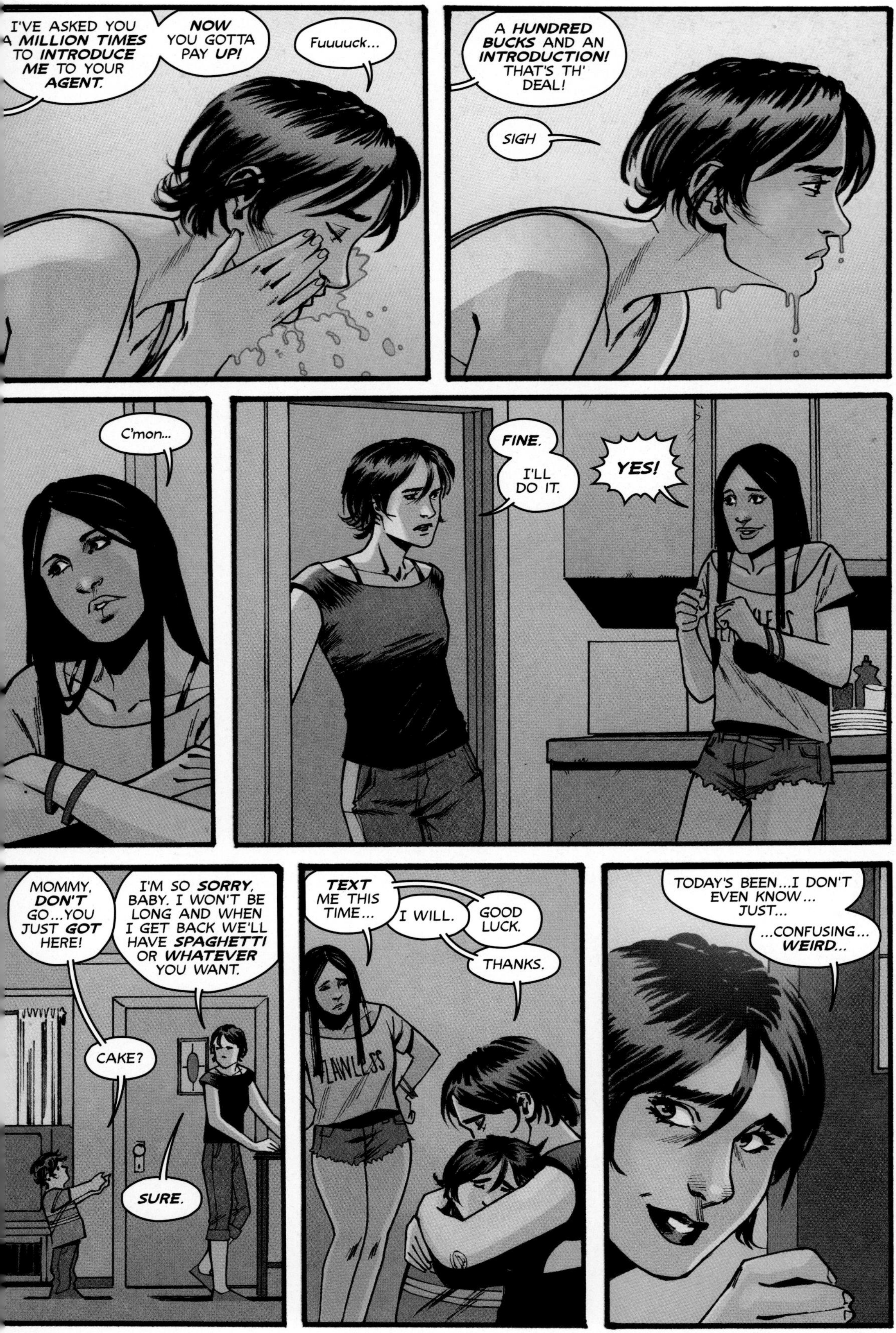
I'VE ASKED YOU A MILLION TIMES TO INTRODUCE ME TO YOUR AGENT.
NOW YOU GOTTA PAY UP!
Fuuuuck...
A HUNDRED BUCKS AND AN INTRODUCTION! THAT'S TH' DEAL!
SIGH
C'mon...
FINE.
I'LL DO IT.
YES!
MOMMY, DON'T GO...YOU JUST GOT HERE!
I'M SO SORRY, BABY. I WON'T BE LONG AND WHEN I GET BACK WE'LL HAVE SPAGHETTI OR WHATEVER YOU WANT.
CAKE?
SURE.
TEXT ME THIS TIME...
I WILL.
GOOD LUCK.
THANKS.
TODAY'S BEEN...I DON'T EVEN KNOW... JUST...
...CONFUSING... WEIRD...

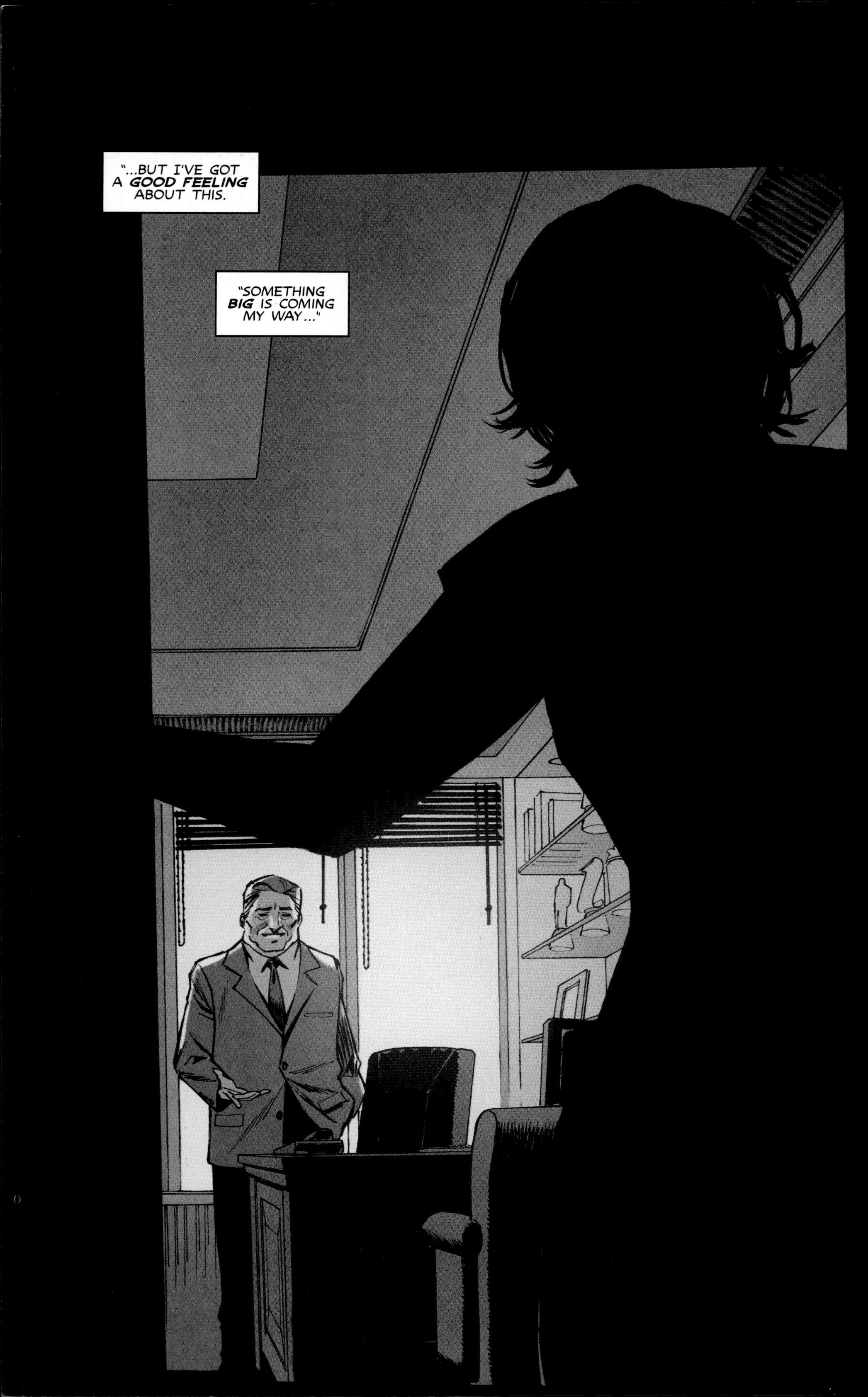
"...BUT I'VE GOT A GOOD FEELING ABOUT THIS.
"SOMETHING BIG IS COMING MY WAY..."

PART 2: 24-7, 365

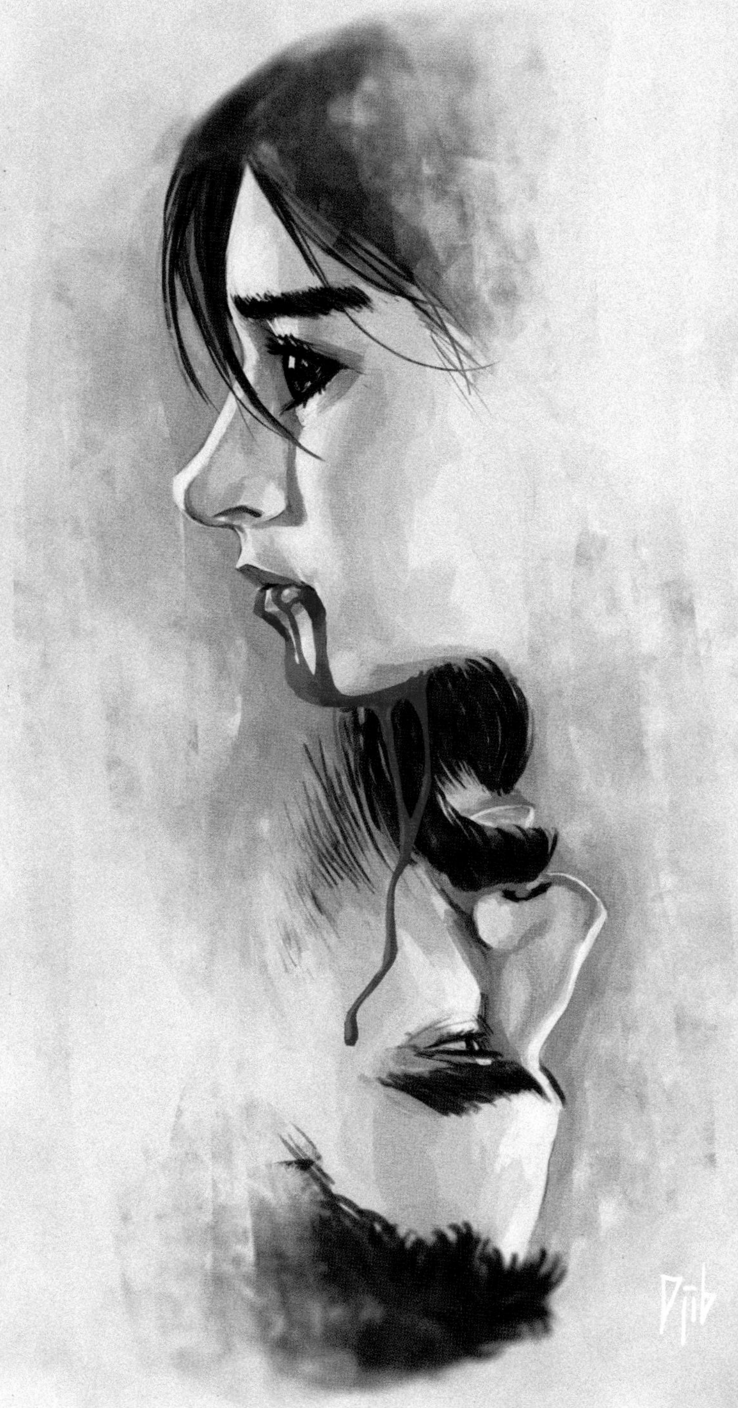

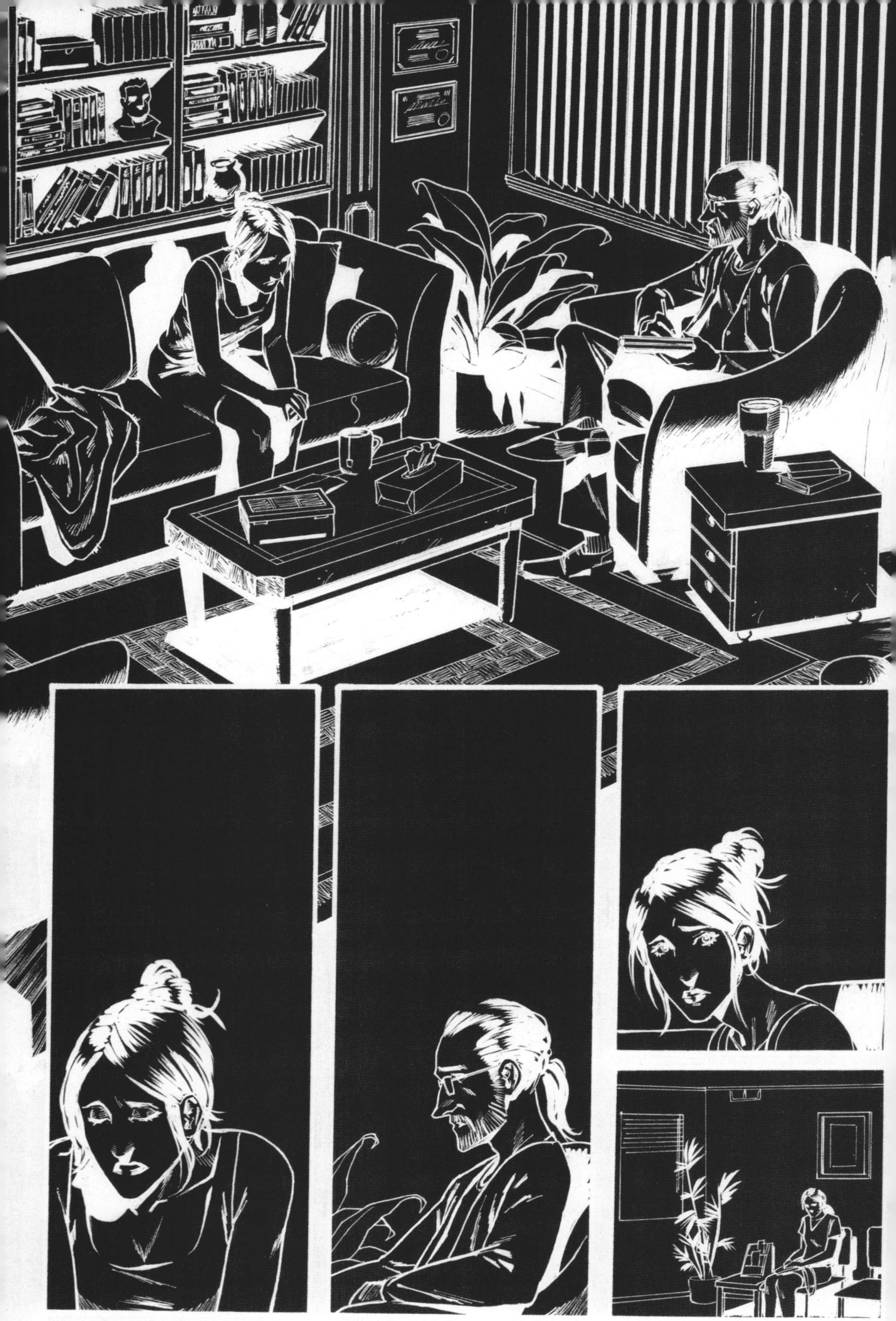

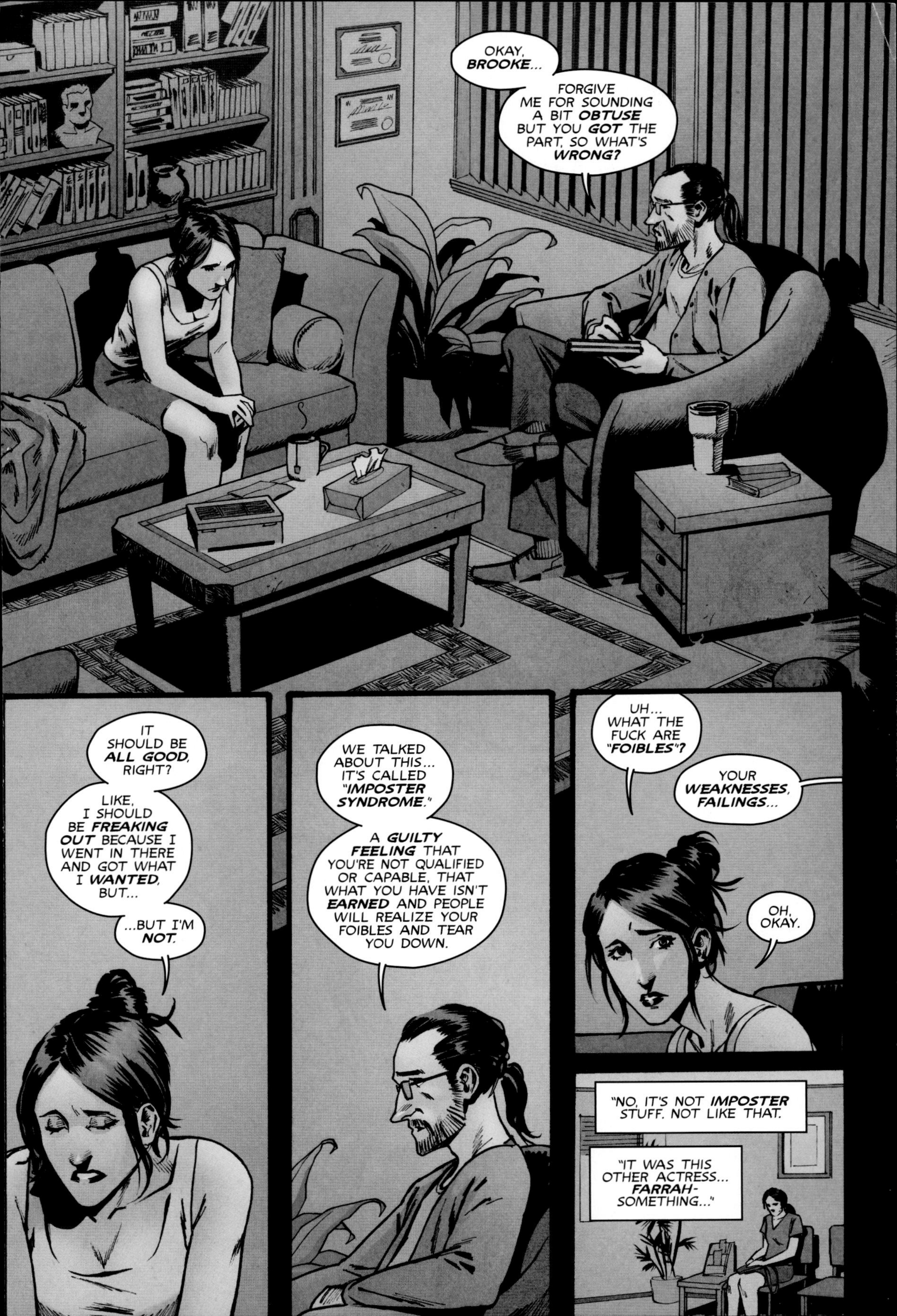
OKAY, BROOKE...
FORGIVE ME FOR SOUNDING A BIT OBTUSE BUT YOU GOT THE PART, SO WHAT'S WRONG?
IT SHOULD BE ALL GOOD, RIGHT?
LIKE, I SHOULD BE FREAKING OUT BECAUSE I WENT IN THERE AND GOT WHAT I WANTED, BUT...
...BUT I'M NOT.
WE TALKED ABOUT THIS... IT'S CALLED "IMPOSTER SYNDROME."
A GUILTY FEELING THAT YOU'RE NOT QUALIFIED OR CAPABLE, THAT WHAT YOU HAVE ISN'T EARNED AND PEOPLE WILL REALIZE YOUR FOIBLES AND TEAR YOU DOWN.
UH... WHAT THE FUCK ARE "FOIBLES"?
YOUR WEAKNESSES, FAILINGS...
OH, OKAY.
"NO, IT'S NOT IMPOSTER STUFF. NOT LIKE THAT.
"IT WAS THIS OTHER ACTRESS... FARRAH-SOMETHING..."

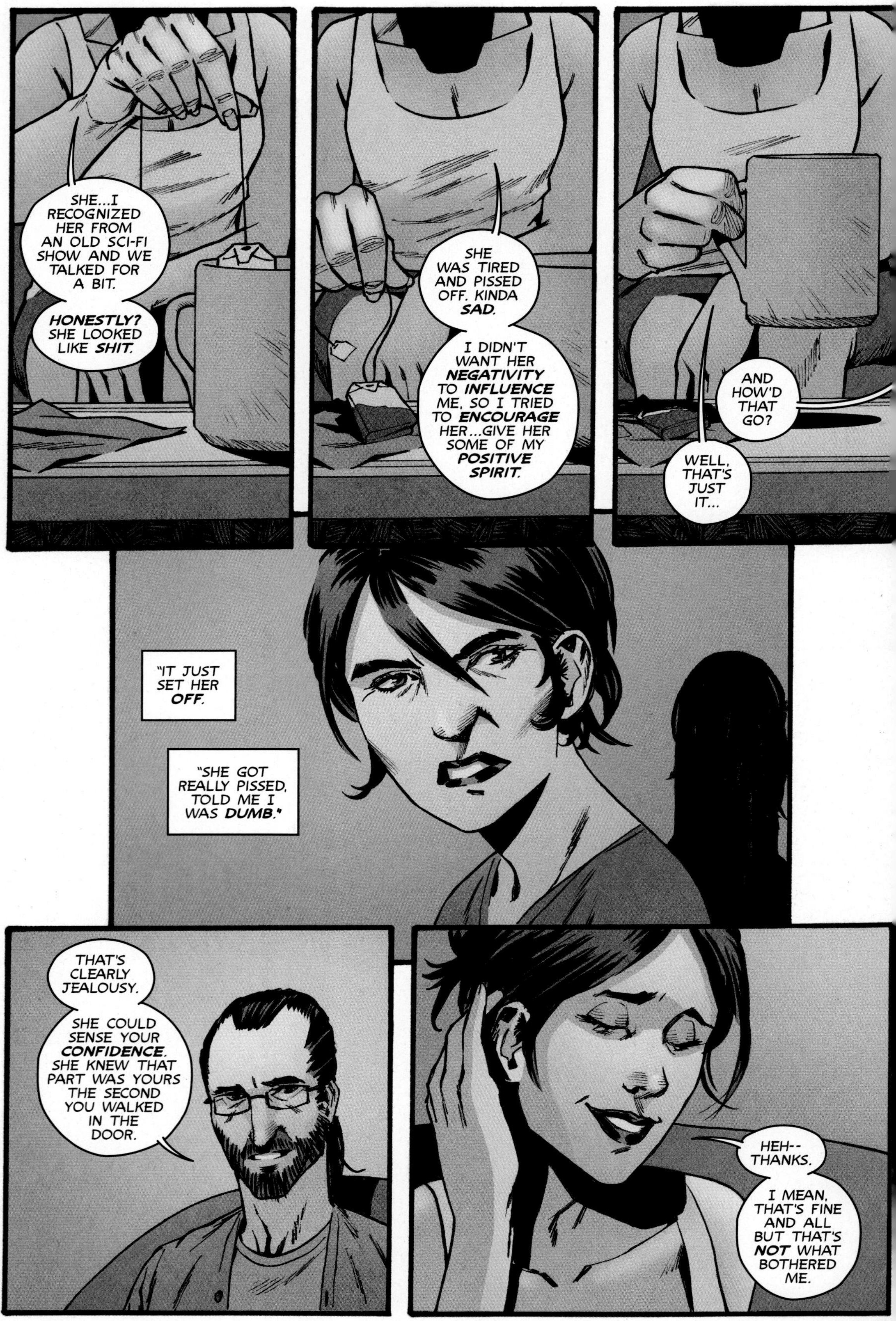
SHE...I RECOGNIZED HER FROM AN OLD SCI-FI SHOW AND WE TALKED FOR A BIT.
HONESTLY? SHE LOOKED LIKE SHIT.
SHE WAS TIRED AND PISSED OFF. KINDA SAD.
I DIDN'T WANT HER NEGATIVITY TO INFLUENCE ME, SO I TRIED TO ENCOURAGE HER...GIVE HER SOME OF MY POSITIVE SPIRIT.
AND HOW'D THAT GO?
WELL, THAT'S JUST IT...
"IT JUST SET HER OFF.
"SHE GOT REALLY PISSED, TOLD ME I WAS DUMB."
THAT'S CLEARLY JEALOUSY.
SHE COULD SENSE YOUR CONFIDENCE. SHE KNEW THAT PART WAS YOURS THE SECOND YOU WALKED IN THE DOOR.
HEH-- THANKS.
I MEAN, THAT'S FINE AND ALL BUT THAT'S NOT WHAT BOTHERED ME.

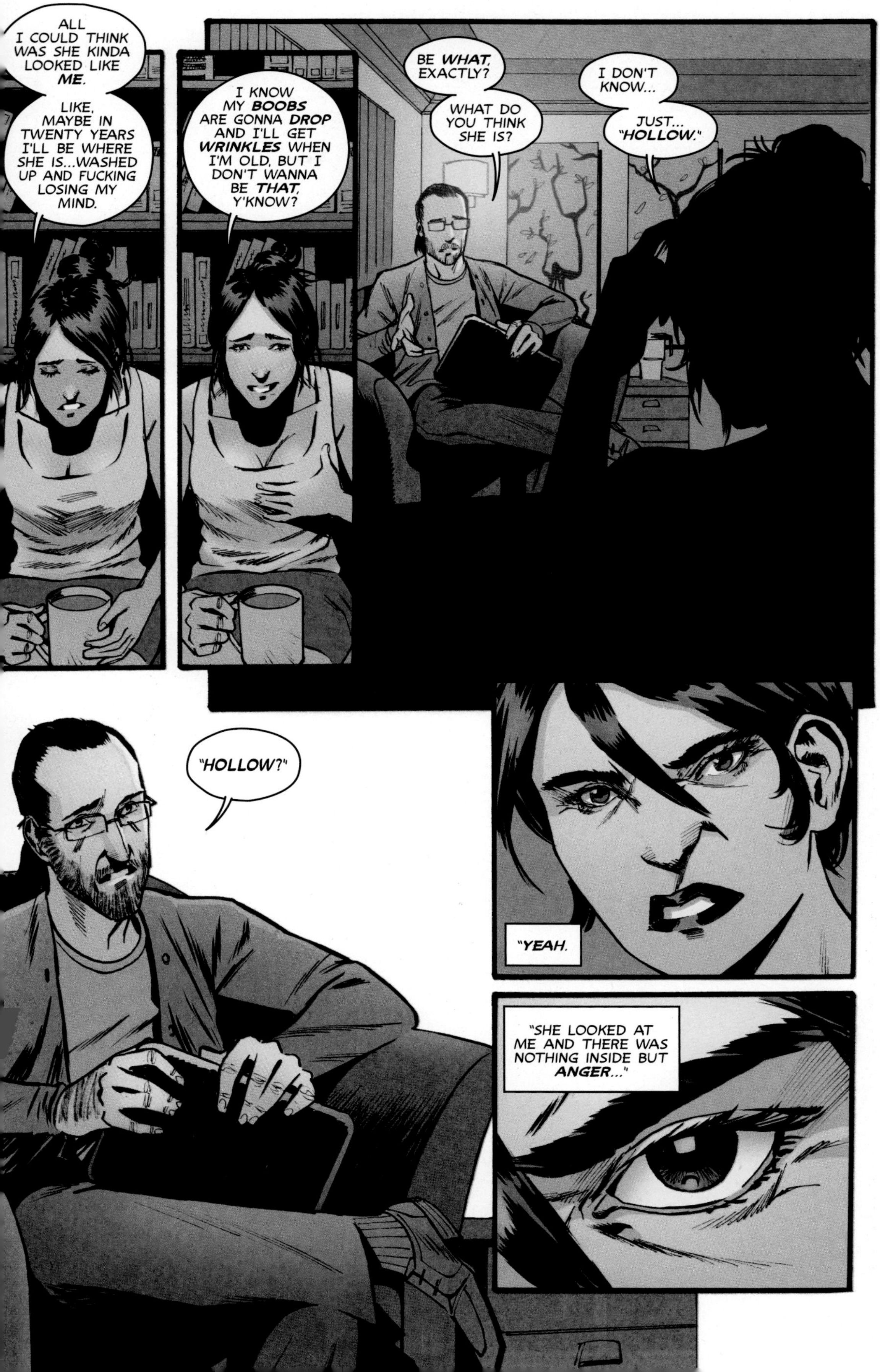
ALL I COULD THINK WAS SHE KINDA LOOKED LIKE ME.
LIKE, MAYBE IN TWENTY YEARS I'LL BE WHERE SHE IS...WASHED UP AND FUCKING LOSING MY MIND.
I KNOW MY BOOBS ARE GONNA DROP AND I'LL GET WRINKLES WHEN I'M OLD, BUT I DON'T WANNA BE THAT, Y'KNOW?
BE WHAT, EXACTLY?
WHAT DO YOU THINK SHE IS?
I DON'T KNOW...
JUST... "HOLLOW."
"HOLLOW?"
"YEAH.
"SHE LOOKED AT ME AND THERE WAS NOTHING INSIDE BUT ANGER..."

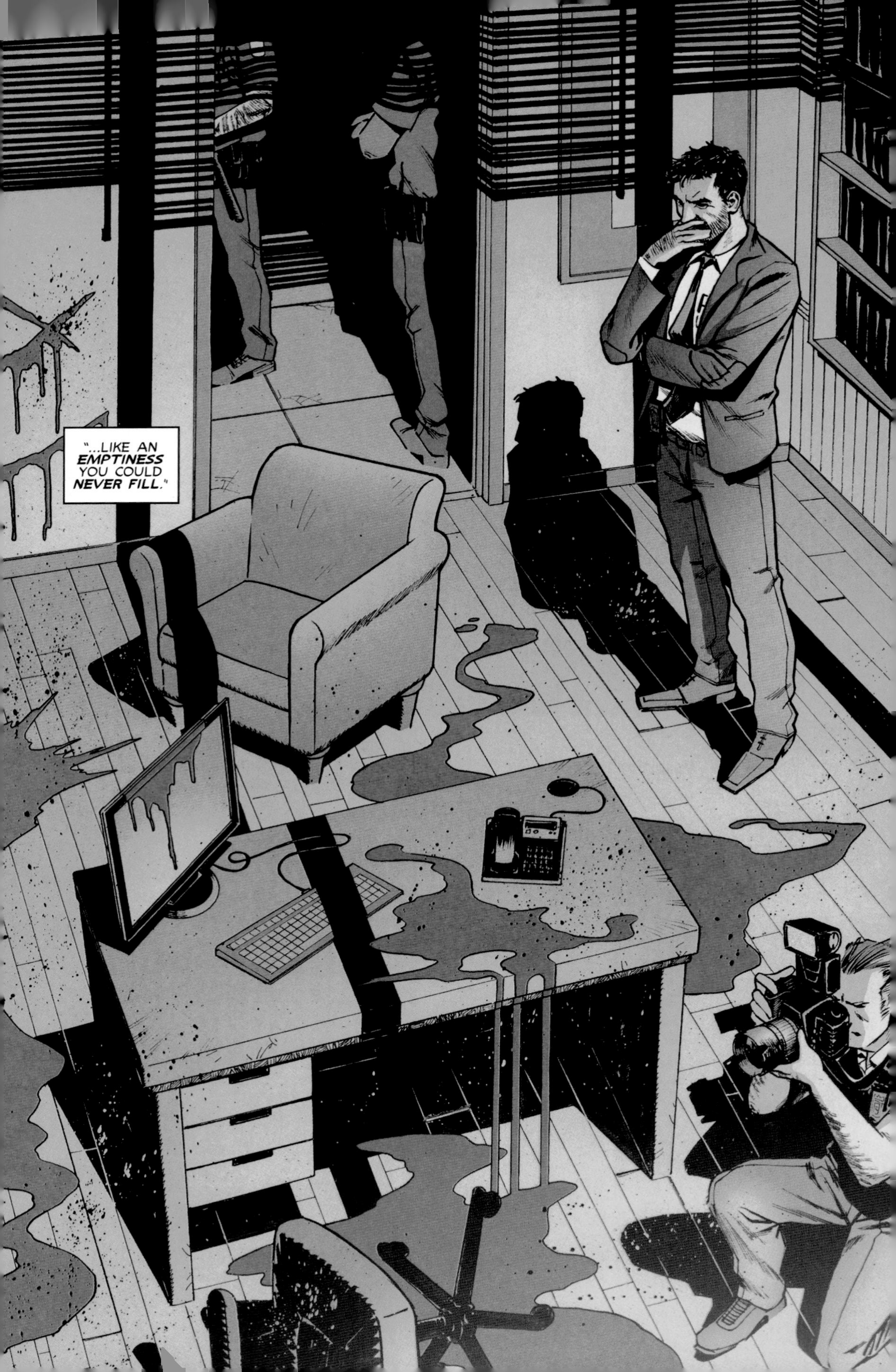
"...LIKE AN EMPTINESS YOU COULD NEVER FILL."

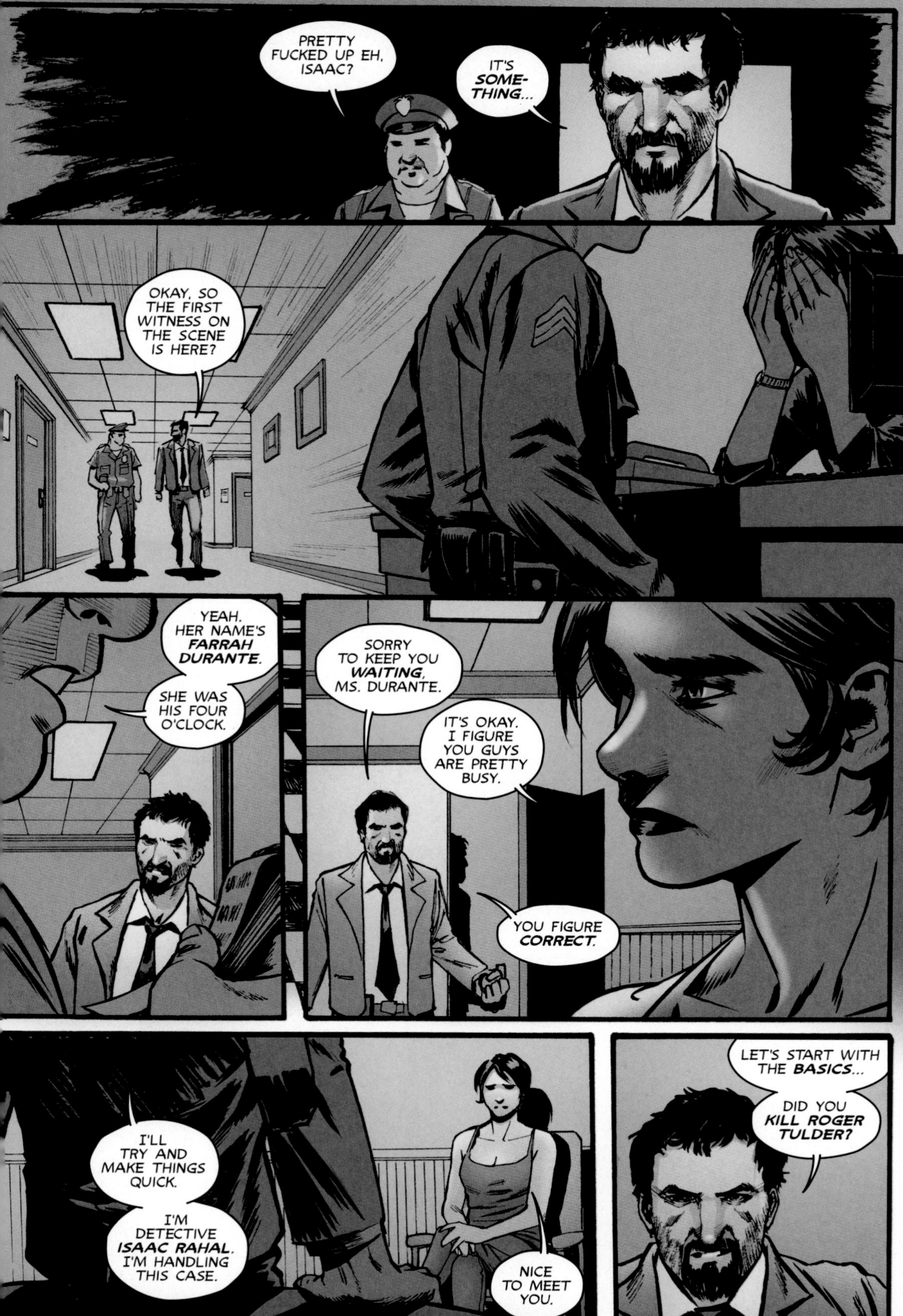
PRETTY FUCKED UP EH, ISAAC?
IT'S SOMETHING...
OKAY, SO THE FIRST WITNESS ON THE SCENE IS HERE?
YEAH. HER NAME'S FARRAH DURANTE.
SHE WAS HIS FOUR O'CLOCK.
SORRY TO KEEP YOU WAITING, MS. DURANTE.
IT'S OKAY. I FIGURE YOU GUYS ARE PRETTY BUSY.
YOU FIGURE CORRECT.
I'LL TRY AND MAKE THINGS QUICK.
I'M DETECTIVE ISAAC RAHAL. I'M HANDLING THIS CASE.
NICE TO MEET YOU.
LET'S START WITH THE BASICS...
DID YOU KILL ROGER TULDER?

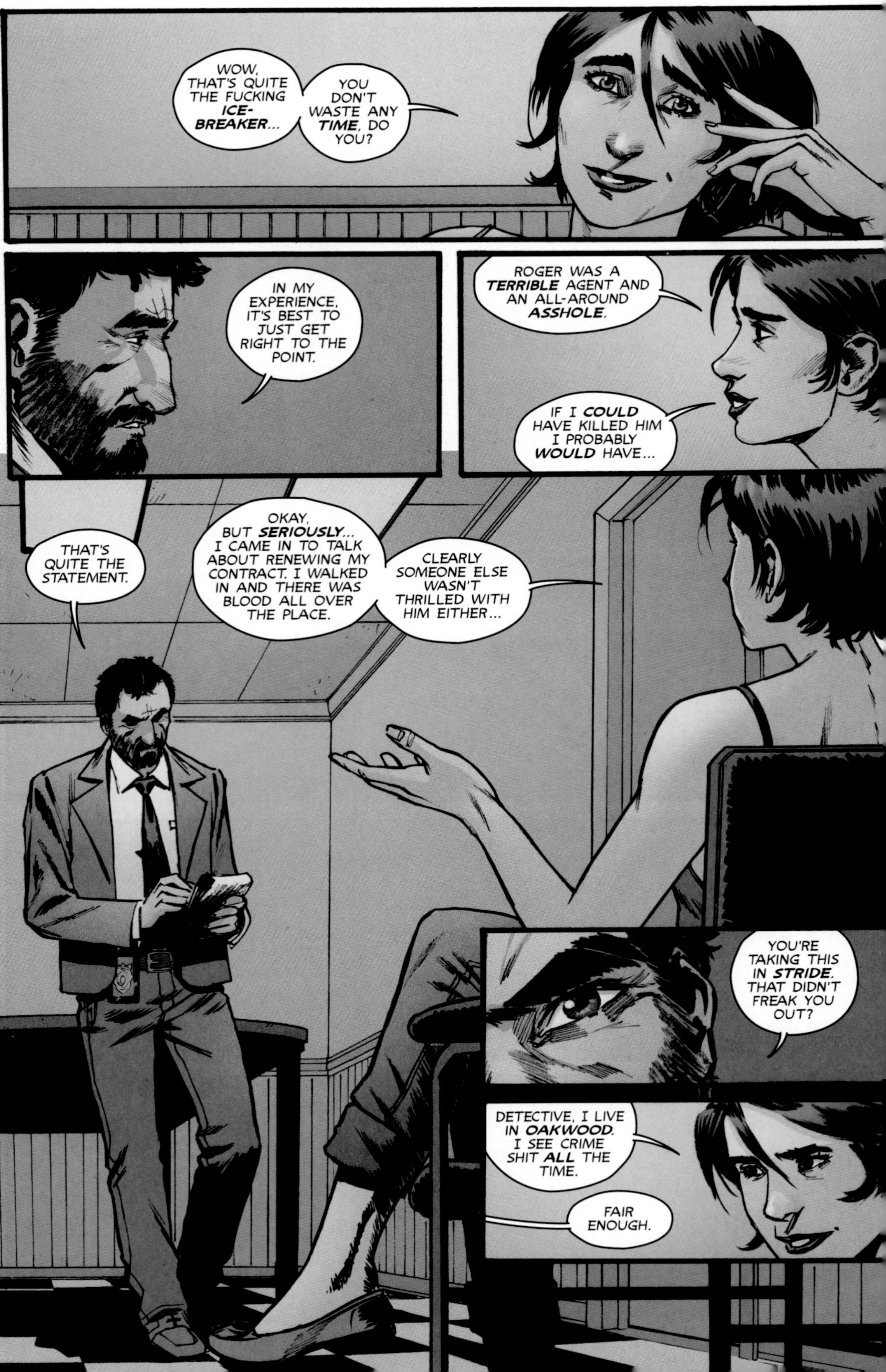
WOW, THAT'S QUITE THE FUCKING ICE-BREAKER...
YOU DON'T WASTE ANY TIME, DO YOU?
IN MY EXPERIENCE, IT'S BEST TO JUST GET RIGHT TO THE POINT.
ROGER WAS A TERRIBLE AGENT AND AN ALL-AROUND ASSHOLE.
IF I COULD HAVE KILLED HIM I PROBABLY WOULD HAVE...
THAT'S QUITE THE STATEMENT.
OKAY, BUT SERIOUSLY... I CAME IN TO TALK ABOUT RENEWING MY CONTRACT. I WALKED IN AND THERE WAS BLOOD ALL OVER THE PLACE.
CLEARLY SOMEONE ELSE WASN'T THRILLED WITH HIM EITHER...
YOU'RE TAKING THIS IN STRIDE. THAT DIDN'T FREAK YOU OUT?
DETECTIVE, I LIVE IN OAKWOOD. I SEE CRIME SHIT ALL THE TIME.
FAIR ENOUGH.

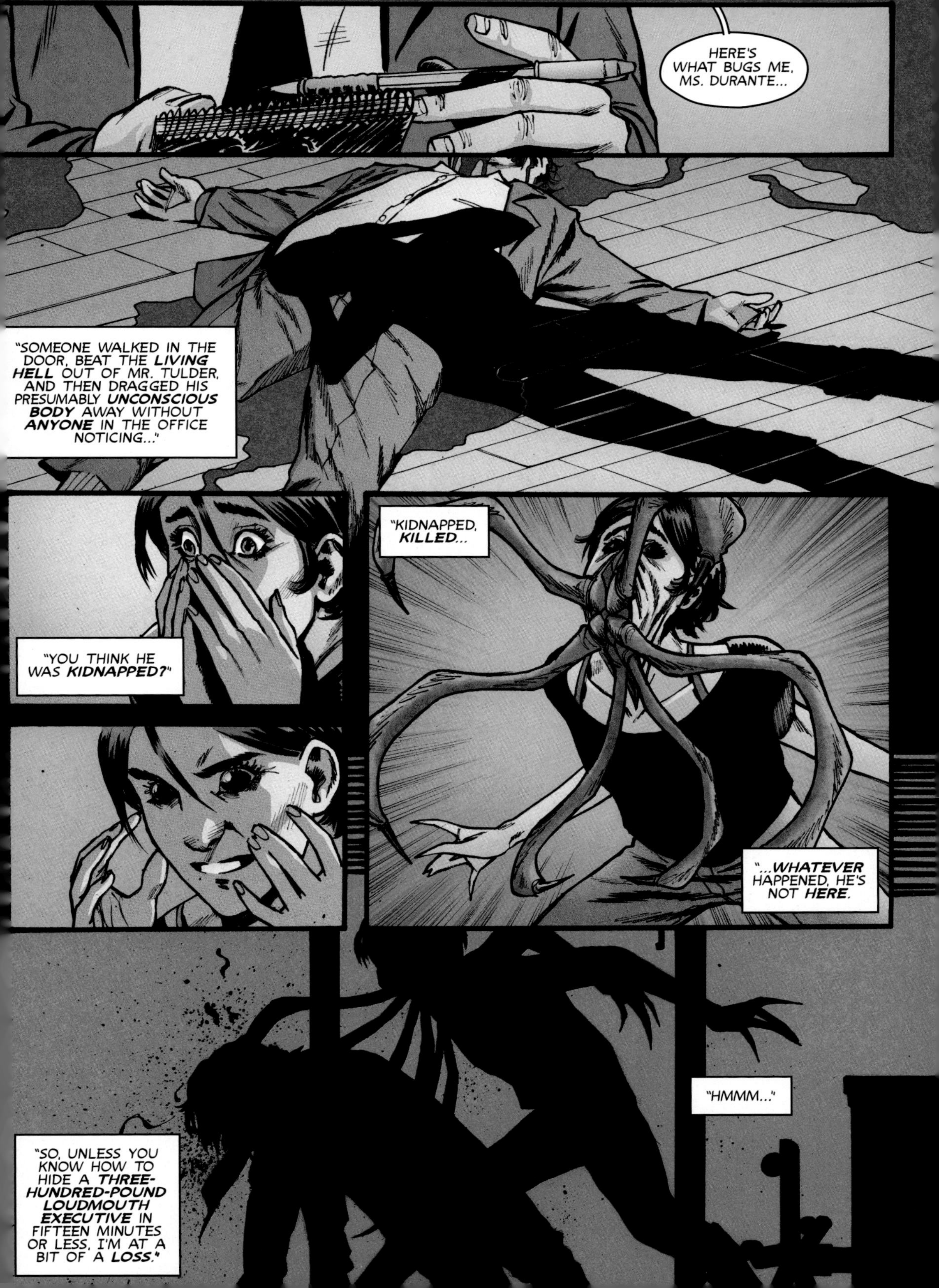

HERE'S WHAT BUGS ME, MS. DURANTE...
"SOMEONE WALKED IN THE DOOR, BEAT THE ***LIVING HELL*** OUT OF MR. TULDER, AND THEN DRAGGED HIS PRESUMABLY ***UNCONSCIOUS BODY*** AWAY WITHOUT ***ANYONE*** IN THE OFFICE NOTICING..."
"YOU THINK HE WAS ***KIDNAPPED?***"
"KIDNAPPED, ***KILLED...***
"...***WHATEVER*** HAPPENED, HE'S NOT ***HERE.***
"HMMM..."
"SO, UNLESS YOU KNOW HOW TO HIDE A ***THREE-HUNDRED-POUND LOUDMOUTH EXECUTIVE*** IN FIFTEEN MINUTES OR LESS, I'M AT A BIT OF A ***LOSS.***"

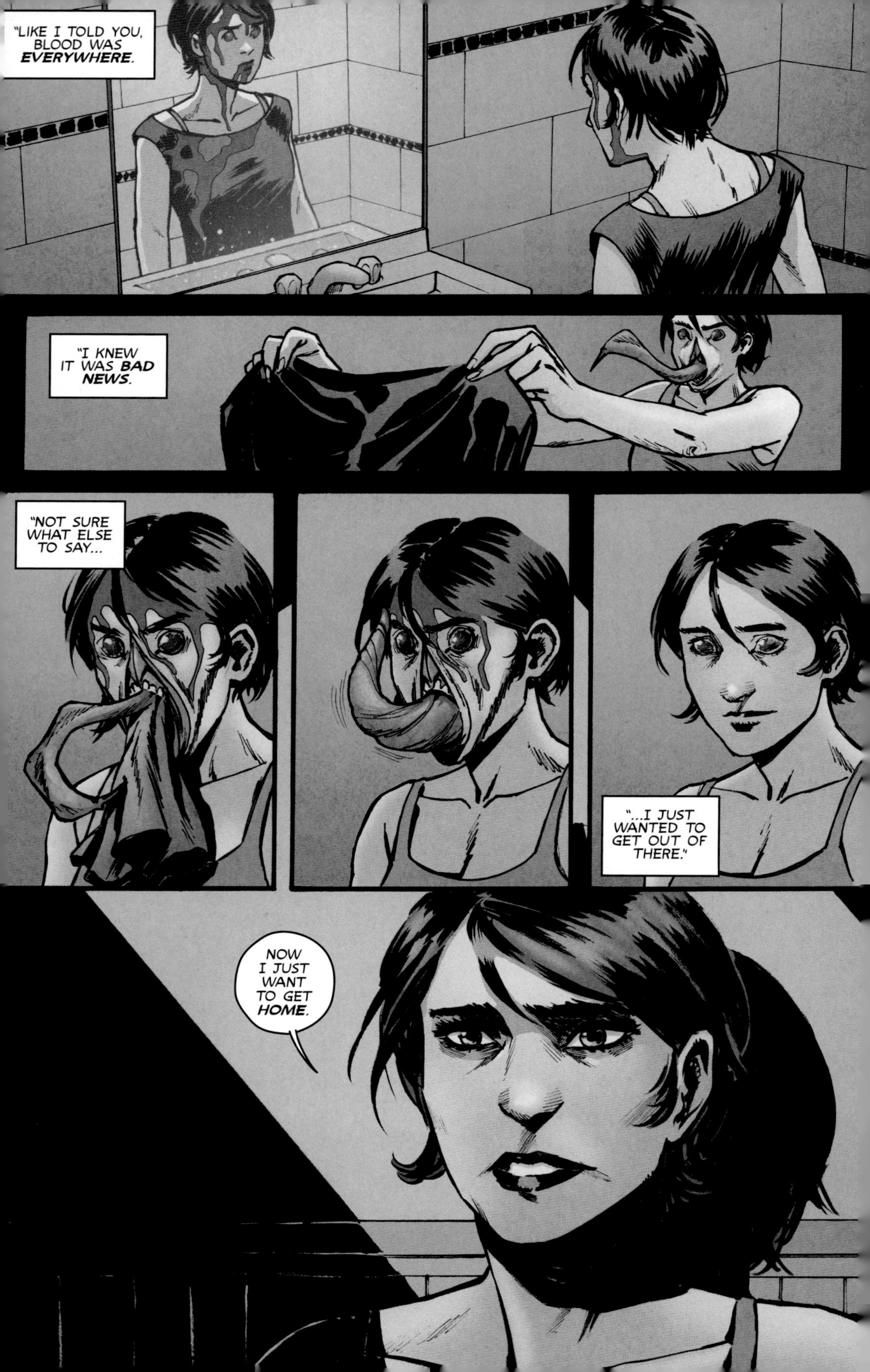
"LIKE I TOLD YOU, BLOOD WAS **EVERYWHERE**.
"I KNEW IT WAS **BAD NEWS**.
"NOT SURE WHAT ELSE TO SAY...
"...I JUST WANTED TO GET OUT OF THERE."
NOW I JUST WANT TO GET **HOME**.

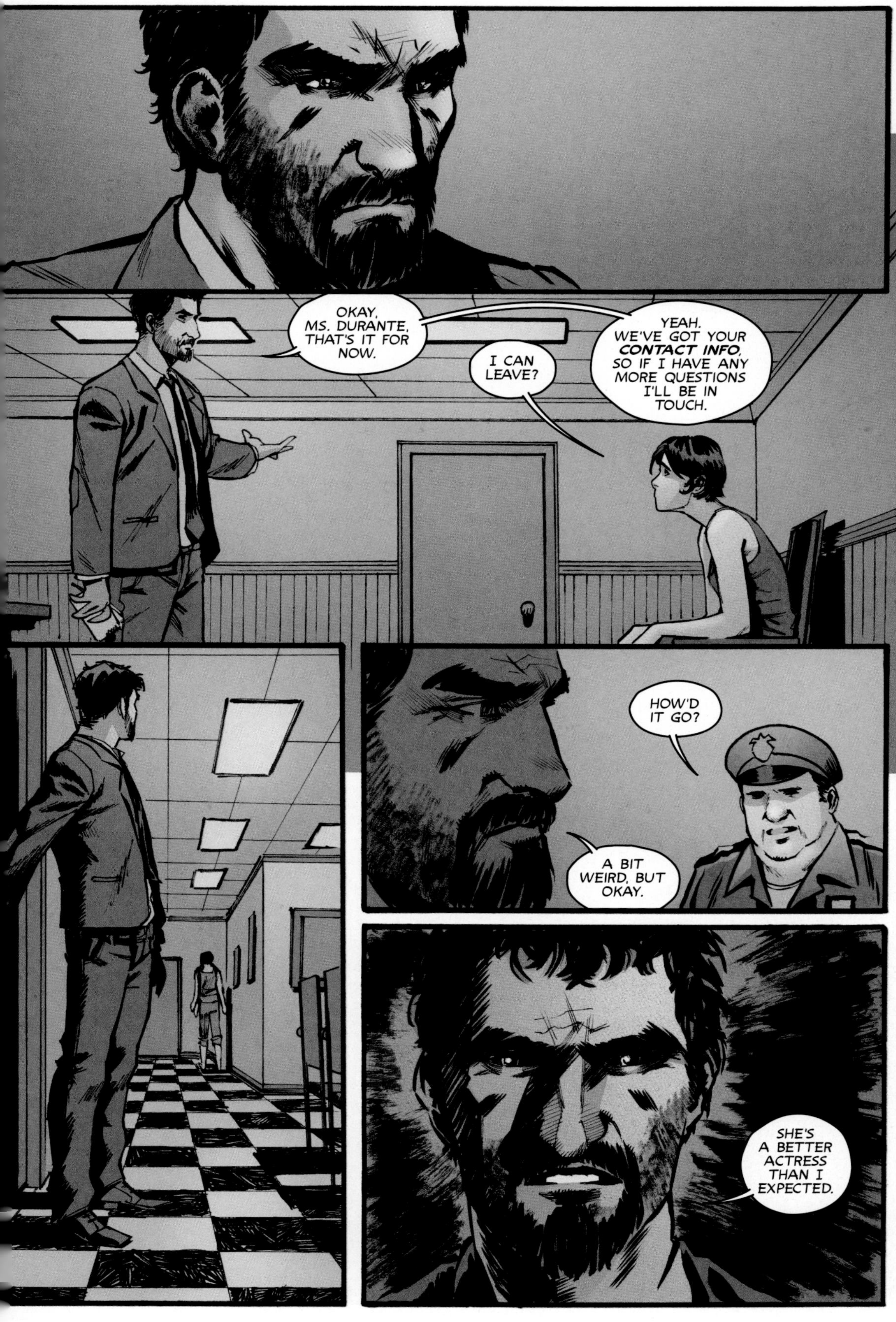
OKAY, MS. DURANTE, THAT'S IT FOR NOW.
I CAN LEAVE?
YEAH. WE'VE GOT YOUR **CONTACT INFO**, SO IF I HAVE ANY MORE QUESTIONS I'LL BE IN TOUCH.
HOW'D IT GO?
A BIT WEIRD, BUT OKAY.
SHE'S A BETTER ACTRESS THAN I EXPECTED.

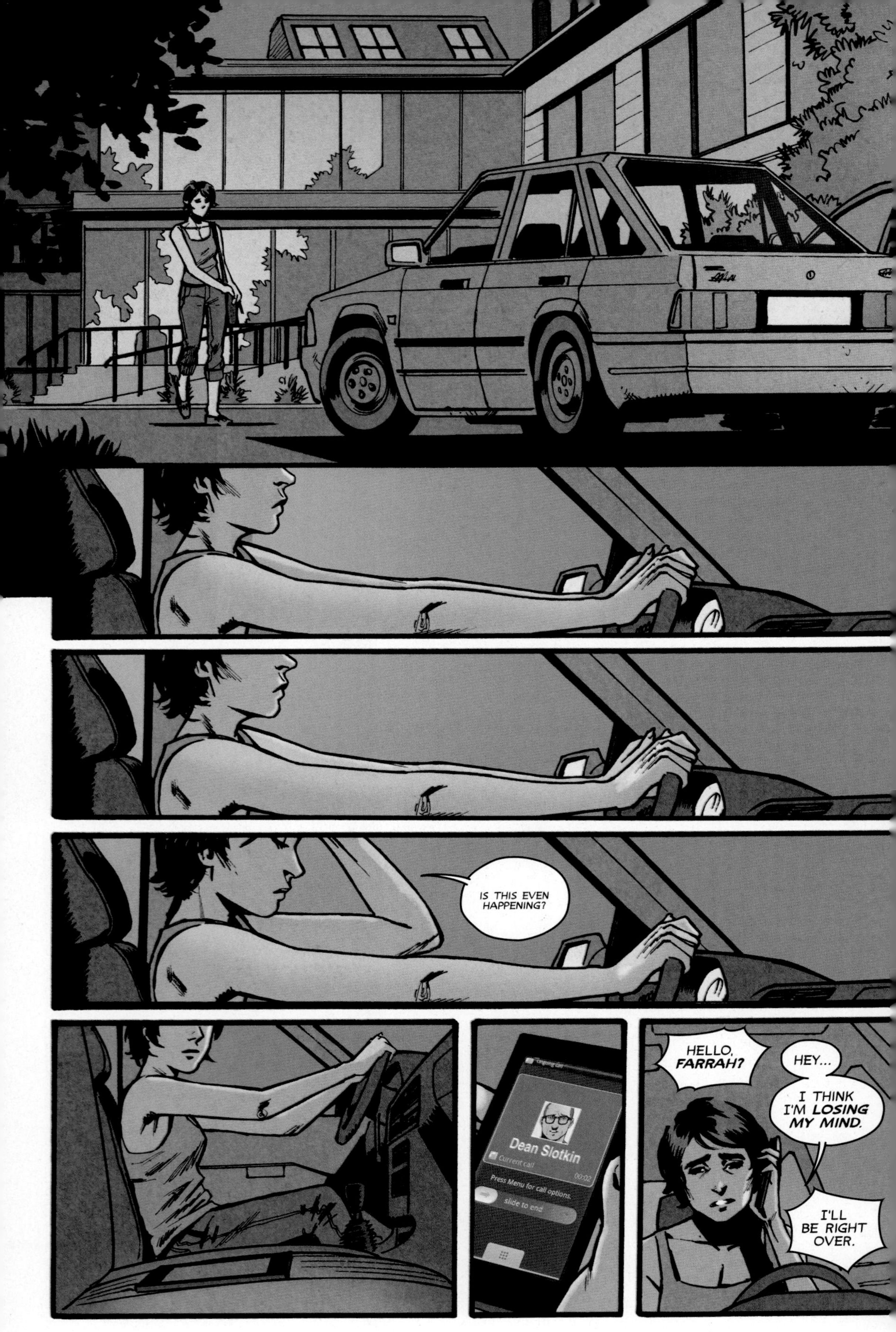
IS THIS EVEN HAPPENING?
Dean Slotkin
Current call
Press Menu for call options.
slide to end
HELLO, FARRAH?
HEY...
I THINK I'M LOSING MY MIND.
I'LL BE RIGHT OVER.

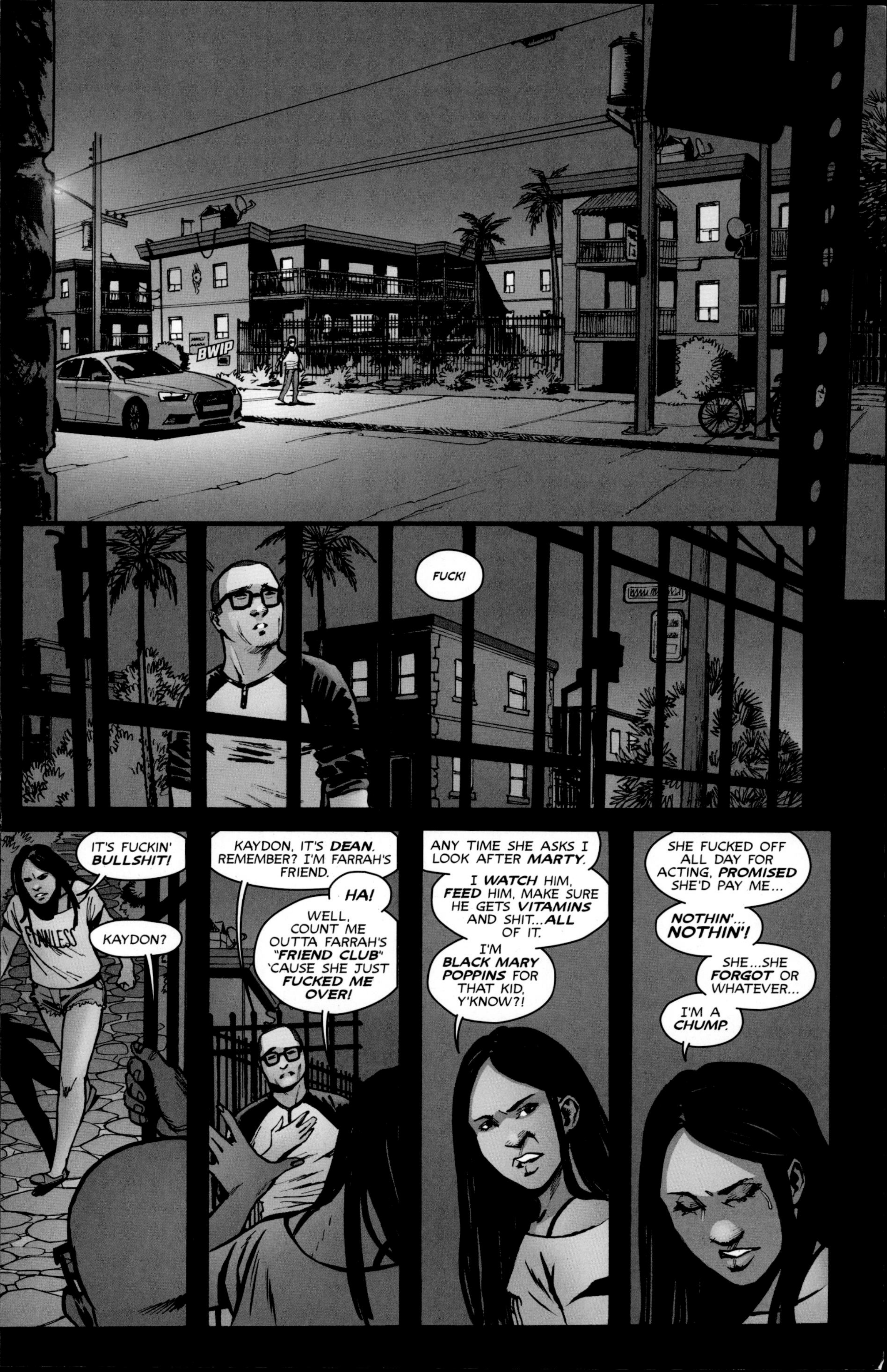
BWIP
FUCK!
IT'S FUCKIN' BULLSHIT!
KAYDON?
KAYDON, IT'S DEAN. REMEMBER? I'M FARRAH'S FRIEND.
HA!
WELL, COUNT ME OUTTA FARRAH'S "FRIEND CLUB" 'CAUSE SHE JUST FUCKED ME OVER!
ANY TIME SHE ASKS I LOOK AFTER MARTY.
I WATCH HIM, FEED HIM, MAKE SURE HE GETS VITAMINS AND SHIT...ALL OF IT.
I'M BLACK MARY POPPINS FOR THAT KID, Y'KNOW?!
SHE FUCKED OFF ALL DAY FOR ACTING, PROMISED SHE'D PAY ME...
NOTHIN'... NOTHIN'!
SHE...SHE FORGOT OR WHATEVER...
I'M A CHUMP.

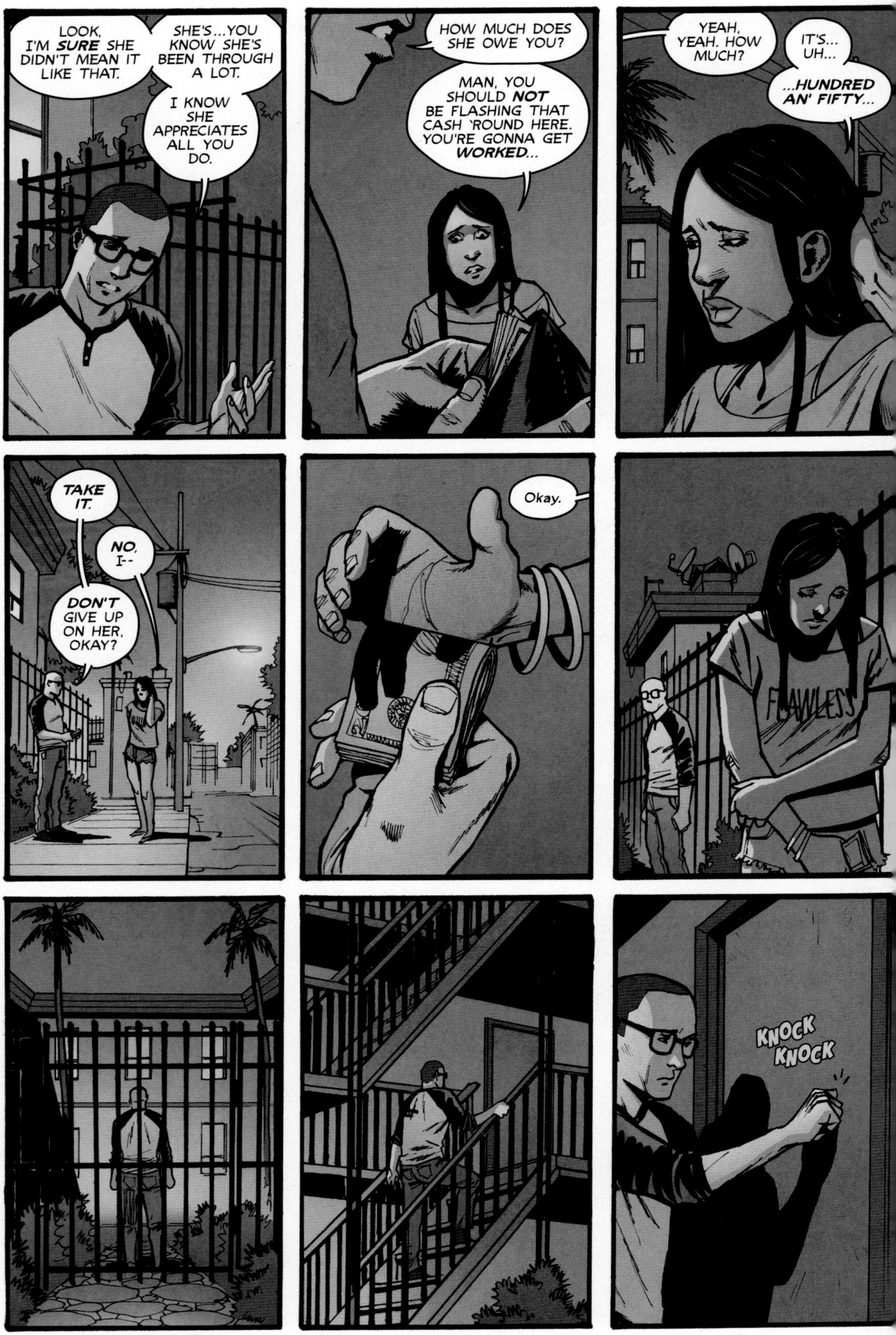
LOOK, I'M SURE SHE DIDN'T MEAN IT LIKE THAT.
SHE'S...YOU KNOW SHE'S BEEN THROUGH A LOT.
I KNOW SHE APPRECIATES ALL YOU DO.
HOW MUCH DOES SHE OWE YOU?
MAN, YOU SHOULD NOT BE FLASHING THAT CASH 'ROUND HERE. YOU'RE GONNA GET WORKED...
YEAH, YEAH. HOW MUCH?
IT'S... UH...
...HUNDRED AN' FIFTY...
TAKE IT.
NO, I--
DON'T GIVE UP ON HER, OKAY?
Okay.
FLAWLESS
KNOCK KNOCK

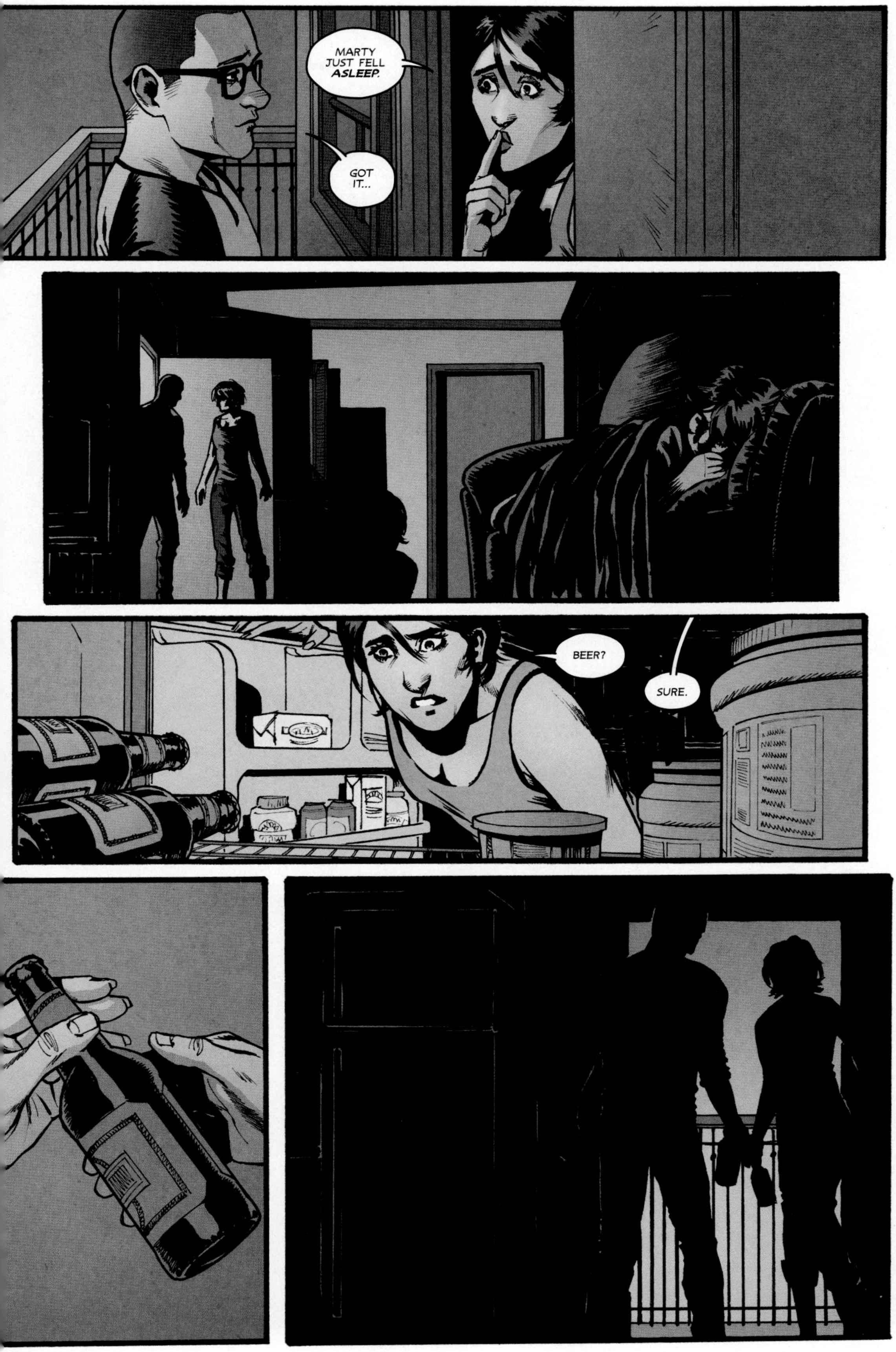
MARTY JUST FELL ASLEEP.
GOT IT...
BEER?
SURE.

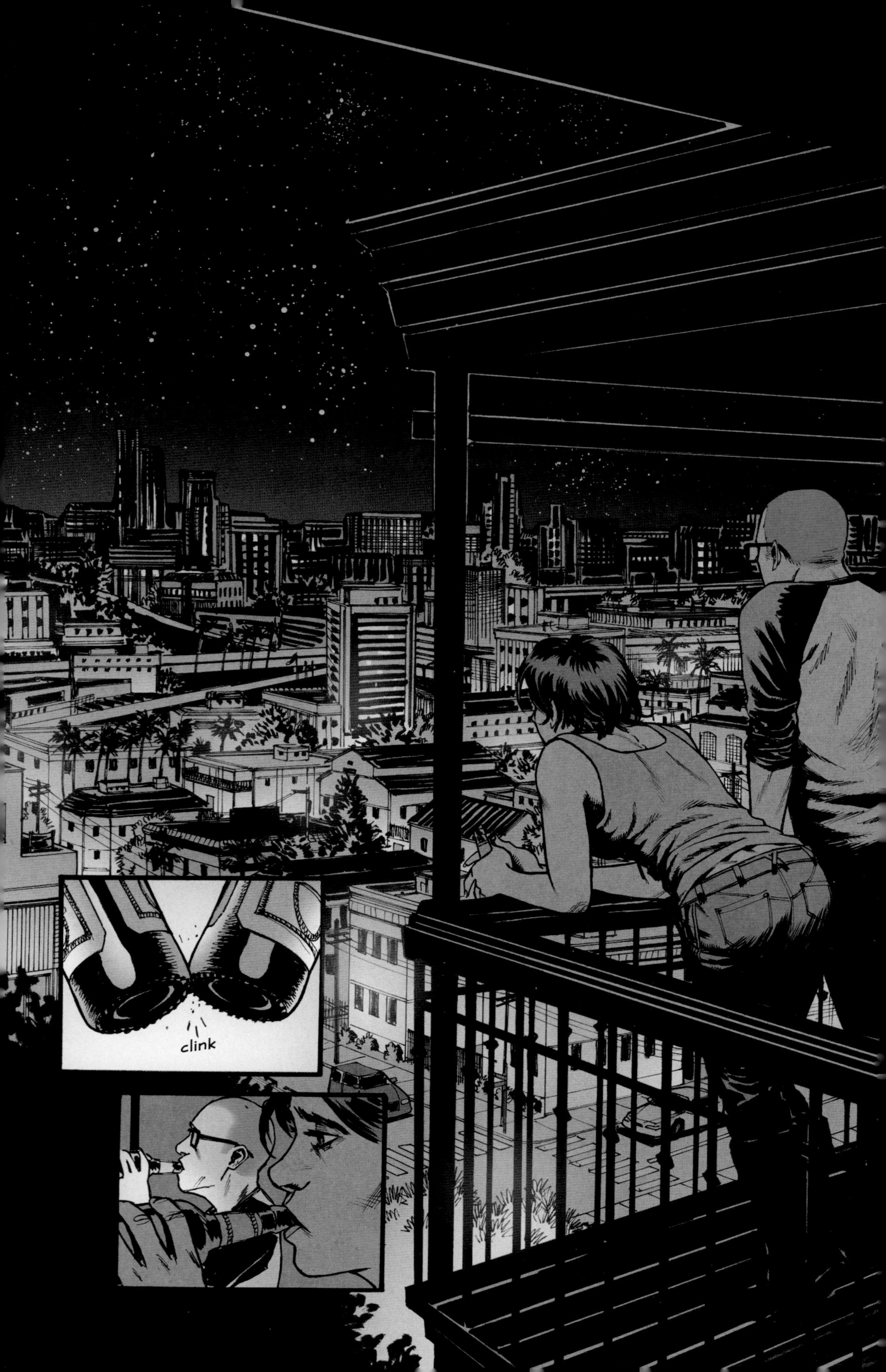
clink

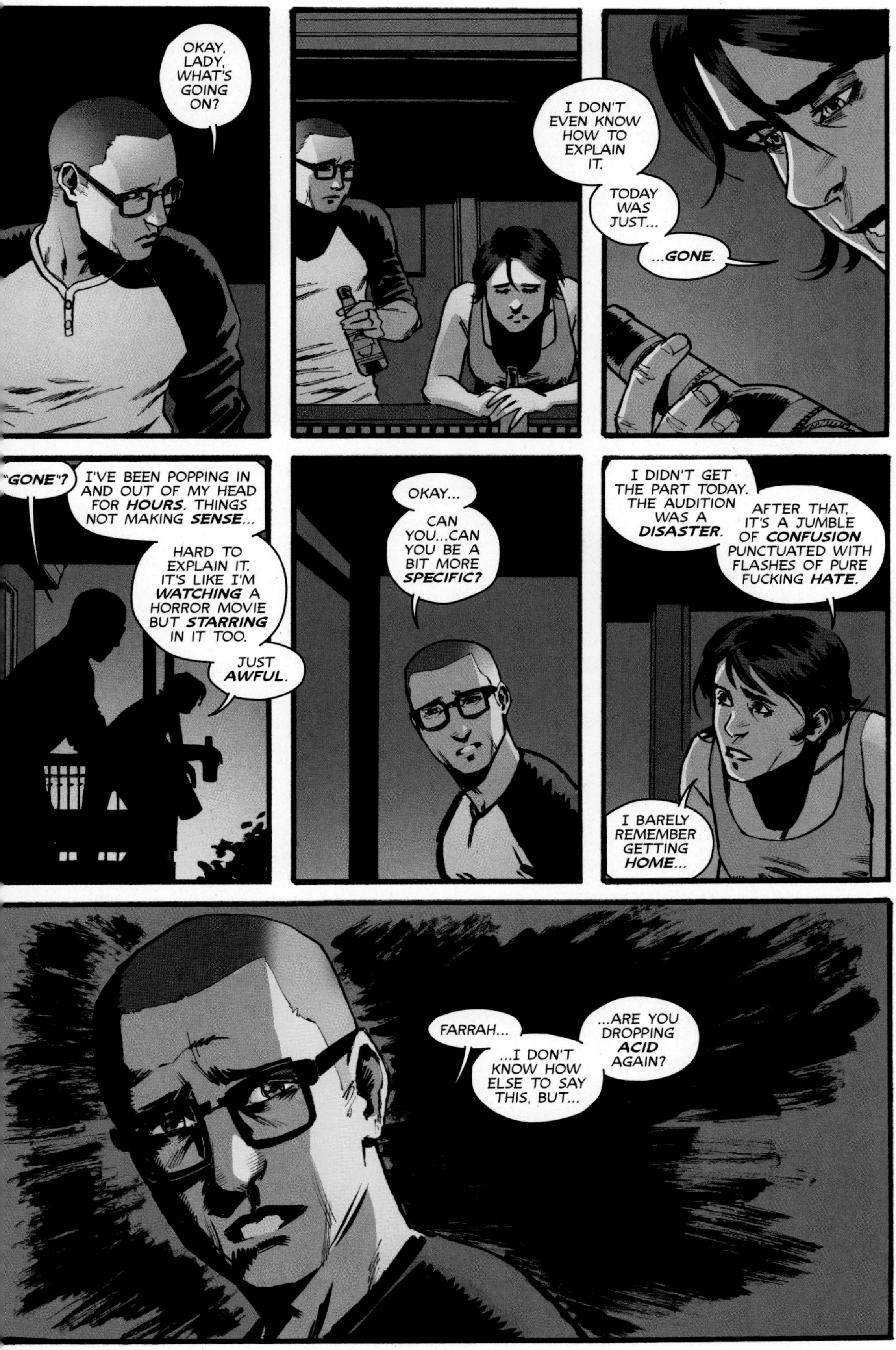
OKAY, LADY, WHAT'S GOING ON?
I DON'T EVEN KNOW HOW TO EXPLAIN IT.
TODAY WAS JUST...
...GONE.
"GONE"?
I'VE BEEN POPPING IN AND OUT OF MY HEAD FOR HOURS. THINGS NOT MAKING SENSE...
HARD TO EXPLAIN IT. IT'S LIKE I'M WATCHING A HORROR MOVIE BUT STARRING IN IT TOO.
JUST AWFUL.
OKAY...
CAN YOU...CAN YOU BE A BIT MORE SPECIFIC?
I DIDN'T GET THE PART TODAY. THE AUDITION WAS A DISASTER.
AFTER THAT, IT'S A JUMBLE OF CONFUSION PUNCTUATED WITH FLASHES OF PURE FUCKING HATE.
I BARELY REMEMBER GETTING HOME...
FARRAH...
...I DON'T KNOW HOW ELSE TO SAY THIS, BUT...
...ARE YOU DROPPING ACID AGAIN?

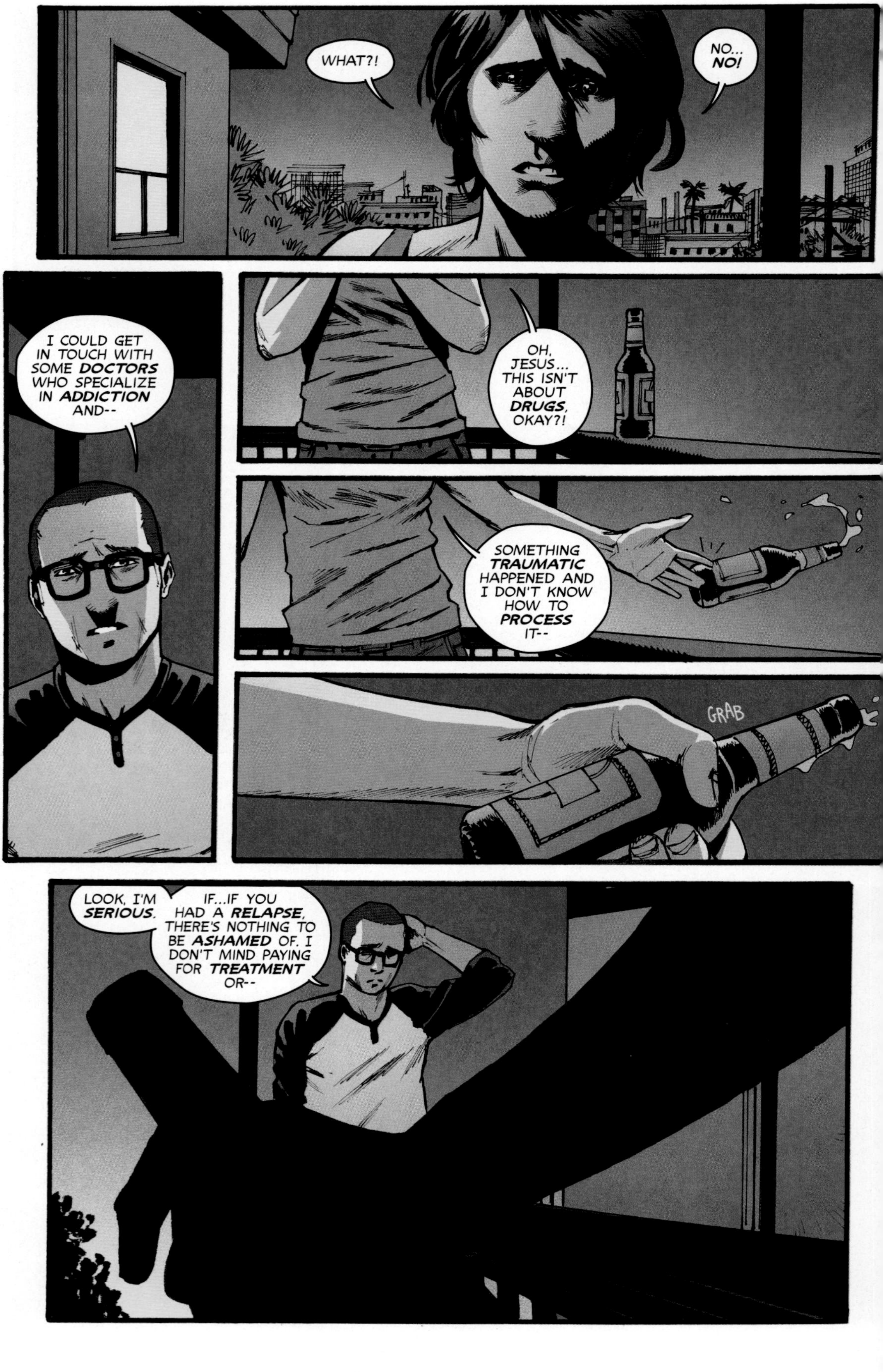
WHAT?!
NO... NO!
I COULD GET IN TOUCH WITH SOME DOCTORS WHO SPECIALIZE IN ADDICTION AND--
OH, JESUS... THIS ISN'T ABOUT DRUGS, OKAY?!
SOMETHING TRAUMATIC HAPPENED AND I DON'T KNOW HOW TO PROCESS IT--
GRAB
LOOK, I'M SERIOUS.
IF...IF YOU HAD A RELAPSE, THERE'S NOTHING TO BE ASHAMED OF. I DON'T MIND PAYING FOR TREATMENT OR--

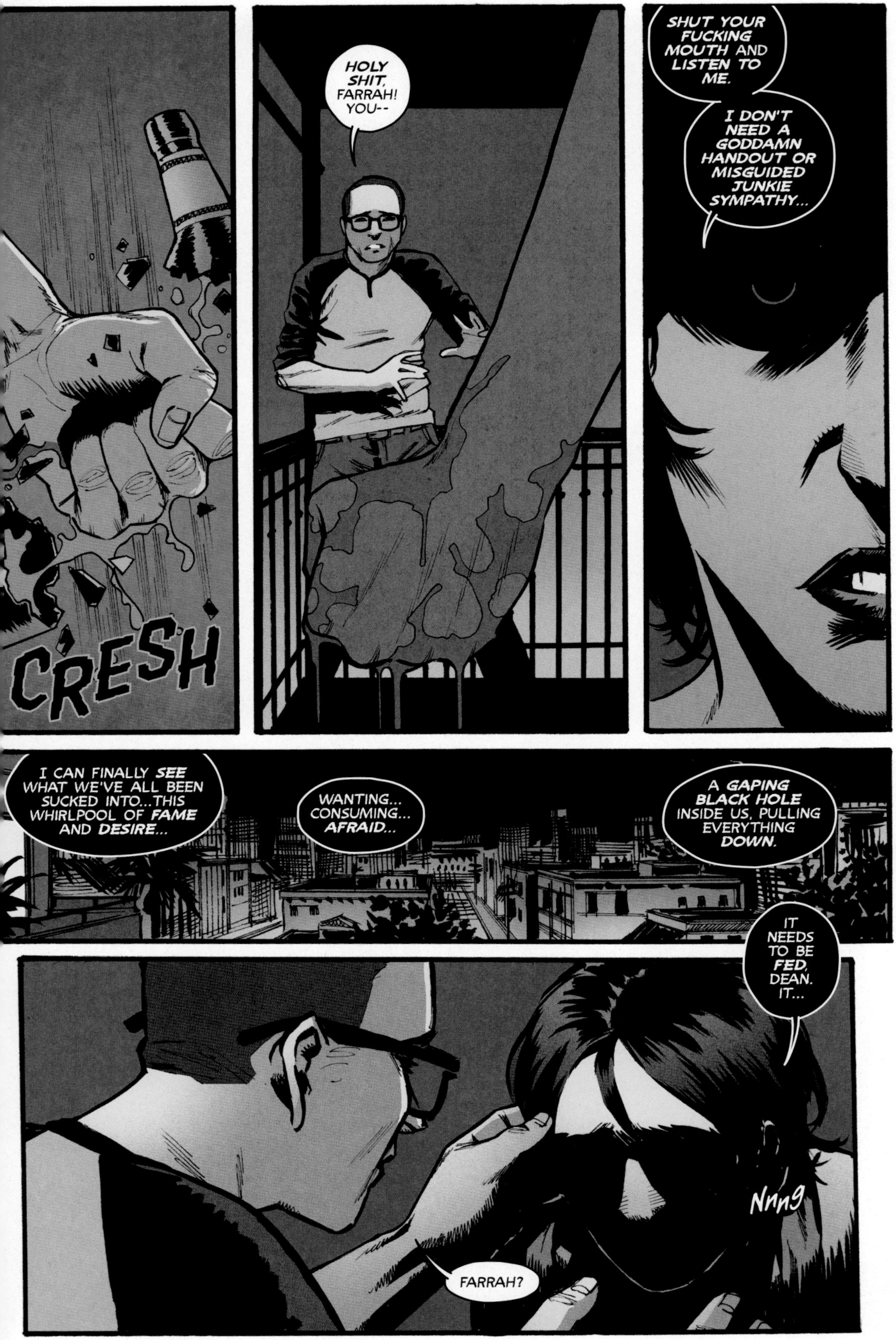
CRESH
HOLY SHIT, FARRAH! YOU--
SHUT YOUR FUCKING MOUTH AND LISTEN TO ME.
I DON'T NEED A GODDAMN HANDOUT OR MISGUIDED JUNKIE SYMPATHY...
I CAN FINALLY SEE WHAT WE'VE ALL BEEN SUCKED INTO...THIS WHIRLPOOL OF FAME AND DESIRE...
WANTING... CONSUMING... AFRAID...
A GAPING BLACK HOLE INSIDE US, PULLING EVERYTHING DOWN.
IT NEEDS TO BE FED, DEAN. IT...
Nnng
FARRAH?

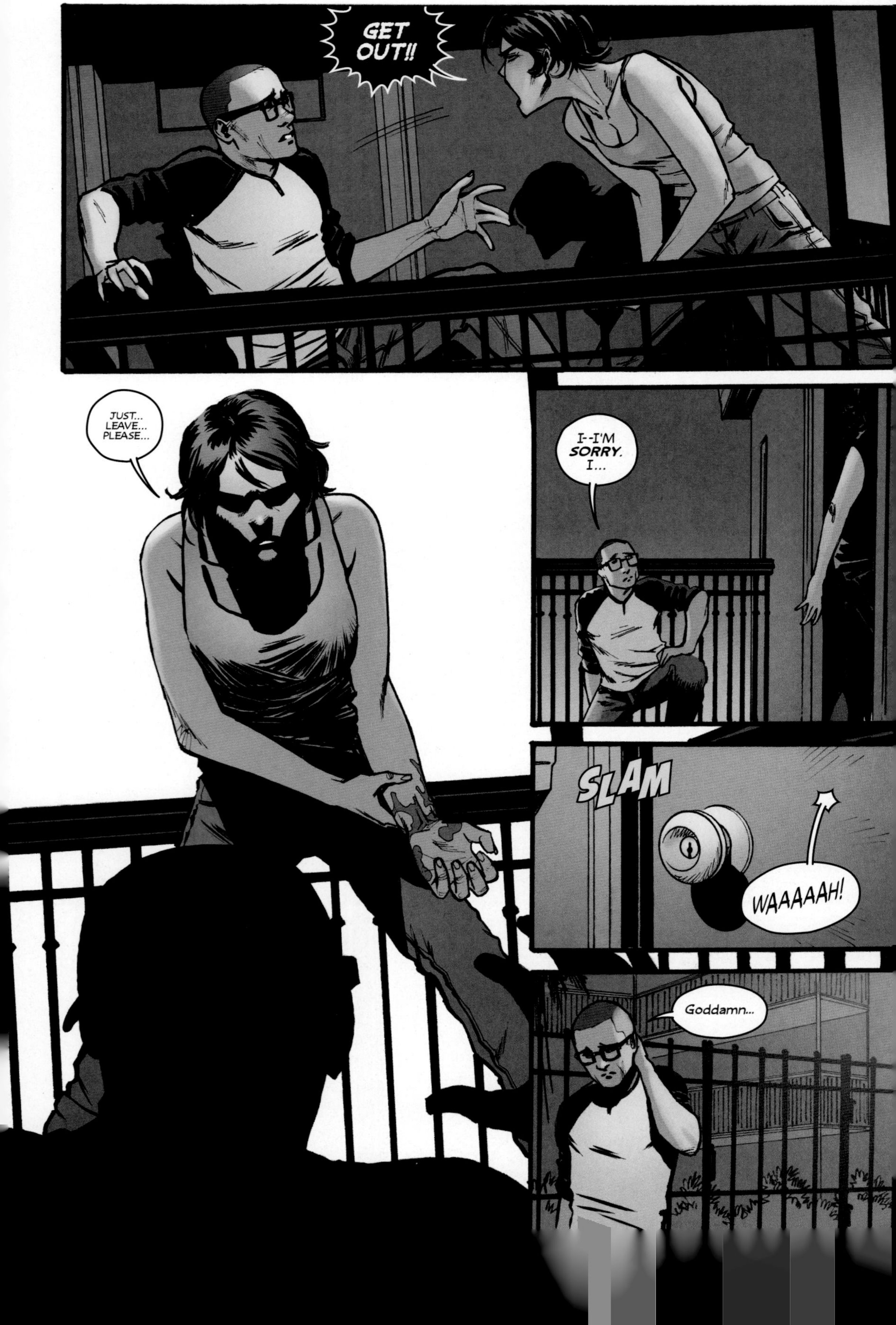
GET OUT!!
JUST... LEAVE... PLEASE...
I--I'M SORRY. I...
SLAM
WAAAAAH!
Goddamn...

WAAAAH!

MARTY... *MARTY!* JUST GIVE ME A SEC HERE...

HEY, BABY, WHY ARE YOU *CRYING?* WHAT'S WRONG?

I HEARD A *MONSTER* ROAR...

SCARED ME.

WELL, MOMMA'S HERE NOW.

Good.

YOU LIE DOWN WHILE MOMMA WATCHES A BIT OF TV, OKAY?

'kay.

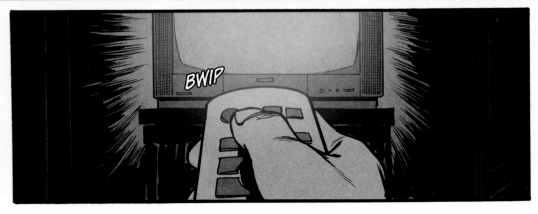

BWIP

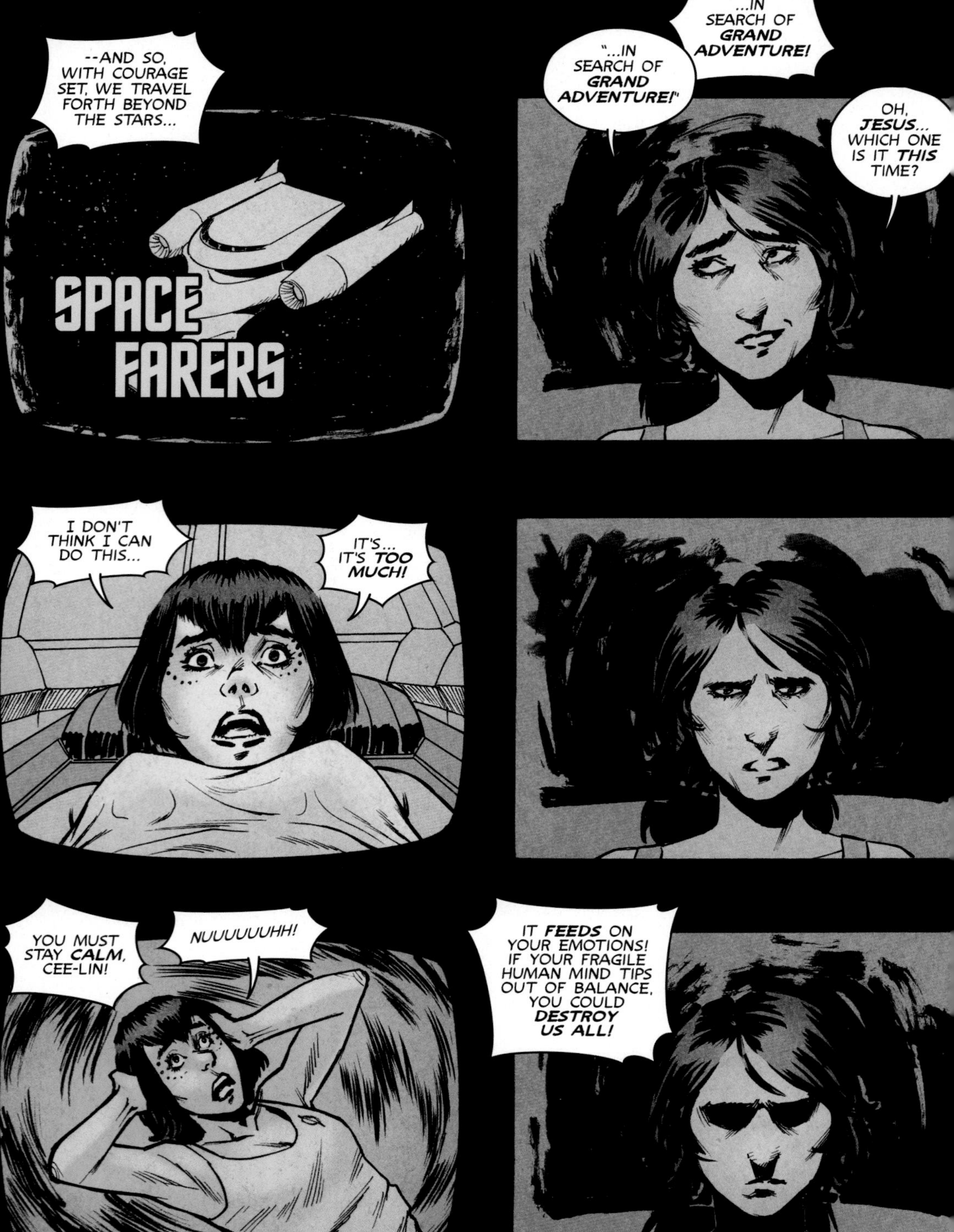
--AND SO, WITH COURAGE SET, WE TRAVEL FORTH BEYOND THE STARS...
SPACE FARERS
...IN SEARCH OF GRAND ADVENTURE!
"...IN SEARCH OF GRAND ADVENTURE!"
OH, JESUS... WHICH ONE IS IT THIS TIME?
I DON'T THINK I CAN DO THIS...
IT'S... IT'S TOO MUCH!
YOU MUST STAY CALM, CEE-LIN!
NUUUUUUHH!
IT FEEDS ON YOUR EMOTIONS! IF YOUR FRAGILE HUMAN MIND TIPS OUT OF BALANCE, YOU COULD DESTROY US ALL!

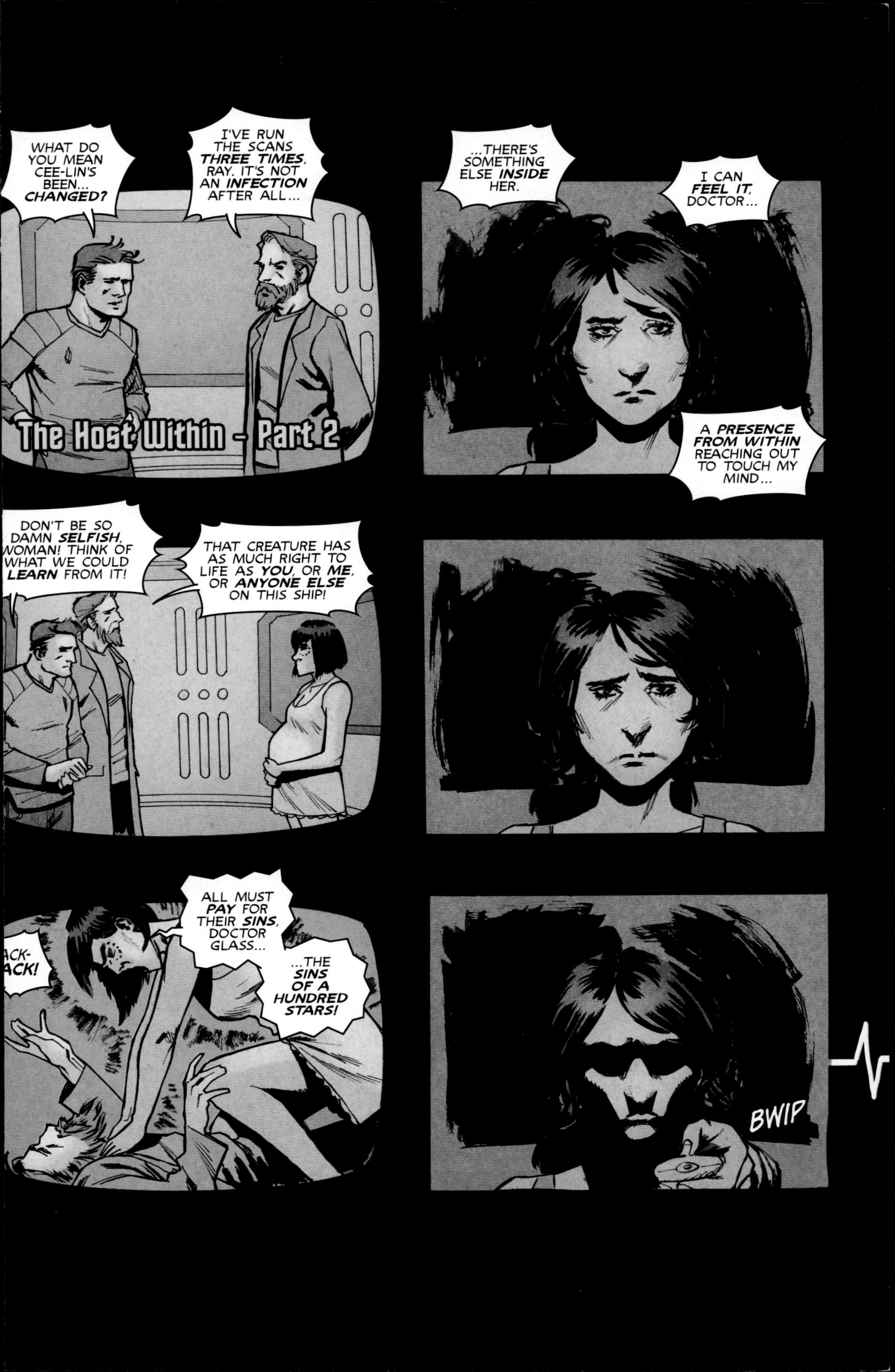
WHAT DO YOU MEAN CEE-LIN'S BEEN... CHANGED?
I'VE RUN THE SCANS THREE TIMES, RAY. IT'S NOT AN INFECTION AFTER ALL...
The Host Within - Part 2
...THERE'S SOMETHING ELSE INSIDE HER.
I CAN FEEL IT, DOCTOR...
A PRESENCE FROM WITHIN REACHING OUT TO TOUCH MY MIND...
DON'T BE SO DAMN SELFISH, WOMAN! THINK OF WHAT WE COULD LEARN FROM IT!
THAT CREATURE HAS AS MUCH RIGHT TO LIFE AS YOU, OR ME, OR ANYONE ELSE ON THIS SHIP!
ACK- ACK!
ALL MUST PAY FOR THEIR SINS, DOCTOR GLASS...
...THE SINS OF A HUNDRED STARS!
BWIP

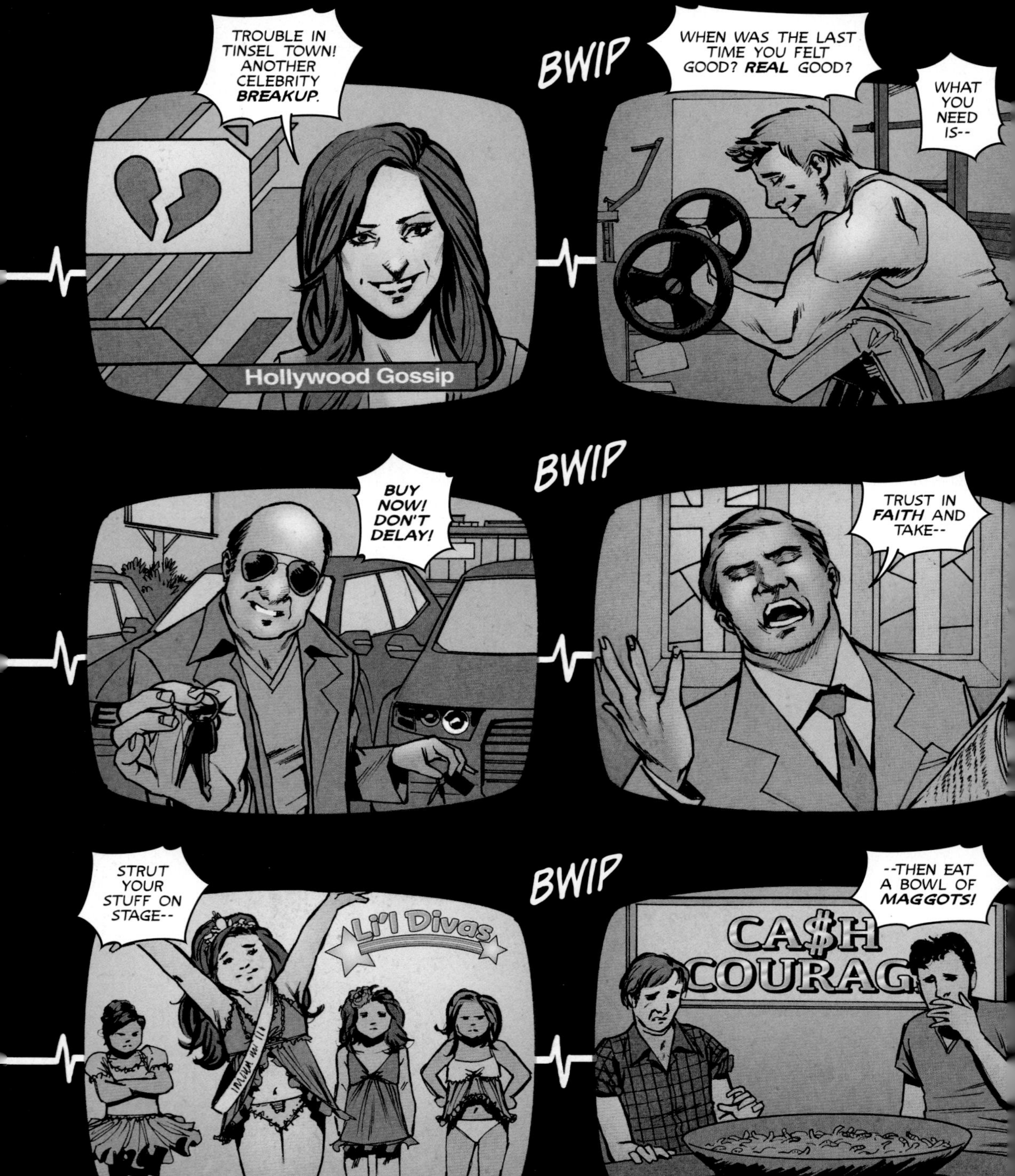
TROUBLE IN TINSEL TOWN! ANOTHER CELEBRITY **BREAKUP**.
Hollywood Gossip
BWIP
WHEN WAS THE LAST TIME YOU FELT GOOD? **REAL** GOOD?
WHAT YOU NEED IS--
BWIP
BUY NOW! DON'T DELAY!
TRUST IN **FAITH** AND TAKE--
BWIP
STRUT YOUR STUFF ON STAGE--
Li'l Divas
--THEN EAT A BOWL OF **MAGGOTS!**
CA$H
COURAG

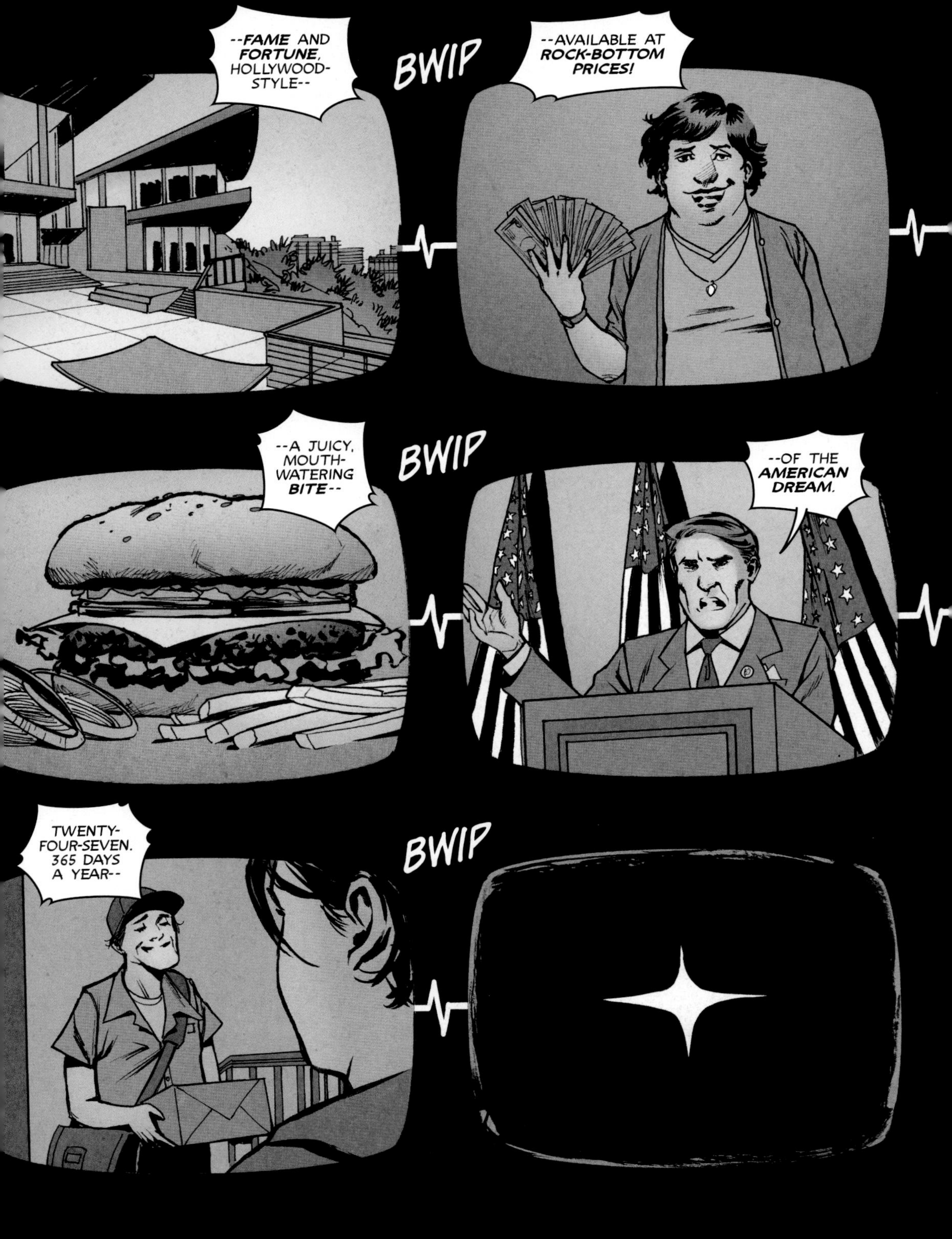
--FAME AND FORTUNE, HOLLYWOOD-STYLE--
BWIP
--AVAILABLE AT ROCK-BOTTOM PRICES!
--A JUICY, MOUTH-WATERING BITE--
BWIP
--OF THE AMERICAN DREAM.
TWENTY-FOUR-SEVEN. 365 DAYS A YEAR--
BWIP

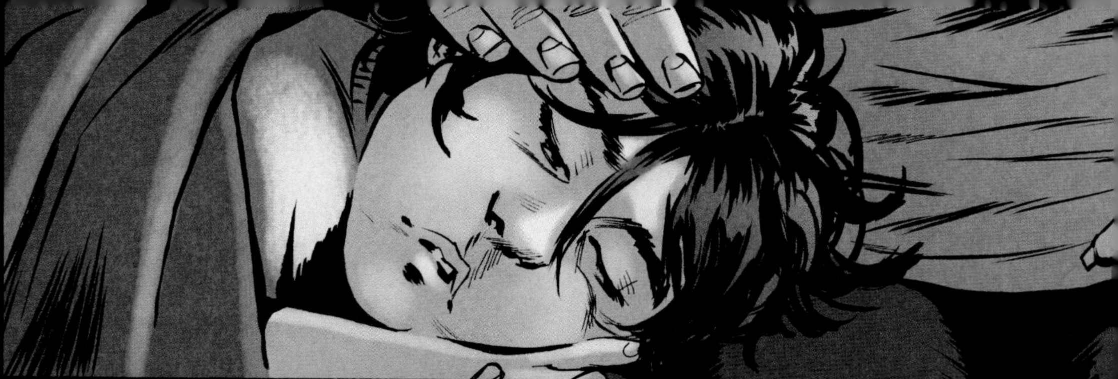
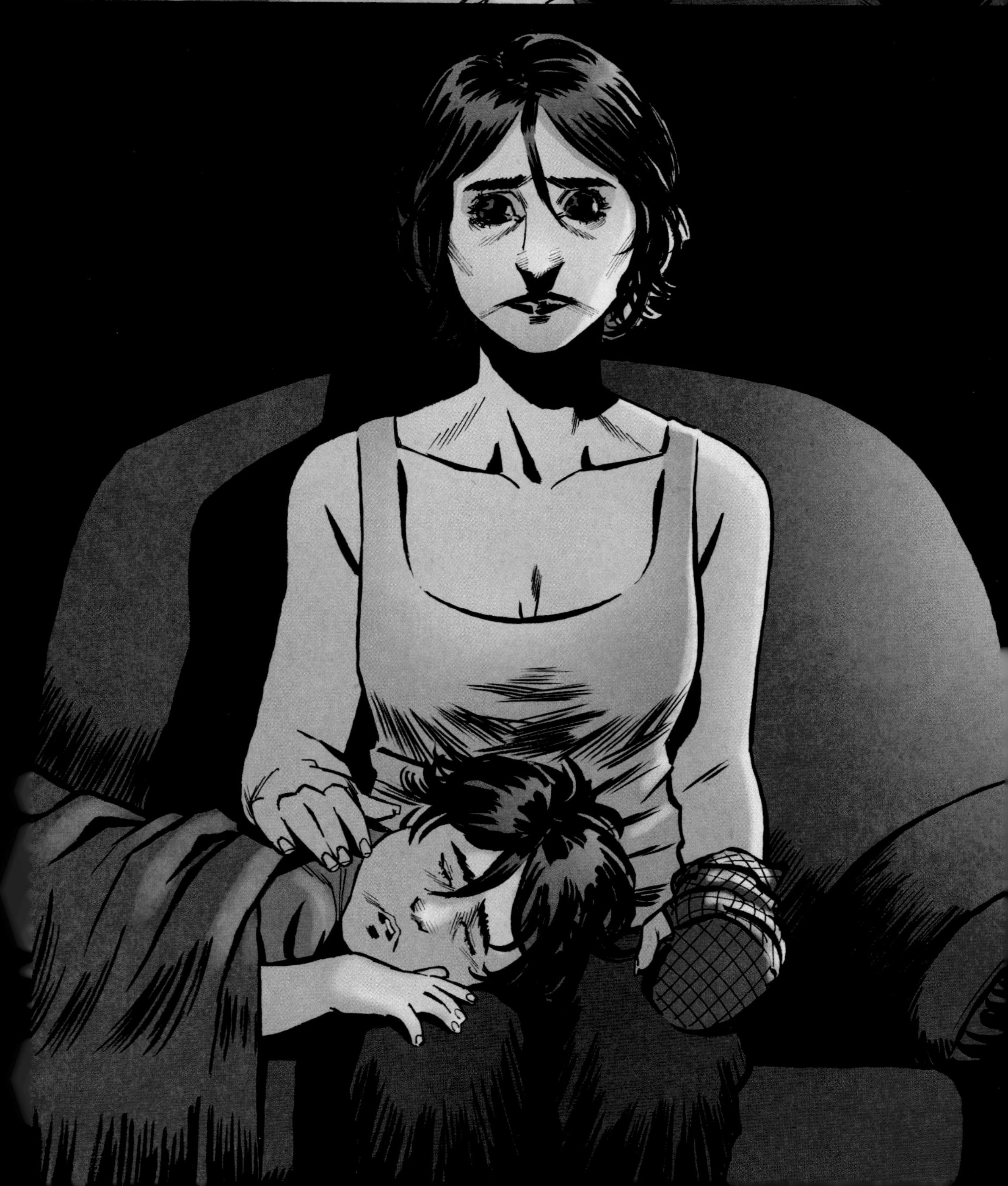

PART 3: MAKING A NEST

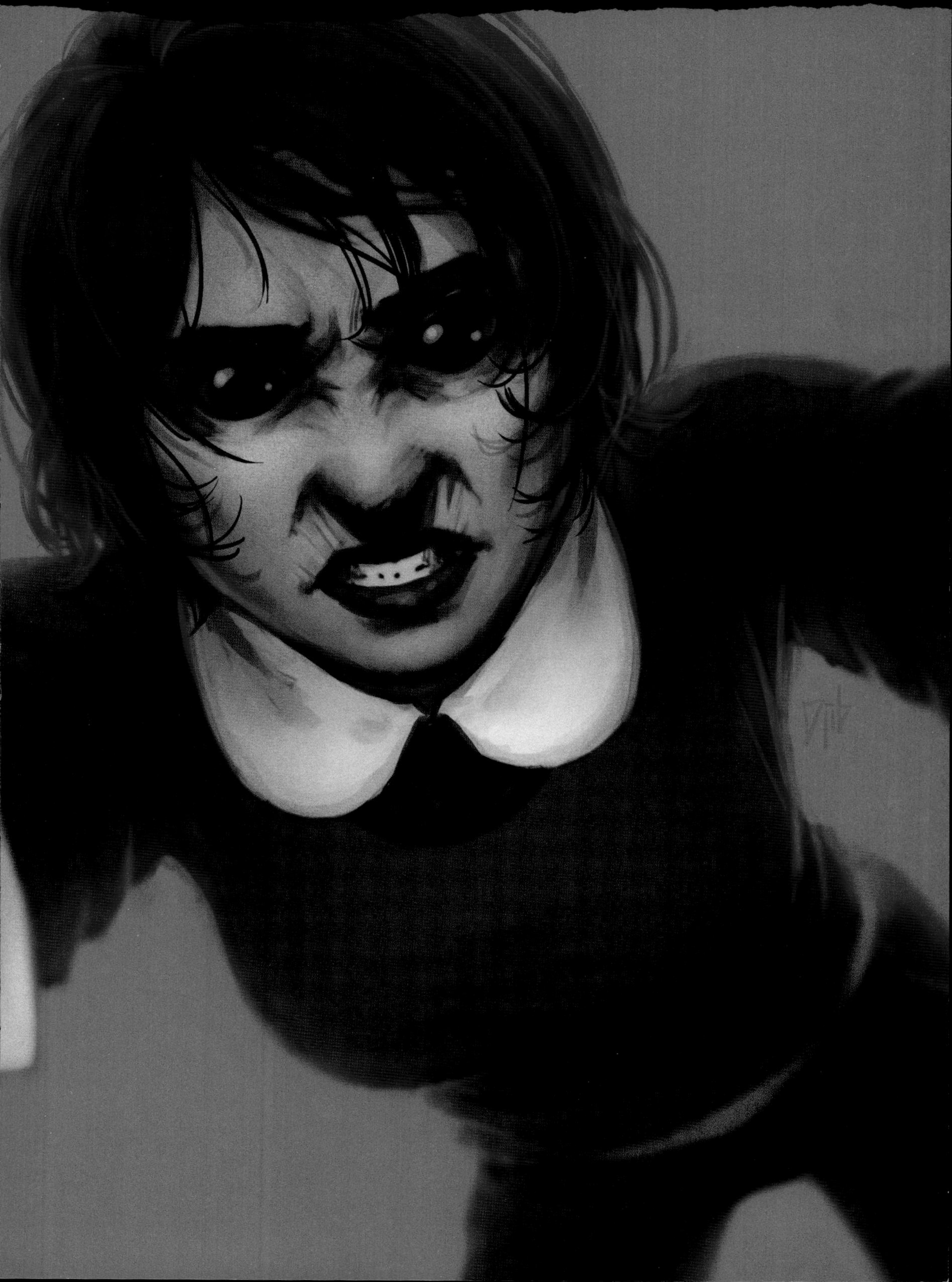

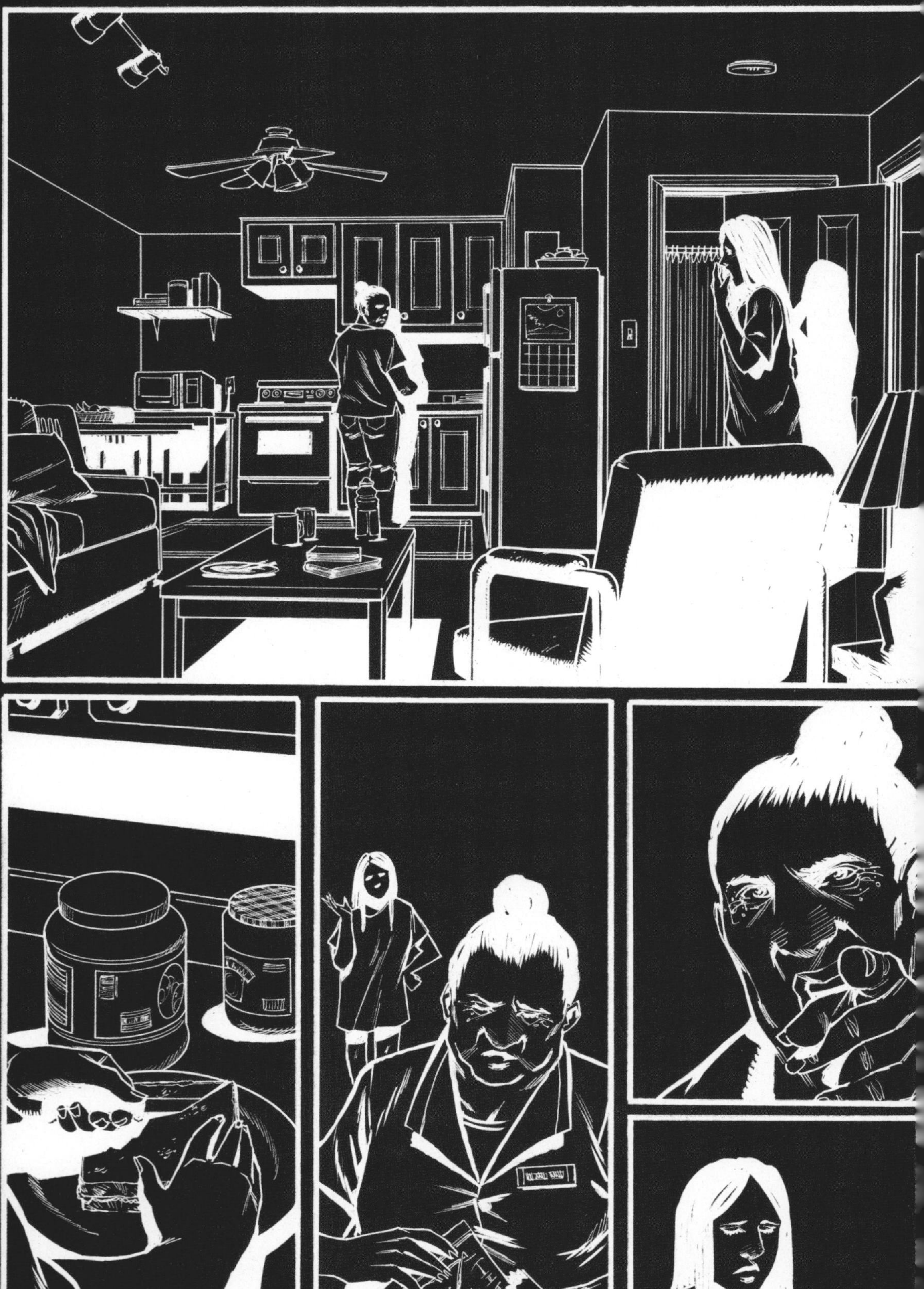

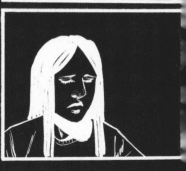

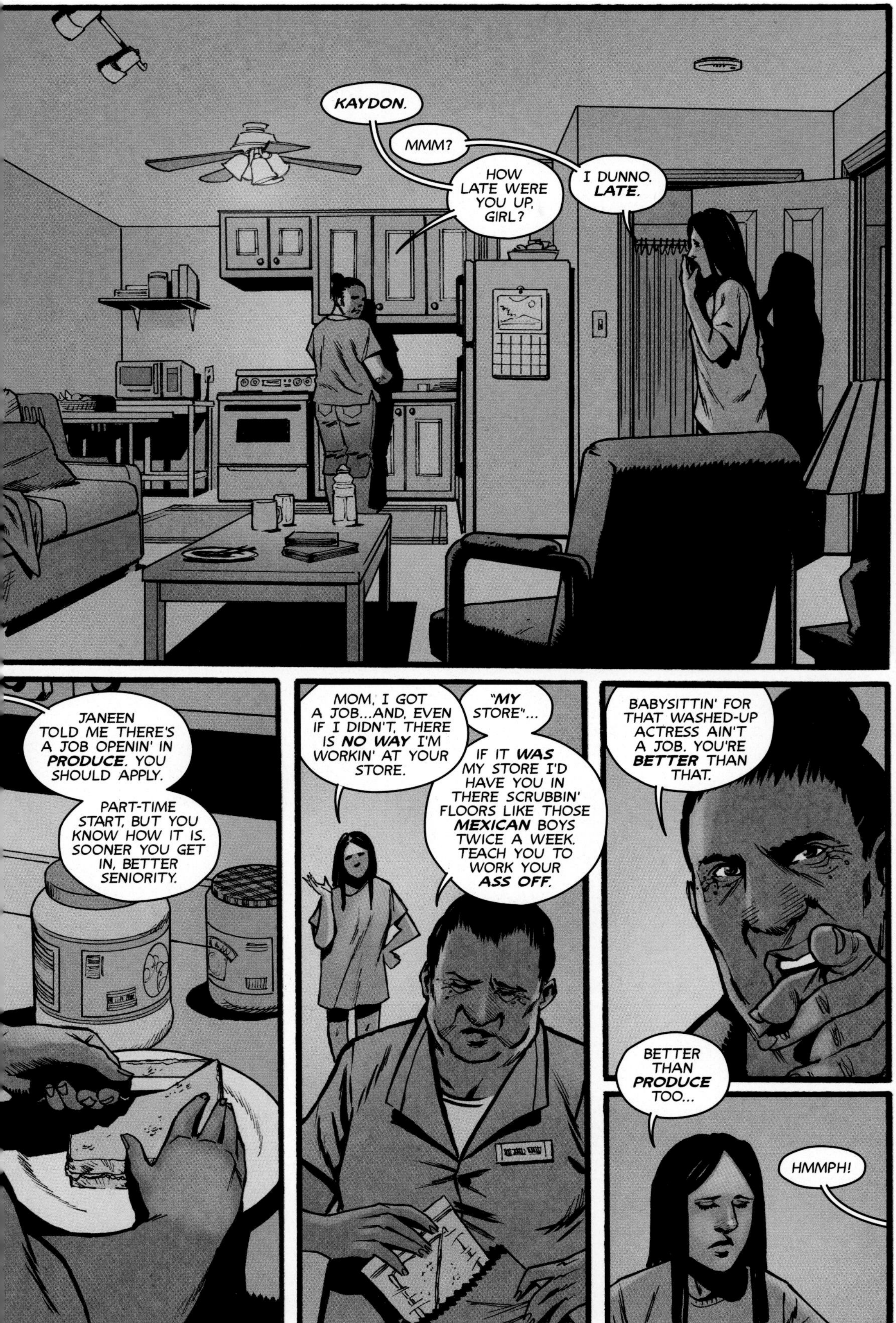
KAYDON.
MMM?
HOW LATE WERE YOU UP, GIRL?
I DUNNO. LATE.
JANEEN TOLD ME THERE'S A JOB OPENIN' IN PRODUCE. YOU SHOULD APPLY.
PART-TIME START, BUT YOU KNOW HOW IT IS. SOONER YOU GET IN, BETTER SENIORITY.
MOM, I GOT A JOB...AND, EVEN IF I DIDN'T, THERE IS NO WAY I'M WORKIN' AT YOUR STORE.
"MY STORE"...
IF IT WAS MY STORE I'D HAVE YOU IN THERE SCRUBBIN' FLOORS LIKE THOSE MEXICAN BOYS TWICE A WEEK. TEACH YOU TO WORK YOUR ASS OFF.
BABYSITTIN' FOR THAT WASHED-UP ACTRESS AIN'T A JOB. YOU'RE BETTER THAN THAT.
BETTER THAN PRODUCE TOO...
HMMPH!

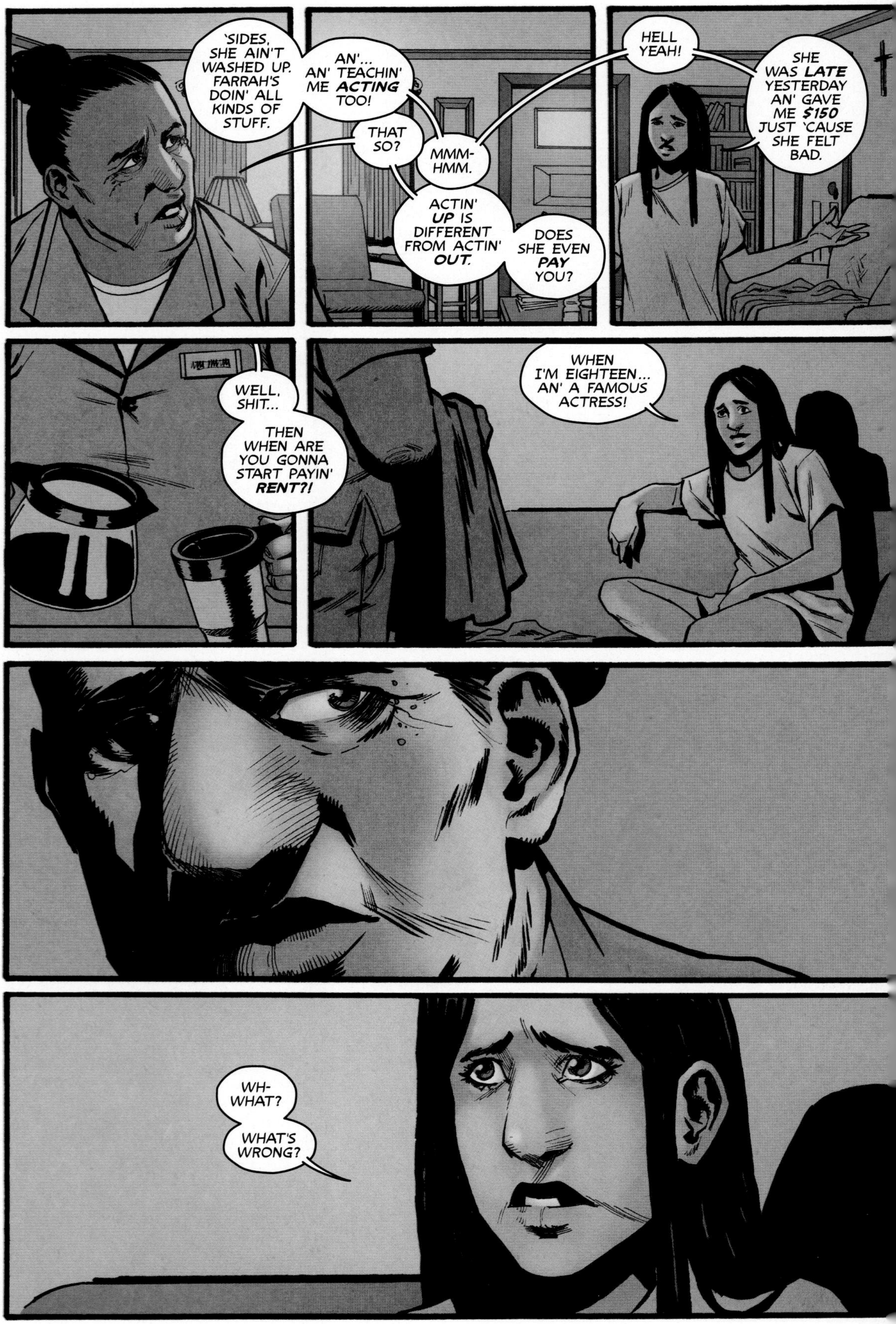

'SIDES, SHE AIN'T WASHED UP. FARRAH'S DOIN' ALL KINDS OF STUFF.
AN'... AN' TEACHIN' ME **ACTING** TOO!
THAT SO?
MMM-HMM.
ACTIN' **UP** IS DIFFERENT FROM ACTIN' **OUT**.
DOES SHE EVEN **PAY** YOU?
HELL YEAH!
SHE WAS **LATE** YESTERDAY AN' GAVE ME **$150** JUST 'CAUSE SHE FELT BAD.
WELL, SHIT...
THEN WHEN ARE YOU GONNA START PAYIN' **RENT?!**
WHEN I'M EIGHTEEN... AN' A FAMOUS ACTRESS!
WH-WHAT?
WHAT'S WRONG?

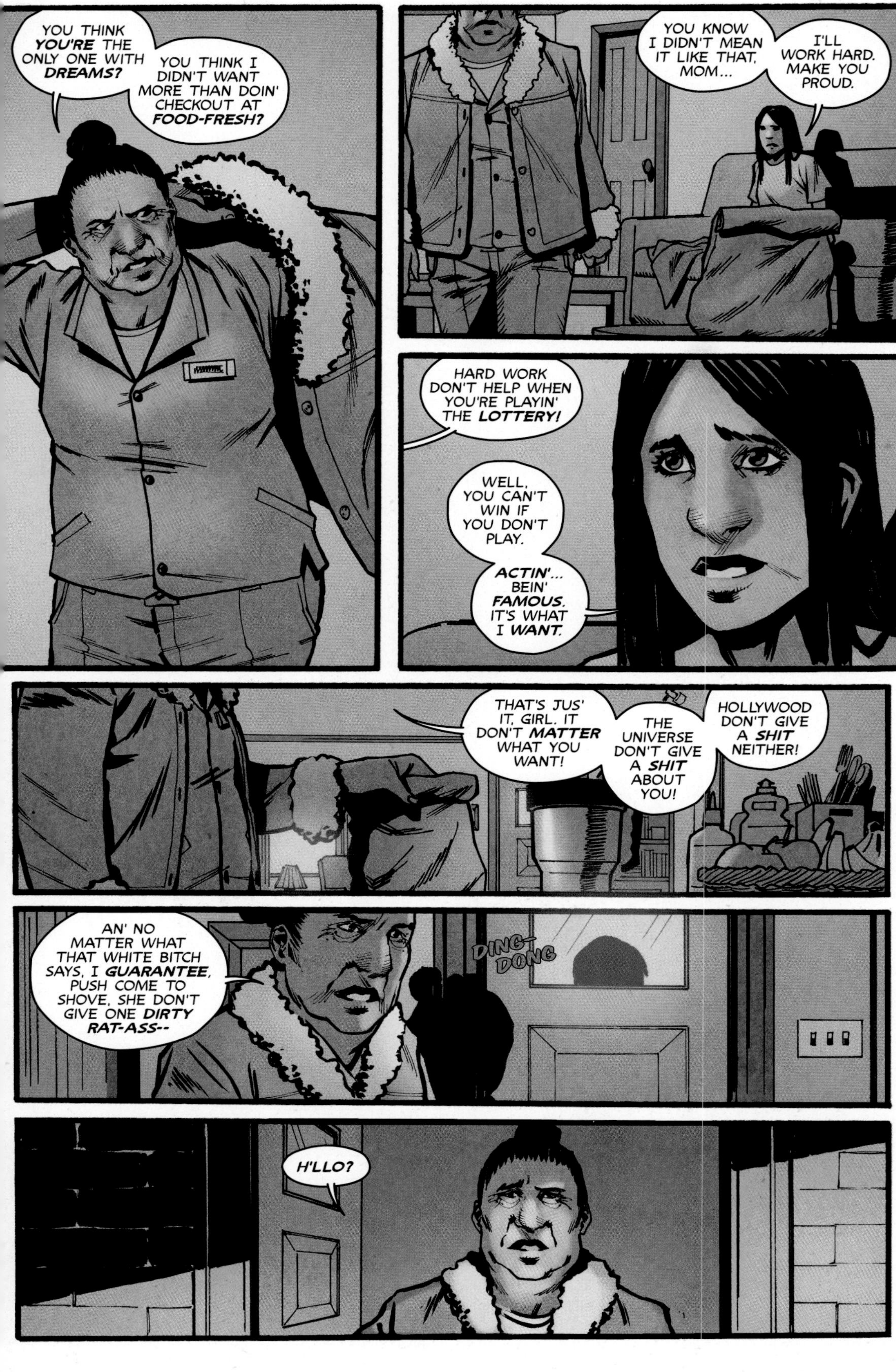
YOU THINK YOU'RE THE ONLY ONE WITH DREAMS?
YOU THINK I DIDN'T WANT MORE THAN DOIN' CHECKOUT AT FOOD-FRESH?
YOU KNOW I DIDN'T MEAN IT LIKE THAT, MOM...
I'LL WORK HARD. MAKE YOU PROUD.
HARD WORK DON'T HELP WHEN YOU'RE PLAYIN' THE LOTTERY!
WELL, YOU CAN'T WIN IF YOU DON'T PLAY.
ACTIN'... BEIN' FAMOUS. IT'S WHAT I WANT.
THAT'S JUS' IT, GIRL. IT DON'T MATTER WHAT YOU WANT!
THE UNIVERSE DON'T GIVE A SHIT ABOUT YOU!
HOLLYWOOD DON'T GIVE A SHIT NEITHER!
AN' NO MATTER WHAT THAT WHITE BITCH SAYS, I GUARANTEE, PUSH COME TO SHOVE, SHE DON'T GIVE ONE DIRTY RAT-ASS--
DING-DONG
H'LLO?

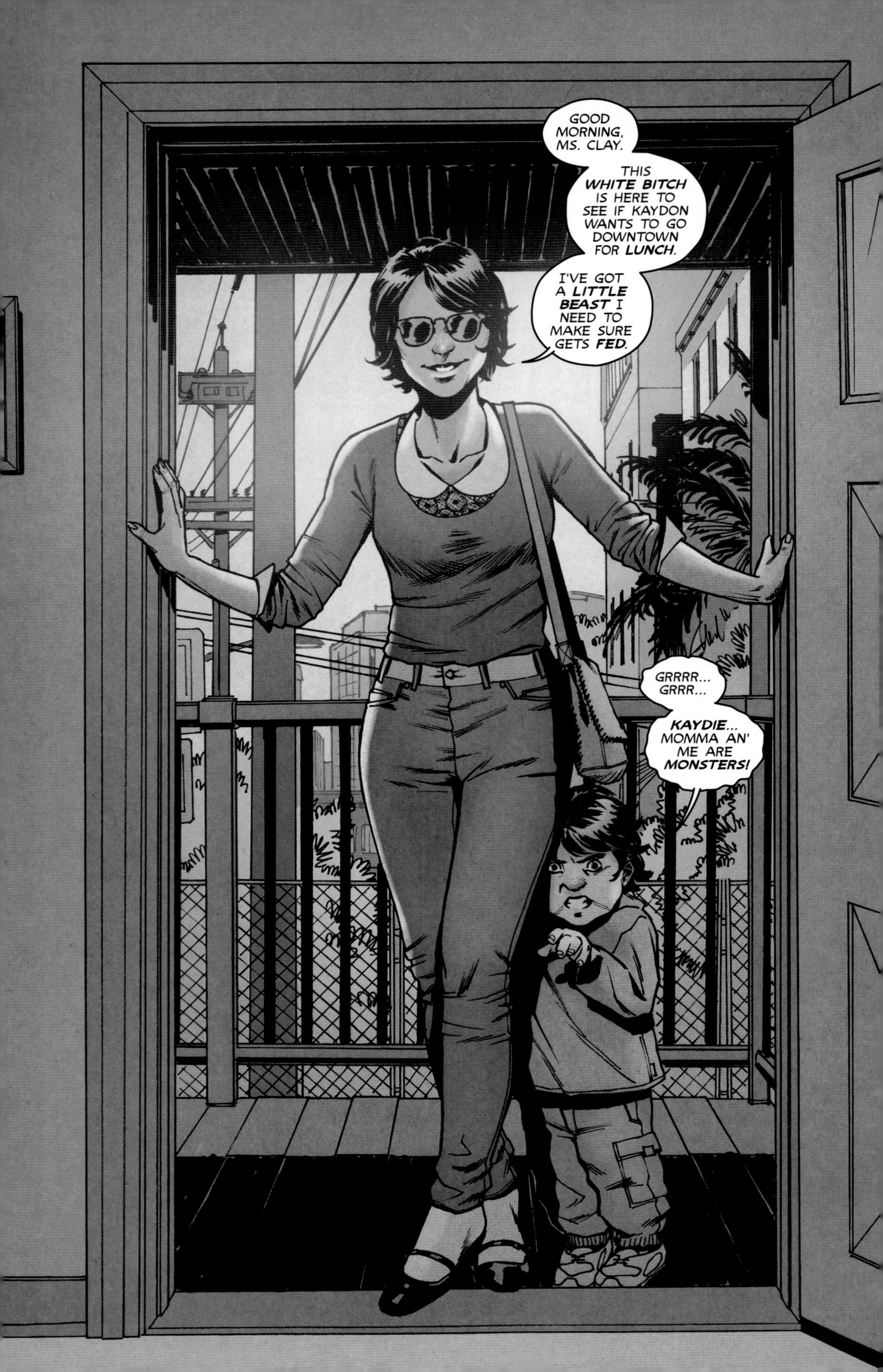
GOOD MORNING, MS. CLAY.
THIS WHITE BITCH IS HERE TO SEE IF KAYDON WANTS TO GO DOWNTOWN FOR LUNCH.
I'VE GOT A LITTLE BEAST I NEED TO MAKE SURE GETS FED.
GRRRR... GRRR...
KAYDIE... MOMMA AN' ME ARE MONSTERS!

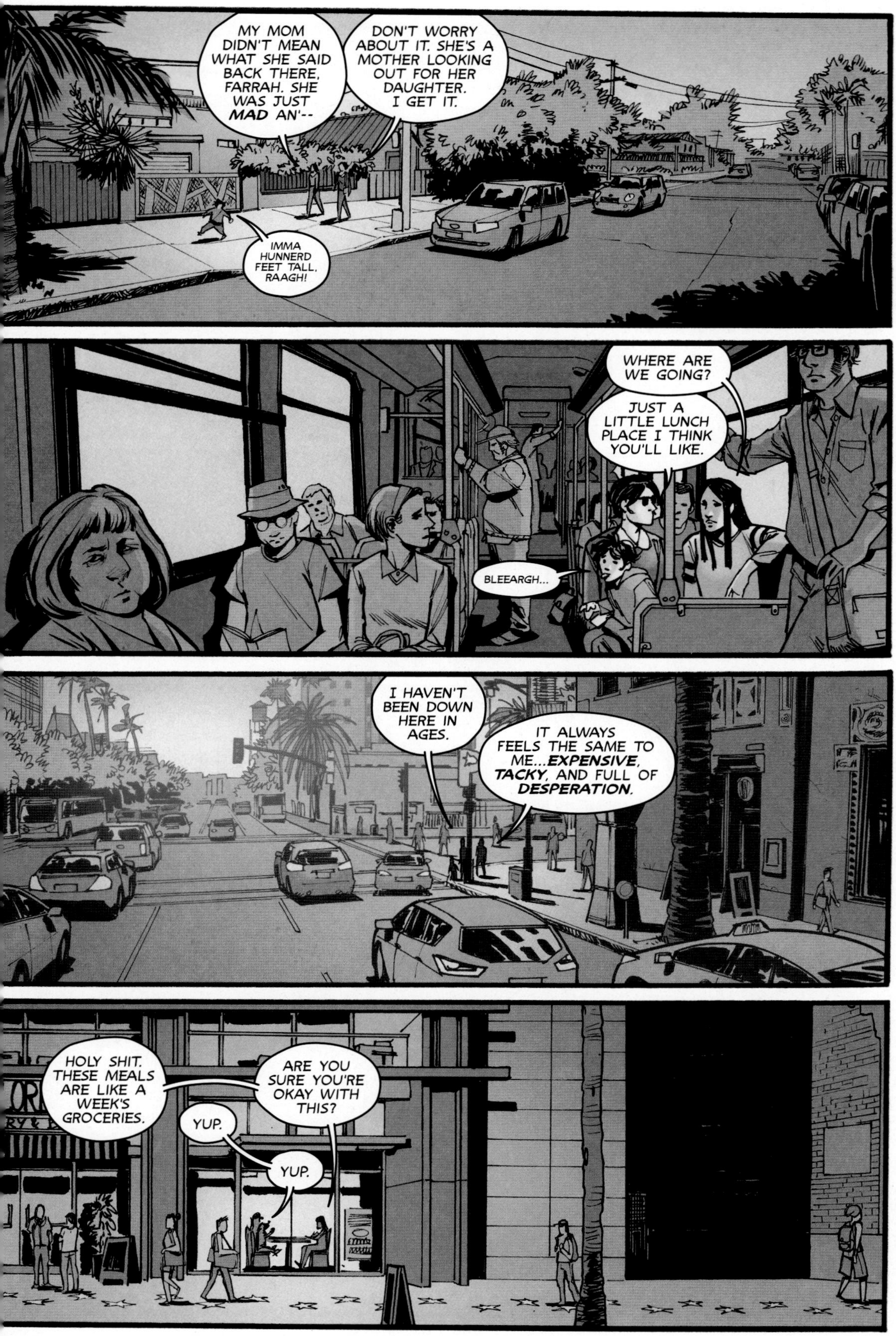
MY MOM DIDN'T MEAN WHAT SHE SAID BACK THERE, FARRAH. SHE WAS JUST *MAD* AN'--
DON'T WORRY ABOUT IT. SHE'S A MOTHER LOOKING OUT FOR HER DAUGHTER. I GET IT.
IMMA HUNNERD FEET TALL, RAAGH!
WHERE ARE WE GOING?
JUST A LITTLE LUNCH PLACE I THINK YOU'LL LIKE.
BLEEARGH...
I HAVEN'T BEEN DOWN HERE IN AGES.
IT ALWAYS FEELS THE SAME TO ME...*EXPENSIVE*, *TACKY*, AND FULL OF *DESPERATION*.
HOLY SHIT. THESE MEALS ARE LIKE A WEEK'S GROCERIES.
ARE YOU SURE YOU'RE OKAY WITH THIS?
YUP.
YUP.

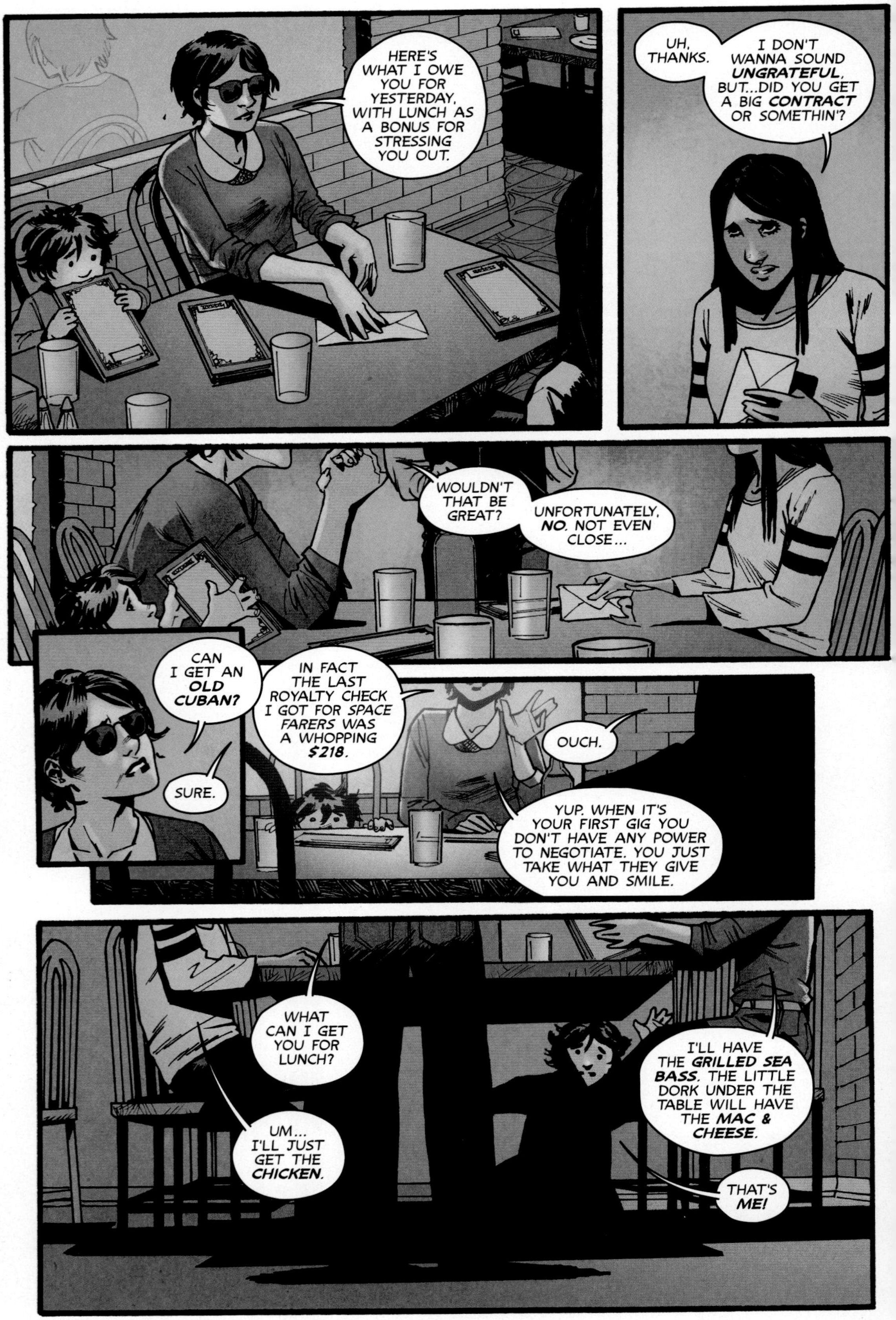
HERE'S WHAT I OWE YOU FOR YESTERDAY, WITH LUNCH AS A BONUS FOR STRESSING YOU OUT.
UH, THANKS.
I DON'T WANNA SOUND UNGRATEFUL, BUT...DID YOU GET A BIG CONTRACT OR SOMETHIN'?
WOULDN'T THAT BE GREAT?
UNFORTUNATELY, NO, NOT EVEN CLOSE...
CAN I GET AN OLD CUBAN?
SURE.
IN FACT THE LAST ROYALTY CHECK I GOT FOR SPACE FARERS WAS A WHOPPING $218.
OUCH.
YUP. WHEN IT'S YOUR FIRST GIG YOU DON'T HAVE ANY POWER TO NEGOTIATE. YOU JUST TAKE WHAT THEY GIVE YOU AND SMILE.
WHAT CAN I GET YOU FOR LUNCH?
UM... I'LL JUST GET THE CHICKEN.
I'LL HAVE THE GRILLED SEA BASS. THE LITTLE DORK UNDER THE TABLE WILL HAVE THE MAC & CHEESE.
THAT'S ME!

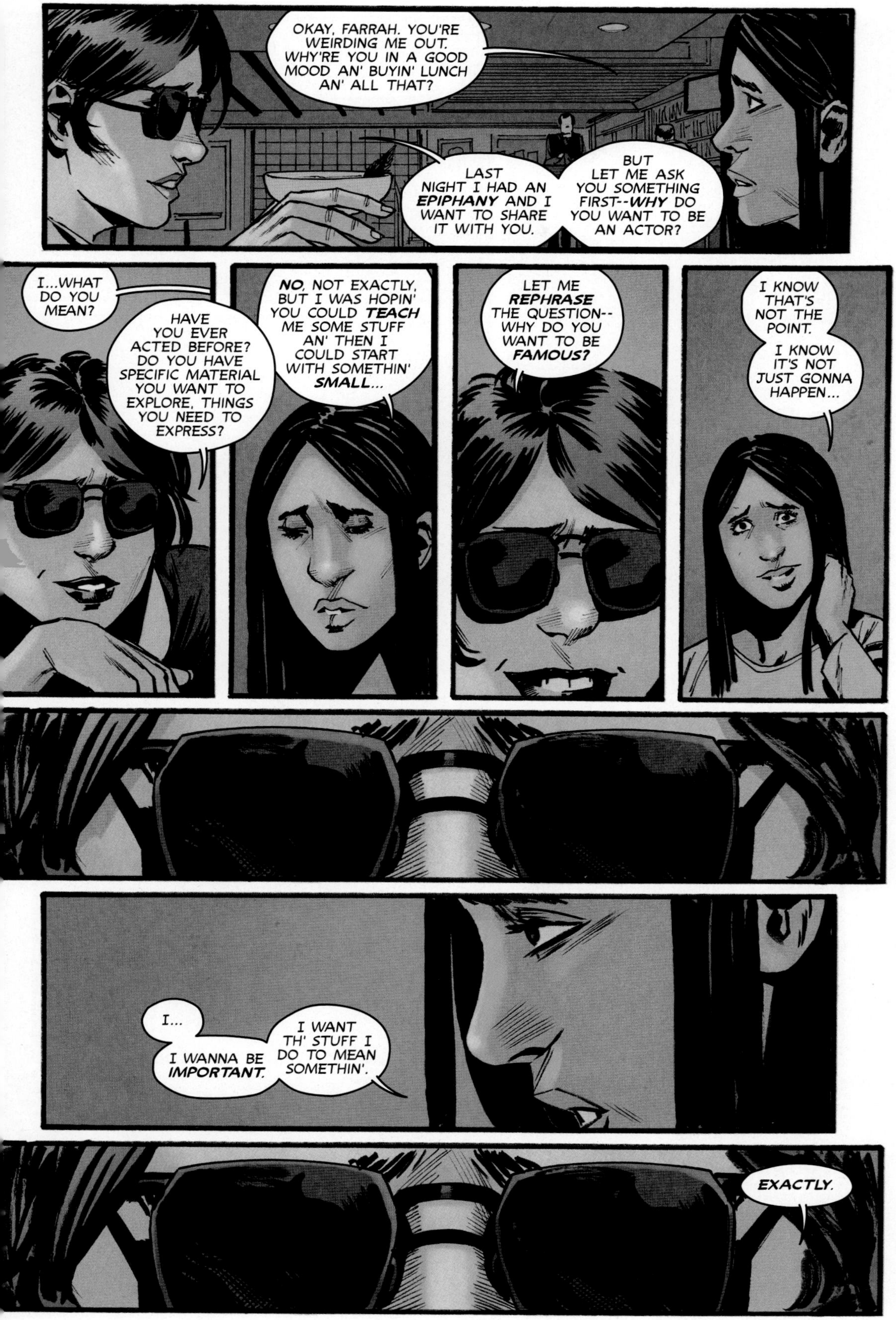
OKAY, FARRAH. YOU'RE WEIRDING ME OUT. WHY'RE YOU IN A GOOD MOOD AN' BUYIN' LUNCH AN' ALL THAT?
LAST NIGHT I HAD AN EPIPHANY AND I WANT TO SHARE IT WITH YOU.
BUT LET ME ASK YOU SOMETHING FIRST--WHY DO YOU WANT TO BE AN ACTOR?
I...WHAT DO YOU MEAN?
HAVE YOU EVER ACTED BEFORE? DO YOU HAVE SPECIFIC MATERIAL YOU WANT TO EXPLORE, THINGS YOU NEED TO EXPRESS?
NO, NOT EXACTLY, BUT I WAS HOPIN' YOU COULD TEACH ME SOME STUFF AN' THEN I COULD START WITH SOMETHIN' SMALL...
LET ME REPHRASE THE QUESTION--WHY DO YOU WANT TO BE FAMOUS?
I KNOW THAT'S NOT THE POINT.
I KNOW IT'S NOT JUST GONNA HAPPEN...
I...
I WANNA BE IMPORTANT.
I WANT TH' STUFF I DO TO MEAN SOMETHIN'.
EXACTLY.

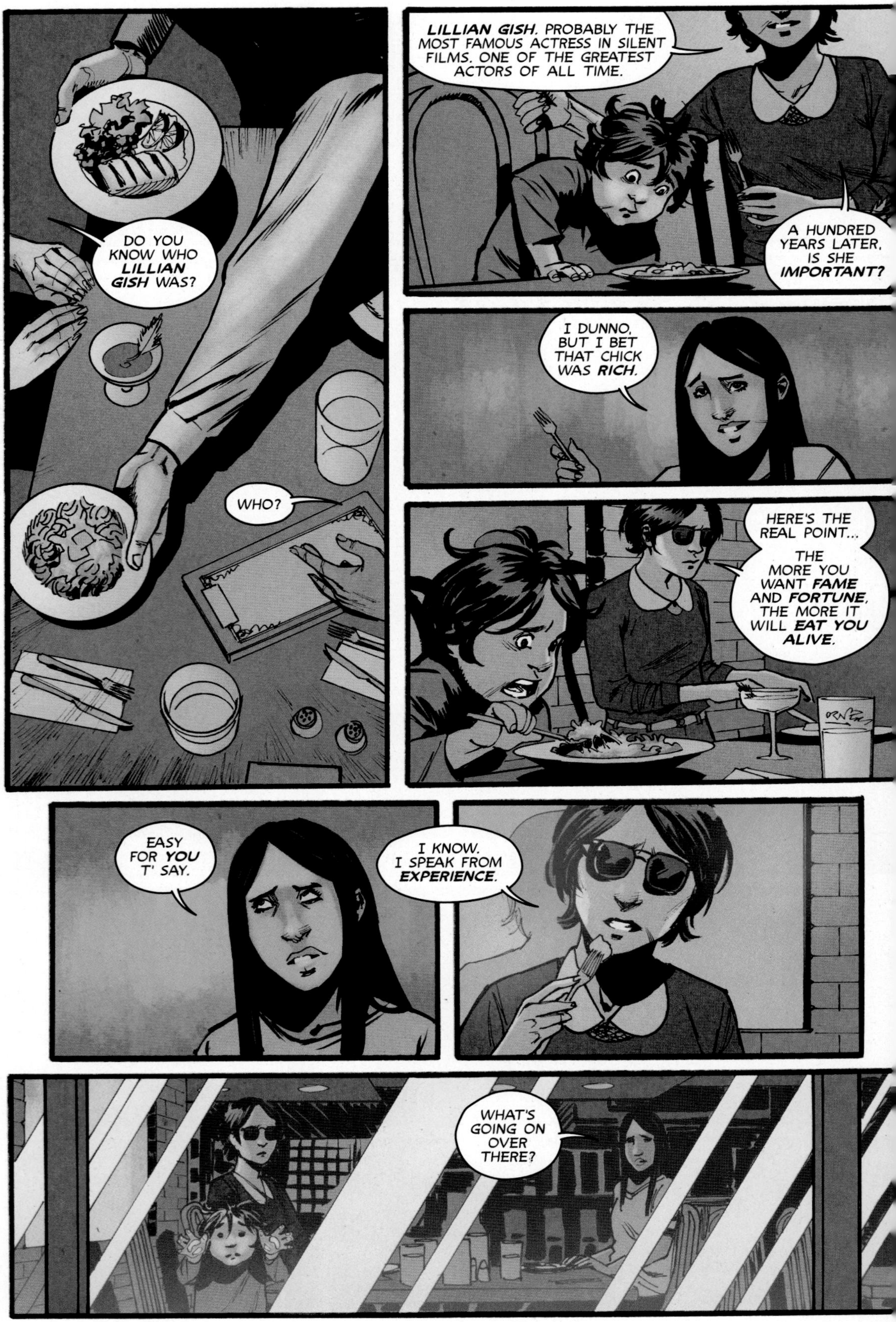
DO YOU KNOW WHO LILLIAN GISH WAS?
WHO?
LILLIAN GISH. PROBABLY THE MOST FAMOUS ACTRESS IN SILENT FILMS. ONE OF THE GREATEST ACTORS OF ALL TIME.
A HUNDRED YEARS LATER, IS SHE IMPORTANT?
I DUNNO, BUT I BET THAT CHICK WAS RICH.
HERE'S THE REAL POINT...
THE MORE YOU WANT FAME AND FORTUNE, THE MORE IT WILL EAT YOU ALIVE.
EASY FOR YOU T' SAY.
I KNOW. I SPEAK FROM EXPERIENCE.
WHAT'S GOING ON OVER THERE?

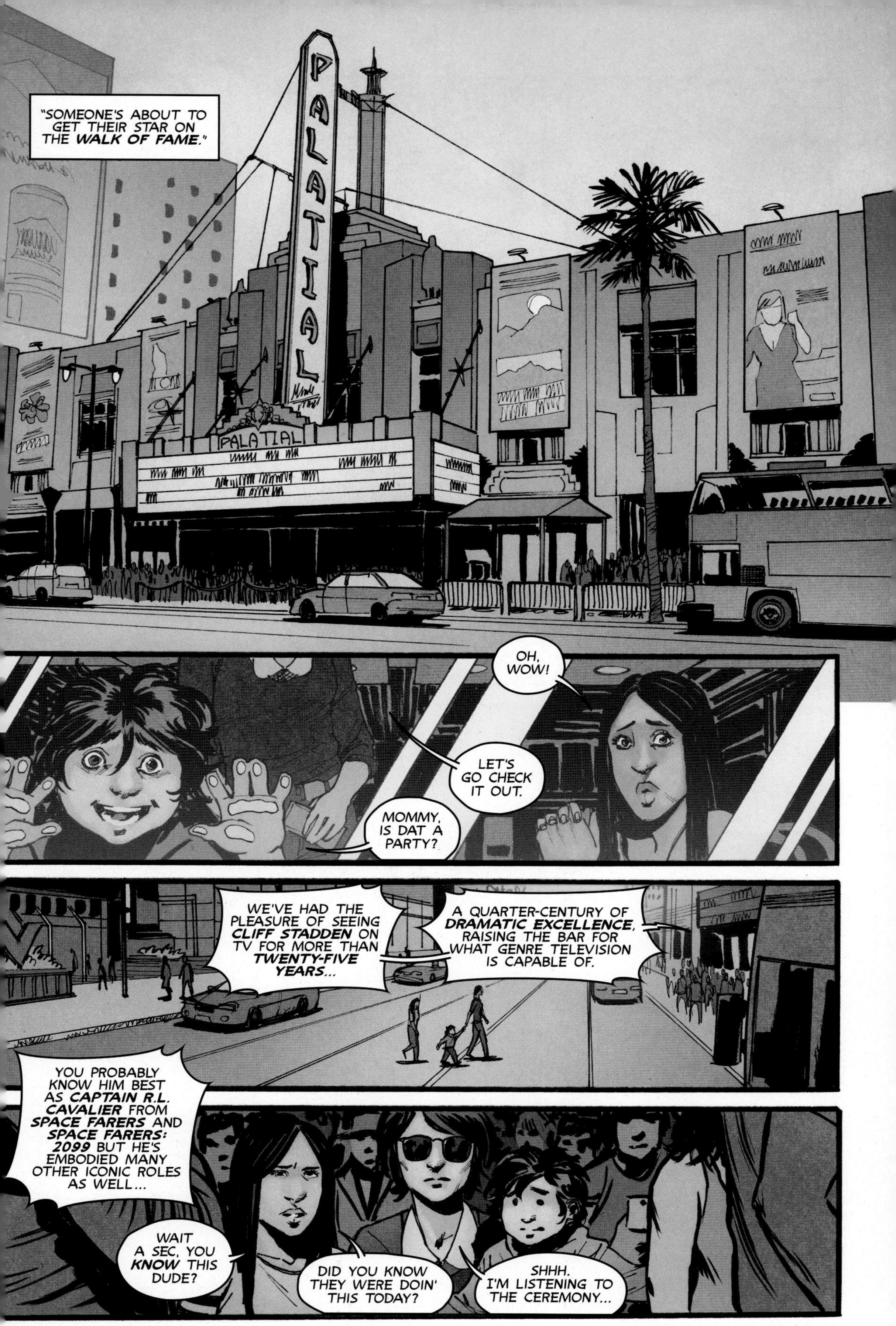

"SOMEONE'S ABOUT TO GET THEIR STAR ON THE WALK OF FAME."
PALATIAL
PALATIAL
OH, WOW!
LET'S GO CHECK IT OUT.
MOMMY, IS DAT A PARTY?
WE'VE HAD THE PLEASURE OF SEEING CLIFF STADDEN ON TV FOR MORE THAN TWENTY-FIVE YEARS...
A QUARTER-CENTURY OF DRAMATIC EXCELLENCE, RAISING THE BAR FOR WHAT GENRE TELEVISION IS CAPABLE OF.
YOU PROBABLY KNOW HIM BEST AS CAPTAIN R.L. CAVALIER FROM SPACE FARERS AND SPACE FARERS: 2099 BUT HE'S EMBODIED MANY OTHER ICONIC ROLES AS WELL...
WAIT A SEC, YOU KNOW THIS DUDE?
DID YOU KNOW THEY WERE DOIN' THIS TODAY?
SHHH. I'M LISTENING TO THE CEREMONY...

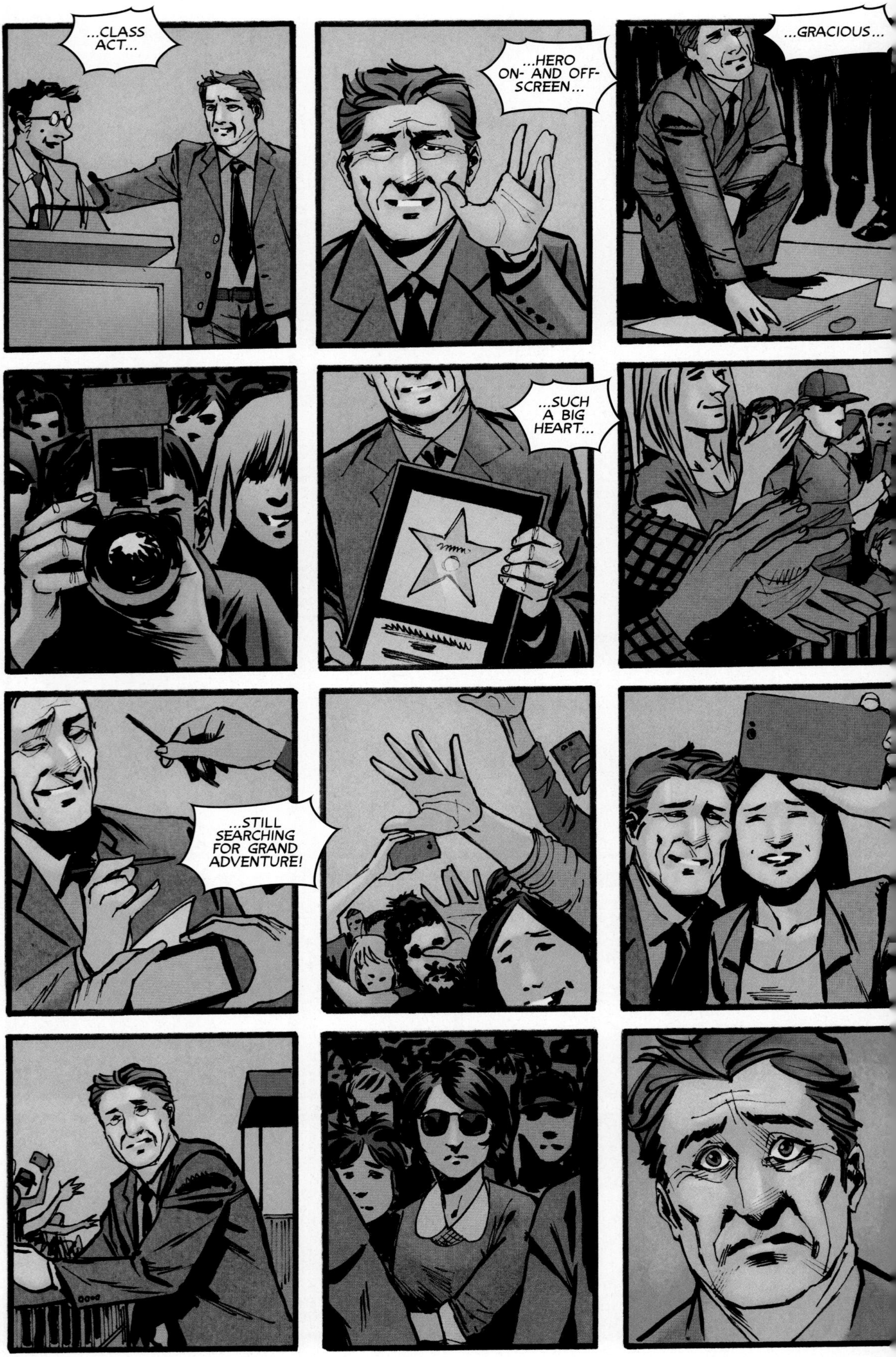
...CLASS ACT...
...HERO ON- AND OFF-SCREEN...
...GRACIOUS...
...SUCH A BIG HEART...
...STILL SEARCHING FOR GRAND ADVENTURE!

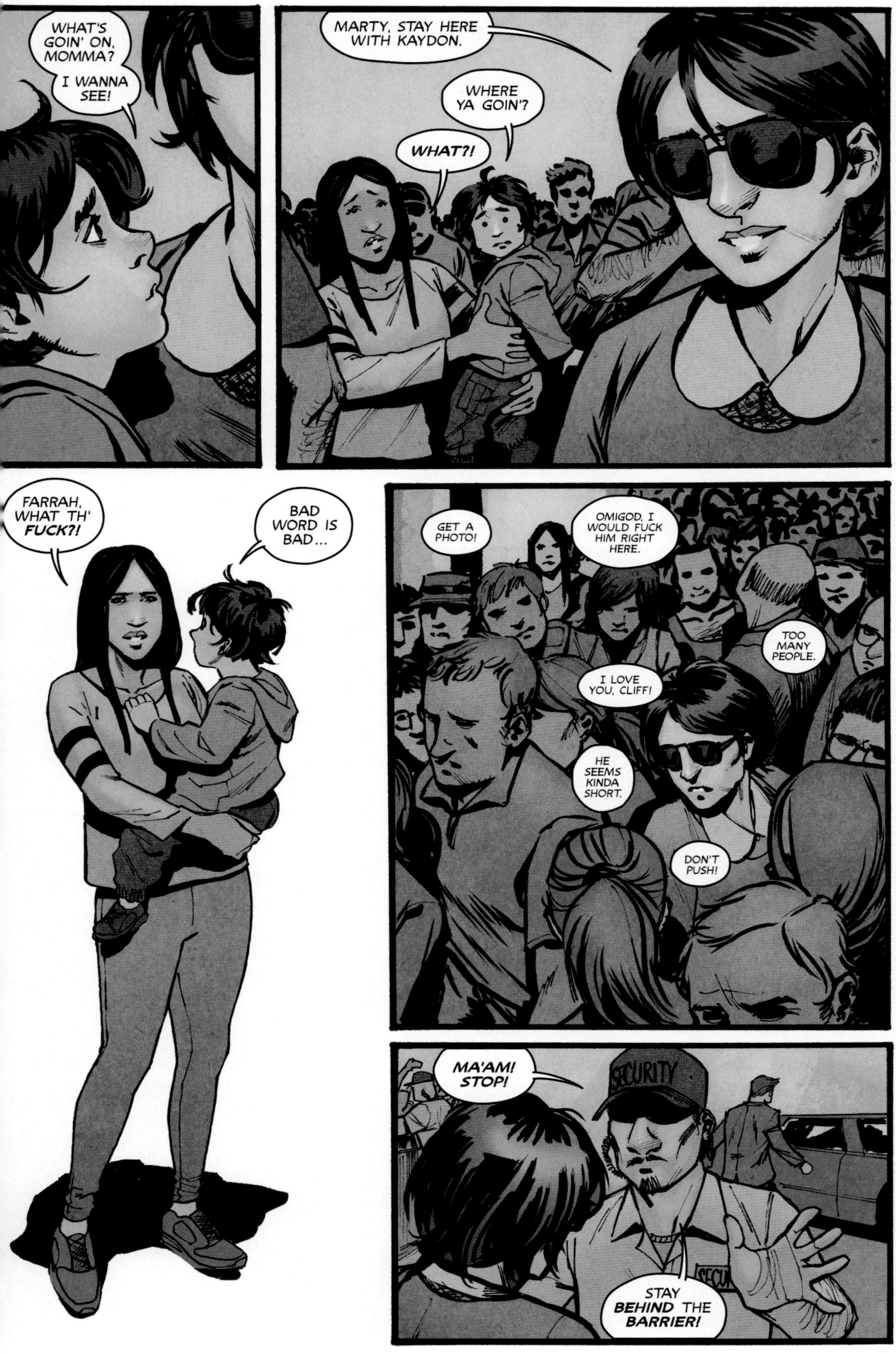
WHAT'S GOIN' ON, MOMMA?
I WANNA SEE!
MARTY, STAY HERE WITH KAYDON.
WHERE YA GOIN'?
WHAT?!
FARRAH, WHAT TH' FUCK?!
BAD WORD IS BAD...
GET A PHOTO!
OMIGOD, I WOULD FUCK HIM RIGHT HERE.
TOO MANY PEOPLE.
I LOVE YOU, CLIFF!
HE SEEMS KINDA SHORT.
DON'T PUSH!
MA'AM! STOP!
SECURITY
STAY BEHIND THE BARRIER!

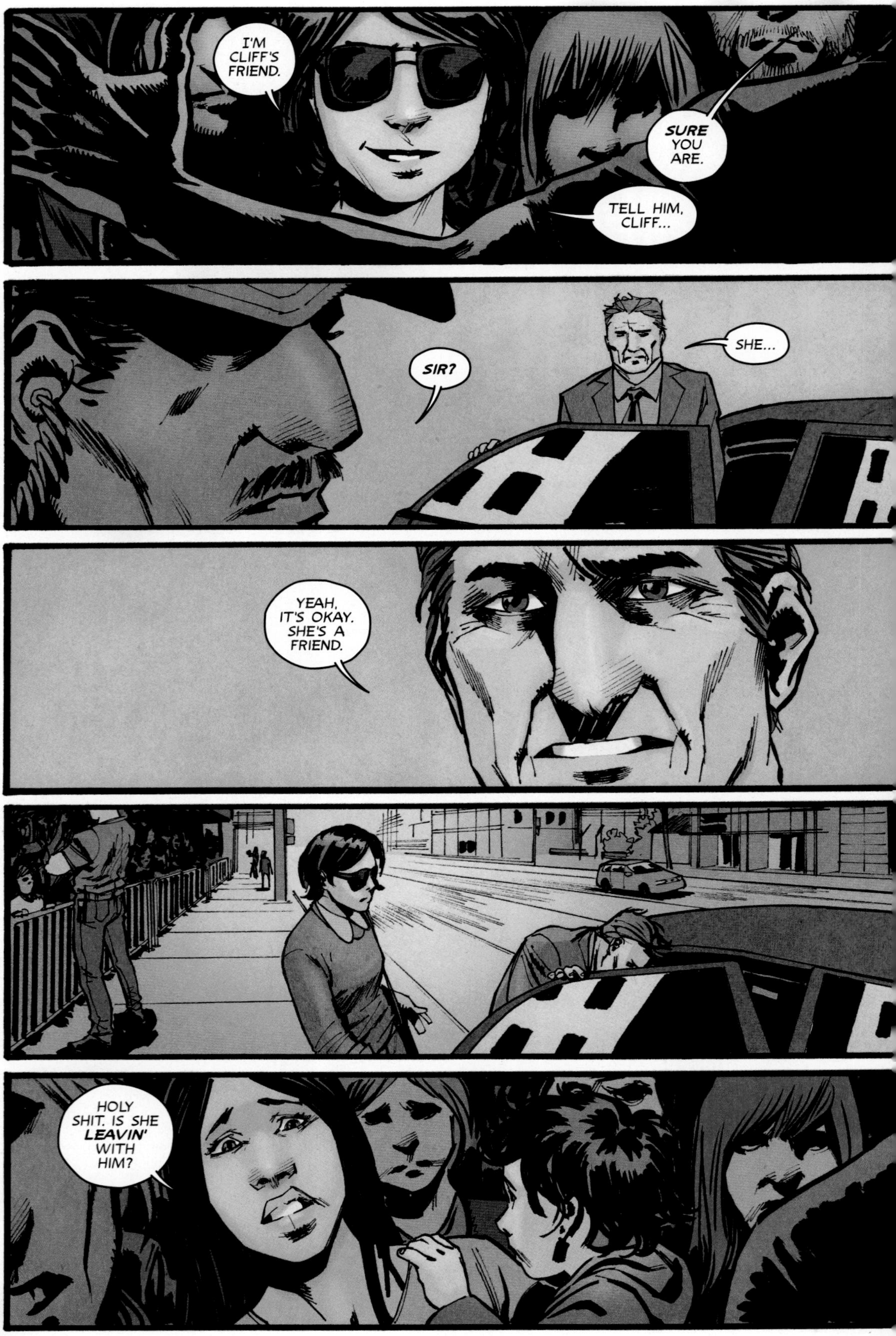

I'M CLIFF'S FRIEND.
SURE YOU ARE.
TELL HIM, CLIFF...
SIR?
SHE...
YEAH, IT'S OKAY. SHE'S A FRIEND.
HOLY SHIT. IS SHE LEAVIN' WITH HIM?

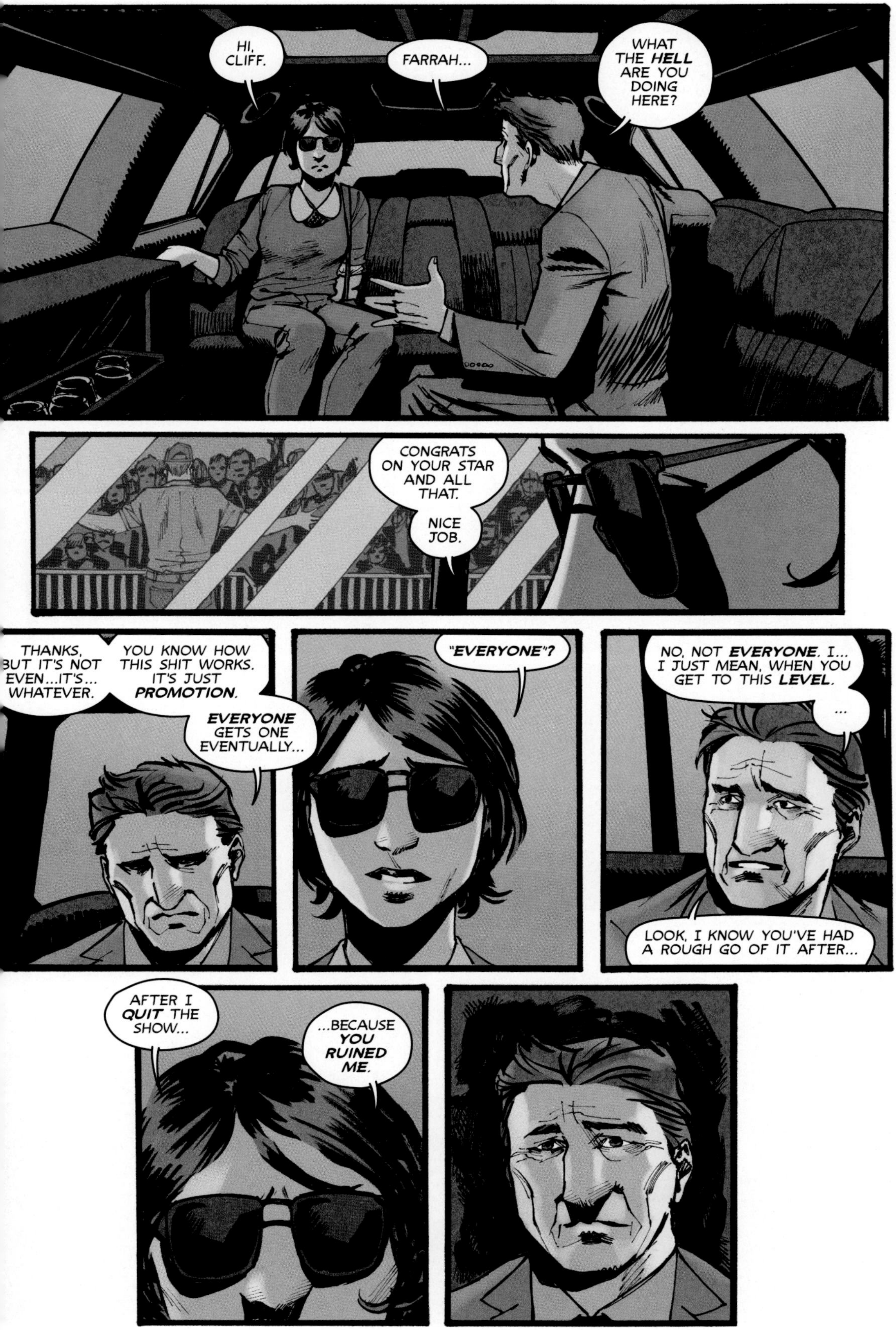
HI, CLIFF.
FARRAH...
WHAT THE **HELL** ARE YOU DOING HERE?
CONGRATS ON YOUR STAR AND ALL THAT.
NICE JOB.
THANKS, BUT IT'S NOT EVEN...IT'S... WHATEVER.
YOU KNOW HOW THIS SHIT WORKS. IT'S JUST **PROMOTION**.
EVERYONE GETS ONE EVENTUALLY...
"**EVERYONE**"?
NO, NOT **EVERYONE**. I... I JUST MEAN, WHEN YOU GET TO THIS **LEVEL**.
...
LOOK, I KNOW YOU'VE HAD A ROUGH GO OF IT AFTER...
AFTER I **QUIT** THE SHOW...
...BECAUSE **YOU RUINED ME**.

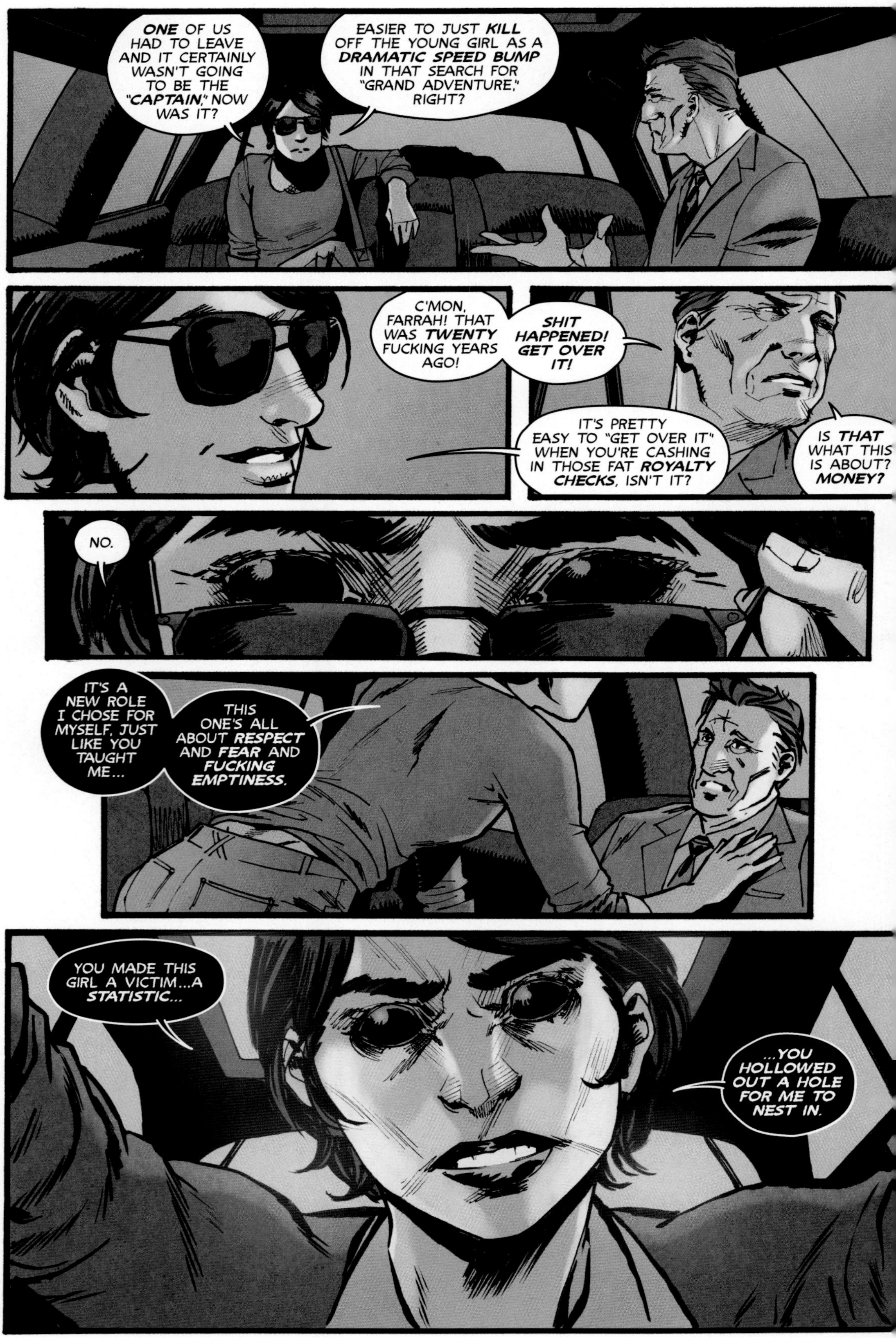
ONE OF US HAD TO LEAVE AND IT CERTAINLY WASN'T GOING TO BE THE "CAPTAIN," NOW WAS IT?
EASIER TO JUST KILL OFF THE YOUNG GIRL AS A DRAMATIC SPEED BUMP IN THAT SEARCH FOR "GRAND ADVENTURE," RIGHT?
C'MON, FARRAH! THAT WAS TWENTY FUCKING YEARS AGO!
SHIT HAPPENED! GET OVER IT!
IT'S PRETTY EASY TO "GET OVER IT" WHEN YOU'RE CASHING IN THOSE FAT ROYALTY CHECKS, ISN'T IT?
IS THAT WHAT THIS IS ABOUT? MONEY?
NO.
IT'S A NEW ROLE I CHOSE FOR MYSELF, JUST LIKE YOU TAUGHT ME...
THIS ONE'S ALL ABOUT RESPECT AND FEAR AND FUCKING EMPTINESS.
YOU MADE THIS GIRL A VICTIM...A STATISTIC...
...YOU HOLLOWED OUT A HOLE FOR ME TO NEST IN.

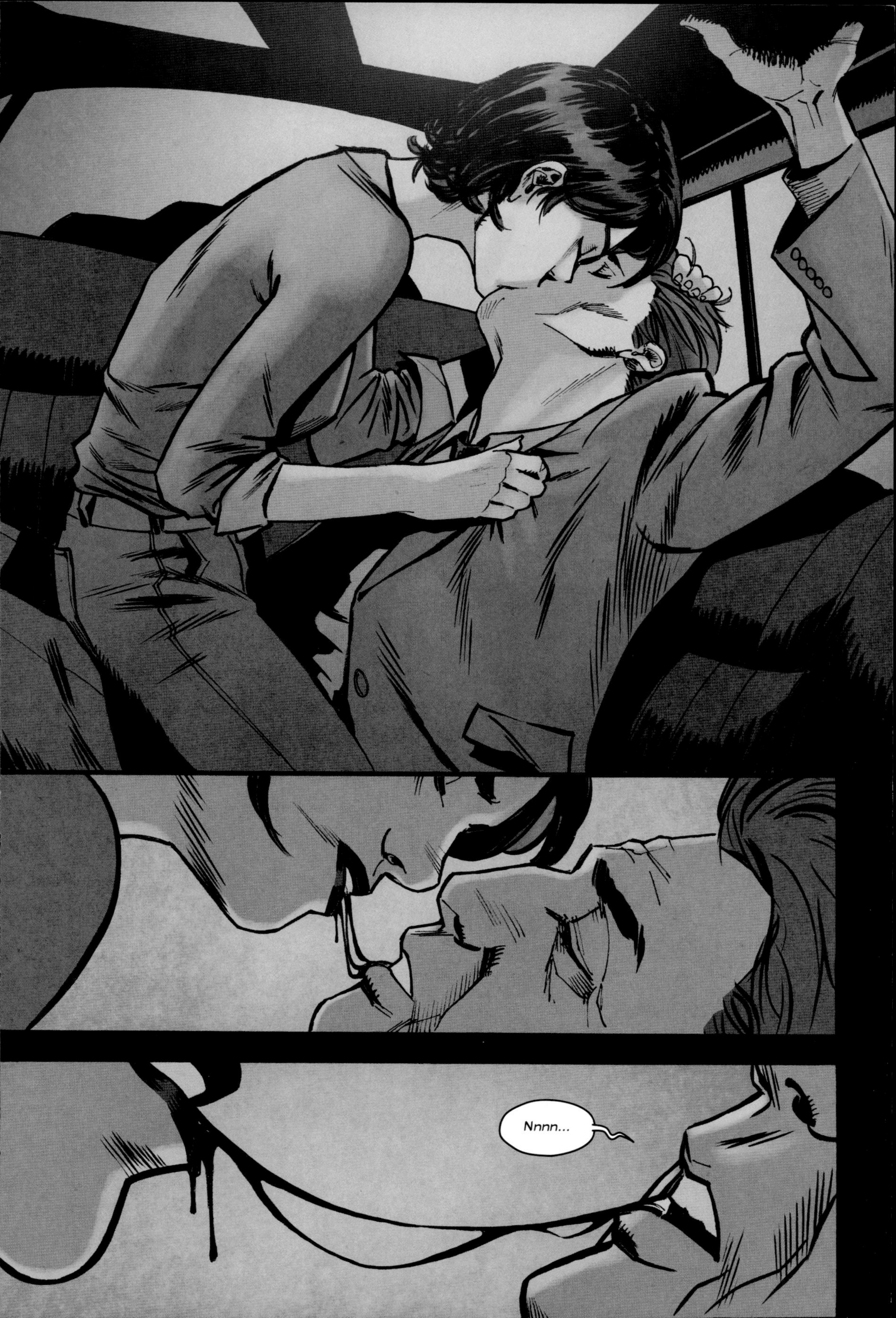
Nnnn...

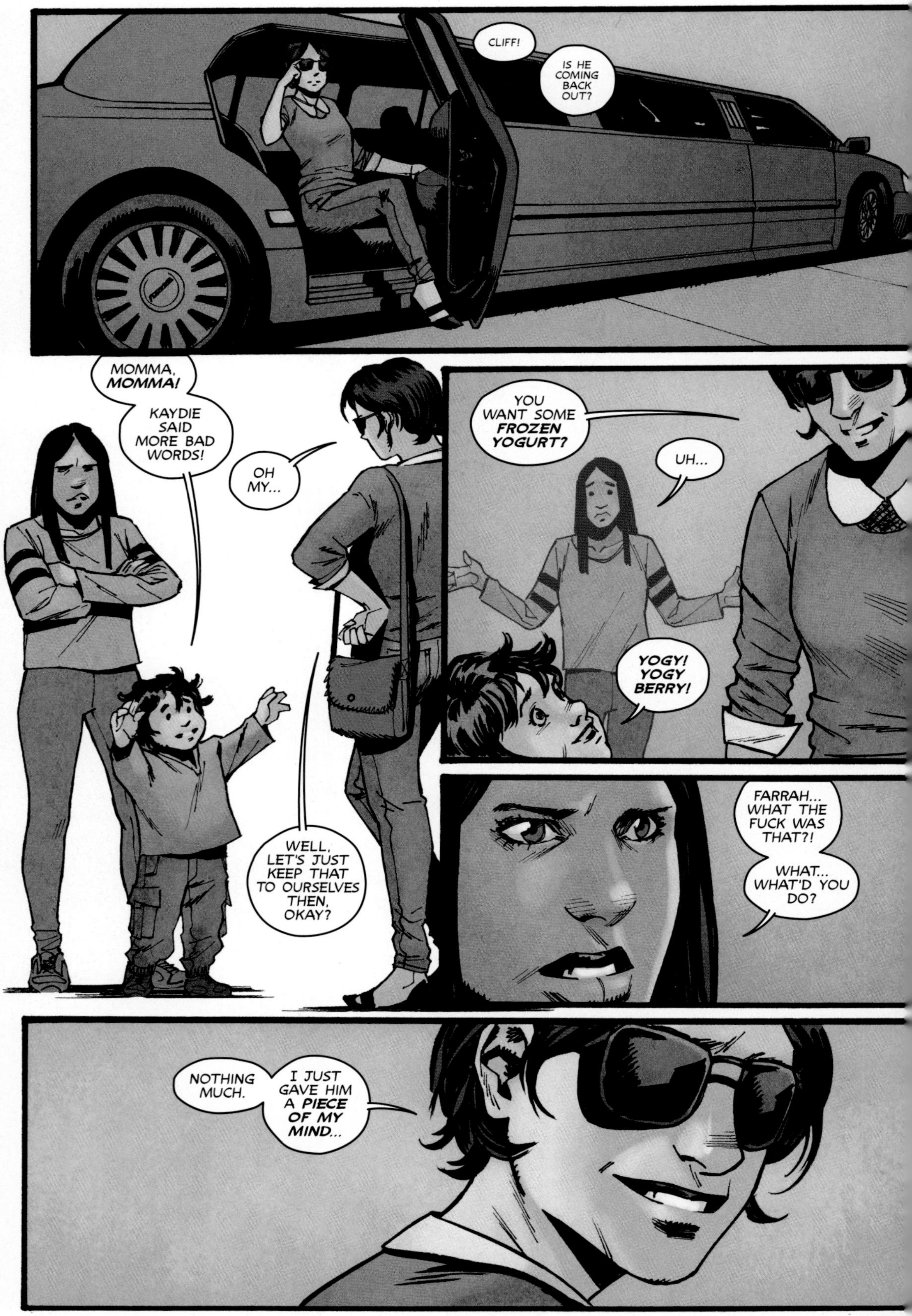
CLIFF!
IS HE COMING BACK OUT?
MOMMA, ***MOMMA!***
KAYDIE SAID MORE BAD WORDS!
OH MY...
WELL, LET'S JUST KEEP THAT TO OURSELVES THEN, OKAY?
YOU WANT SOME ***FROZEN YOGURT?***
UH...
YOGY! YOGY BERRY!
FARRAH... WHAT THE FUCK WAS THAT?!
WHAT... WHAT'D YOU DO?
NOTHING MUCH.
I JUST GAVE HIM A ***PIECE OF MY MIND...***

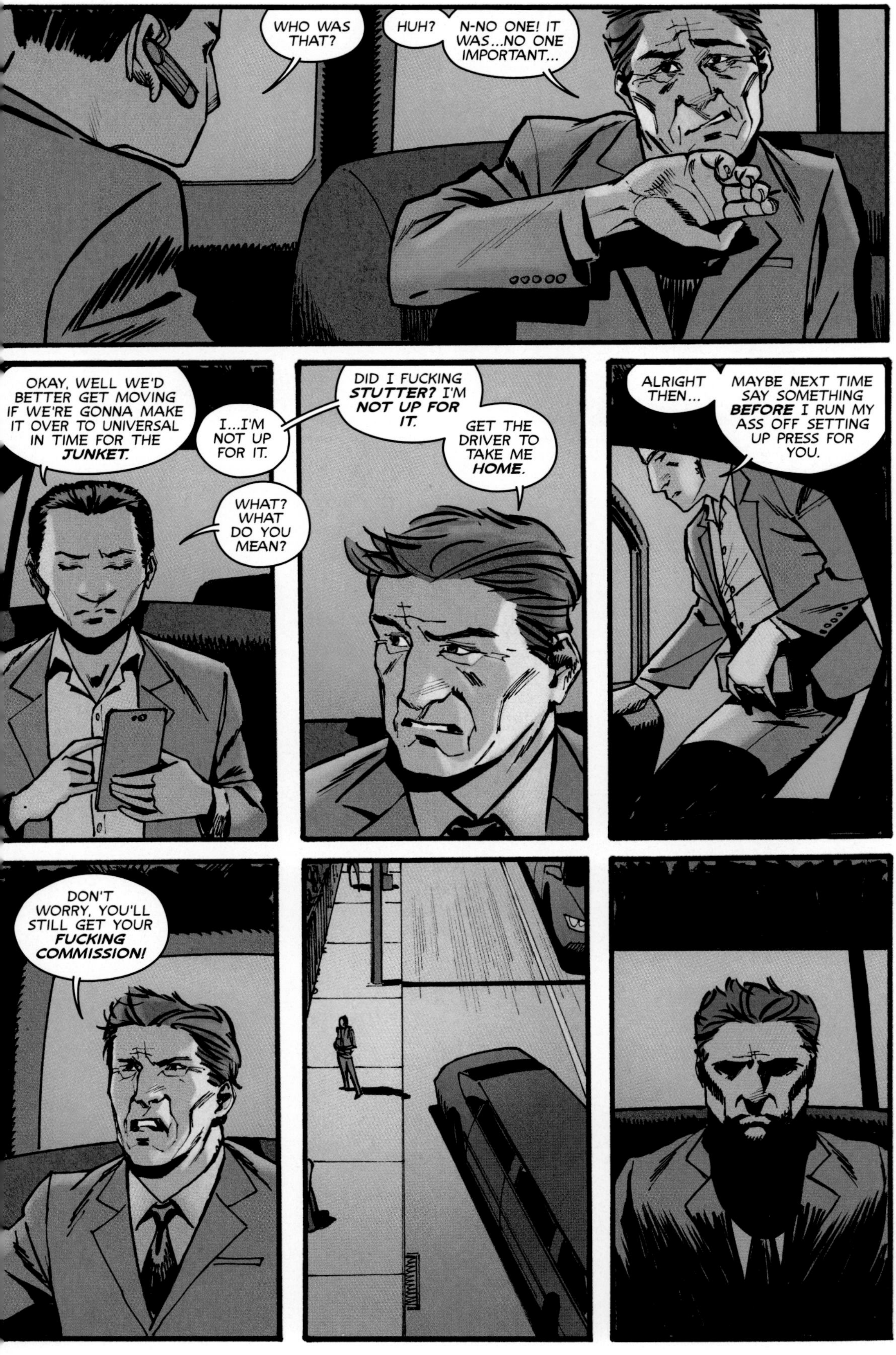
WHO WAS THAT?
HUH?
N-NO ONE! IT WAS...NO ONE IMPORTANT...
OKAY, WELL WE'D BETTER GET MOVING IF WE'RE GONNA MAKE IT OVER TO UNIVERSAL IN TIME FOR THE JUNKET.
I...I'M NOT UP FOR IT.
WHAT? WHAT DO YOU MEAN?
DID I FUCKING STUTTER? I'M NOT UP FOR IT.
GET THE DRIVER TO TAKE ME HOME.
ALRIGHT THEN...
MAYBE NEXT TIME SAY SOMETHING BEFORE I RUN MY ASS OFF SETTING UP PRESS FOR YOU.
DON'T WORRY, YOU'LL STILL GET YOUR FUCKING COMMISSION!

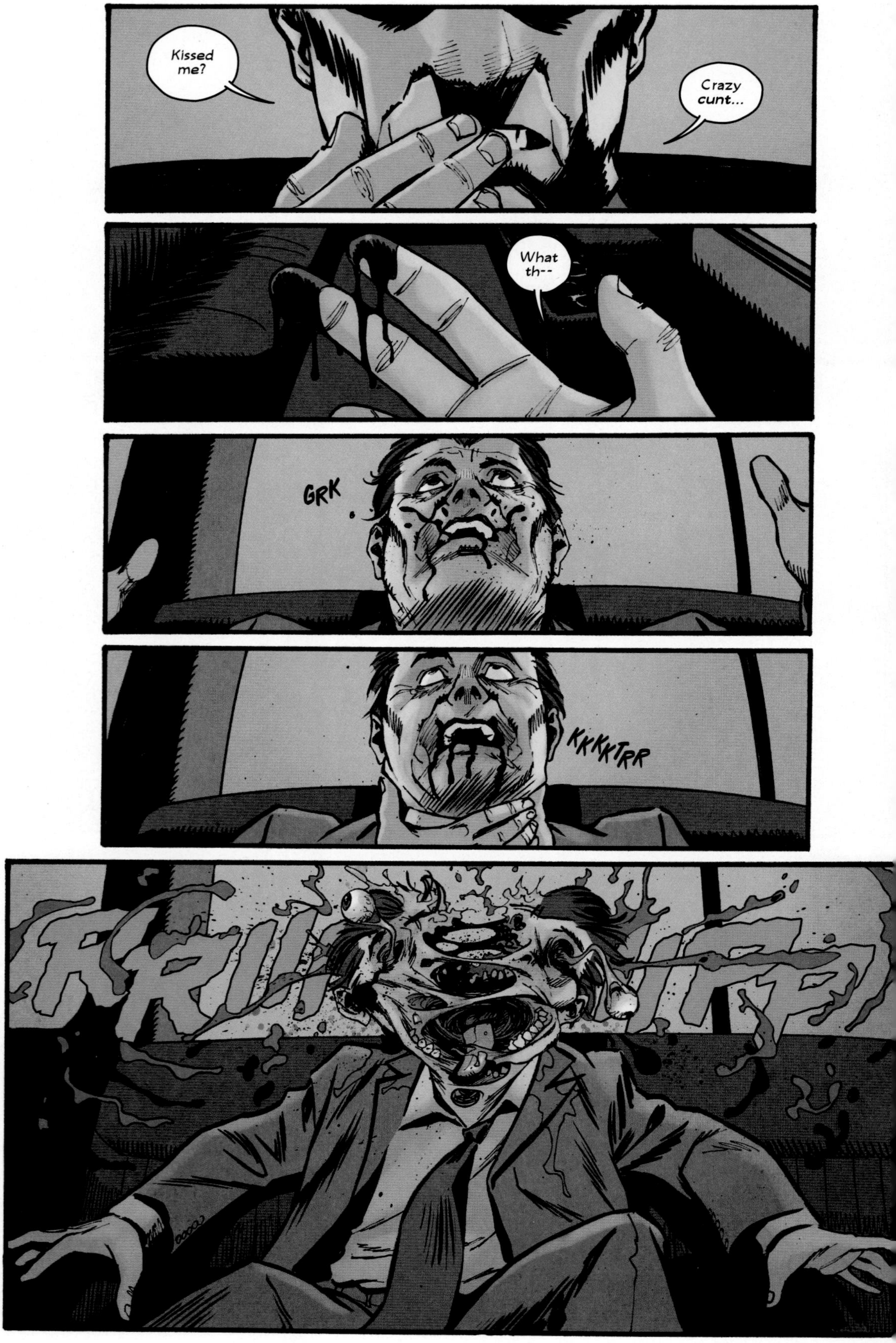
Kissed me?
Crazy cunt...
What th--
GRK
KKKKTRR

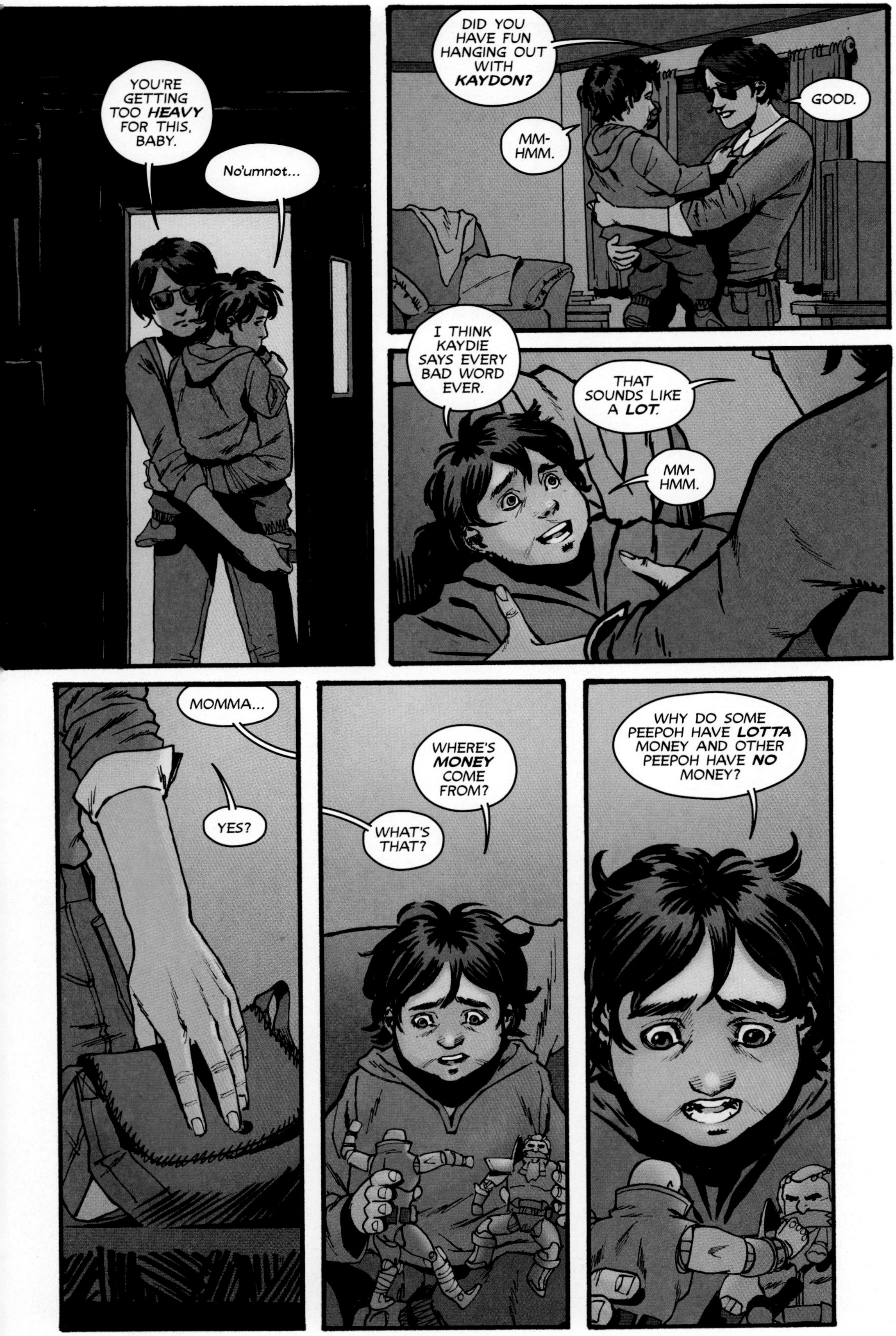

YOU'RE GETTING TOO HEAVY FOR THIS, BABY.
No'umnot...
DID YOU HAVE FUN HANGING OUT WITH KAYDON?
MM-HMM.
GOOD.
I THINK KAYDIE SAYS EVERY BAD WORD EVER.
THAT SOUNDS LIKE A LOT.
MM-HMM.
MOMMA...
YES?
WHERE'S MONEY COME FROM?
WHAT'S THAT?
WHY DO SOME PEEPOH HAVE LOTTA MONEY AND OTHER PEEPOH HAVE NO MONEY?

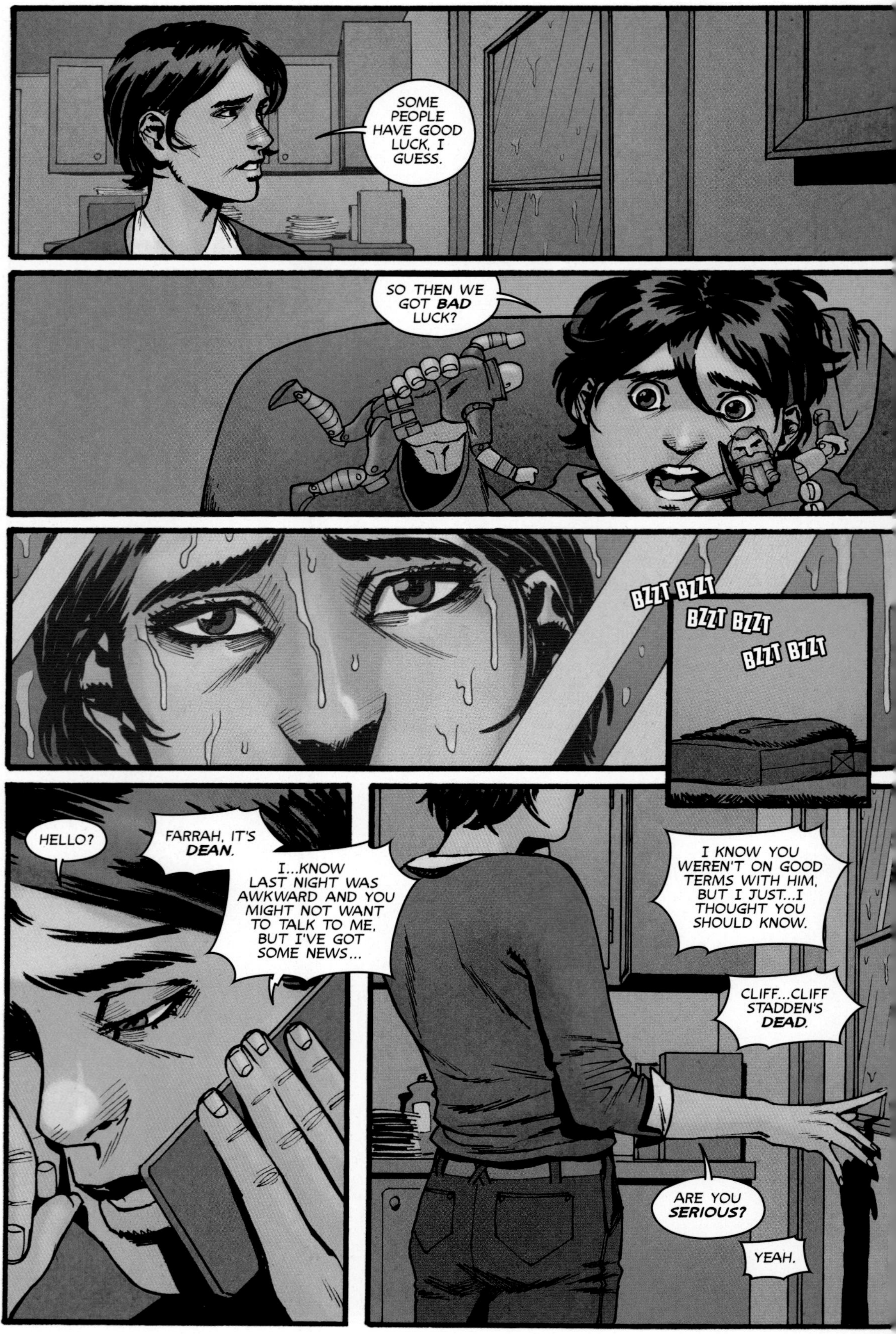

SOME PEOPLE HAVE GOOD LUCK, I GUESS.
SO THEN WE GOT **BAD** LUCK?
BZZT BZZT
BZZT BZZT
BZZT BZZT
HELLO?
FARRAH, IT'S **DEAN.**
I...KNOW LAST NIGHT WAS AWKWARD AND YOU MIGHT NOT WANT TO TALK TO ME, BUT I'VE GOT SOME NEWS...
I KNOW YOU WEREN'T ON GOOD TERMS WITH HIM, BUT I JUST...I THOUGHT YOU SHOULD KNOW.
CLIFF...CLIFF STADDEN'S **DEAD.**
ARE YOU **SERIOUS?**
YEAH.

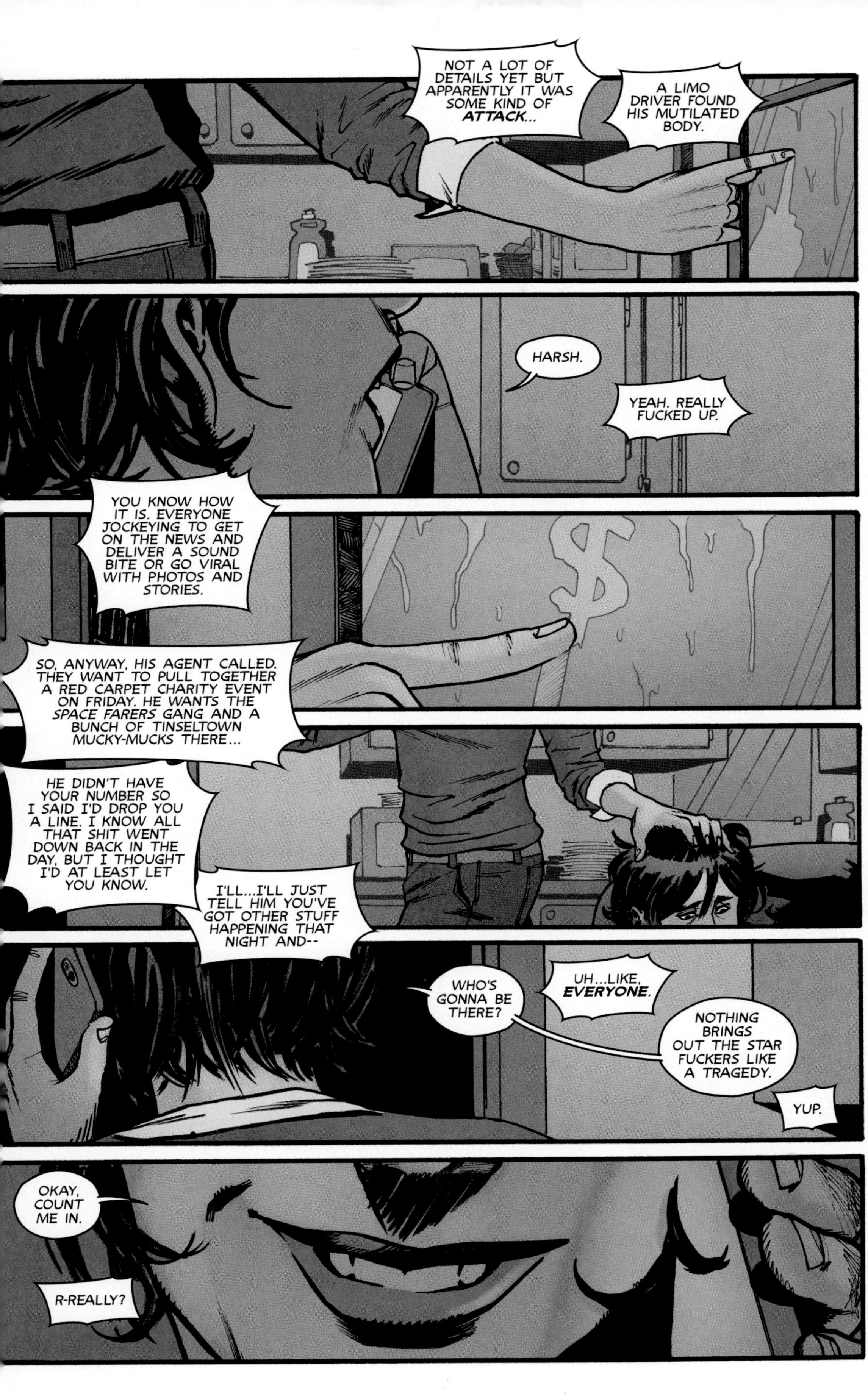
NOT A LOT OF DETAILS YET BUT APPARENTLY IT WAS SOME KIND OF ATTACK...
A LIMO DRIVER FOUND HIS MUTILATED BODY.
HARSH.
YEAH. REALLY FUCKED UP.
YOU KNOW HOW IT IS. EVERYONE JOCKEYING TO GET ON THE NEWS AND DELIVER A SOUND BITE OR GO VIRAL WITH PHOTOS AND STORIES.
SO, ANYWAY, HIS AGENT CALLED. THEY WANT TO PULL TOGETHER A RED CARPET CHARITY EVENT ON FRIDAY. HE WANTS THE SPACE FARERS GANG AND A BUNCH OF TINSELTOWN MUCKY-MUCKS THERE...
HE DIDN'T HAVE YOUR NUMBER SO I SAID I'D DROP YOU A LINE. I KNOW ALL THAT SHIT WENT DOWN BACK IN THE DAY, BUT I THOUGHT I'D AT LEAST LET YOU KNOW.
I'LL...I'LL JUST TELL HIM YOU'VE GOT OTHER STUFF HAPPENING THAT NIGHT AND--
WHO'S GONNA BE THERE?
UH...LIKE, EVERYONE.
NOTHING BRINGS OUT THE STAR FUCKERS LIKE A TRAGEDY.
YUP.
OKAY, COUNT ME IN.
R-REALLY?

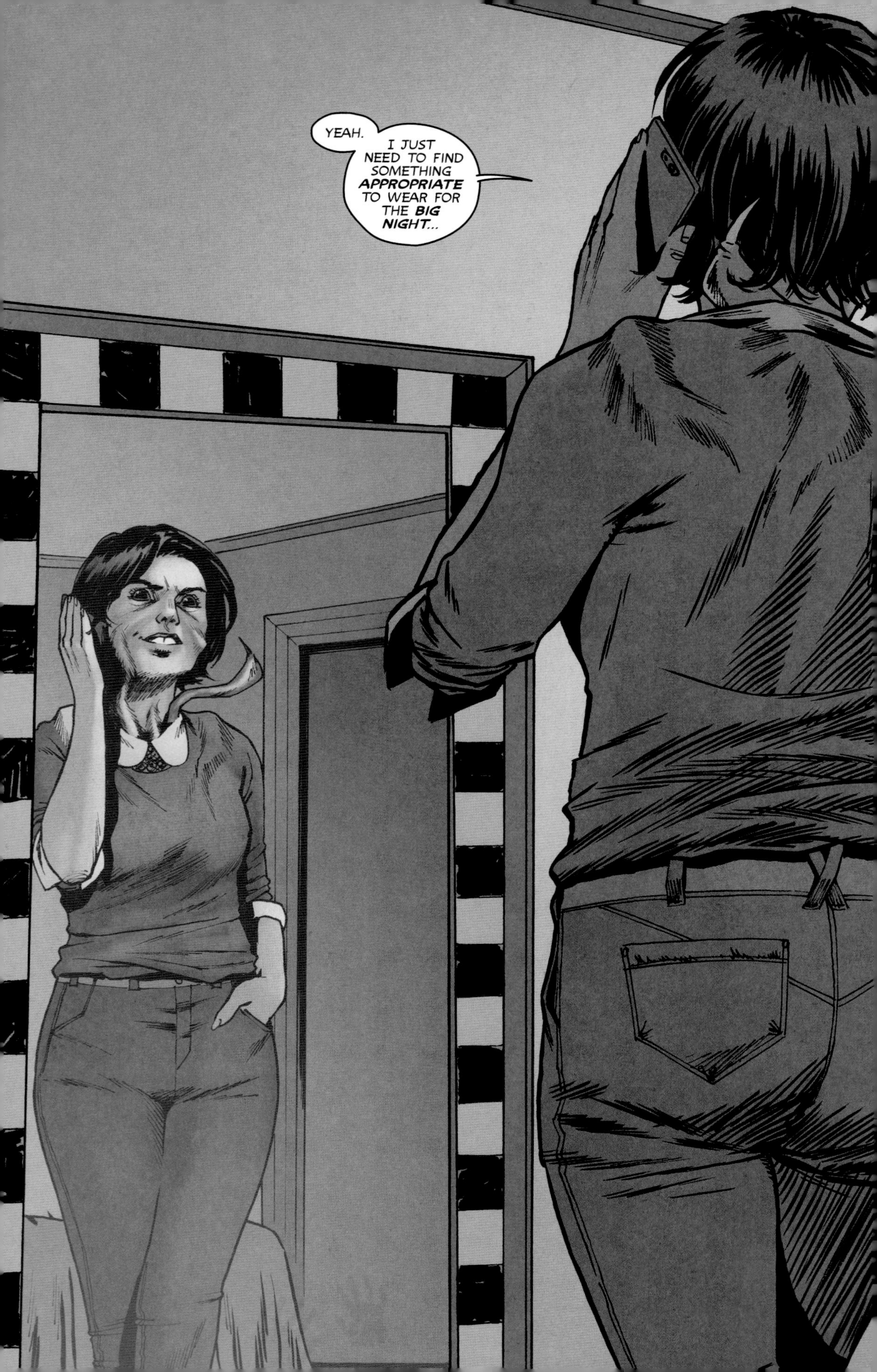
YEAH.
I JUST NEED TO FIND SOMETHING APPROPRIATE TO WEAR FOR THE BIG NIGHT...

PART 4: PLAYING THE PART

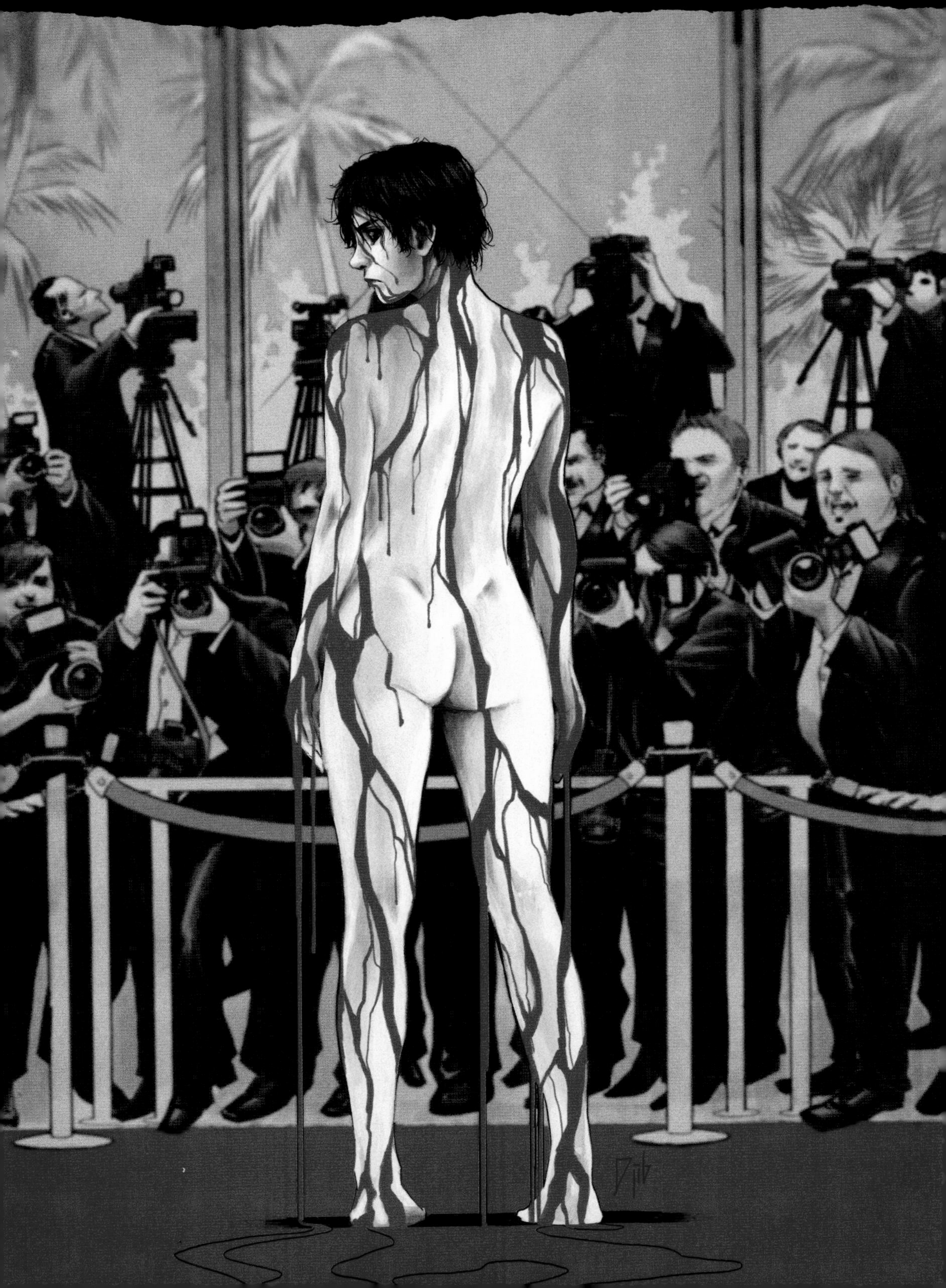

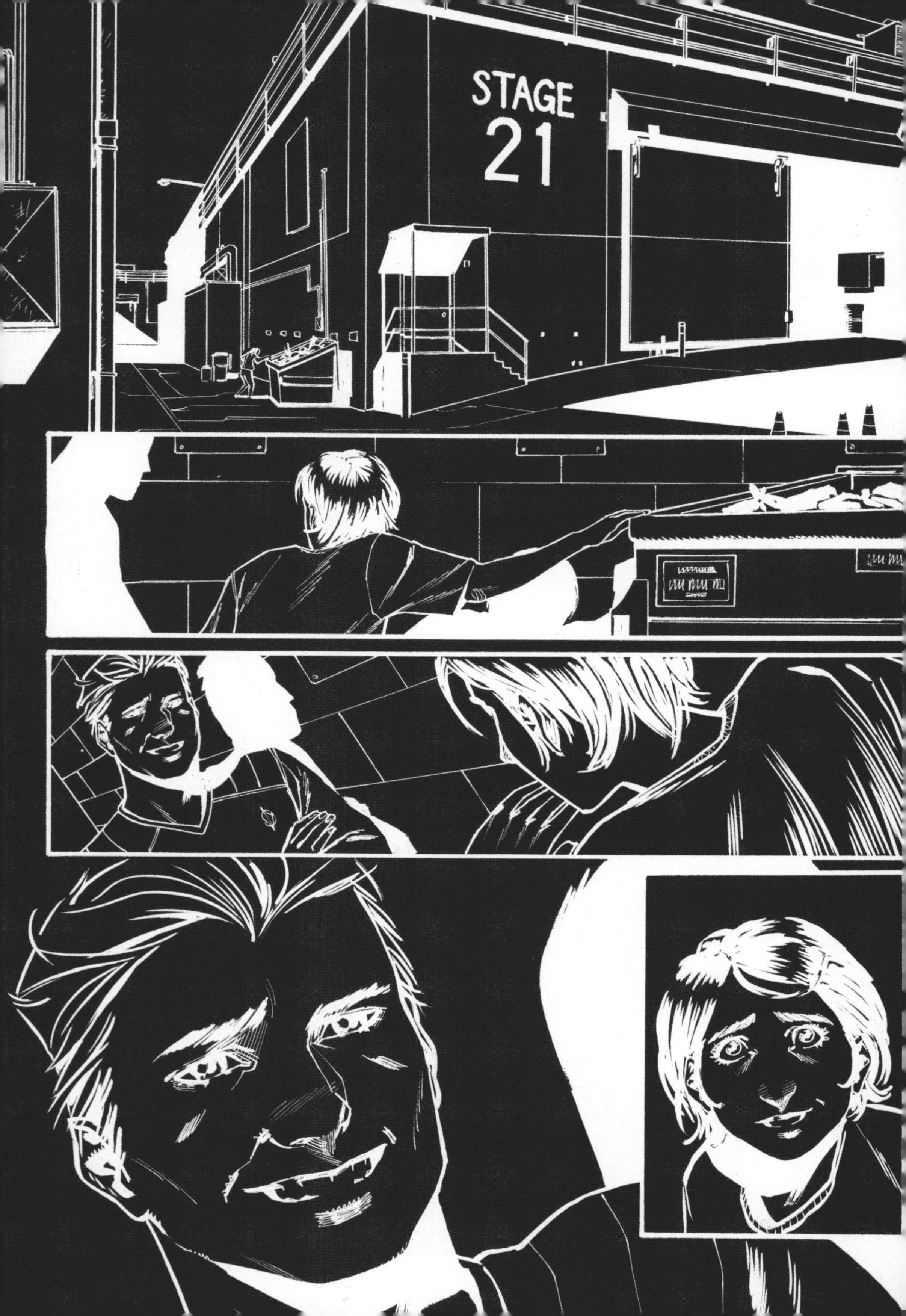
STAGE
21

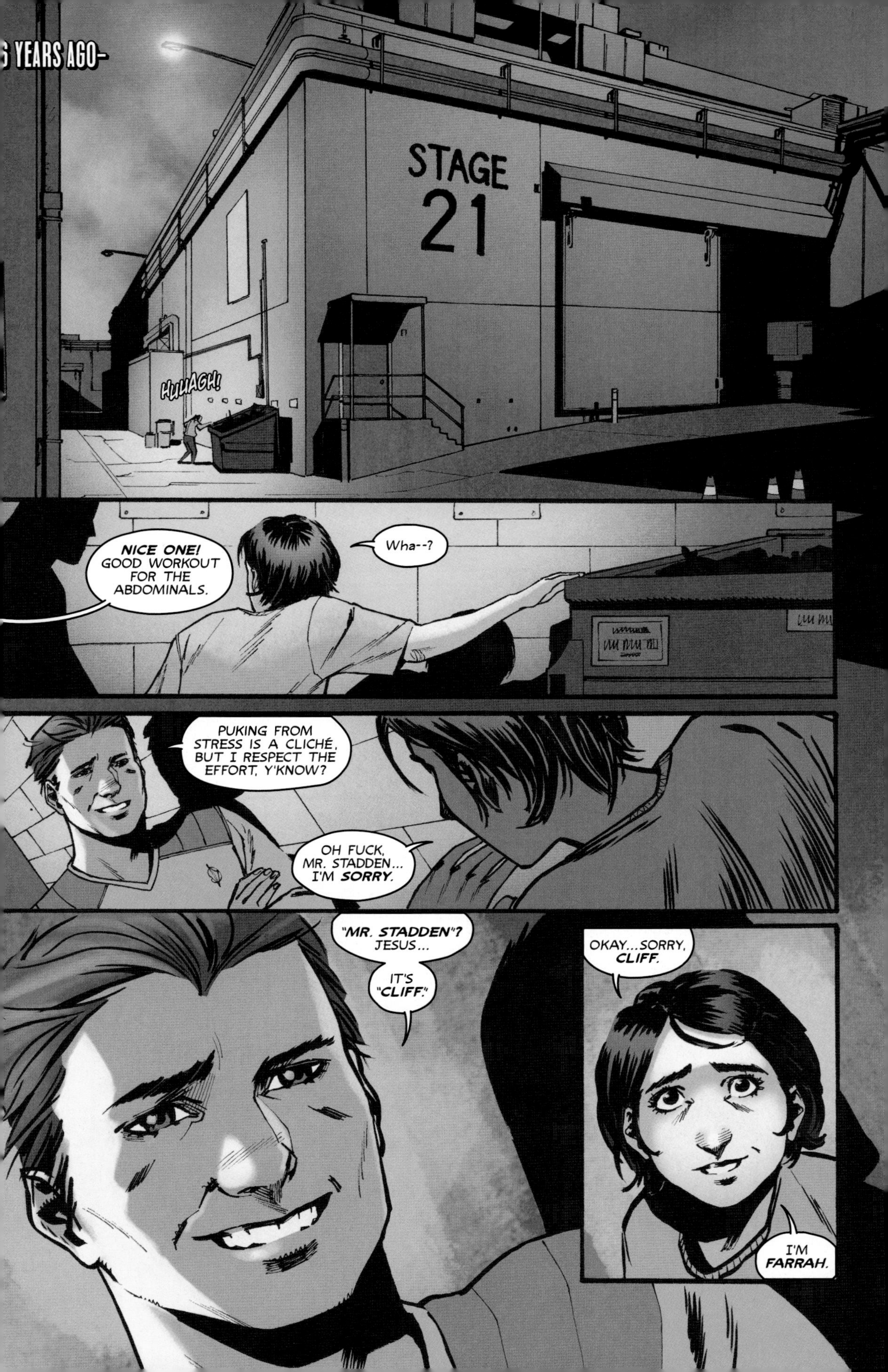
YEARS AGO-
STAGE 21
HUUAGH!
NICE ONE! GOOD WORKOUT FOR THE ABDOMINALS.
Wha--?
PUKING FROM STRESS IS A CLICHÉ, BUT I RESPECT THE EFFORT, Y'KNOW?
OH FUCK, MR. STADDEN... I'M SORRY.
"MR. STADDEN"? JESUS...
IT'S "CLIFF."
OKAY...SORRY, CLIFF.
I'M FARRAH.

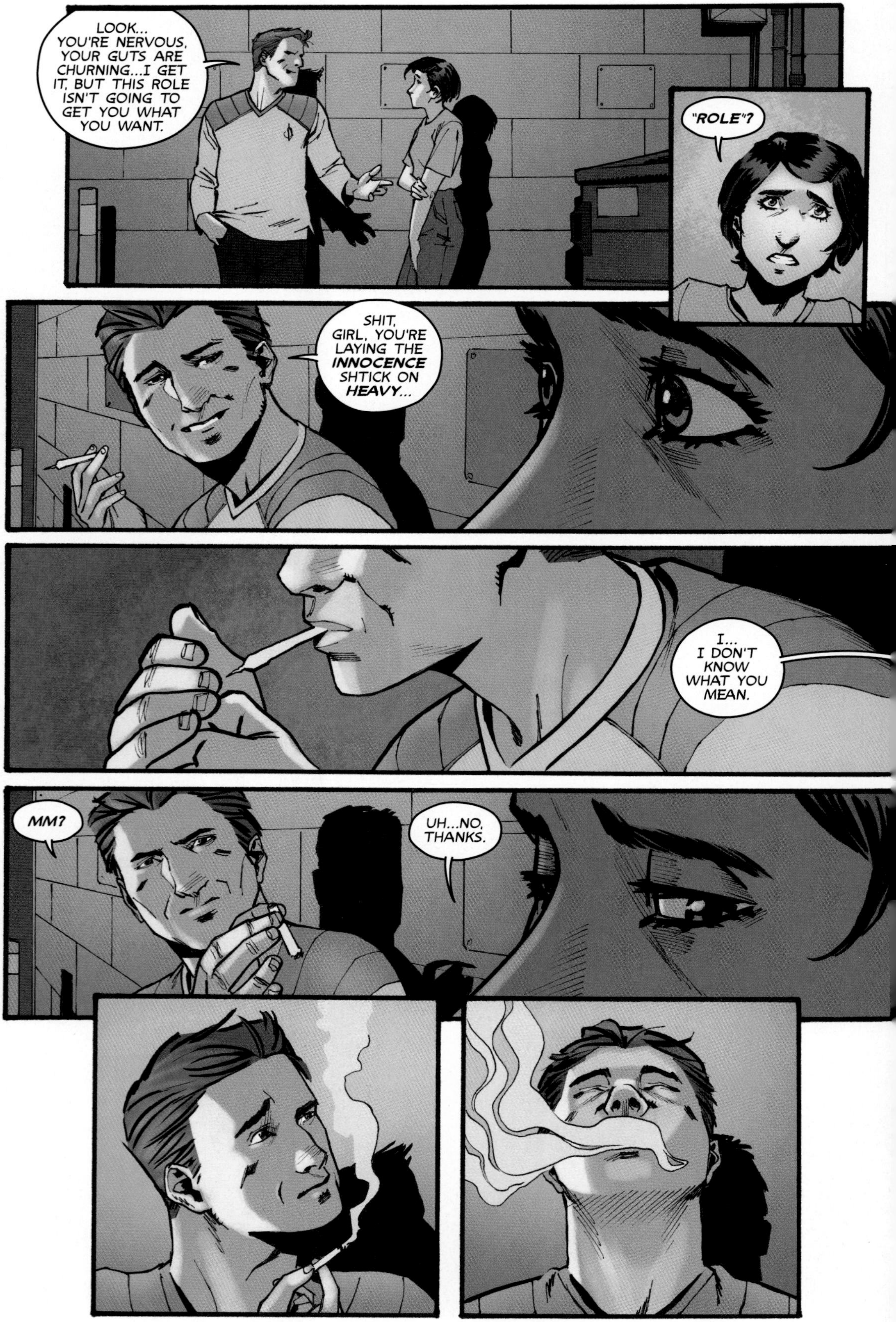
LOOK... YOU'RE NERVOUS, YOUR GUTS ARE CHURNING...I GET IT, BUT THIS ROLE ISN'T GOING TO GET YOU WHAT YOU WANT.
"ROLE"?
SHIT, GIRL, YOU'RE LAYING THE INNOCENCE SHTICK ON HEAVY...
I... I DON'T KNOW WHAT YOU MEAN.
MM?
UH...NO, THANKS.

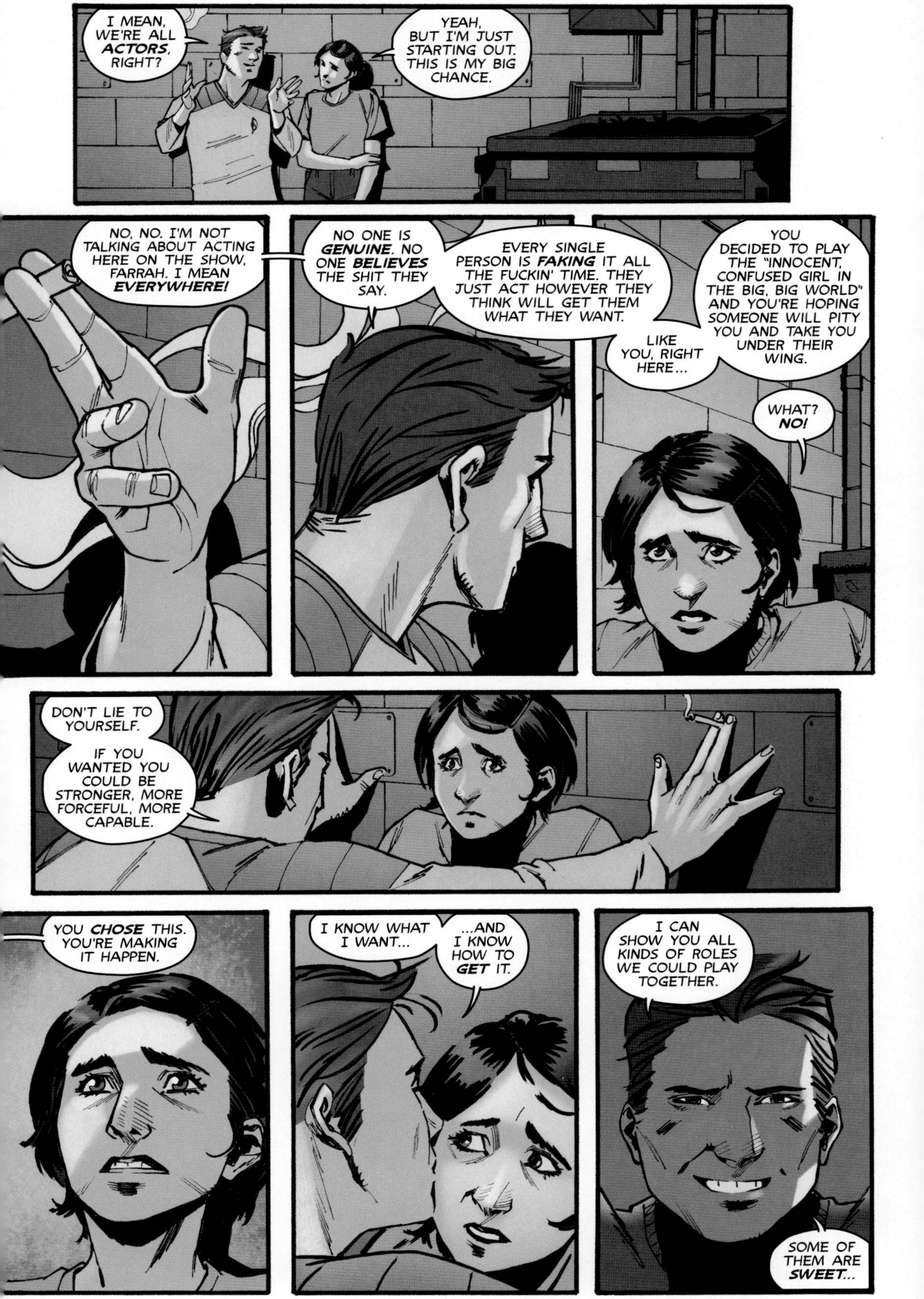
I MEAN, WE'RE ALL ACTORS, RIGHT?
YEAH, BUT I'M JUST STARTING OUT. THIS IS MY BIG CHANCE.
NO, NO. I'M NOT TALKING ABOUT ACTING HERE ON THE SHOW, FARRAH. I MEAN EVERYWHERE!
NO ONE IS GENUINE. NO ONE BELIEVES THE SHIT THEY SAY.
EVERY SINGLE PERSON IS FAKING IT ALL THE FUCKIN' TIME. THEY JUST ACT HOWEVER THEY THINK WILL GET THEM WHAT THEY WANT.
LIKE YOU, RIGHT HERE...
YOU DECIDED TO PLAY THE "INNOCENT, CONFUSED GIRL IN THE BIG, BIG WORLD" AND YOU'RE HOPING SOMEONE WILL PITY YOU AND TAKE YOU UNDER THEIR WING.
WHAT? NO!
DON'T LIE TO YOURSELF.
IF YOU WANTED YOU COULD BE STRONGER, MORE FORCEFUL, MORE CAPABLE.
YOU CHOSE THIS. YOU'RE MAKING IT HAPPEN.
I KNOW WHAT I WANT...
...AND I KNOW HOW TO GET IT.
I CAN SHOW YOU ALL KINDS OF ROLES WE COULD PLAY TOGETHER.
SOME OF THEM ARE SWEET...

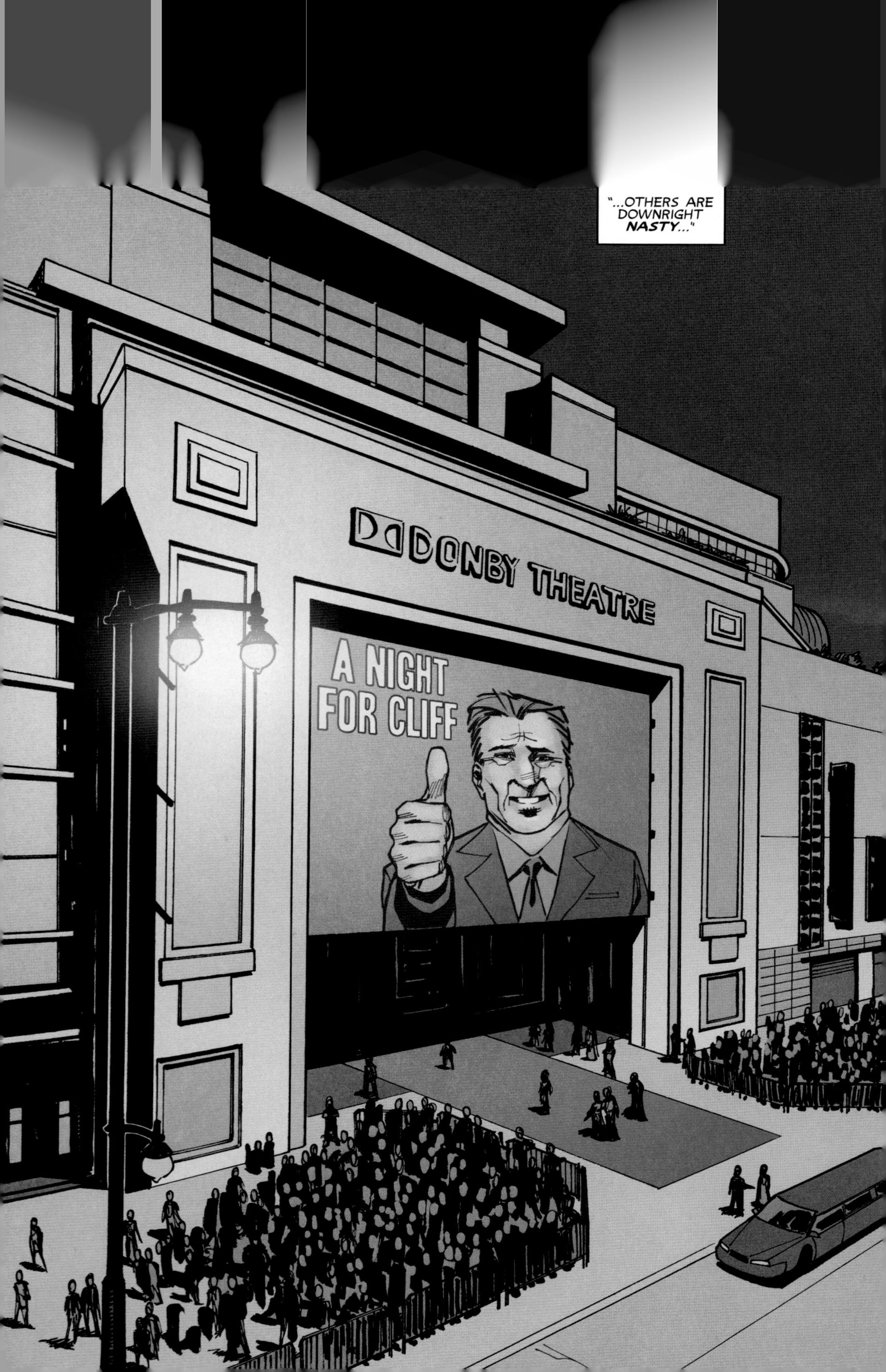
"...OTHERS ARE DOWNRIGHT NASTY..."
DONBY THEATRE
A NIGHT FOR CLIFF

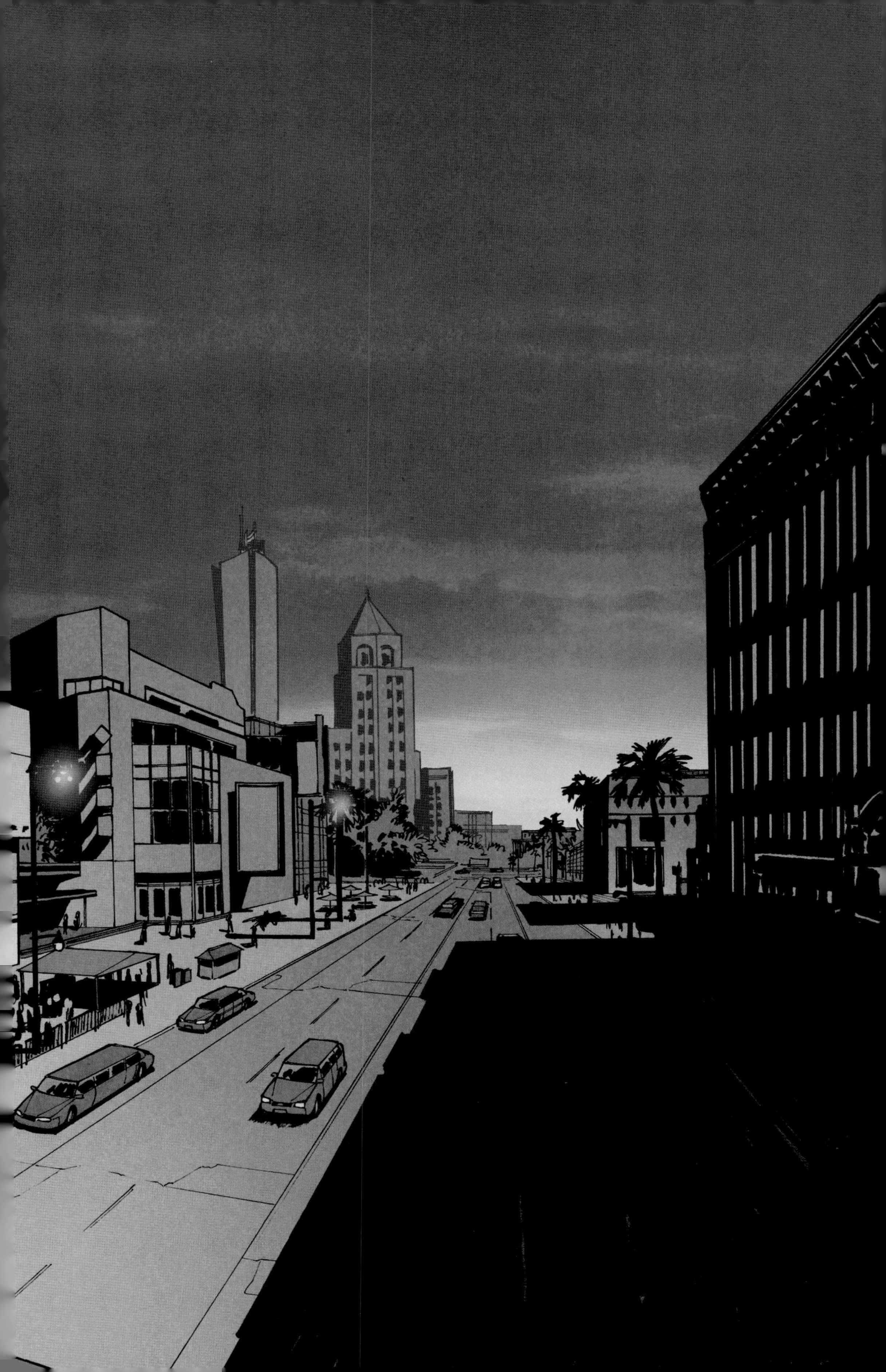

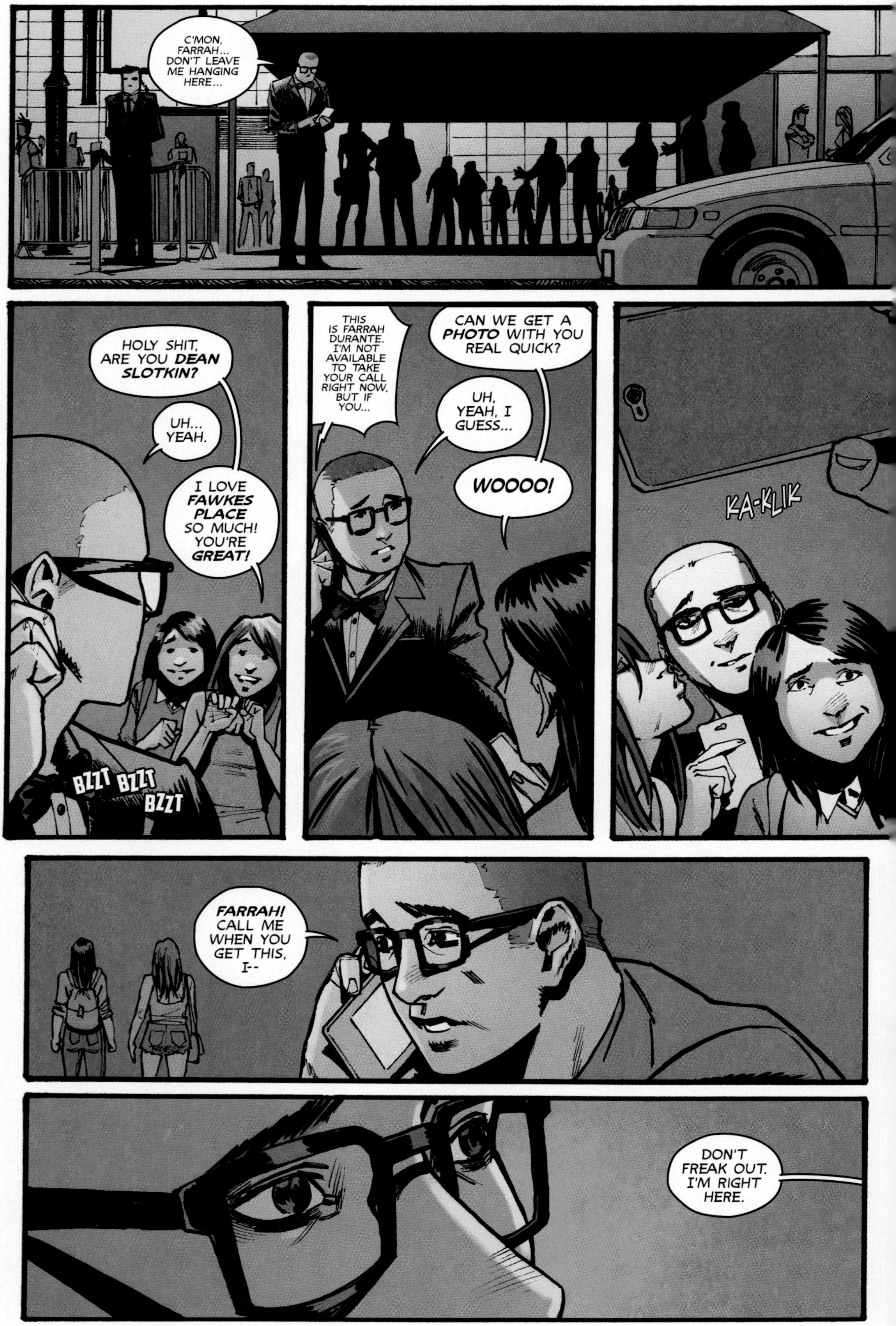
C'MON, FARRAH... DON'T LEAVE ME HANGING HERE...
HOLY SHIT, ARE YOU DEAN SLOTKIN?
UH... YEAH.
I LOVE FAWKES PLACE SO MUCH! YOU'RE GREAT!
BZZT BZZT BZZT
THIS IS FARRAH DURANTE. I'M NOT AVAILABLE TO TAKE YOUR CALL RIGHT NOW, BUT IF YOU...
CAN WE GET A PHOTO WITH YOU REAL QUICK?
UH, YEAH, I GUESS...
WOOOO!
KA-KLIK
FARRAH! CALL ME WHEN YOU GET THIS, I--
DON'T FREAK OUT. I'M RIGHT HERE.

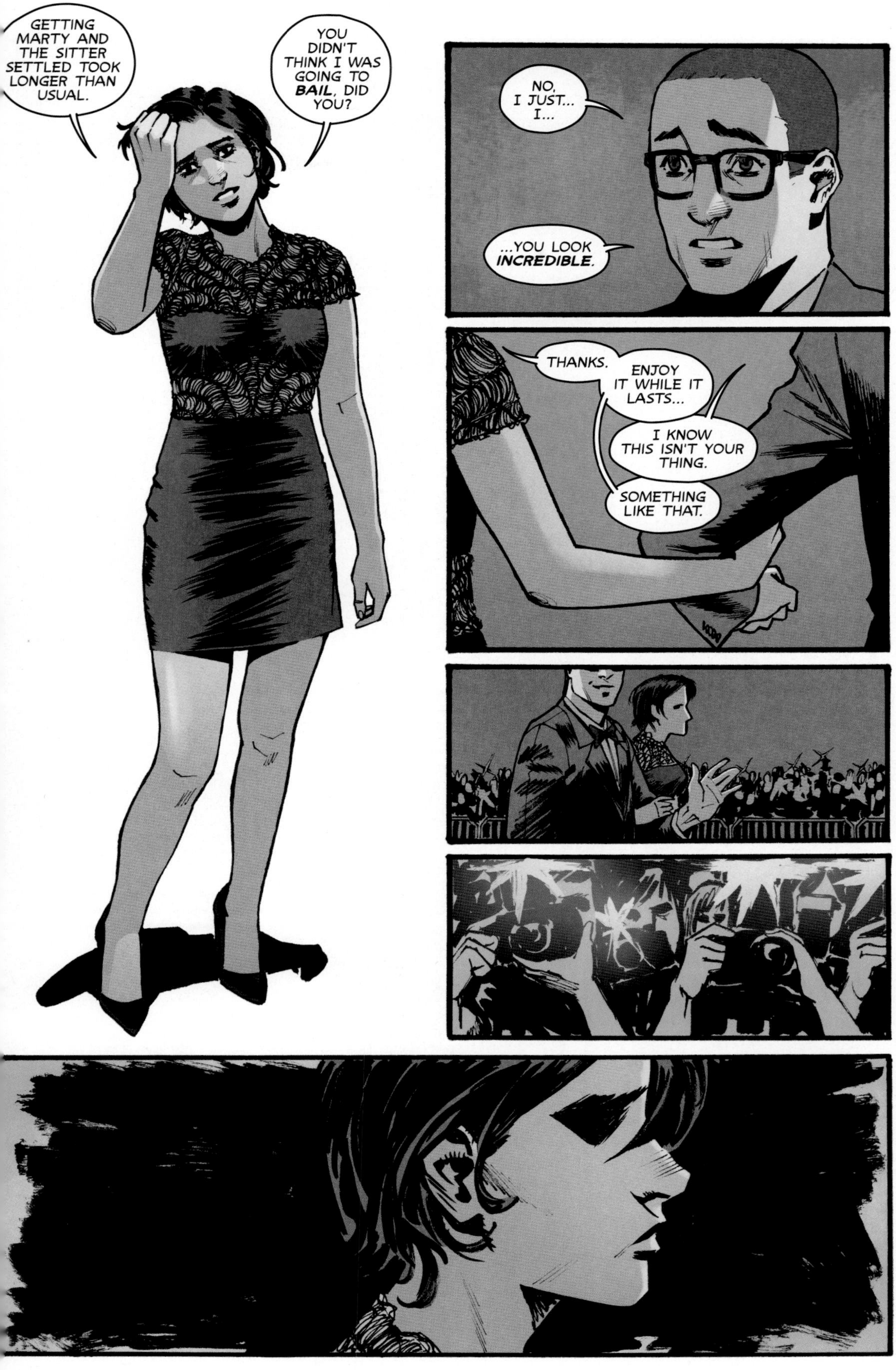
GETTING MARTY AND THE SITTER SETTLED TOOK LONGER THAN USUAL.
YOU DIDN'T THINK I WAS GOING TO BAIL, DID YOU?
NO, I JUST... I...
...YOU LOOK INCREDIBLE.
THANKS.
ENJOY IT WHILE IT LASTS...
I KNOW THIS ISN'T YOUR THING.
SOMETHING LIKE THAT.

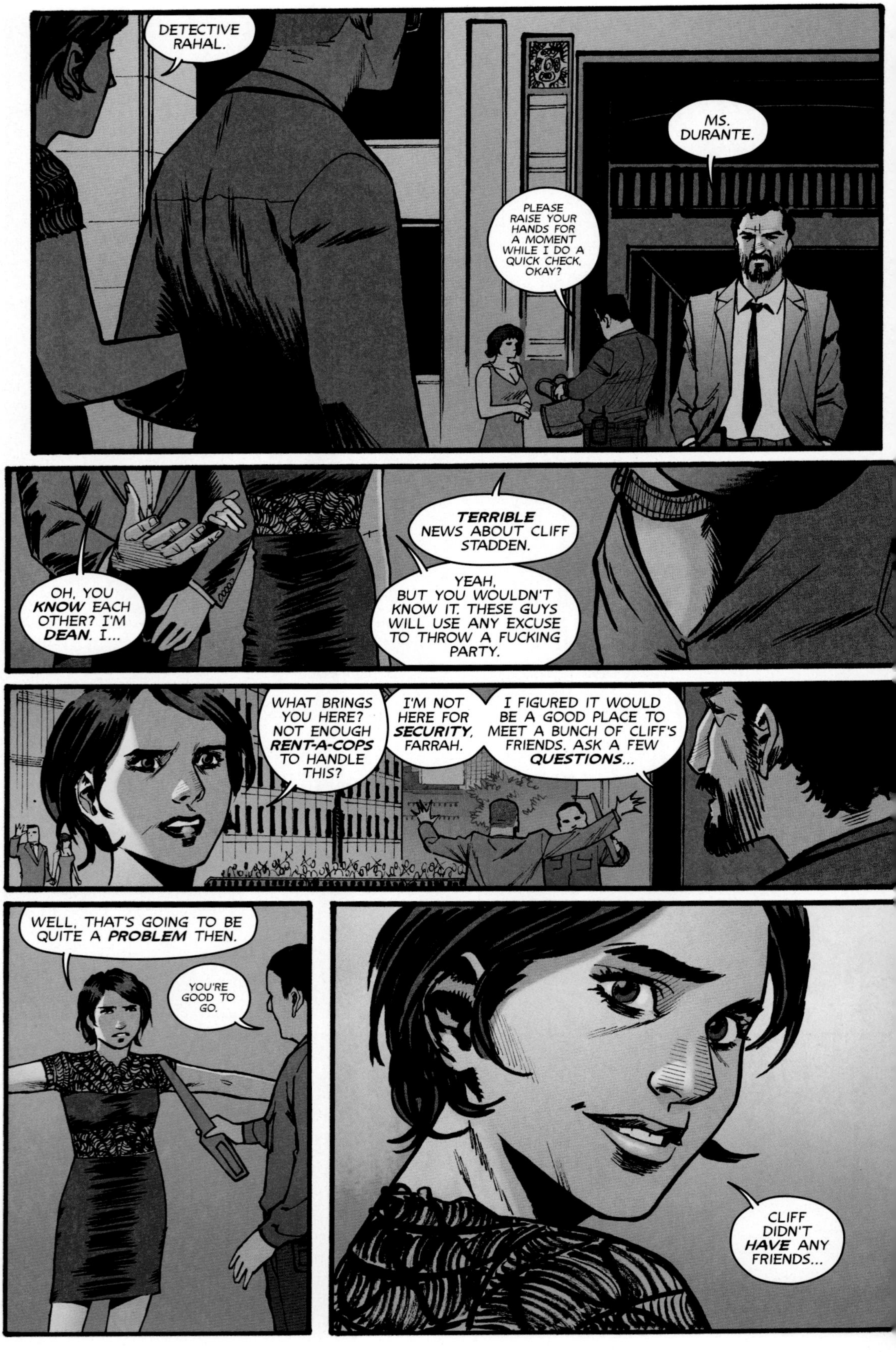
DETECTIVE RAHAL.
MS. DURANTE.
PLEASE RAISE YOUR HANDS FOR A MOMENT WHILE I DO A QUICK CHECK, OKAY?
TERRIBLE NEWS ABOUT CLIFF STADDEN.
OH, YOU KNOW EACH OTHER? I'M DEAN. I...
YEAH, BUT YOU WOULDN'T KNOW IT. THESE GUYS WILL USE ANY EXCUSE TO THROW A FUCKING PARTY.
WHAT BRINGS YOU HERE? NOT ENOUGH RENT-A-COPS TO HANDLE THIS?
I'M NOT HERE FOR SECURITY, FARRAH.
I FIGURED IT WOULD BE A GOOD PLACE TO MEET A BUNCH OF CLIFF'S FRIENDS. ASK A FEW QUESTIONS...
WELL, THAT'S GOING TO BE QUITE A PROBLEM THEN.
YOU'RE GOOD TO GO.
CLIFF DIDN'T HAVE ANY FRIENDS...

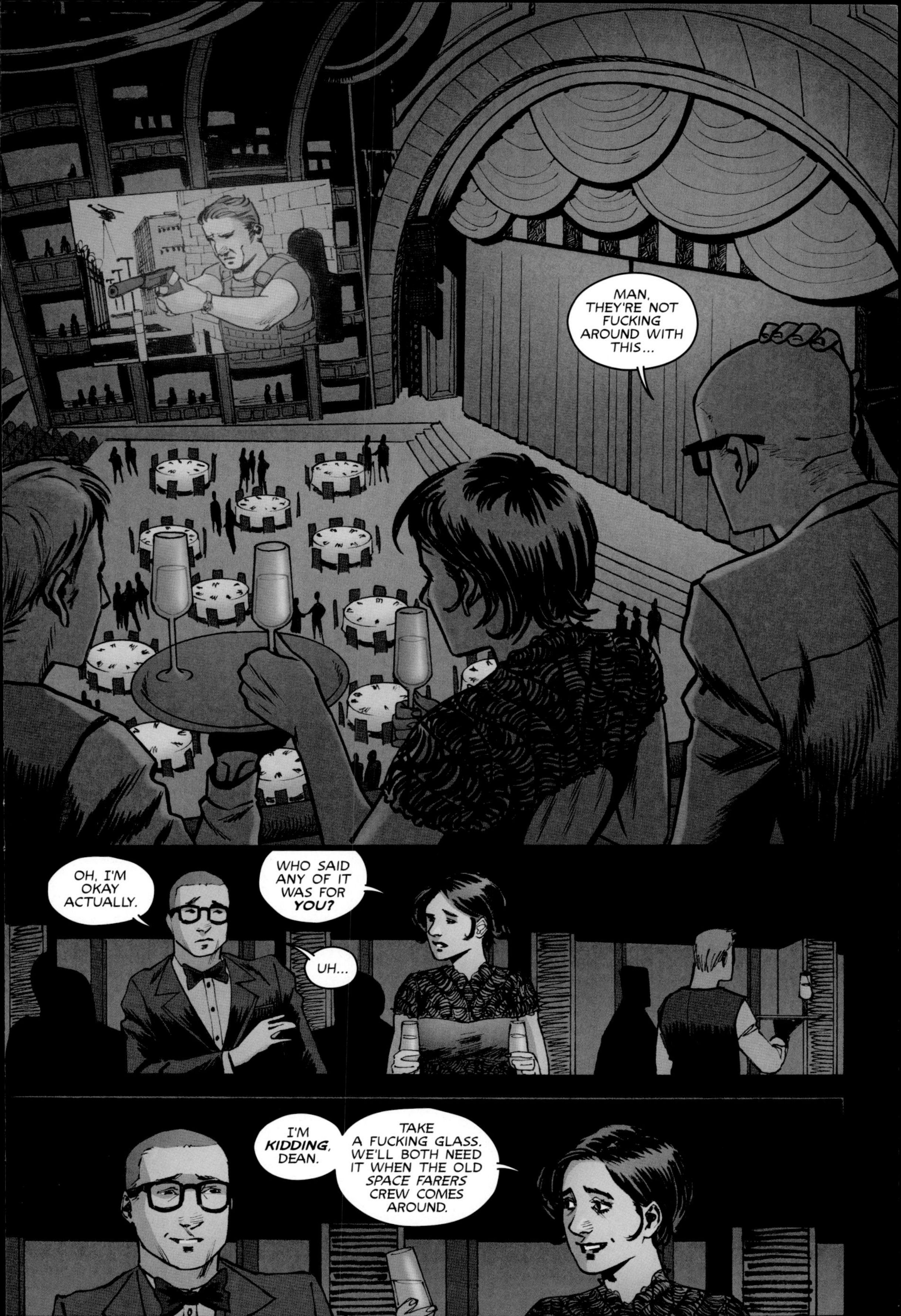
MAN, THEY'RE NOT FUCKING AROUND WITH THIS...
OH, I'M OKAY ACTUALLY.
WHO SAID ANY OF IT WAS FOR **YOU?**
UH...
I'M **KIDDING**, DEAN.
TAKE A FUCKING GLASS. WE'LL BOTH NEED IT WHEN THE OLD *SPACE FARERS* CREW COMES AROUND.

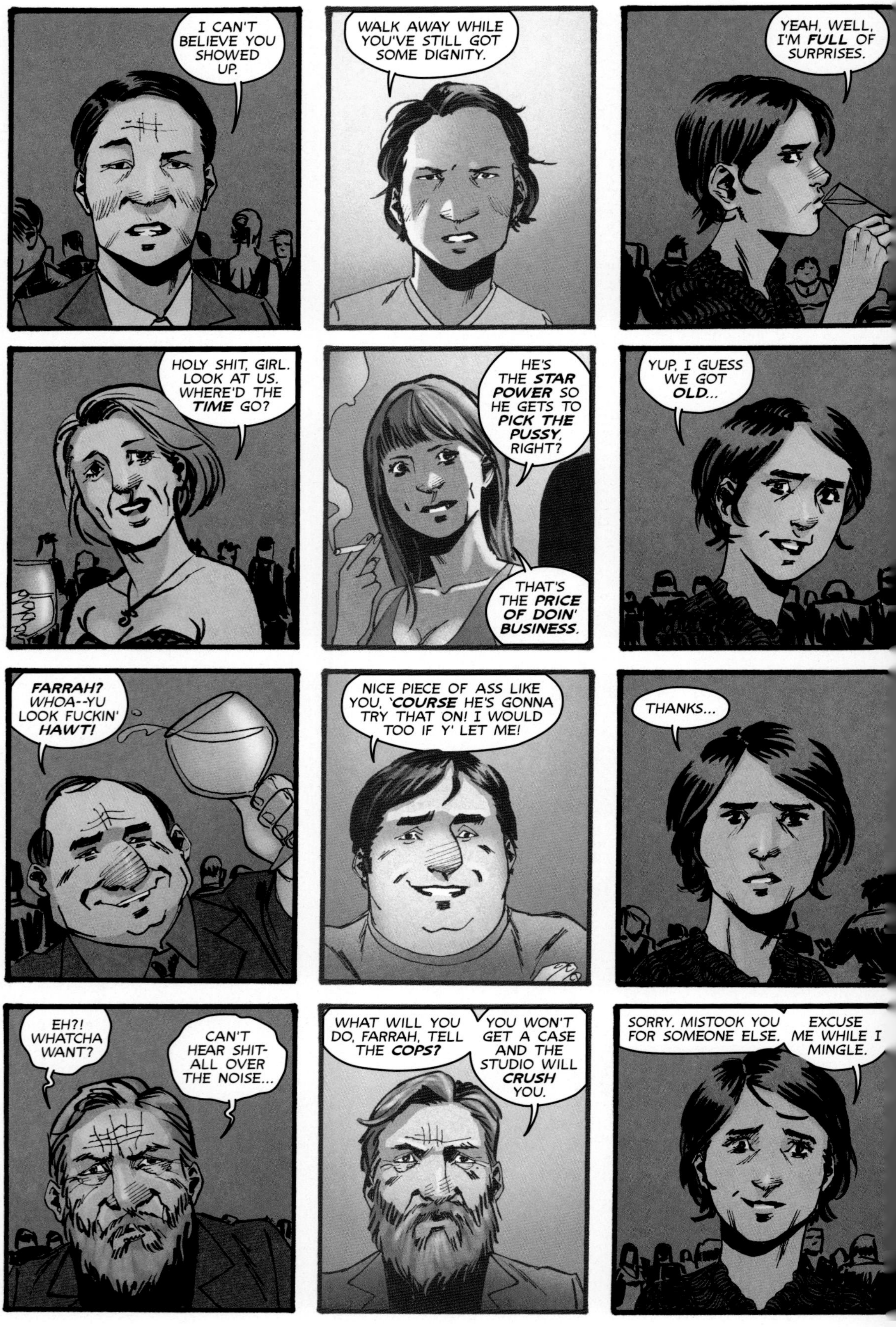
I CAN'T BELIEVE YOU SHOWED UP.
WALK AWAY WHILE YOU'VE STILL GOT SOME DIGNITY.
YEAH, WELL, I'M FULL OF SURPRISES.
HOLY SHIT, GIRL. LOOK AT US. WHERE'D THE TIME GO?
HE'S THE STAR POWER SO HE GETS TO PICK THE PUSSY, RIGHT?
THAT'S THE PRICE OF DOIN' BUSINESS.
YUP, I GUESS WE GOT OLD...
FARRAH? WHOA--YU LOOK FUCKIN' HAWT!
NICE PIECE OF ASS LIKE YOU, `COURSE HE'S GONNA TRY THAT ON! I WOULD TOO IF Y' LET ME!
THANKS...
EH?! WHATCHA WANT?
CAN'T HEAR SHIT-ALL OVER THE NOISE...
WHAT WILL YOU DO, FARRAH, TELL THE COPS?
YOU WON'T GET A CASE AND THE STUDIO WILL CRUSH YOU.
SORRY. MISTOOK YOU FOR SOMEONE ELSE.
EXCUSE ME WHILE I MINGLE.

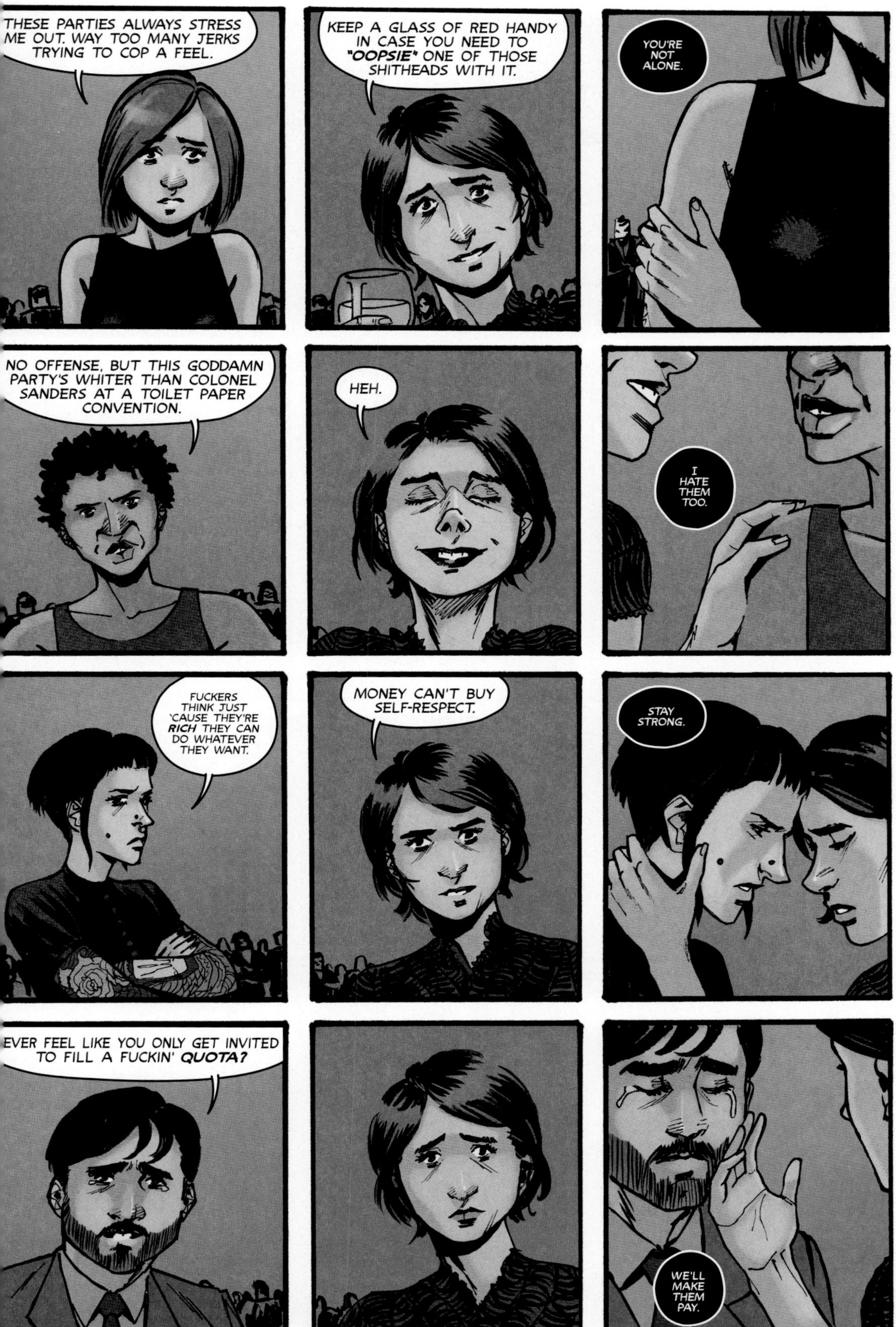
THESE PARTIES ALWAYS STRESS ME OUT. WAY TOO MANY JERKS TRYING TO COP A FEEL.
KEEP A GLASS OF RED HANDY IN CASE YOU NEED TO "OOPSIE" ONE OF THOSE SHITHEADS WITH IT.
YOU'RE NOT ALONE.
NO OFFENSE, BUT THIS GODDAMN PARTY'S WHITER THAN COLONEL SANDERS AT A TOILET PAPER CONVENTION.
HEH.
I HATE THEM TOO.
FUCKERS THINK JUST 'CAUSE THEY'RE RICH THEY CAN DO WHATEVER THEY WANT.
MONEY CAN'T BUY SELF-RESPECT.
STAY STRONG.
EVER FEEL LIKE YOU ONLY GET INVITED TO FILL A FUCKIN' QUOTA?
WE'LL MAKE THEM PAY.

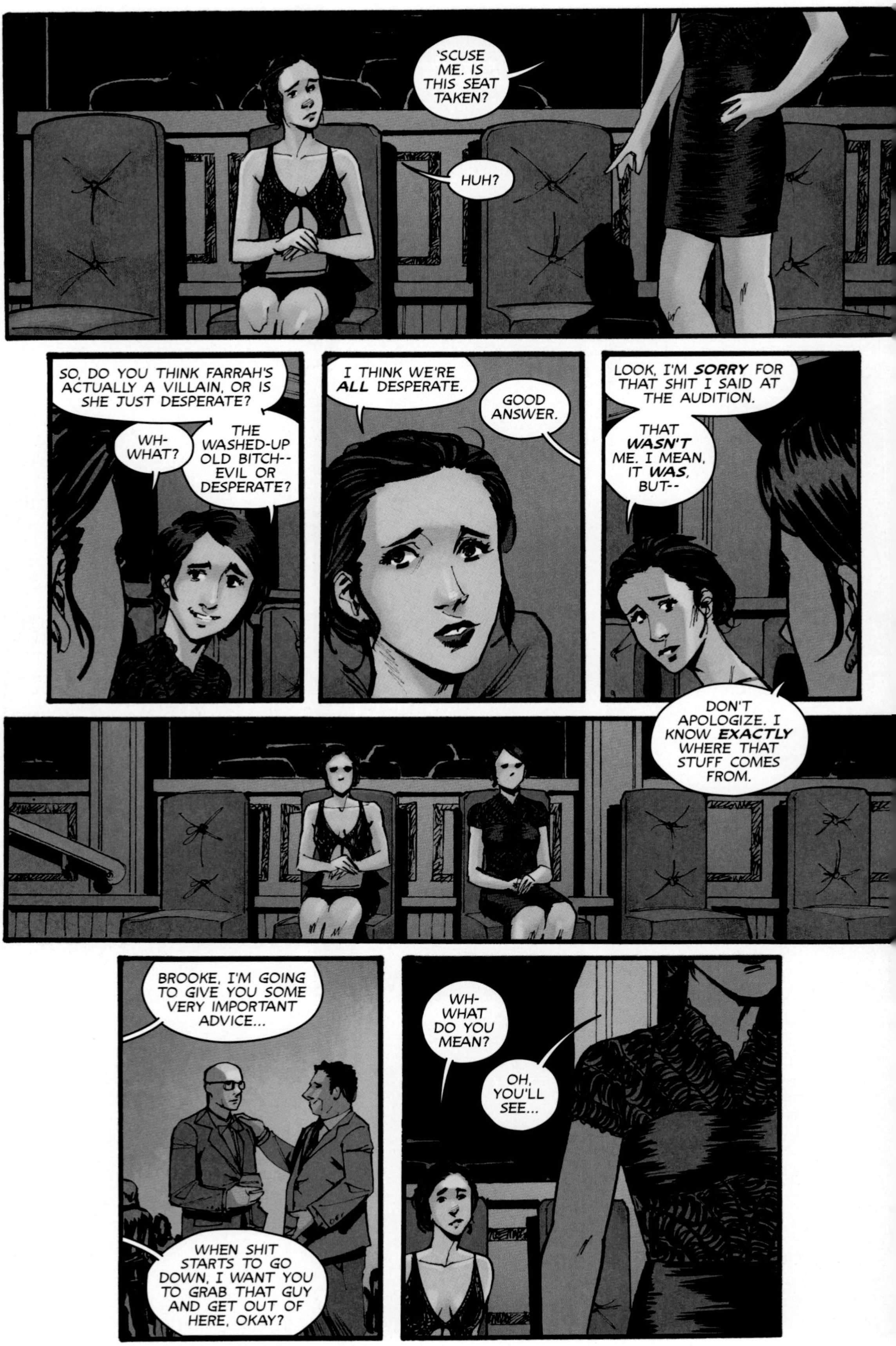
'SCUSE ME. IS THIS SEAT TAKEN?
HUH?
SO, DO YOU THINK FARRAH'S ACTUALLY A VILLAIN, OR IS SHE JUST DESPERATE?
WH- WHAT?
THE WASHED-UP OLD BITCH-- EVIL OR DESPERATE?
I THINK WE'RE ALL DESPERATE.
GOOD ANSWER.
LOOK, I'M SORRY FOR THAT SHIT I SAID AT THE AUDITION.
THAT WASN'T ME. I MEAN, IT WAS, BUT--
DON'T APOLOGIZE. I KNOW EXACTLY WHERE THAT STUFF COMES FROM.
BROOKE, I'M GOING TO GIVE YOU SOME VERY IMPORTANT ADVICE...
WHEN SHIT STARTS TO GO DOWN, I WANT YOU TO GRAB THAT GUY AND GET OUT OF HERE, OKAY?
WH- WHAT DO YOU MEAN?
OH, YOU'LL SEE...

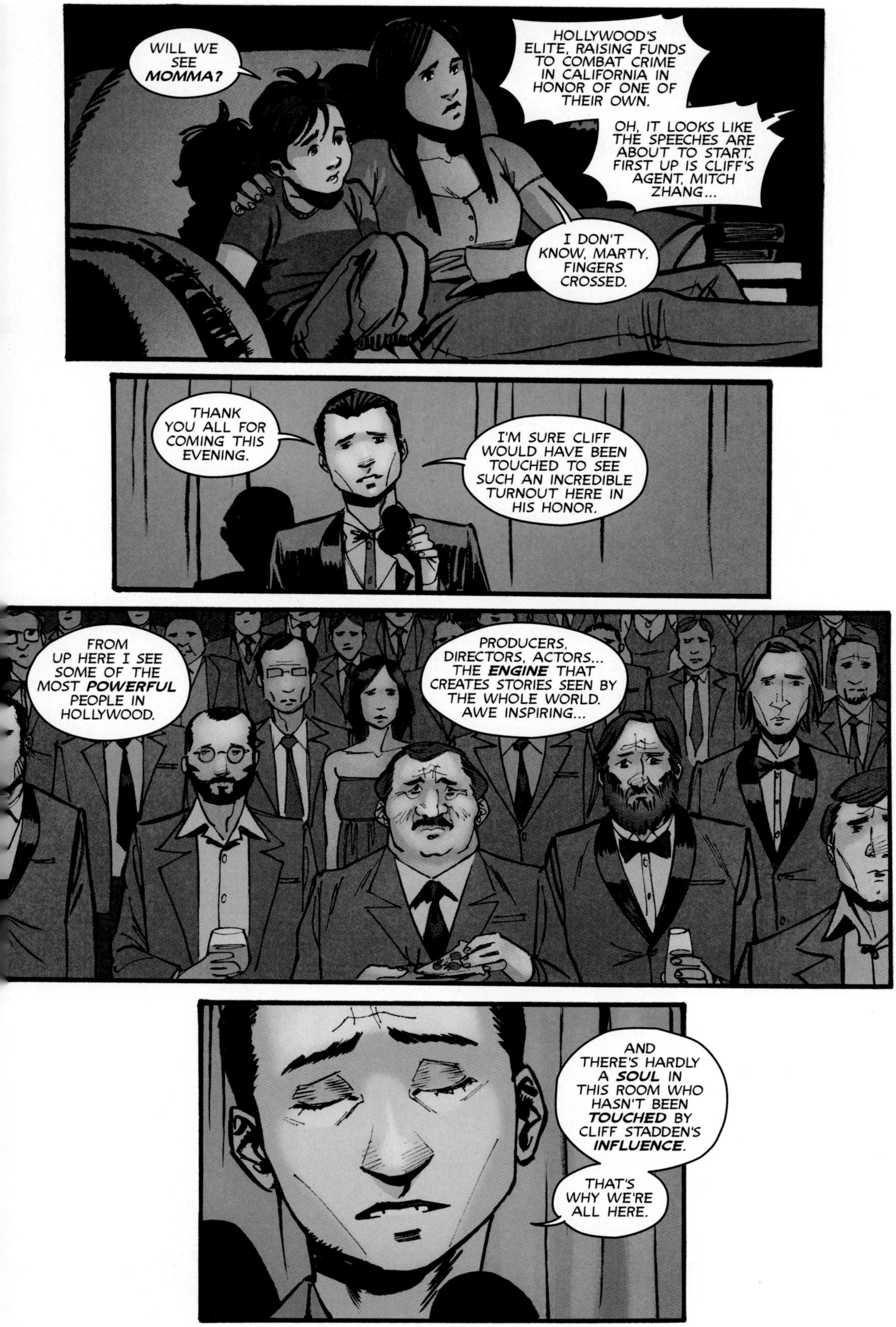
WILL WE SEE MOMMA?
HOLLYWOOD'S ELITE, RAISING FUNDS TO COMBAT CRIME IN CALIFORNIA IN HONOR OF ONE OF THEIR OWN.
OH, IT LOOKS LIKE THE SPEECHES ARE ABOUT TO START. FIRST UP IS CLIFF'S AGENT, MITCH ZHANG...
I DON'T KNOW, MARTY. FINGERS CROSSED.
THANK YOU ALL FOR COMING THIS EVENING.
I'M SURE CLIFF WOULD HAVE BEEN TOUCHED TO SEE SUCH AN INCREDIBLE TURNOUT HERE IN HIS HONOR.
FROM UP HERE I SEE SOME OF THE MOST POWERFUL PEOPLE IN HOLLYWOOD.
PRODUCERS, DIRECTORS, ACTORS... THE ENGINE THAT CREATES STORIES SEEN BY THE WHOLE WORLD. AWE INSPIRING...
AND THERE'S HARDLY A SOUL IN THIS ROOM WHO HASN'T BEEN TOUCHED BY CLIFF STADDEN'S INFLUENCE.
THAT'S WHY WE'RE ALL HERE.

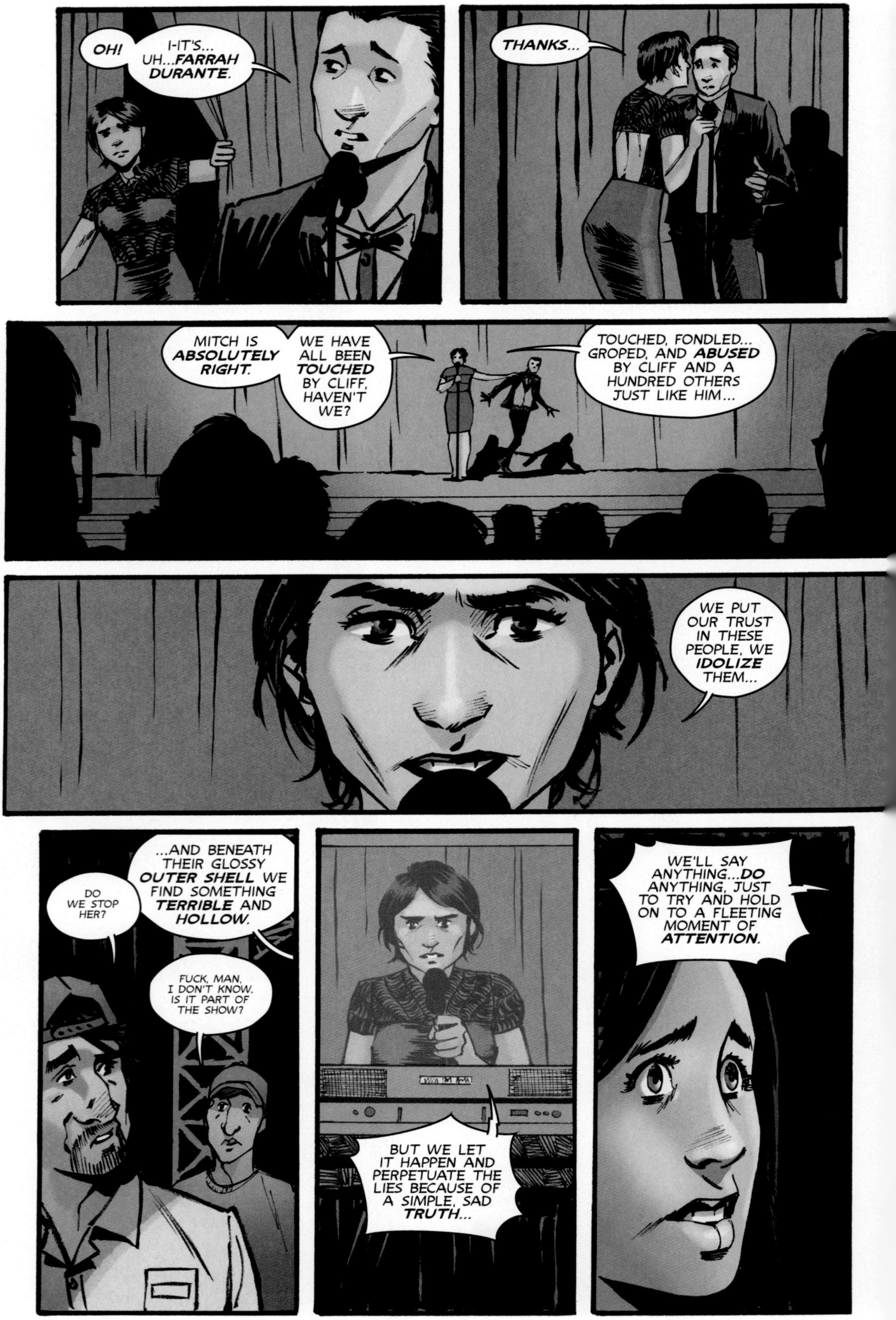
OH!
I-IT'S... UH...FARRAH DURANTE.
THANKS...
MITCH IS ABSOLUTELY RIGHT.
WE HAVE ALL BEEN TOUCHED BY CLIFF, HAVEN'T WE?
TOUCHED, FONDLED... GROPED, AND ABUSED BY CLIFF AND A HUNDRED OTHERS JUST LIKE HIM...
WE PUT OUR TRUST IN THESE PEOPLE, WE IDOLIZE THEM...
...AND BENEATH THEIR GLOSSY OUTER SHELL WE FIND SOMETHING TERRIBLE AND HOLLOW.
DO WE STOP HER?
FUCK, MAN, I DON'T KNOW. IS IT PART OF THE SHOW?
BUT WE LET IT HAPPEN AND PERPETUATE THE LIES BECAUSE OF A SIMPLE, SAD TRUTH...
WE'LL SAY ANYTHING...DO ANYTHING, JUST TO TRY AND HOLD ON TO A FLEETING MOMENT OF ATTENTION.

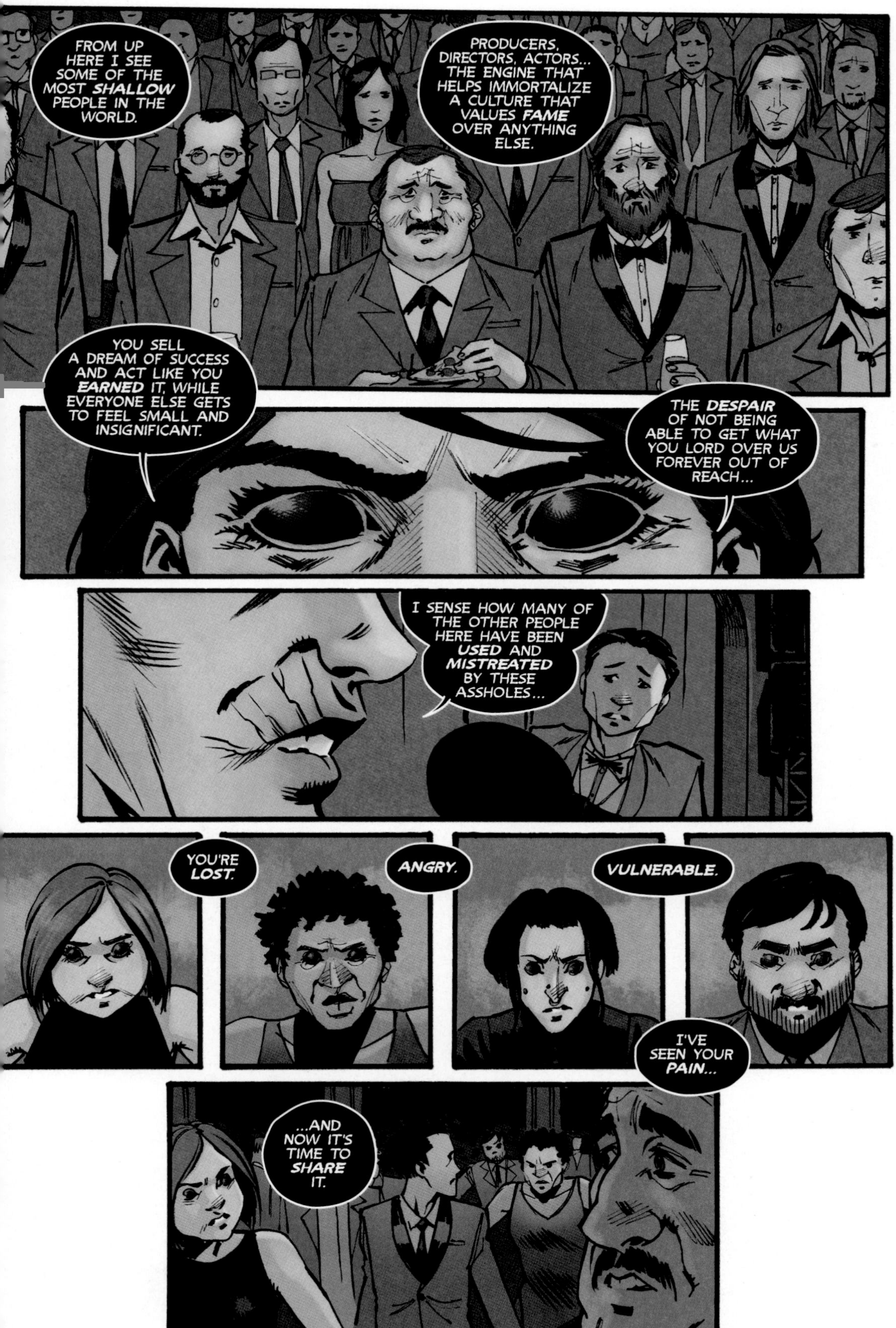
FROM UP HERE I SEE SOME OF THE MOST SHALLOW PEOPLE IN THE WORLD.
PRODUCERS, DIRECTORS, ACTORS... THE ENGINE THAT HELPS IMMORTALIZE A CULTURE THAT VALUES FAME OVER ANYTHING ELSE.
YOU SELL A DREAM OF SUCCESS AND ACT LIKE YOU EARNED IT, WHILE EVERYONE ELSE GETS TO FEEL SMALL AND INSIGNIFICANT.
THE DESPAIR OF NOT BEING ABLE TO GET WHAT YOU LORD OVER US FOREVER OUT OF REACH...
I SENSE HOW MANY OF THE OTHER PEOPLE HERE HAVE BEEN USED AND MISTREATED BY THESE ASSHOLES...
YOU'RE LOST.
ANGRY.
VULNERABLE.
I'VE SEEN YOUR PAIN...
...AND NOW IT'S TIME TO SHARE IT.

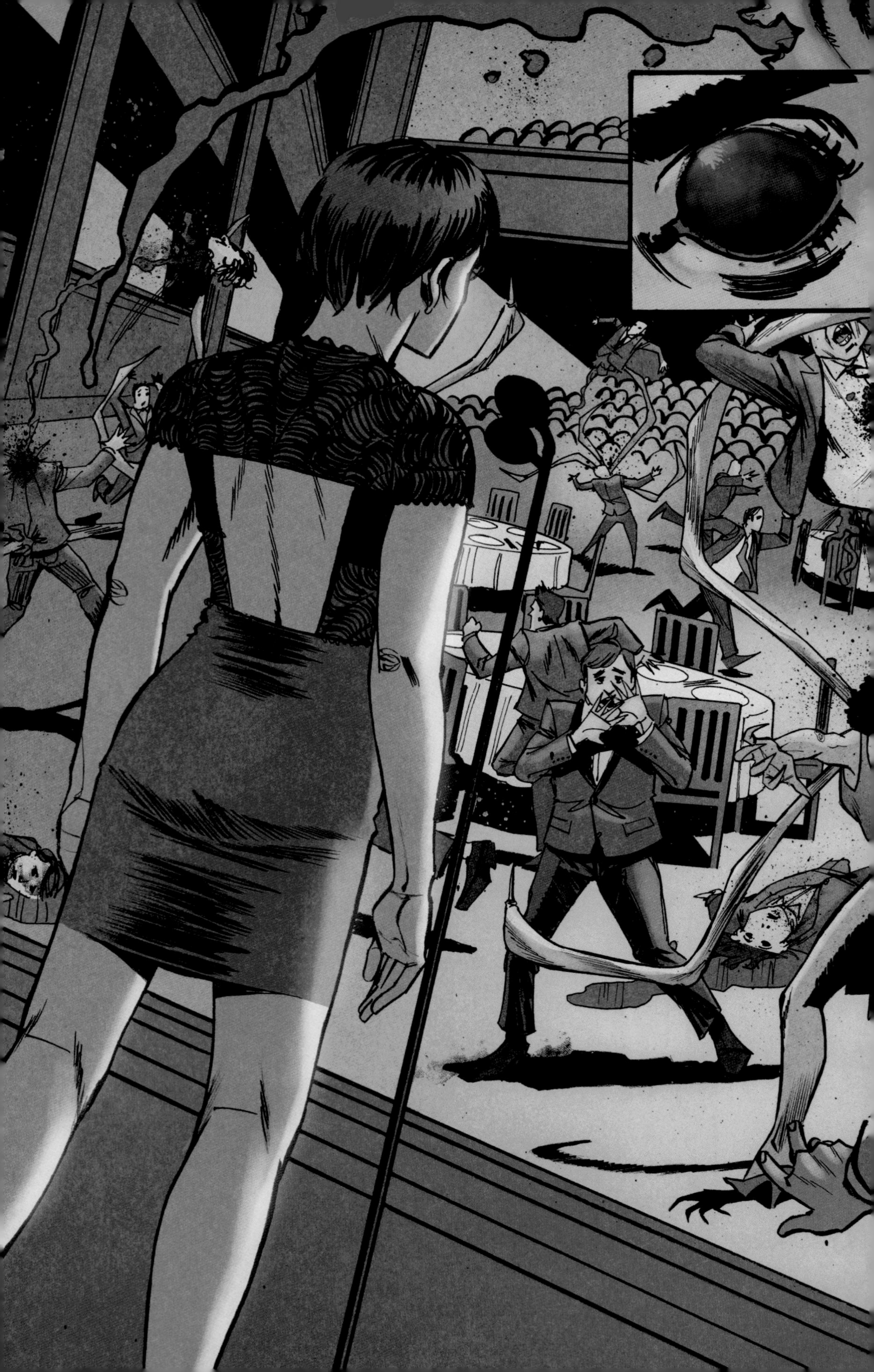

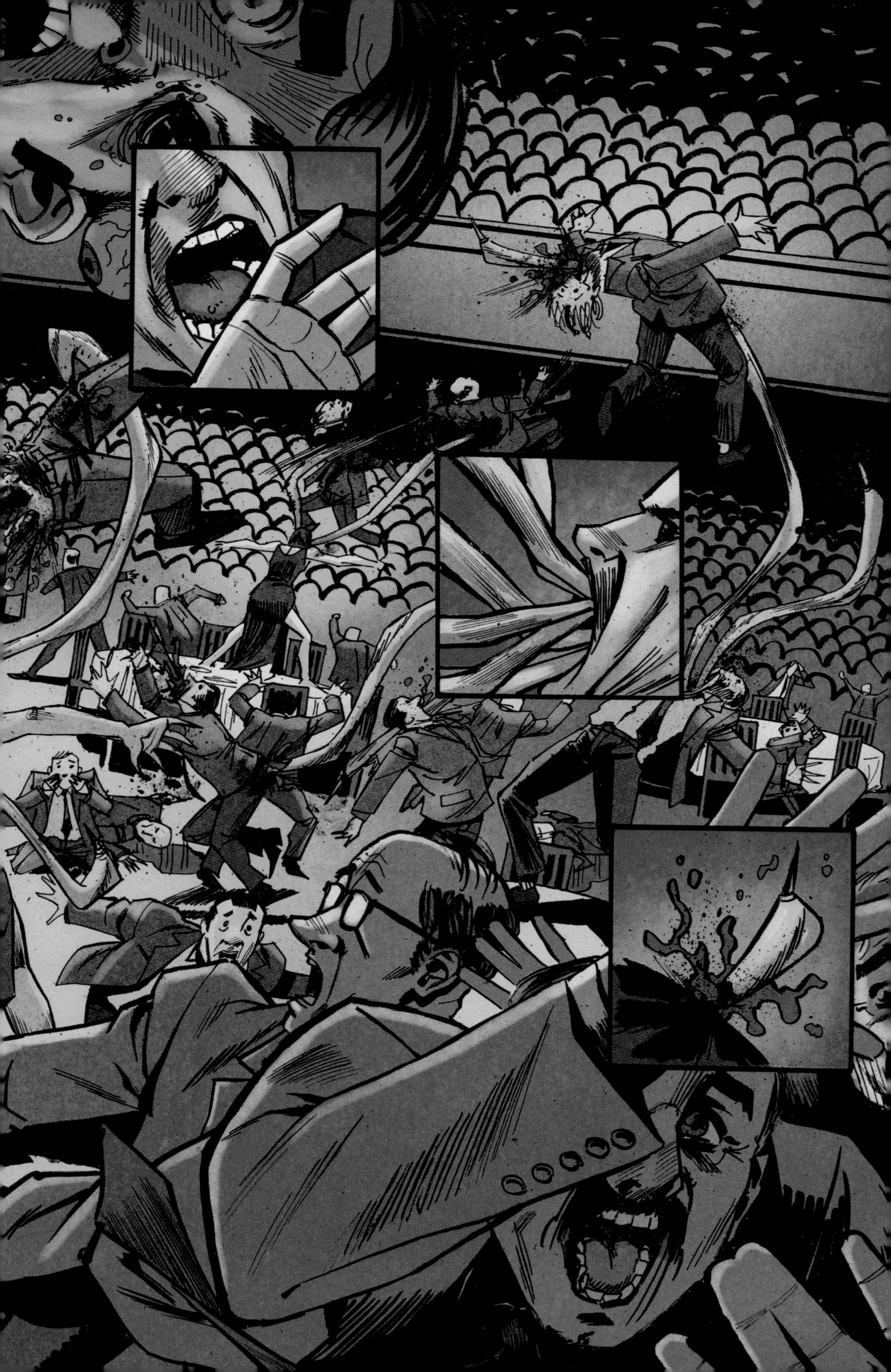

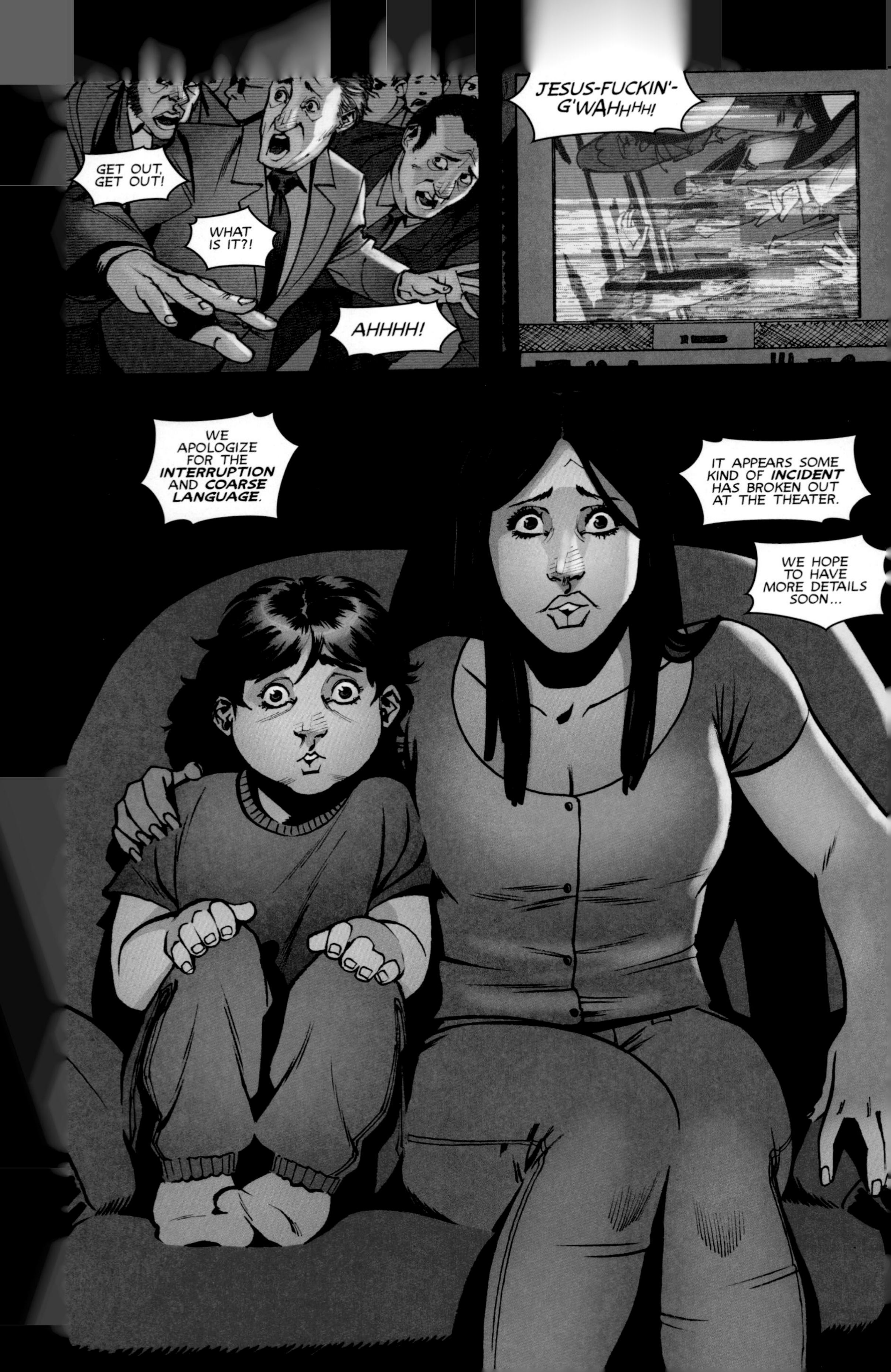
GET OUT, GET OUT!
WHAT IS IT?!
AHHHH!
JESUS-FUCKIN'-G'WAHHHH!
WE APOLOGIZE FOR THE **INTERRUPTION** AND **COARSE LANGUAGE.**
IT APPEARS SOME KIND OF **INCIDENT** HAS BROKEN OUT AT THE THEATER.
WE HOPE TO HAVE MORE DETAILS SOON...

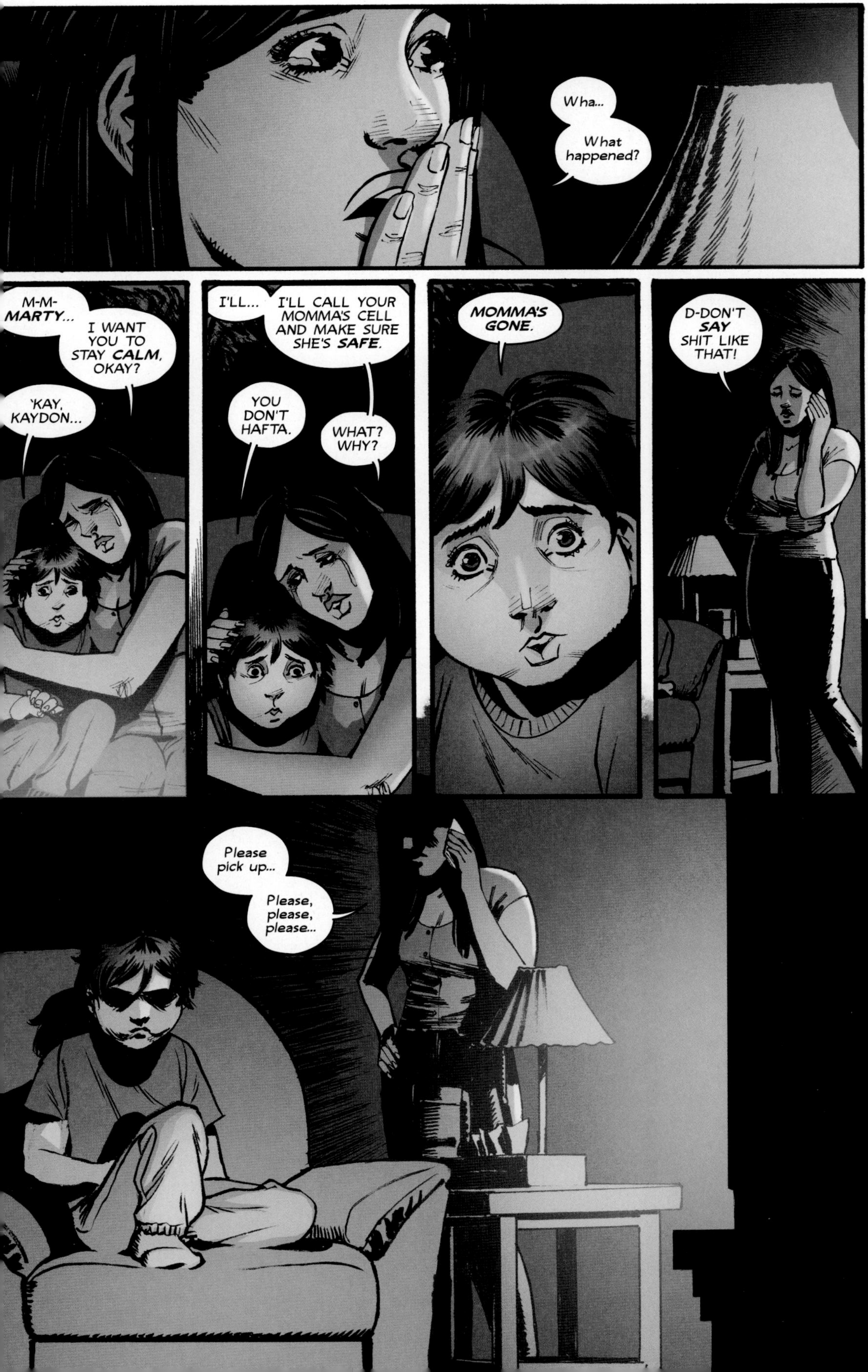
Wha...
What happened?
M-M-MARTY...
I WANT YOU TO STAY CALM, OKAY?
'KAY, KAYDON...
I'LL...
I'LL CALL YOUR MOMMA'S CELL AND MAKE SURE SHE'S SAFE.
YOU DON'T HAFTA.
WHAT? WHY?
MOMMA'S GONE.
D-DON'T SAY SHIT LIKE THAT!
Please pick up...
Please, please, please...

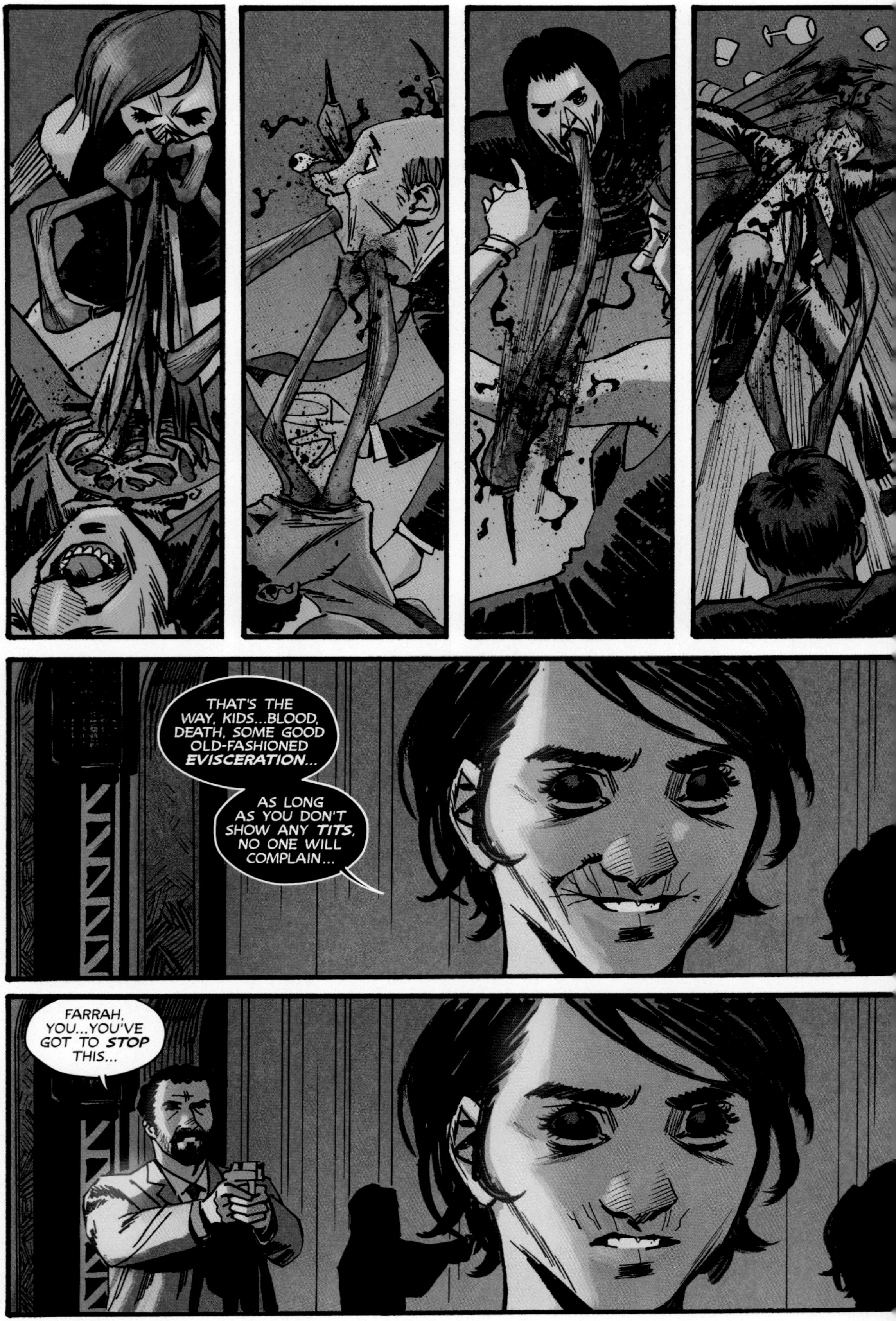
THAT'S THE WAY, KIDS...BLOOD, DEATH, SOME GOOD OLD-FASHIONED EVISCERATION...
AS LONG AS YOU DON'T SHOW ANY TITS, NO ONE WILL COMPLAIN...
FARRAH, YOU...YOU'VE GOT TO STOP THIS...

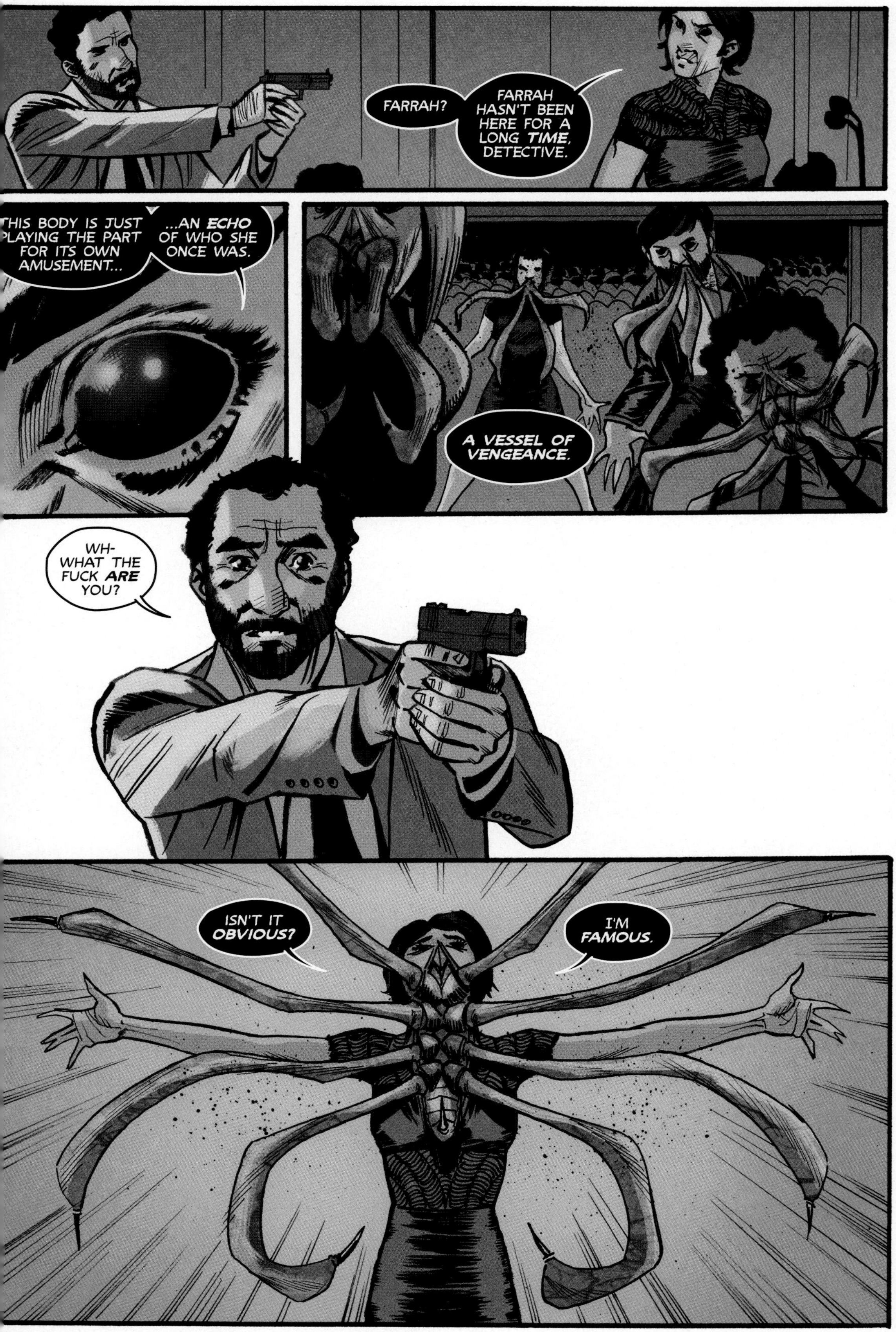
FARRAH?
FARRAH HASN'T BEEN HERE FOR A LONG TIME, DETECTIVE.
THIS BODY IS JUST PLAYING THE PART FOR ITS OWN AMUSEMENT...
...AN ECHO OF WHO SHE ONCE WAS.
A VESSEL OF VENGEANCE.
WH- WHAT THE FUCK ARE YOU?
ISN'T IT OBVIOUS?
I'M FAMOUS.

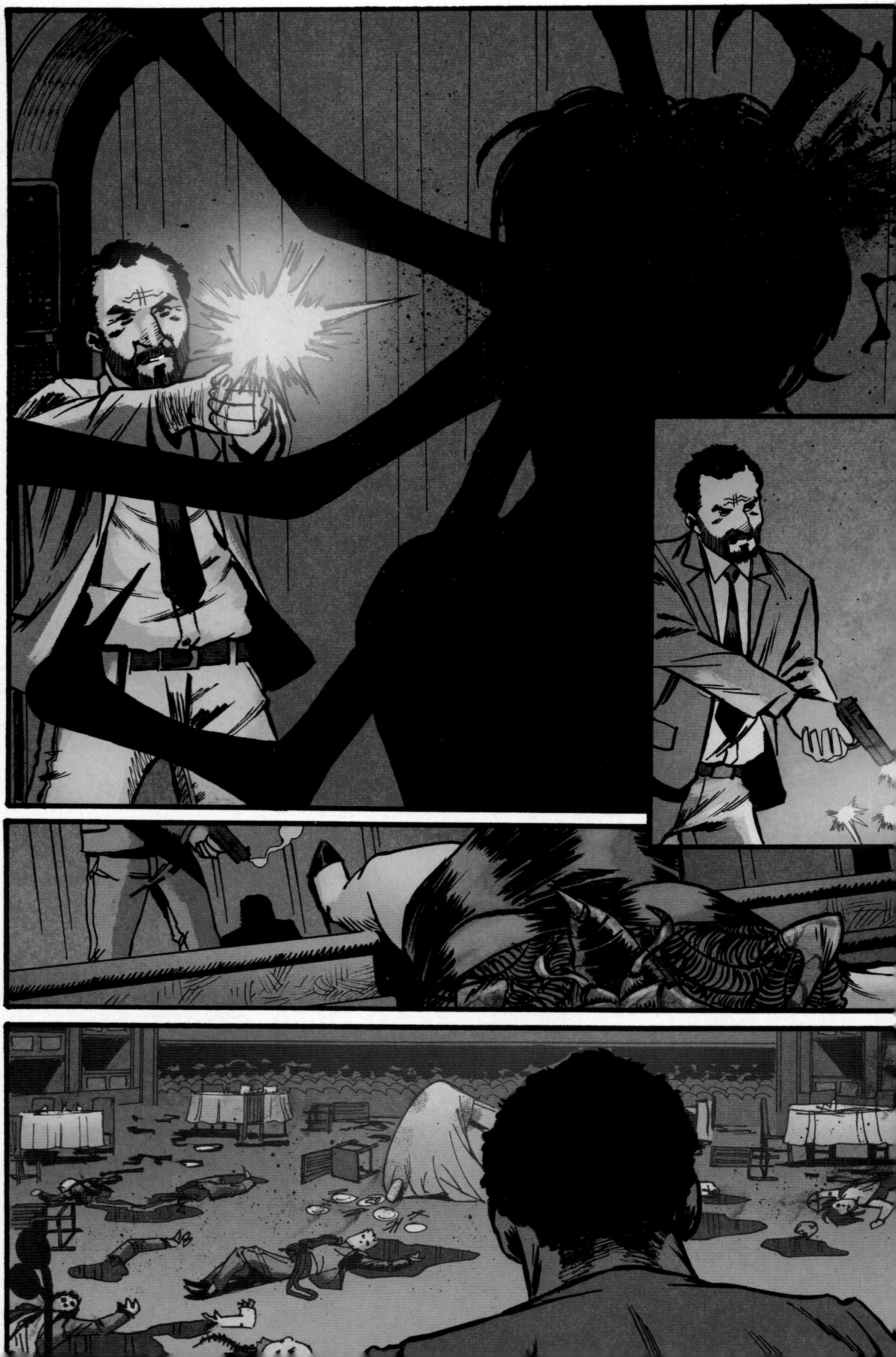

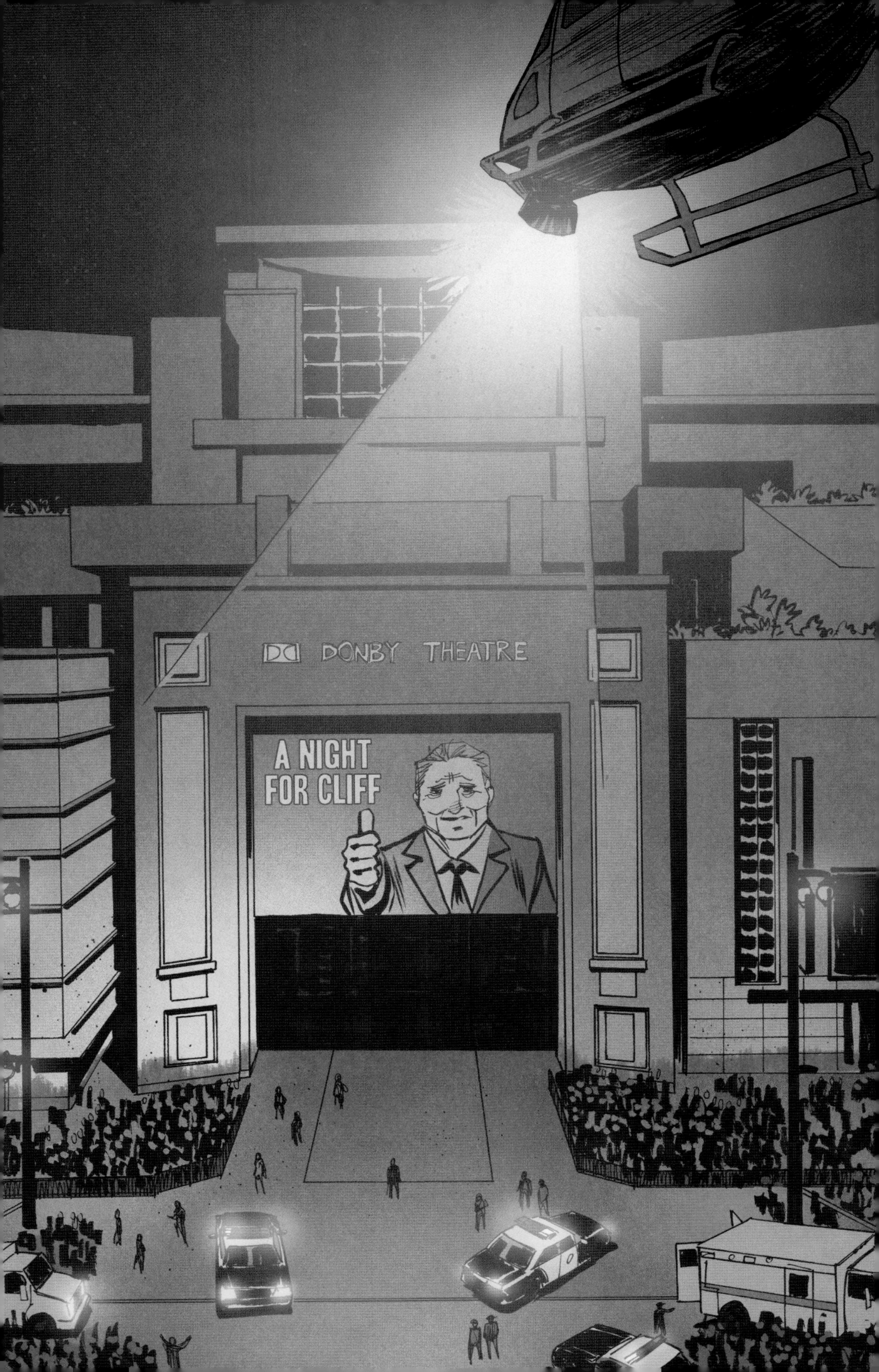
DONBY THEATRE
A NIGHT FOR CLIFF

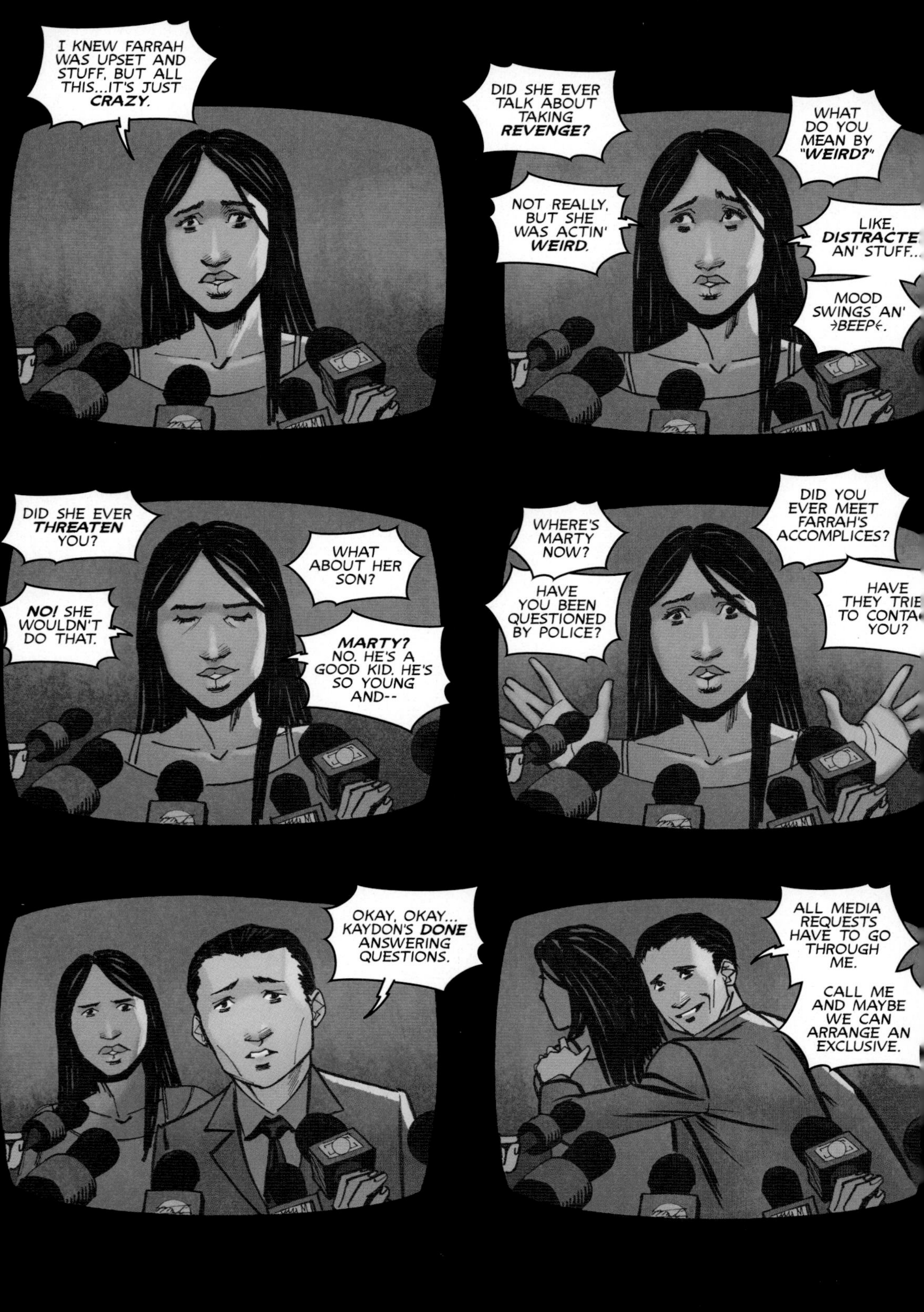
I KNEW FARRAH WAS UPSET AND STUFF, BUT ALL THIS...IT'S JUST **CRAZY**.
DID SHE EVER TALK ABOUT TAKING **REVENGE?**
NOT REALLY, BUT SHE WAS ACTIN' **WEIRD**.
WHAT DO YOU MEAN BY "**WEIRD?**"
LIKE, **DISTRACTE** AN' STUFF...
MOOD SWINGS AN' ›BEEP‹.
DID SHE EVER **THREATEN** YOU?
NO! SHE WOULDN'T DO THAT.
WHAT ABOUT HER SON?
MARTY? NO. HE'S A GOOD KID. HE'S SO YOUNG AND--
WHERE'S MARTY NOW?
DID YOU EVER MEET FARRAH'S ACCOMPLICES?
HAVE YOU BEEN QUESTIONED BY POLICE?
HAVE THEY TRIE TO CONTA YOU?
OKAY, OKAY... KAYDON'S **DONE** ANSWERING QUESTIONS.
ALL MEDIA REQUESTS HAVE TO GO THROUGH ME.
CALL ME AND MAYBE WE CAN ARRANGE AN EXCLUSIVE.

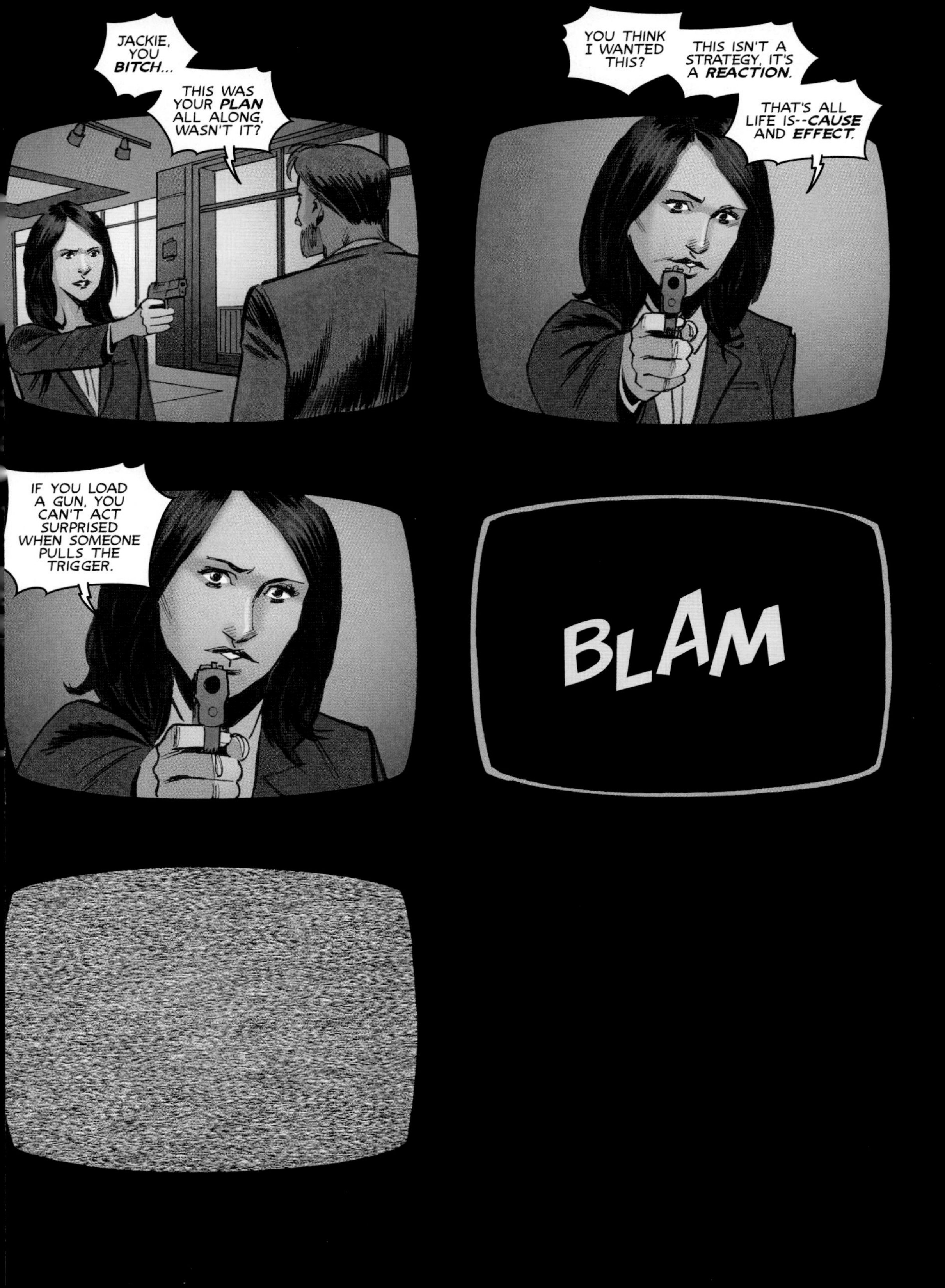
JACKIE, YOU BITCH...
THIS WAS YOUR PLAN ALL ALONG, WASN'T IT?
YOU THINK I WANTED THIS?
THIS ISN'T A STRATEGY, IT'S A REACTION.
THAT'S ALL LIFE IS--CAUSE AND EFFECT.
IF YOU LOAD A GUN, YOU CAN'T ACT SURPRISED WHEN SOMEONE PULLS THE TRIGGER.
BLAM

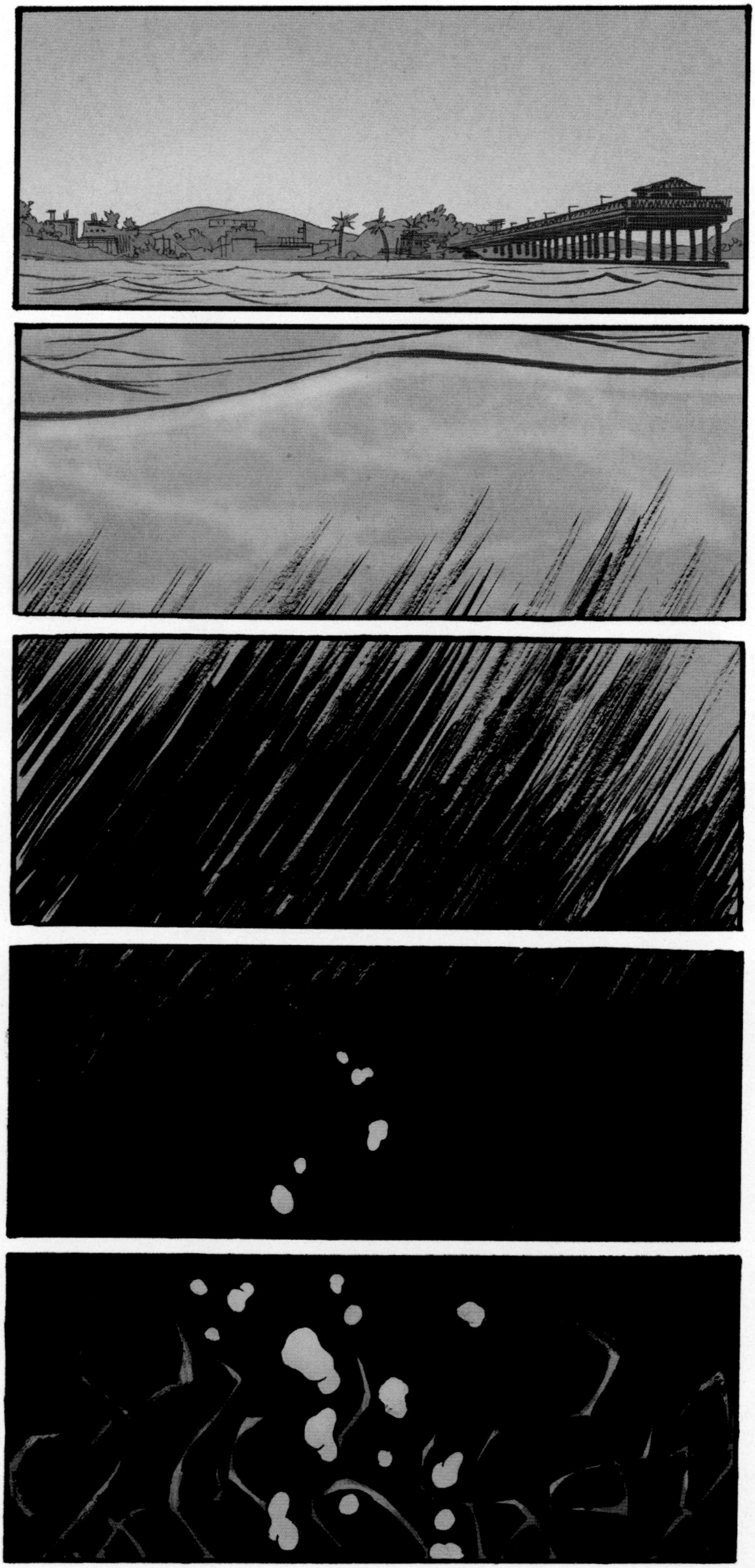

TO BE CONTINUED

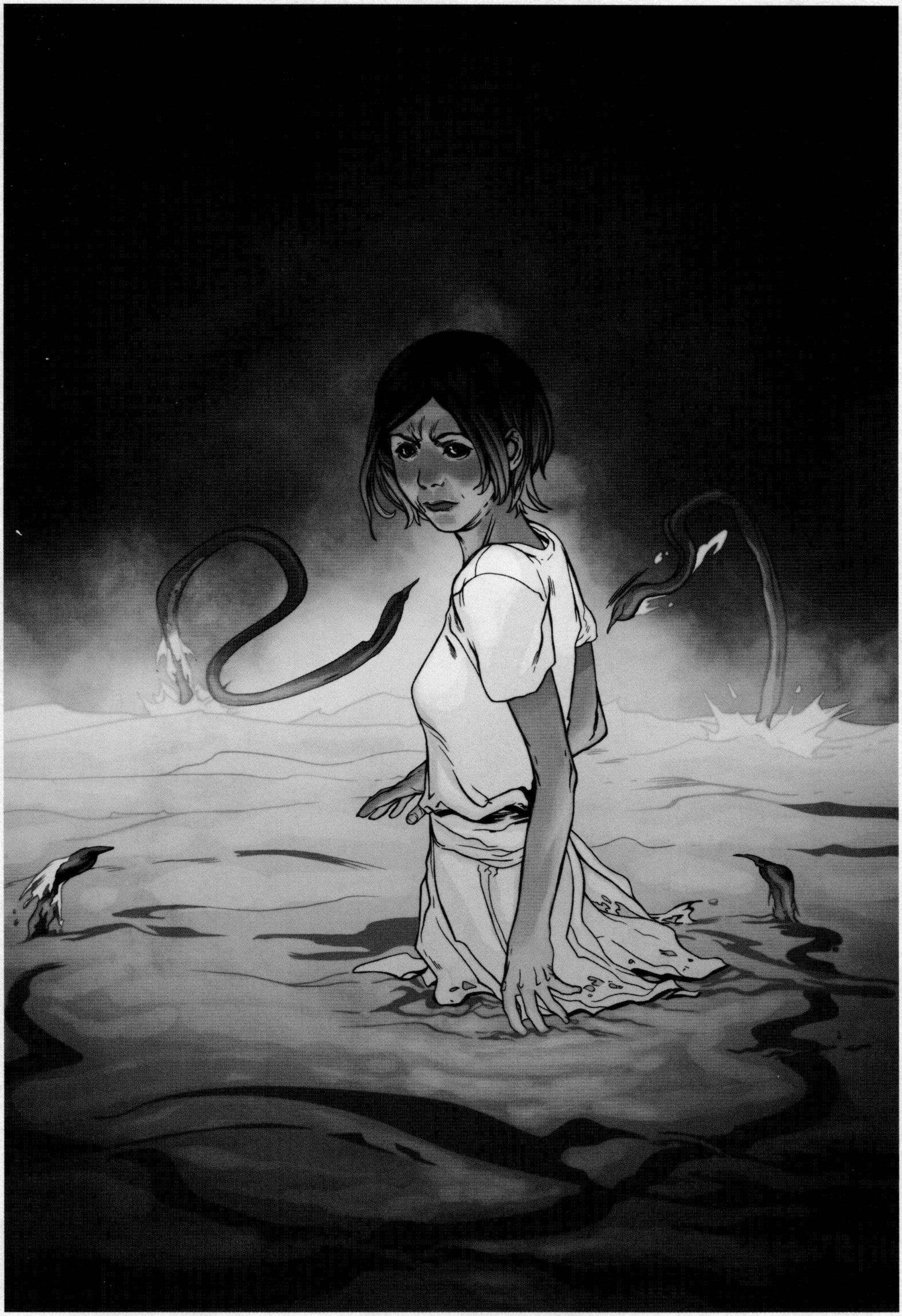

GLITTERBOMB #1 (Cover B)

Line Art by Stevan Cummings, Colors by Djibril Morissette-Phan

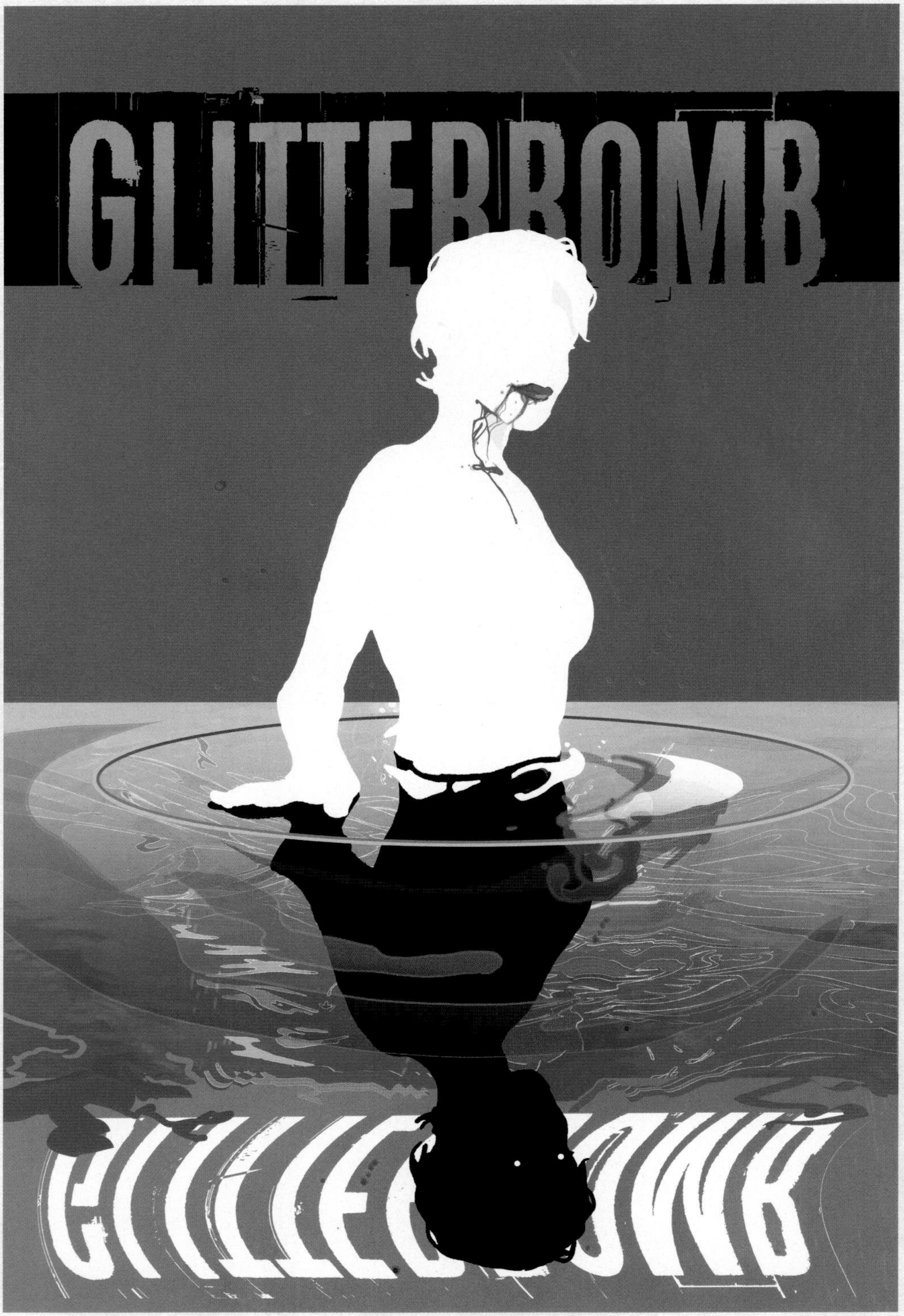
GLITTERBOMB

GLITTERBOMB #1 (Rose City Comic Con Cover)

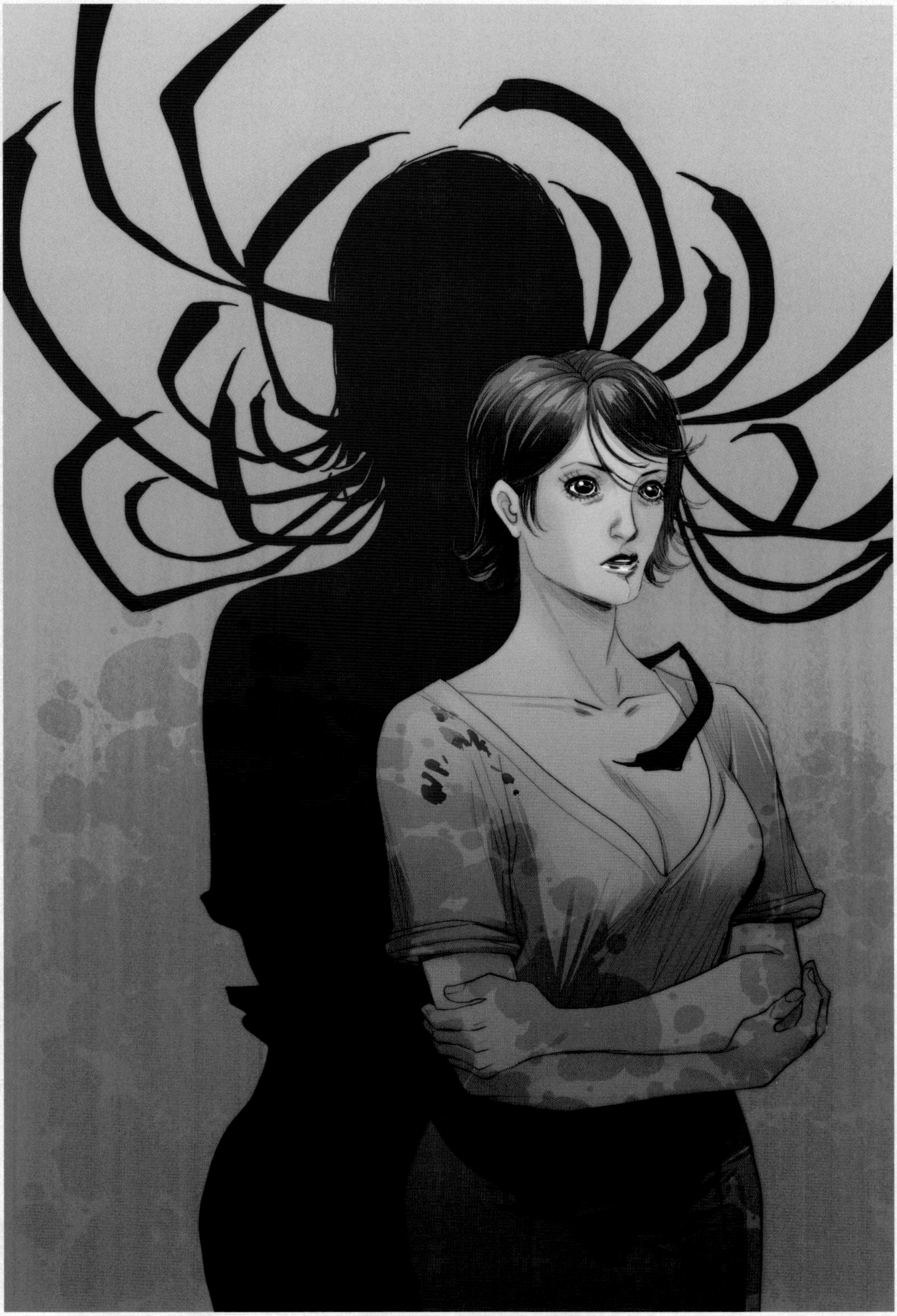

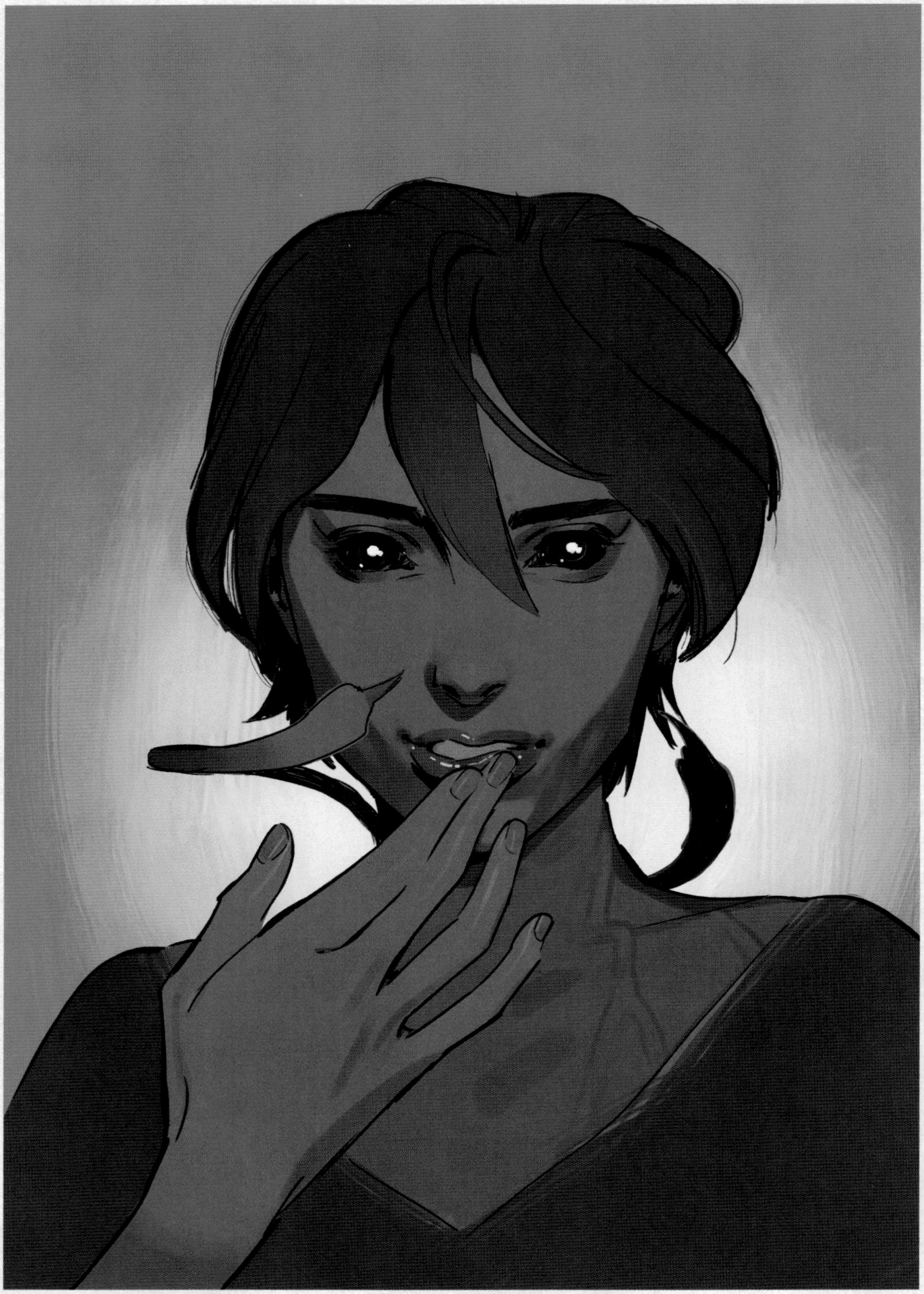

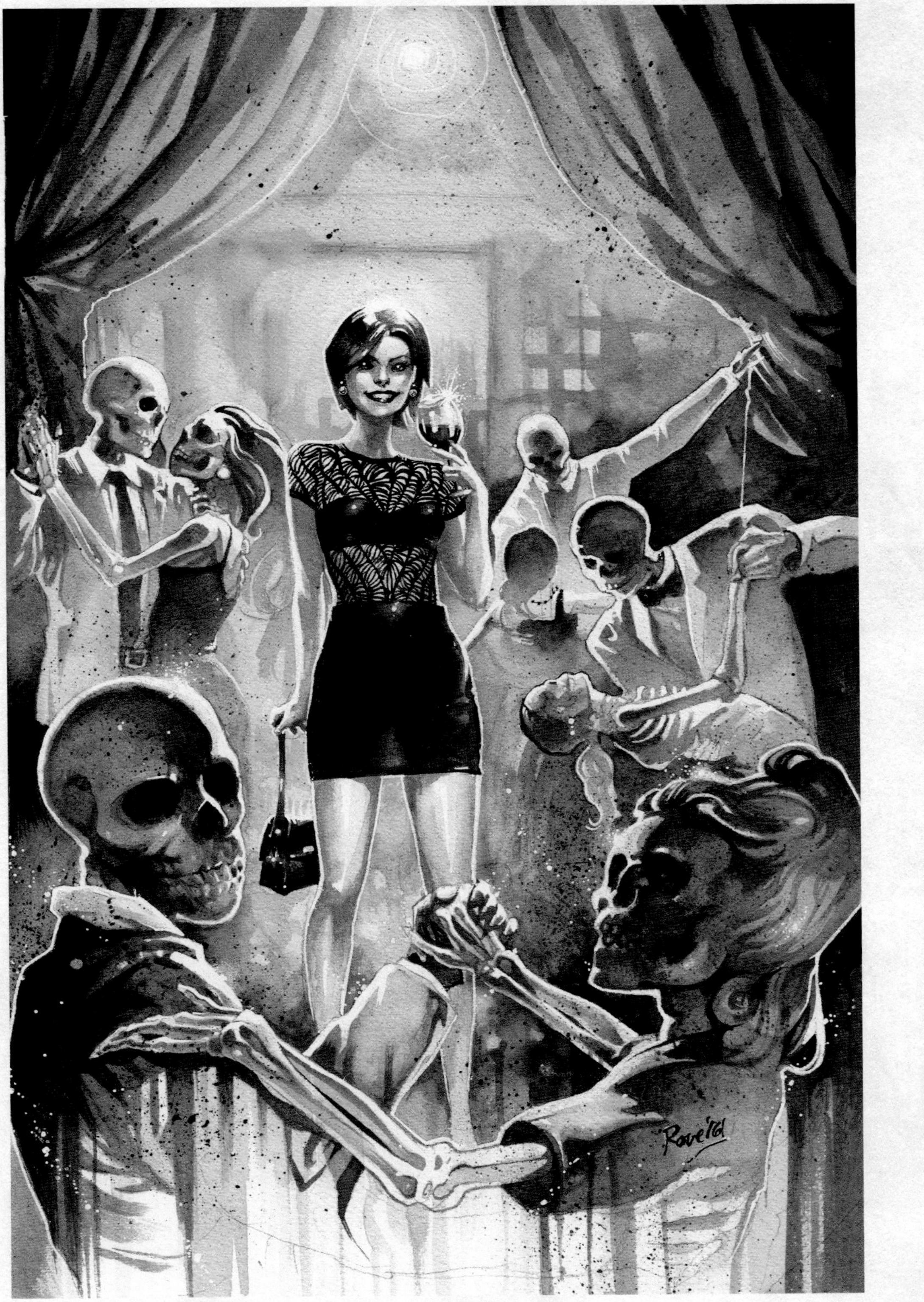
Rove'21

GLITTERBOMB #4 (Cover B)

CHARACTER DESIGN SKETCHES

Art by Djibril Morissette-Phan. Notes by Jim Zub from his design document.

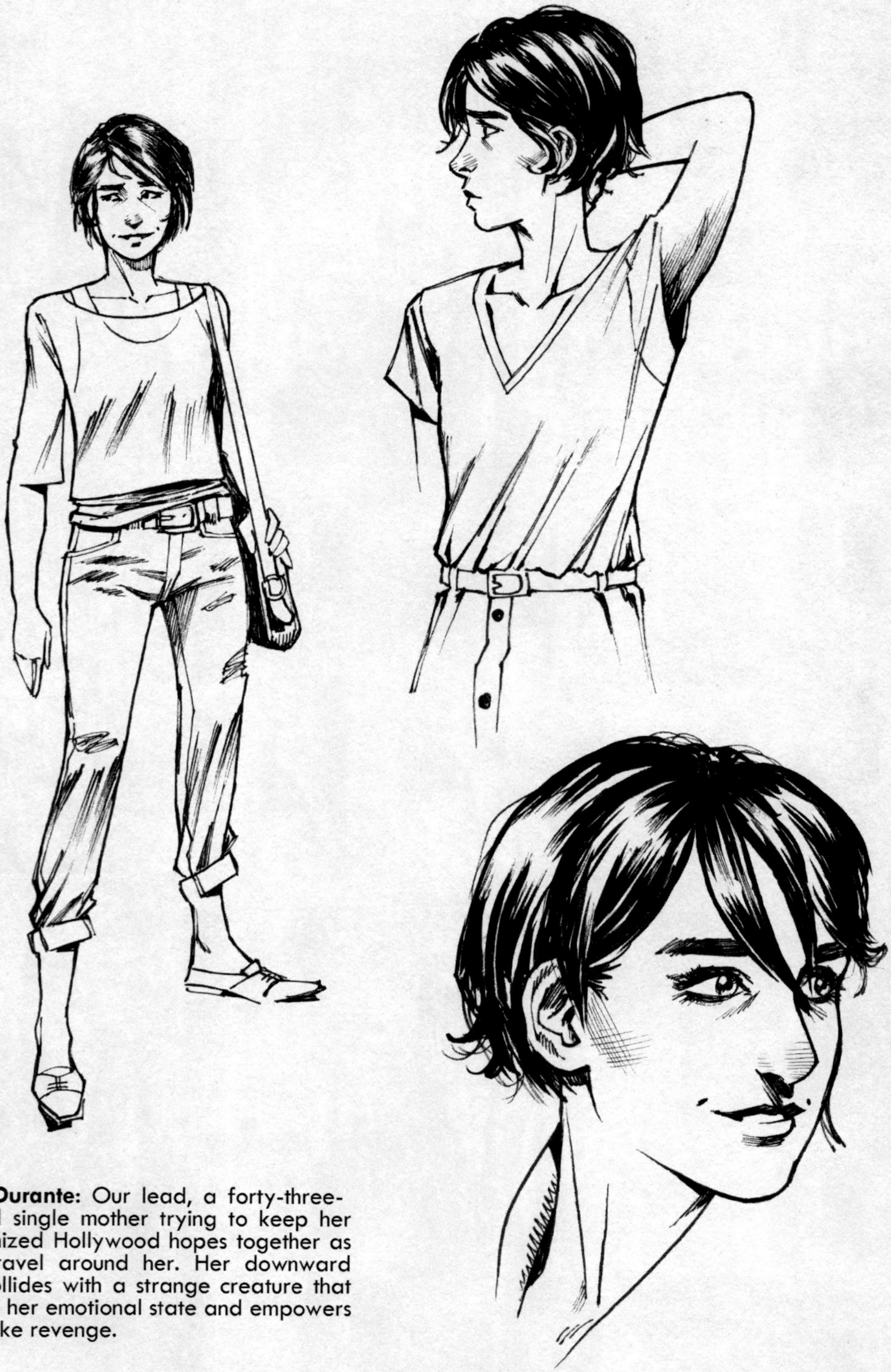

Farrah Durante: Our lead, a forty-three-year-old single mother trying to keep her disorganized Hollywood hopes together as they unravel around her. Her downward spiral collides with a strange creature that feeds on her emotional state and empowers her to take revenge.

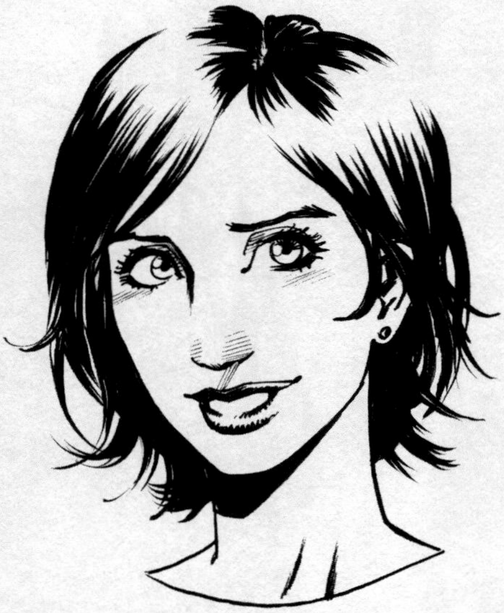

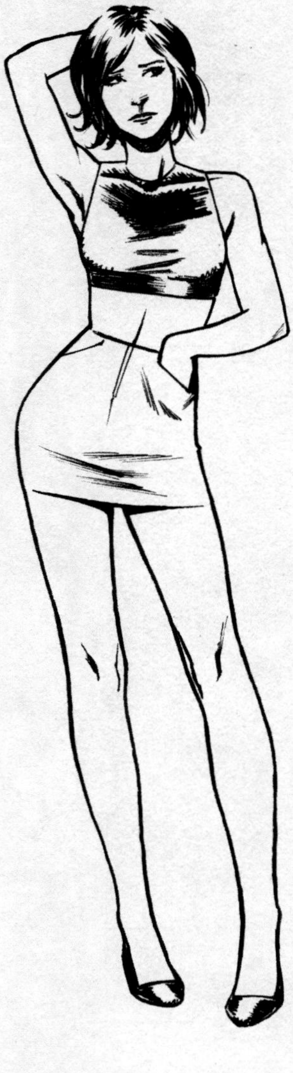

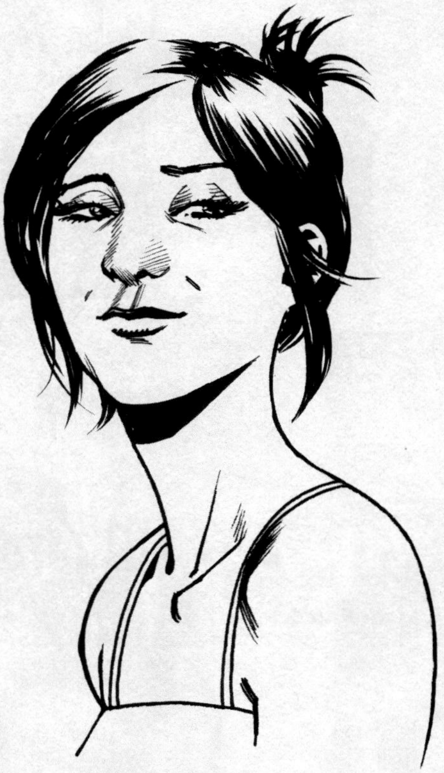

Brooke Vixy: A twenty-year-old up-and-coming actress who has the skill and looks to make it big. She doesn't look the exact same, but there should be a sense that Brooke is like a younger version of Farrah, the actress she could have been if she'd had the drive and confidence early in her career and hadn't been abused and pushed to the sidelines. Brooke will be one of the focal points of Farrah's anger.

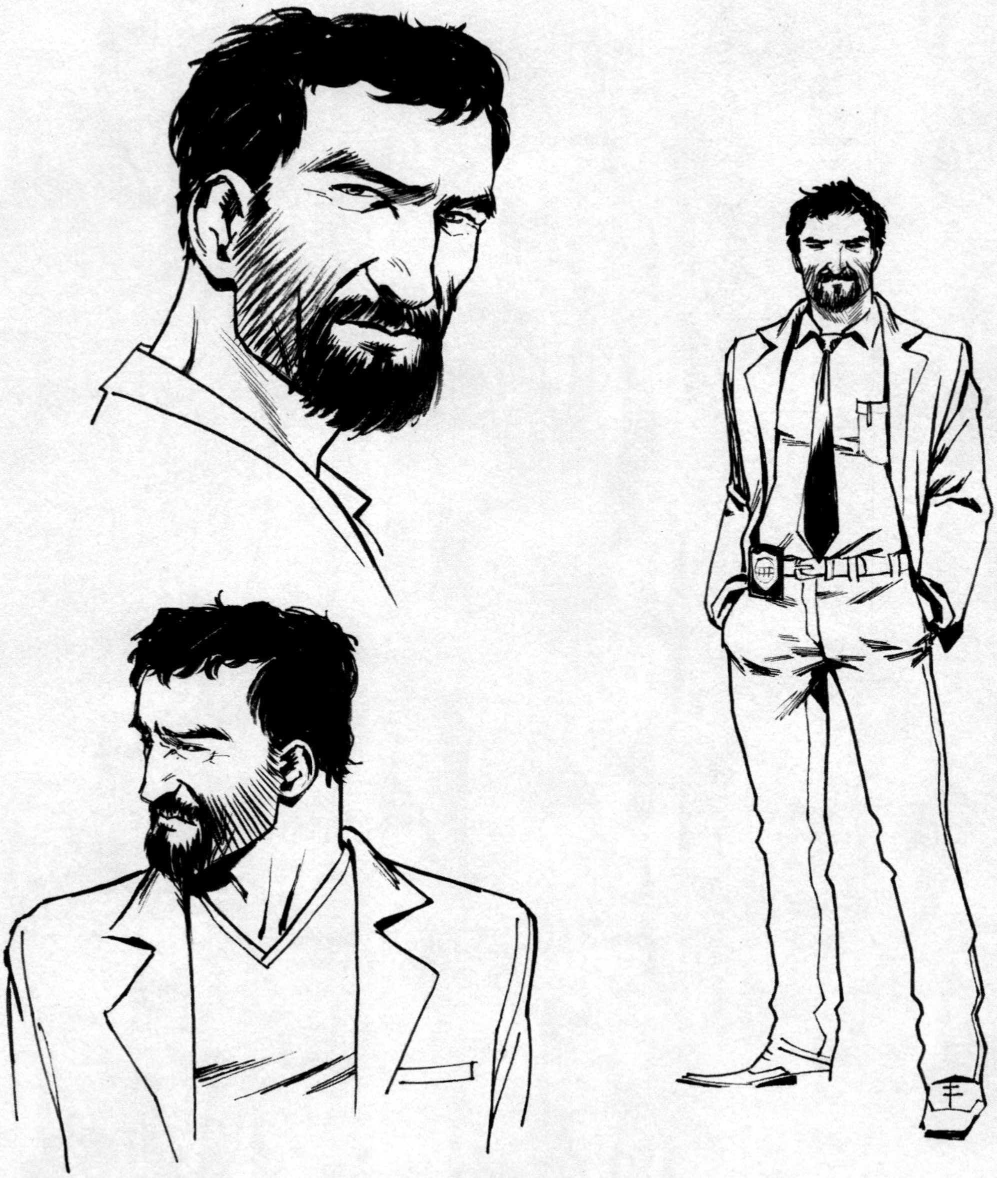

Isaac Rahal: A forty-six-year-old police officer of Arab descent, but he was born in America so that aspect of him is reflected in his skin tone and facial features but not clothes or attitude.

He's the detective in charge of the serial murder investigation that spins out of Farrah's killing spree. Isaac is intensely cynical and assumes the worst in people, which will serve him well as he digs through Hollywood's heartless fame machine to try and find out what's going on.

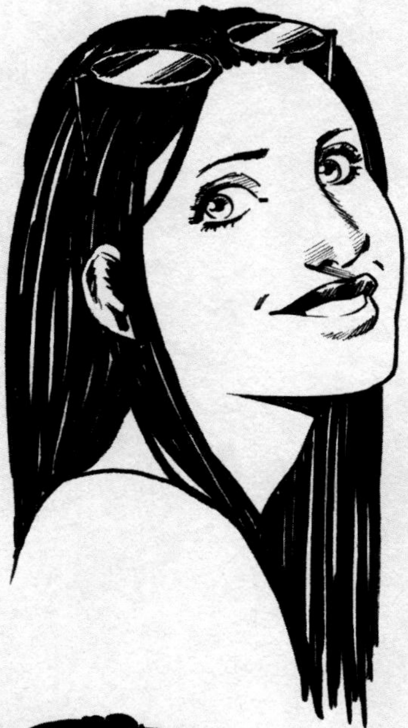

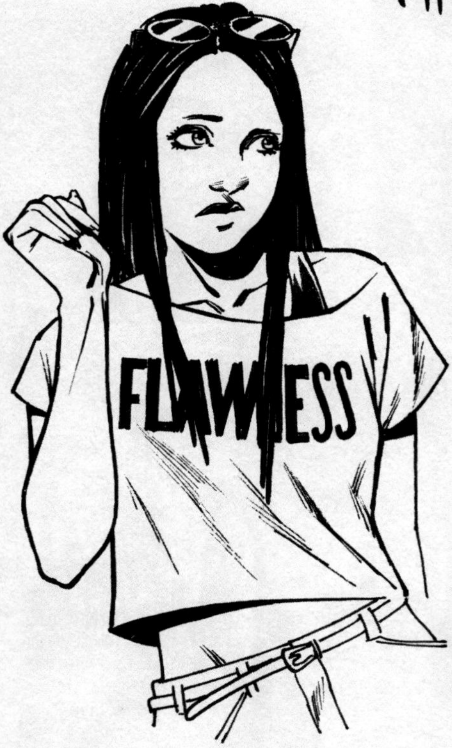

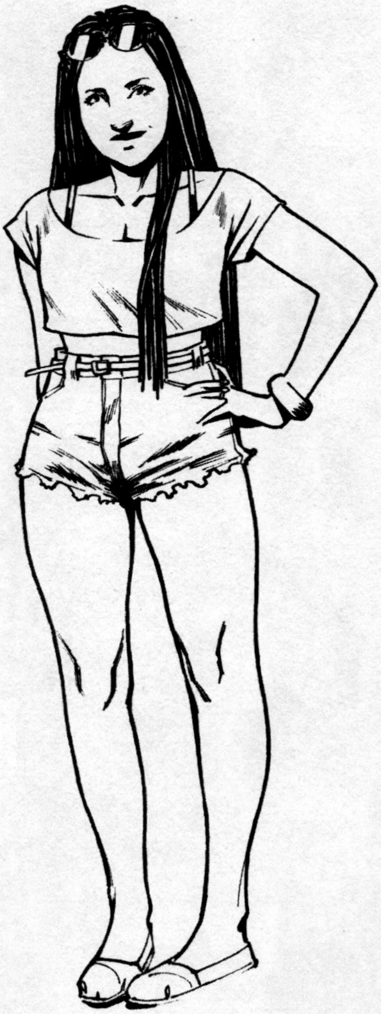

Kaydon Klay: A seventeen-year-old African-American girl from a struggling family who wants to be an actress. She babysits young Marty for Farrah and thinks she can help her get representation and break in to the acting business.

Kaydon is our way of showing a fame-seeker outside of the Hollywood system, someone who is going to get pulled into this maelstrom of ego and destruction.

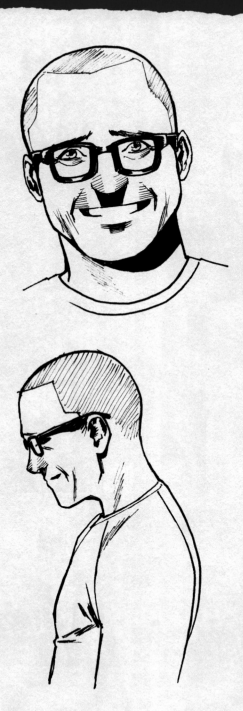

Dean Slotkin: An old friend and confidant, as well as a far more successful actor, Dean wants to help Farrah but she keeps him at arm's length and, once the creature starts her on a path of destruction, she tries to push him away so he won't see what she's become or get killed by it.

Martin Durante: Farrah's four-year-old son. Even with a stable home and two focused parents Marty would be a handful to take care of but with Farrah (and sometimes Kaydon) barely holding things together, it's nowhere near enough.

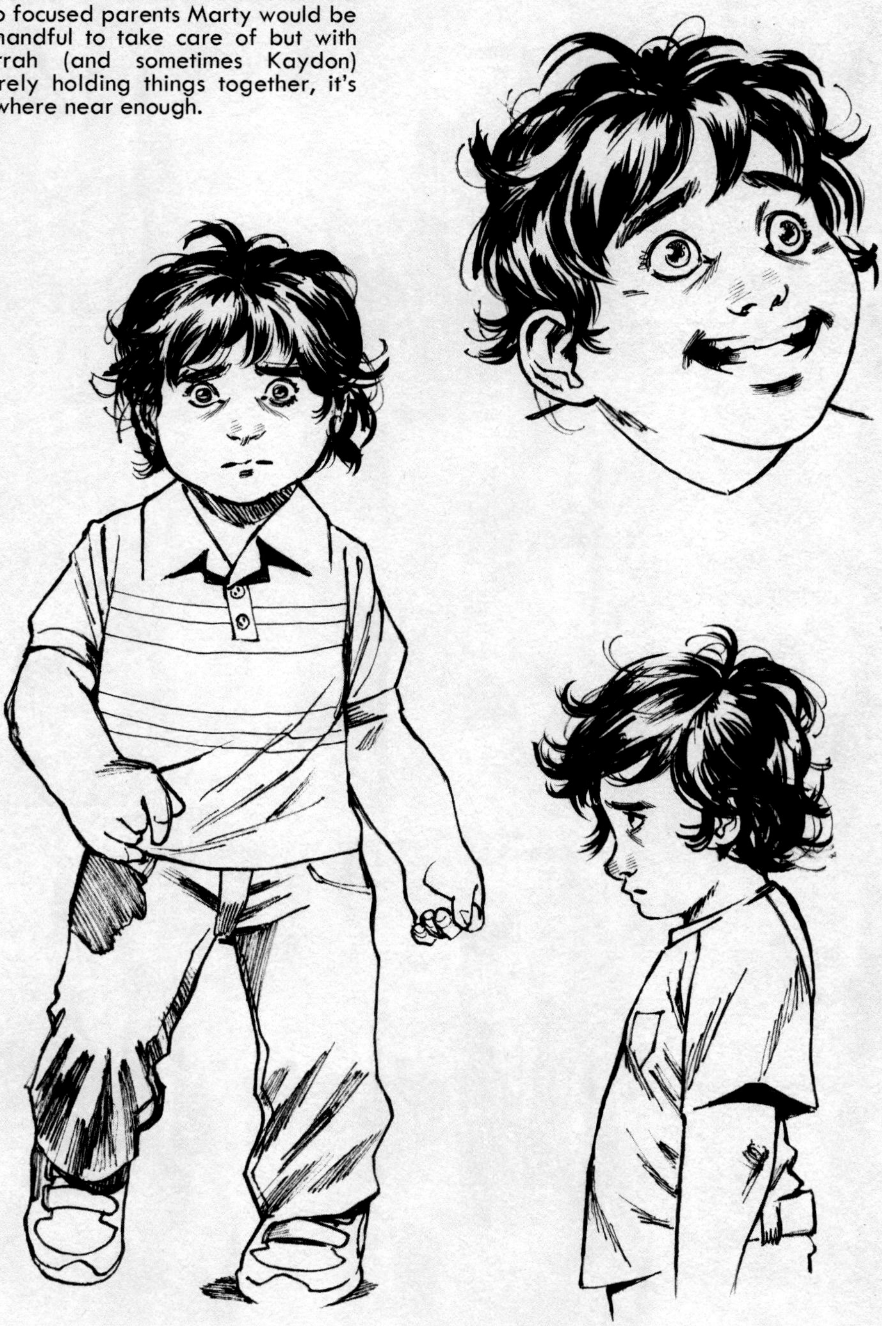

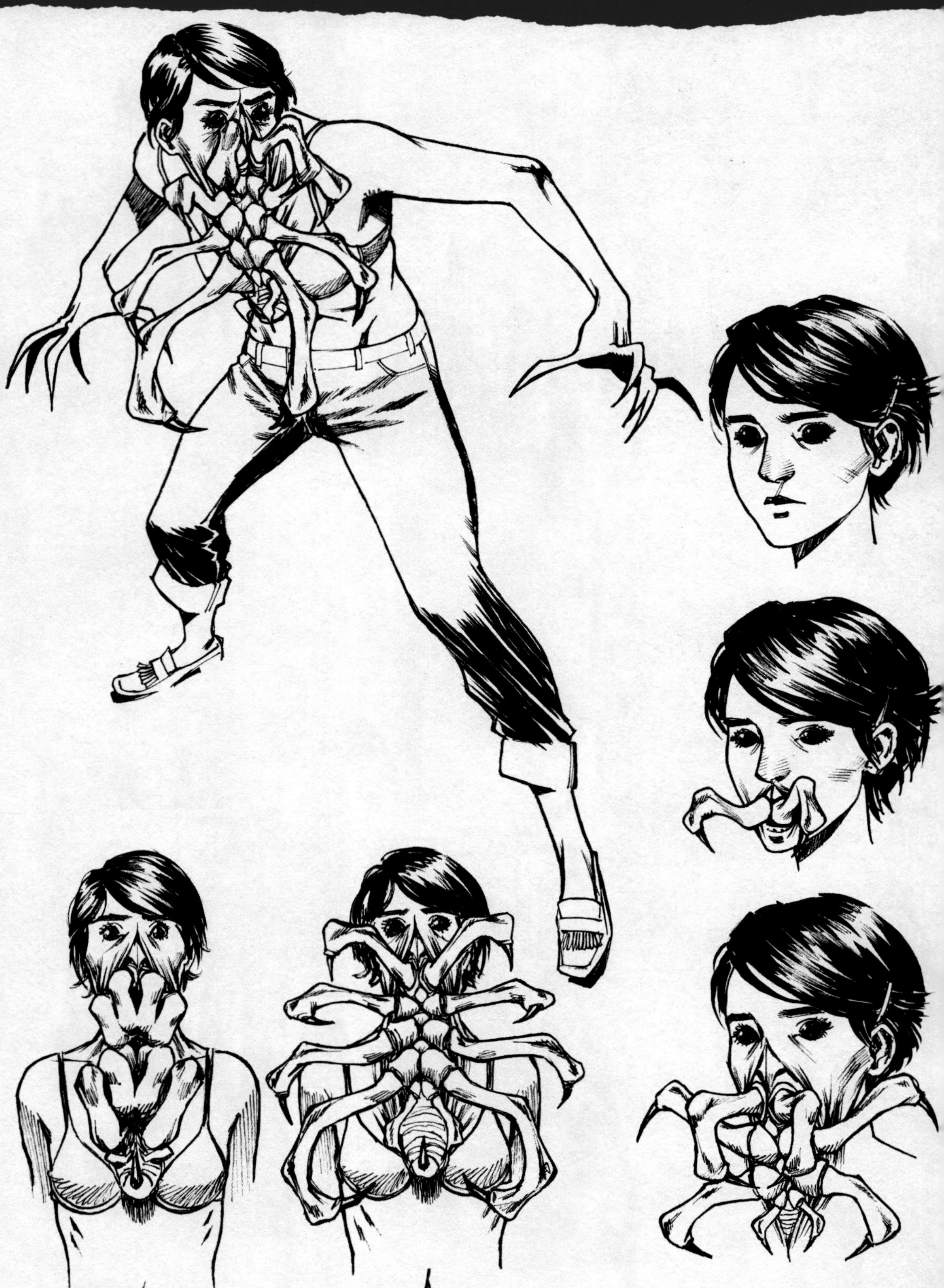

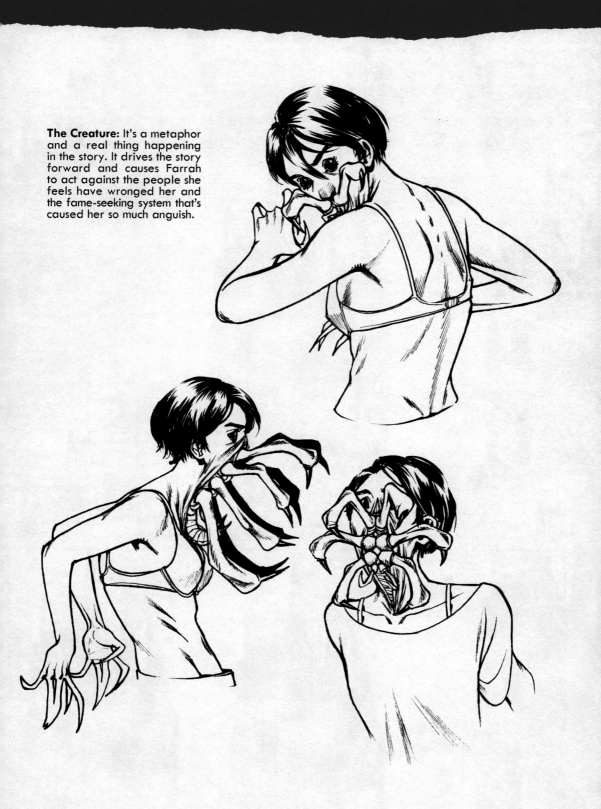

The Creature: It's a metaphor and a real thing happening in the story. It drives the story forward and causes Farrah to act against the people she feels have wronged her and the fame-seeking system that's caused her so much anguish.

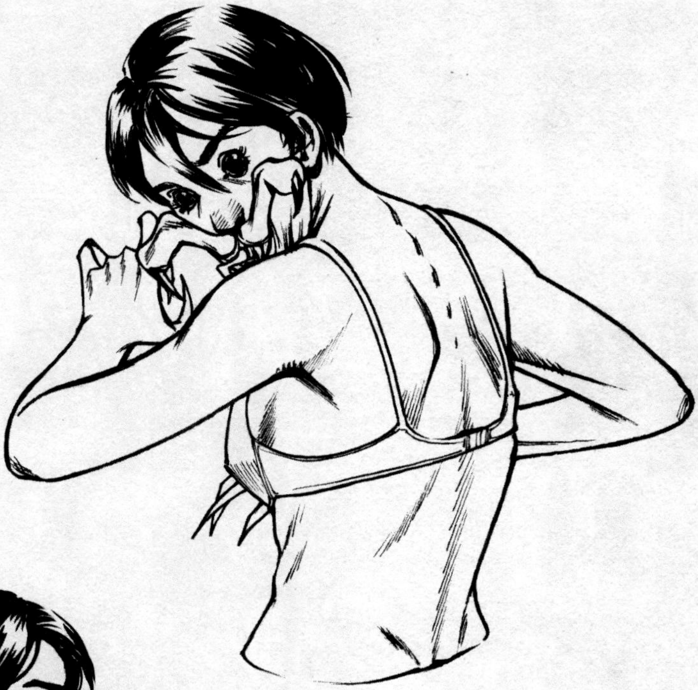

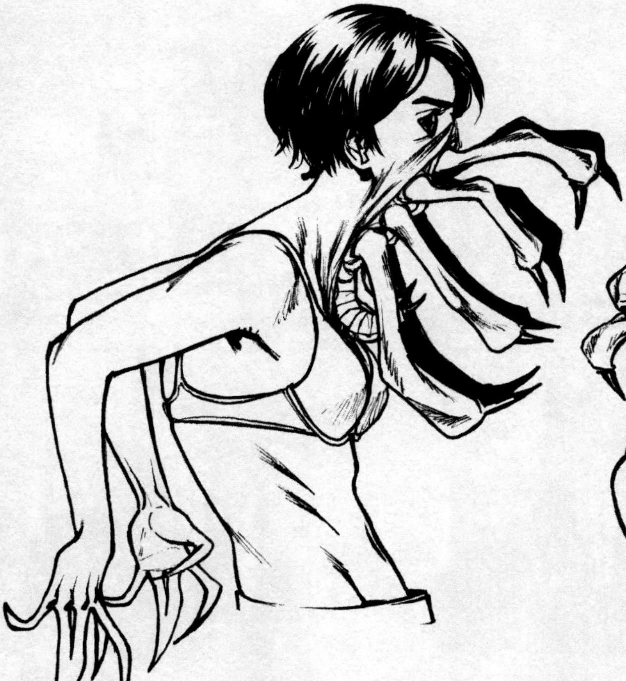

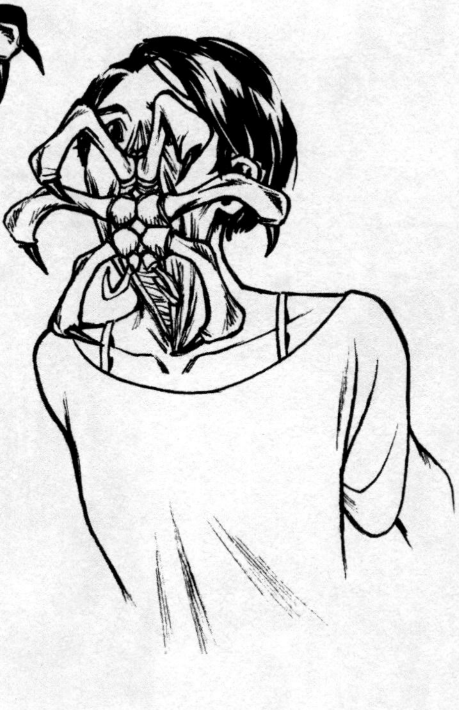

AN OSCAR WINNER BULLIED ME SO BADLY THAT I QUIT THE FILM INDUSTRY

George hoisted me up on top of a plastic picnic table in the middle of the front office and began dry-humping me. He pinned me in place as the table legs scooted back against the wall with his bodily force. The front doors opened, letting the fall air chill my exposed skin.

He was laughing. They were all laughing.

I thought there were only five people in the front lobby — a few producers, the production manager, the director, maybe a driver from transportation, a production assistant or two. I remember people saying to me later, when we were alone — not in front of anyone who could fire us — "I can't believe he did that! If we worked anywhere else, he'd be fired."

"Yeah," I said. I thought the same thing.

But none of us did anything about it.

What could I do? I was pretty low on the food chain. And my bosses all saw it. All guffawed. Enjoyed the show. I wasn't a person. I was an expendable.

I gave up my home to be part of this movie crew; moved all my belongings into storage and was living in a Motel 8 off an Omaha highway with a great view of the parking lot — everything a girl dreams of when she works her way up in the film business.

I wish that was the only time George humiliated me in front of people. But it wasn't. He took pleasure in making jokes at my expense, asking me if I wanted to act in the porn the characters in the movie watch, telling me I was stupid.

He didn't know me. He didn't care that I spent seven years working in production already, that I worked for Spelling Television and produced my own show, that I took the steps down in rank to help my friend and, in theory, myself.

"I need your help," Victor said over a call. "Linda can't go out of town, and I hoped you'd be willing to live in Omaha for three months and help me on the movie. They [the producers] want me to hire locals, but I can't trust them — they don know anything." To sweeten the deal he said, "It's low-buc get but a negative pick-up from Paramount. The pay isn good, but I need someone who knows how to run an offic

I thought the call was heaven-sent. I had served my husban with divorce papers and wanted to put as much distanc between me and the man who spent five years emotionall abusing me. I wanted to fill all my holes back in and prov I still had worth. I was at my best at work.

And there was Victor's cheery voice over the phone, laughin giving me an escape route. If I said yes, I had three days t put my house on the market, my things in storage, and 1,50 miles between me and my soon-to-be ex.

Little did I know I had "victim" written on my forehead. Th deciding to leave didn't mean the first door was an exit.

"Yes," I told Victor. And I went to be his production coordinat

George wasn't the only man on set to treat me disrespectfull But he was the only one to apologize. After calling me a idiot at a production meeting for asking how he preferre his paperwork, he wrote me an apology note.

"I shouldn't have done that. Sorry."

When he gave it to me, he told me I reminded him of h soon-to-be ex-wife. He was in the process of divorcing he and leaving his small child because he started an affair wi the gorgeous lead actress on the movie he wrapped befor this low-budget one. He and his big-budget girlfriend wer better than us. His brown eyes laughed, and I wondered this was the bullshit he fed his ex-wife, too.

I thumbtacked George's apology in public view behind m desk. I figured if he had the audacity to embarrass me i public, he should publicly apologize. There was still som fight in me.

One of the six producers on the film was a jerk, too. It wa Jake's first time as a producer. He came from post-productio

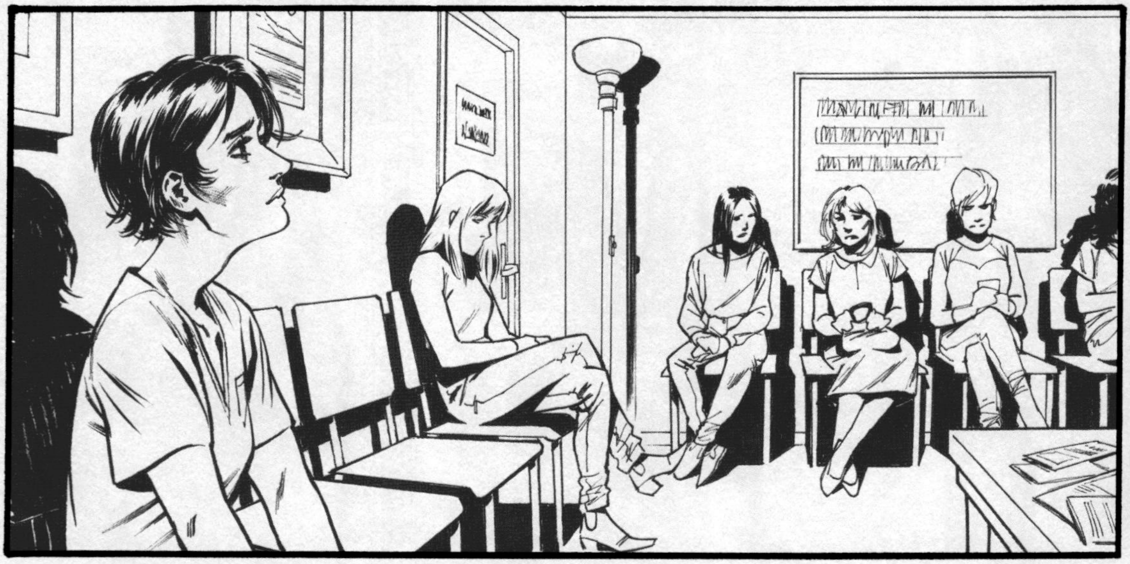

nd didn't have much time on set. He overcompensated by nforming the office staff of what our jobs entailed. The first ay on location he had his assistant hand me a printout of a roduction coordinator's jobs and responsibilities. It was ironic.

ake asked me to forge SAG sheets, changing the working ours of actors. I told him no. He threatened me to get me to o it. I said no. He said the producers didn't want to get in rouble. But they had no issue with hammering me down.

Just do it," he insisted. "We'll get in big trouble."

s if I wouldn't.

ake called me one morning from location while I was in the roduction office.

How could you let us run out of film? Why are you including ort ends in the total? What the fuck is wrong with you?"

'm not the camera department," I responded. "I don't fill in e totals on the production report, and if you don't want short nds in the total, talk to the director of photography, the first ssistant camera, second assistant camera or loader. All on set."

e slammed the phone down on me. He conveniently forgot at, according to the paperwork he gave me, a production oordinator wasn't allowed on set. That my job had me firmly lanted in the production office across town. Any time I asked visit set, they wouldn't let me.

stayed. I'd chat with my friend, Victor, the one who hired me. Ve talked about how clueless Jake was. We laughed at how y assistant kept trying to get me fired because she wanted y job. We laughed at how terrible it was that I couldn't keep good production assistant because they wouldn't work the 2- to 14-hour days for less than $100 a day. We sat in his ffice and commiserated about how the producers told us ach to do opposite things. Then he'd leave for set, and I'd be lone with a girl who wanted my job and bosses who used me s a punching bag.

hought I could take it. I wanted to prove I was strong. I could andle all the bullshit. I was smart. I spent years learning all bout each department so I could help solve problems. I had omething to prove.

ut having something to prove is a waste of time and energy.

e director, Alexander, had a problem with me. You see, I efused to forge the SAG sheets. And I had the nerve to send whole script to a minor. Sending scripts to the cast was part f my job, but he didn't want the minor's family to read the ript. He didn't want the parents to back out because of the ene of the actors watching porn or the lesbian relationship in e movie. Which is what happened.

lexander called the production office and asked for me. was the first time in eight weeks the director spoke to me rectly.

ell me Jake made you do it."

s tone was terse. I imagined his temples sweating and his ick, black-rimmed glasses sliding down is hot face.

"Do what?" I asked. I had no idea what he was fuming about.

"Send the script. Tell me Jake made you do it."

Looking back, I know at this moment everyone else would have said, "Yes, Jake made me do it"; would have told the up-and-coming director that their tormentor told them to do it. I could've made myself the hero. I could have moved up the food chain and saved myself. I wish I had said yes. But I thought the truth mattered. I didn't want to join in the blame game.

"No, he didn't," I whispered.

"Who the fuck do you think you are?" Alexander cursed me out for a good minute or two. He called me every nasty, derogatory term and anything else his quick wit thought of. He drowned me under his tidal wave of rage.

Calm came over my mind as my body began to shake with fear and fury and inferiority. I kept my voice flat.

"I'm going to have to stop you there," I said. "No one talks to me that way."

"Fuck you," the director said.

My floodgate burst.

"I don't know who the fuck you think you're talking to, but no one talks to me like that," I repeated. I leaned forward on my desk. I needed its strength. I couldn't fall. My voice grew powerful. All the pain they inflicted on me was returned tenfold. I remember enjoying it. The phones started ringing off the hook again. I had work to do. I was over being the punching bag. "Fuck you!" I yelled, and I hung up on him.

"Holly, phone," my assistant said. She held the receiver toward me. She was across the room at her desk. Her eyes reflected her brain's calculations about the probability of me being fired and her opportunity to take my job. "Line two is Victor."

"Hi, Victor." I sank into my chair. "I think I may be fired."

He laughed. "I heard the whole thing." He had been standing next to Alexander and heard my side, too.

I wasn't fired. Alexander waited to dole out his punishment.

It was the day before our Thanksgiving holiday. We had worked six-day weeks, and it had been a long time since many of the crew had seen their families. Family members came to Omaha and took up residence with us in the Motel 8 to share a rubbery turkey dinner and 12 hours off. My mom was kindhearted enough to visit and lift my spirits.

To make up for the hell I dealt with, the second assistant director, Sean, invited me to set the day before Thanksgiving. He placed me as an extra in a scene. I sat in position during rehearsal, and just before Alexander was about to shoot, he asked me to leave.

Sean couldn't believe it.

"Let her stay," he said.

"No."

Without a word, I got up. As I walked off the set, Alexander spoke.

"Get back to the office," he said. "I don't want you on my set. At all."

Alexander didn't know my mom was on set that day, too, working as an extra with me. The assistant directors made sure she got camera time. Their apology to me.

Mom saw how they treated me, how I let myself be dismissed. She saw how small I'd become.

The worst day came not so long after that.

An art department truck was in an accident at the high school we used as the main film location. The cube truck hit a passenger vehicle, killing the teenage driver.

How could we stay? How could we finish the movie? How would we continue filming at the scene of a student's death? How did the movie matter now?

My phone blew up with calls. Red lights flashed across the phone. There was no way to answer them all.

"You'll probably get some calls," Jake said. His voice was soft. "Don't tell them anything."

"What could I tell them? I wasn't there."

Ringing filled the space between us.

"Don't pick up."

"What if it's one of our producers? The director? You?"

"Fine, pick up, but take messages. Don't tell them anything."

Jake didn't come to the office, and neither did the other producers. I don't recall handing it well, and I may have shared a producer's phone number in addition to taking messages.

I sat in the room under fluorescent lights and cried thinking about the kid who died and his family. I thought about the 20-something-year-old who killed a teenager because of a movie. Maybe he was on his way to pick up a prop or drop off paint. It was too terrible.

I think that's when I broke.

I lost my taste for the business and all the belittling I endured. How could a movie be more important than the people working on it? The idea that I had to know more and be tougher because I was a woman didn't feel right.

On the last day of filming, I walked away from the business.

George and Alexander saw their careers take off. Alexander was nominated for an Academy Award or two. People talk about his genius. George is a first assistant director on A-list blockbusters and became a producer for Alexander. (His actress girlfriend dumped him and married Hollywood royalty.)

I don't think of any of them fondly. I wonder if they're still u to their old tricks. I wonder if the actors who looked up t them and the viewers of their movies knew how misogynist they were if they'd still be successful.

And I know the answer is yes.

I lost any passion I had for the art. I didn't understand wh I let myself be treated so badly. I couldn't wrap my bra around why being good at my job wasn't enough. I ge therapy. I found my voice and backbone, built boundarie filled in my holes and remembered my worth.

I didn't want to be bitter. I wanted to be whole. It wa immensely hard work putting a grown woman back together

When I ventured back into production years later, I realize it was still filled with people proving they could do it. Provin they were better than others around them by shitting o them, backstabbing and stealing creativity.

But I no longer needed to prove my worth to famous stranger I didn't need to prove I was strong enough to take the abus I learned I had my own creative longings, and I didn't nee anyone's approval to pursue them, and I certainly didn have the desire to give my ideas or self away anymore.

I elected to thrive away from the abuses of Hollywood. An by walking away, I learned I no longer found myself force on my back, on top of a table locked in place and shaking I didn't require a desk to steady my voice. I found my ow legs, my own worth and voice.

© 2016 by Holly Raychelle Hughes. Originally published in XO Jane. Reprinted by permission of the auth